THE COMPANY OF WOMEN

Charlotte
A widowed working mother from Brooklyn

Clare
A would-be nun forced into her family's
Madison Avenue business

Elizabeth
The once-lovely wife of an alcoholic

Mary Rose
Broadway movie usher, suffering the scars of
a brutal marriage

Muriel
A bitter spinster

Friends in common devotion to

Father Cyprian
a compelling and controversial priest

FIVE WOMEN AND A PRIEST
all dedicated to

Felicitas
Charlotte's daughter, the brilliant and beautiful
spiritual child they share. She is their hope for
the future . . .

Please turn the page for rave reviews of
THE COMPANY OF WOMEN

Also by Mary Gordon
Published by Ballantine Books:

FINAL PAYMENTS

the Company of Women

Mary Gordon

BALLANTINE BOOKS • NEW YORK

Grateful acknowledgment is made to the following for permission to reprint previously published material:

Random House, Inc., and Faber and Faber Ltd.: Twenty-one lines from "The Common Life" from *W. H. Auden: Collected Poems* by W. H. Auden, edited by Edward Mendelson. Copyright © 1963 by W. H. Auden. Reprinted by permission of Random House, Inc., and Faber & Faber Ltd.

Abkco Music, Inc.: Lyrics from "Under My Thumb" by Mick Jagger and Keith Richard. © 1966 by Abkco Music, Inc. All rights reserved. Used by permission.

Library of Congress Catalog Card Number: 80-5284

ISBN 0-345-29861-6

This edition published by arrangement with Random House, Inc.

Manufactured in the United States of America

First International Ballantine Books Edition: September 1981
First Ballantine Books Edition: January 1982

To my mother

What draws
singular lives together in the first place,
　　loneliness, lust, ambition,

or mere convenience, is obvious, why they drop
　　or murder one another
clear enough: how they create, though, a common
　　　world
　　between them, like Bombelli's

impossible yet useful numbers, no one
　　has yet explained. Still, they do
manage to forgive impossible behavior,
　　to endure by some miracle

conversational tics and larval habits
　　without wincing . . .

　　　　　The ogre will come in any case:
　　so Joyce has warned us. Howbeit,
fasting or feasting, we both know this: without
　　the Spirit we die, but life

without the Letter is in the worst of taste,
　　and always, though truth and love
can never really differ, when they seem to,
　　the subaltern should be truth.

　　　　—W. H. Auden, "The Common Life"

PART I

1963

I

Felicitas Maria Taylor was called after the one virgin martyr whose name contained some hope for ordinary human happiness. This joke was made for the first time at Felicitas' baptism in May of 1949 by one of her three godmothers. There were three because Felicitas' mother could not decide among her friends. So great an honor did Charlotte Taylor consider it that she could not bear to deprive any of the three women she deeply loved of the privilege of being godmother to her child. The pastor would permit only one female sponsor's name on the baptismal certificate, so Charlotte made the women draw straws. Clare, who drew the longest straw, signed her name to the certificate. But Father Cyprian Leonard, who performed the actual ceremony, allowed Elizabeth and Mary Rose and Clare to stand together at the font with Charlotte's brother Jack and make the responses. Which was Cyp all over, Charlotte said.

It was because of Father Cyprian that Charlotte, Clare, Elizabeth and Mary Rose had met, in 1932, when he had inaugurated the first of his series of weekend retreats for working women. One Friday evening a month, these women came from their jobs to the silent convent of Our Lady of Sorrows to pray in silence, to be served by silent nuns and to listen to the sermons and confessional advice of Father Cyprian. Charlotte took the train from Brooklyn, where she worked as a secretary in the insurance firm of Tom O'Brien; Elizabeth, who had been genteelly raised in New Orleans, but whose husband had lost all his money because of drink, walked from whatever elementary school she was, at the time, teaching at: she could not bear buses or trains. Clare took a taxi from Madison Avenue and Fifty-seventh Street, where she now man-

aged what had been her father's store, one of the finest
leather-goods establishments in New York City. Mary
Rose took the Broadway bus; she was an usher at a
movie theater on Broadway and Forty-third Street. And
Muriel Fisher, who looked after her mother and took in
typing, came down from Worcester, Massachusetts. She
had met Father Cyprian when he preached a mission in
her parish. She was never one of them.

They attended Father Cyprian's retreat every month
from 1932 until the war, when Father Cyprian became a
chaplain. After the war, the retreat movement seemed to
fade. But the women saw one another often, even after
Charlotte's marriage to Frank Taylor in June 1946, and
they never lost touch with Father Cyprian. When he left
the Paracletists and became a secular priest, they could,
for four years, only write to him—out west or up in Canada. But in 1959, he settled in the western New York
town of Orano, where he had been born. He lived in a
furnished room and filled in for priests who were sick or
on vacation. Then in June 1963, he bought the piece of
land where his parents' home had been and began to
build his own house on it.

Every summer since 1959, for the first three weeks of
August, Charlotte, who had been widowed six months after her child's birth, took Felicitas and traveled to Orano
with Elizabeth and Clare and Mary Rose. They stayed in
a motel and visited Father Cyprian. Muriel, who had
been on her own since her mother died in 1957, spent the
warm part of the year—May through November—in
Orano. She had a room in a tourist house where the land-
lady remembered Father Cyprian as a boy.

Each time she went to mass, Felicitas heard her name
read during the part of the canon where the prayers of
virgin martyrs were invoked: Felicitas, Perpetua, Agatha,
Lucy, Cecilia, Anastasia. She was glad she had not been
called Perpetua—it suggested a doggy patience; Agatha
meant inevitable spinsterhood; and Cecilia was shanty
Irish. She could have done something with Lucy, but it
was the loss of Anastasia she most regretted. She thought
of Ingrid Bergman. She thought of the Russian crown
jewels. From the time she was twelve to the time she was

fourteen, her favorite books were *Jane Eyre* and *Ardeth Wilson, Flight Nurse.* In both books, the women ended up with the men they had always loved, who, having begun by being fierce and resisting, ended up faithful, humbled, maimed.

Felicitas lied to her friends about the way she spent her summers. She knew it was very odd. Nearly everything about her family was odd, but her friends didn't have to know it. She could keep the truth from them as she could keep them from her house. She could say to them, "My mother works," and they would understand that they couldn't come over. To have a working mother was slightly dangerous in 1963. None of Felicitas' friends' mothers worked, and Felicitas stressed the danger; she had made her friends afraid to see the inside of her house. She did not know what they imagined, but she knew that it was some horror. Charlotte never thought to ask Felicitas why she never brought her friends home. She never thought of Felicitas as having friends her own age. For Charlotte, her friends were her daughter's.

Every year in May, Felicitas began lying about the summer. When she was smaller, she did not have to lie because she spoke to no one. But now she had friends. And her friends would have thought it a very odd way to spend the summer. They would not have wanted to be her friends anymore.

She had thought of making a joke of it, saying, "God, I'm trapped. I have to go away to this crazy place in the country with my mother's old-fart friends and this priest who's off his rocker." She could have tapped her forehead as she spoke, indicating insanity. But she did not want to make fun of Father Cyprian, even to amuse her friends.

There was no one she could tell about Father Cyprian. It would have been death to her to go a year without seeing him. But how could she say to her friends that the deepest pleasure of her life was riding to the six o'clock mass alone with Father Cyprian in the front of his red pickup? The light then made her see the world as fragile and beautiful. And there was the other light that came through the windows—always of a different church, for Father Cyprian belonged to no one parish—the light she sat in, praying, with his back to her in his beautiful vest-

ments—grass green for the feria, blue for feasts of Our
Lady. She wanted always to be there kneeling, looking
at his black shoes below the black cuffs of his trousers
and the long white alb. They were serious and blessed
and devotional. They were at the center of things. God
was that: nothing not vital. She wanted Him to come to
her. She wanted to take in God. *"Domine, non sum
dignus."* She said the prayer but did not mean it. She believed she was worthy. Her soul she saw as glass filled
with sky or water, as beautiful, as light, as silvery and as
important. That was her soul, light let through some transparent thing, cool light refreshed by water. The side of
God apart from punishment or care. The God that
breathed, breathed over all. The thin, transparent God
that barely left a shadow. She watched the feet of Father
Cyprian as she opened her mouth. She prayed in her soul
for light, a life of light, a life essential as those shoes, as
serious.

How could she tell all that to her friends, who were interested that year in TV doctors?

She was always the one who rode in the pickup with Father Cyprian. This annoyed Muriel Fisher. As she climbed
in, Felicitas could see Muriel's face. She was smiling that
fake smile again.

Muriel smiled because you were supposed to smile at
children if you didn't have any. But she had never liked
Felicitas, not since she discovered that she was the only
one of the women who had not been asked to be her godmother. She had not even been invited to the baptism.
But she believed she had hidden her feelings. One had to
in her position or risk being called sour. All those names
for the spirit taken from food or drink: dryness, bitterness, sourness. And the sweetness that is God. Dry, bitter,
sour, as if the soul were curds left out or vinegar. What
was it that she lacked that she could not name but must
pray for? In confession he warned her of it, and on their
walks. Then she grew bitter when he warned her of bitterness: "Sarah was called mocking." She thought at such
times of Sarah, wife to the patriarch, whose womb was
barren but who conceived in her great age. "It had ceased

to be with Sarah after the manner of women," Muriel
would think, watching him and the child drive away.

After the manner of women. It was blood they meant
when they said women. She could imagine in her body a
dry clot of blood, like the juice on the plate around meat
that had been left out. Change of life. Her life had not
changed. Dry, bitter, sour. But she, living with her
mother, taking in typing for the priests at the college, was
fired by love, brushed through with fire, violent. He said,
"I warn you of these things, these small imperfections, because I know you to be an extraordinary soul." Where,
then, was bitterness in her, and dryness, and the sourness
that was the smell only of exhaustion? Her soul was
brushed, clean, warm, sweet. A small house. His house.
The house she would make for him. She would die for
him. They would die together.

She did not love the child.

But he must not know that. The one time she had said
anything—"It isn't good for her, all that attention. You
spoil her. She'll expect that from life. I only say it for her
own good. She's bound to be disappointed. No one will
ever talk to her again like that, as you do"—he had
simply replied, "She is our only hope."

She knew what he meant. She knew he was right to
say it. They would die, and only one of them would leave
a child. The coarsest of them, of all their souls the least
extraordinary: Charlotte. A good soul, said Father. What
was it a man wanted with her? White skin, teeth. Breasts
for what? Big bolsters, pillows for some head. The man's
head. But the man was dead, and there was only the
child. Their only hope.

Muriel had never, in the long, rich catalog of her en-
vies, envied the offspring of anyone until she had seen
that the trick impressed him: the trick of a child, that
child, who need do nothing to be loved, while she, Muriel, studied, thought, refined herself to a thin white slice
of moon so that her love for him would be what he most
admired: cold, the love of the spirit, knife-sharp, always
on the verge of disappearing.

Charlotte thought privately that Muriel could be called
scrupulous. Of all the girls, Muriel took the longest in

confession. "What the hell does she have to say that's so goddamn interesting?" said Charlotte to Elizabeth, itchy in her pew. "What the hell does she do up there in Worcester?"

Between Charlotte and Muriel now there was emnity, for Charlotte, the only one of them who was a creature of instinct, perceived danger in Muriel's hatred for her child.

In her pew, Charlotte told Elizabeth all the Philadelphia jokes she could remember, substituting the name Worcester. "Two guys were in a boxing match. The winner got a week in Worcester. The loser got two weeks in Worcester."

Elizabeth loved jokes but could never remember them. She shook with laughter, kneeling, preparing for the sacrament. Of all women, she loved Charlotte best; of all loves, her love for Charlotte was the least frail. Charlotte, oldest of thirteen children, brooked no nonsense from the world. She paid all Elizabeth's bills; Elizabeth had only to sign the checks. Once during the Depression, Charlotte was at Elizabeth's house, having breakfast in her nightgown. A bill collector came to the door. Elizabeth, the daughter of a lady and a gentleman, dressed before breakfast in a suit, stockings and high heels, could not speak for shame at the man who chomped his cigar in her living room and would not remove his hat.

"Take off your hat. You're in the presence of ladies," said Charlotte, five ten in her slippers.

"This *lady* is up to her neck in debt," said the bill collector, taking off his hat.

"Talk to me about it. I represent her attorney," said Charlotte.

It turned out that Elizabeth had not paid her bills because she could not. Elizabeth's husband had left her. In the twenties, when he had money, he had given her perfumed cigarettes, stockings with her name embroidered at the top. In the thirties, broke, he drank and wept and left her with a little boy of five who everyone could tell would die young. Taking nothing, he had left a note on the table, which said, "My dear, it is simply better this way."

"What the hell is better about it?" said Charlotte, whom Elizabeth had called and asked to come along. "You'll stay up nights wondering. And God knows you need your sleep, you of all people. And I know you, you'll stop eating."

She had not been able to pay her bills not only because they were for more money than she had but also because she did not know how to. When Charlotte had made the bill collector leave, she said to Elizabeth, "Let's see 'em."

Meaning the bills.

Elizabeth turned, silent and ashamed, to her mother's dresser, where she kept the bills in a locked drawer. She gave them to Charlotte, unopened.

"Why didn't you open them?" asked Charlotte, chewing on her pen. Her energy made Elizabeth weep, for she knew she was all wrong, purely wrong. Her husband had left her, her child was dying and she could not open her bills.

"Why didn't you open them?" repeated Charlotte.

"I didn't know what to do with them."

Elizabeth began to sob, for the pure, infantile shame of it. Charlotte was opening the envelopes with a fruit knife. She looked up, pushing her glasses onto the top of her head.

"Don't act like a goddamn fool. You're a schoolteacher."

Even now, Elizabeth did not know why that sentence had stopped her fear. Perhaps it was that the sight of Charlotte adding numbers in columns was the visible sign of her faith, taking chaos, taking fear and shaping them with fingers that did not taper, did not curve. It was the perfect simplicity of the one round number that Charlotte created out of the slime of those bills that was a miracle to her. She could have knelt before her friend. She could believe her capable of cures. And her signature on the loan, co-signer, was the promise of salvation: the round, open vowels of the name that promised ruin would not cover her, she would not drown.

They all took care of their mothers and did not know about men, thought Elizabeth, laughing at old jokes in gratitude for her friend's rescue thirty years ago. Charlotte did and she did, which made them different, which set them apart. Not that they ever spoke of it, not that it ever interested them, *all that,* as Charlotte would have called it. Still, it was something they knew that the rest of them did not.

Muriel had tried to win Elizabeth, knowing her love of quiet, for which Charlotte had no gift. She would suggest walks, for which Charlotte had no gift. She stayed for months with Father Cyprian, and Elizabeth understood Muriel's look when all of them drove up, Charlotte and Clare and Mary Rose and the child (the child that Elizabeth loved as she had loved her own dead boy). It was the look of the victim of a robbery—all she treasured was exposed, divided, her great stone cut. But Elizabeth could also feel the bitterness, the styptic heart of Muriel that contracted at the sight of the child.

It was strange where life took you, thought Elizabeth, watching Felicitas and Father Cyprian drive away in the red pickup. She thought of herself at Felicitas' age, a Catholic girl in New Orleans. She understood what Felicitas felt driving in the truck with Cyprian: the extreme honor, the hard, durable pride of such company. That she had had with her father, walking along the streets with him, the Southern streets of Catholic New Orleans, where her father tipped his beautiful hat, his perfect straw hat, to ladies. That was the seal of all her romance: to be so deeply honored by the proximity of such a man, a hero, a gentleman.

"Gentlemen bear burdens ladies do not know," her mother had said. And yet her mother had hated her father, had driven him to the high room he lived in, in the boardinghouse run by the woman who was not a lady, whom he did not wish Elizabeth to see. Only once did she see that room, and then she saw what would be to her always the image of male loneliness: her father's two military brushes on his bare deal dresser. That was grand, that was honorable, that solitariness. There was something in men one could not touch, despite the attempts that women made with their clean, warm houses, their protecting furniture, their beds and open bodies. In a man who was a gentleman there was still a solitariness they could not touch. And Elizabeth saw what Muriel did not see: she could not comfort Cyprian, because Cyprian was a gentleman.

After all, there is very little that I know, thought Elizabeth, looking at the pickup, looking down at her hands. The hands of an old woman, she thought. I am sixty-one. Sometimes I think there is nothing I do not know. I know what these women do not. Charlotte knows things I will never know, but I know things she does not. I have a talent for silence for a quiet life. I would, of all things, give that to the child.

She remembered the first time she had met Charlotte, had met any of the women, had met Cyprian. John was still with her, but she was teaching. How grateful she was that her father, fearing some disaster, had sent her to normal school so that she could, astonishingly, make money, keep them going while John sat, drunk, shocked by what had happened to the money. She went out, teaching the children of immigrants, postal workers, stock clerks, men who fixed radios, women who cleaned other people's houses, women who worked in laundries, men who disappeared. It exhausted her. She had not been born to such work, and one weekend a month, to recuperate, she made a retreat at the convent of Our Lady of Sorrows.

How beautiful it was, the smell of wax, the veins of the marble on the cold floors, the nuns, French, silent, civilized, their accents suggesting the Europe she was promised but did not see. They were gifted, as she was gifted, in silence, and had gifts of the eye which so few in the Church had. Pictures of angels, Virgins simple against simple gold. They always saved a private room for her, they said. And for that room her soul thirsted, the plain white bed, the crucifix, the window opening out to nothing she need care for. Her room, overnight.

But that one weekend, a summer one, the sisters had no private rooms. Tears came to Elizabeth's eyes, tears of pure loss, and Mother André had opened her fine, clever hands and said, "Mrs. McCullough, I will try."

They put her in a room full of noise, women laughing for the last time until Sunday night, one in particular whom she did not wish to speak to. She decided to spend her days in the chapel, the library.

What had happened, Elizabeth tried to remember after thirty-one years. What was it that Charlotte had said to make Elizabeth turn around, and in that turning know,

"This is the face of someone I will love"? Life is full of
such misses; the right word could so easily not have been
spoken. Was it the tilt of Charlotte's head, her way of saying "Don't kid me" or "P.S., who did he think he was
talking to?" or "I'm nuts about that one"? Elizabeth had
turned, and suddenly it was as if she were walking toward
a stove, a heat she did not know she had been secretly
yearning for. She laughed. And Charlotte magically
opened the circle in which all these years she had been
warmed and fed and bolstered.

That was the first time she had heard Cyprian preach.
She could remember that. He had spoken of the Holy
Ghost, and the grandeur of his words was as demanding
and as beautiful as her father's.

After that weekend, Charlotte had said, "Come to dinner at my family's place. Bring your little boy."

She loved Charlotte's family as she had loved no other
family, because there was no family like them. The six-
foot mother; the father, tiny, always ready to lose his temper, of which no one was afraid; the brothers, carrying
basketballs, carrying lumber; the beautiful sisters, all engaged. Charlotte supported the family by working for Mr.
O'Brien because her father, who was a jeweler, could not
find work in those bad times. "If people are starving to
death, they don't want rings," Charlotte had said matter-
of-factly. At twenty-five Charlotte was supporting fourteen people. She did not understand why Elizabeth had
marveled; you did what had to be done. Elizabeth did not
think Charlotte would ever marry, although she had an
attachment to a man, Frank Taylor, who had left the seminary, for she could not dream of anyone leaving such a
family.

That first weekend, Elizabeth's son had gone into convulsions. Charlotte's mother had simply picked him up
and immersed him in a sinkful of cold water. Then she
turned him over, the blond child, blue, stiff, shaking. And
then Charlotte's mother did something extraordinary. She
put her finger up his rectum. And the child's convulsions
stopped. His skin turned a normal color. He began to
breathe. And Charlotte's mother said, "My youngest was
like this at your boy's age." And for a moment, Elizabeth
believed her child would not die.

After that, Elizabeth spent nearly every weekend with
Charlotte. Charlotte would drive into Manhattan and
bring Elizabeth and her child to Long Island, leaving
John to drink and weep and fall asleep at the kitchen table, dressed in a suit, as if he believed he would go back
to the office.

And once a month, Elizabeth and Charlotte made retreats with Father Cyprian. Then he established a following: Clare and Mary Rose and Muriel. And thirty
years later, here they were, in western New York, an
hour south of Buffalo, where Cyprian was.

It was clear to Elizabeth that Felicitas was the only one
who could comfort Father Cyprian, the only one with
whom he was not lonely. He would weep as they
sat around him on the floor. He would say, "This is what
is left." And they would remember, all of them, how he
had filled churches and the lines in front of his confessional. Then Felicitas would look up at him and he would
hold her and be comforted.

How could Muriel forgive that? How could she love the
child after that? And yet she had to love her, for the child
was their hope. It was a queer life that Felicitas would
have, a hard life, but how fortunate, Elizabeth thought,
to be like Mary, Martha's sister, like Felicitas, the favored one, the chosen.

It was ridiculous to hate a kid, Charlotte thought. How
could you hate a fourteen-year-old kid? Partly it was Cyprian's fault, she could see that. He encouraged Muriel to
spend all those months in Orano, which was too much,
for Charlotte's money. The way Muriel hung around Cyprian gave Charlotte the willies. Anyone could see there
was something fishy about it. But that was Cyprian. What
he didn't want to see he didn't see. Personally, Charlotte
didn't get it. Muriel bored the hell out of her. And Cyprian liked a laugh. She guessed it was because Muriel was
a brain and liked to use words like "spiritual dryness" and
talk about the gifts of the Holy Ghost over dinner. But
Muriel wasn't half the brain Elizabeth was, only Elizabeth didn't go shooting her mouth off about actual grace
and corporal works of mercy. And what aggravated Charlotte was that she could see Muriel trying to pretend she

was Cyprian's goddamn wife, talking about the bargains
at the grocery store when all she had was some half-assed
hot plate in the tourist house and one pot. To piss in,
thought Charlotte, mentally accusing herself of sins.

Of course, Felicitas didn't help matters any, but that
was Felicitas. Charlotte could see that it burned Muriel
up, Felicitas' riding in the pickup with Cyprian every day
after mass. So she told the kid to soft-pedal it a little, just
every now and then to offer to ride in the car with the
others. Just offer.

"Why should I," said Felicitas. Felicitas had it in her
to have a fresh mouth. Charlotte had to admit it, even if
it was her own kid.

"Just to keep the peace."

"Look, she's up here the whole goddamn summer. She
can ride in his truck the whole frigging time except for
three weeks."

"Don't use the word 'frigging.' "

"Why?"

"It's vulgar."

"Well, then, she's up here the whole goddamn time,
and I'm the one he wants to ride in the truck with him.
He happens to have a lot of stuff to say to me that's very
important that's not for anyone else to hear."

That was Felicitas. Ask her to pour oil on troubled wa-
ters and she'd light a match.

Well, she was just like her father. Charlotte had known
Frank all her life. They had gone to Incarnation School
together until eighth grade, when the boys were separated
and sent to the brothers. At fifteen, Frank had gone to the
prep seminary and had moved on to the senior sem when
he was finished there. All that time, she wrote to him, serious letters; she listened to his stories, his descriptions of
his life, his advice on prayer. Then when he was twenty-
four, he left the seminary. For fifteen years, he made a
living on the fringes of church life, as a failed medical
student might take a job with a pharmaceutical company.
For fifteen years, he took Charlotte to movies, to baseball games, to the Black Friars' Catholic theater in New
Jersey. Finally, when he was thirty-nine, he asked her to
marry him.

She was surprised. Her life with her family, her friends

and Father Cyprian had so absorbed her that she had forgotten that she had not married. "Sure," she said to
Frank, "why not?" Only Cyprian had been against it.

Frank and Cyprian. Men friends. Cyprian never got
over his death. When she had turned to Cyprian, really
at the end of her rope, turned to him as her confessor, he
had written her with such rage. "Do not speak to me of
your sorrow. Your sorrow is nothing to mine. I will never
have anyone like him in my life again. At least you have
a child of his loins. I have nothing. I am completely
alone."

Charlotte would never forgive him for that letter, but
she fought against it, against that part of her nature. None
of the other girls was tempted as she was; none of them
was burdened as she was, hotheaded, hot of heart. The
things she had said to people along the line. Unforgivable.
God knew she should be able to forgive someone a few
words in a moment of grief. But she could not forgive
Cyprian and she would not forget, and those words sat
like a cat, crouched, angry, in her soul, although she had
prayed to God for a clear soul, a cool soul, prayed that
God would make her as nice as Elizabeth.

Cyprian thought she was stupid. That was what he
meant when he said, "Charlotte is the salt of the earth."
He had to do that with people, have that one little sentence about everyone, as if he couldn't remember who
was who without it. She was the salt of the earth and Elizabeth was one of God's doves and Clare had a mind like
a man's and Mary Rose was a ray of sunlight and Muriel
was an extraordinary soul. Something in Cyprian made
him do that, as if he had to pin people down so he
wouldn't lose track of anybody.

He couldn't do that to Frank; he didn't even try—he
knew better. Of course, Cyp had about as clear a view of
Frank as she didn't know what, the Amazon.

But Cyprian was no help to her as far as Frank was
concerned. He was always behind every crackpot scheme
Frank came up with. All the magazines she had to co-sign
loans for, the projects to make liturgical greeting cards.
Fine in the head, but Frank had two mouths to feed. Fat
chance. When Charlotte left her family's house to marry
Frank, the day of her wedding her father handed her a

slip of paper, folded, on which he had written, "You will work t'll the day you die."

The way her family carried on when she told them she was going to get married, you'd have thought she was sixteen and running off with the iceman instead of thirtyeight and marrying an educated gentleman. Cyprian was furious. He said Frank would be tying himself down to bringing in the bacon when it was the Holy Spirit, the salvation of the Church on earth, that was his great work. She remembered having a vision of Frank chained to a slab of bacon the size of a house and laughing, and then wondering if she had committed a sin of disrespect against the clergy. Even Elizabeth had said, "He's an awfully different sort of man." But she thought Charlotte and Frank should get married. She could see they were crazy about each other, although she wouldn't have put it that way. She was too much of a lady. But she said she thought it would be wonderful if Frank and Charlotte had a child.

When the nursing nun at the hospital told Frank that Felicitas was born, he fell to his knees, kissed the hem of her habit and started saying the *Te Deum*. That's what the nun said. Charlotte didn't remember a goddamn thing, she was so knocked out from the dope they gave her. She was loopy for weeks. Frank would come into the room and tell her how beautiful the baby was, but they didn't let Charlotte have her because she had been too knocked out for the Caesarean. She got this crazy idea in her head—it was all that lying around, it'd give anyone ideas—that there was something wrong with the baby. That was why they wouldn't show it to her. She'd have dreams about a baby with clubfeet, or a red shape on her face like a starfish, or fins for arms, or fish eyes with no pupils, blind as a kitten's. Finally Frank made the nun bring the baby in to her, and doped up as she was, she could see her child was perfectly beautiful. Frank held the baby's hands and said, "See those hands? The future is in those hands."

Sometimes she wished everyone would let up on the kid. She had it rough enough, with a father who died when he was six months old and a mother who worked. That day, when Felicitas was four days old and Frank said that to her about the future being in Felicitas' hands,

she thought it was a lot of hot air. But that was because
the dope had made her so gassy she would've given fifty
dollars for a fart. And the nuns did just about nothing for
her, spent all their time with the Jewish patients, trying to
convince them they were goddamn angels of mercy and
not out for converts. Besides, the Jewish patients got a lot
of baskets of fruit, and nuns were always on the lookout
for a free feed. And the Jews always left the nuns money,
and Charlotte would've been goddamned if she'd give a
nun money for doing her job. Charlotte had a roommate
in the hospital who was Jewish; a lovely person, not vulgar at all, from Germany or somewhere.

But even then, sick as she was, she didn't like the way
Frank was carrying on about Felicitas and the great work
she had ahead of her. A six-pound baby, for God's sake.
But when Frank talked like that it was the time they were
the closest, it was the time she felt the most important.

The thing about people was they always wanted to
feel they were more important than they were, more than
just themselves. That was why she felt sorry for people
who didn't believe in God. Who were they but poor
slobs? It wouldn't have been enough for Charlotte. When
Charlotte prayed, she knew she was part of something.
She didn't think about it, like Frank or Cyprian or Muriel or even Elizabeth, but it was there all the same. She
was not alone.

Cyprian didn't even see Felicitas until Frank was dead.
Felicitas was six and Cyprian was back from Canada.
God knew why he ever got the idea to go to Canada. It
was after he left the Pracletists and had gone out west
and that hadn't panned out. That was Cyprian, he wanted
something different, so he pretty much walked out on
everything and took this crazy parish in Sudbury, where
he worked with the Indians who worked in some crazy
kind of mine, sulfur or phosphorus or one of those yellow
things. Well, she had to hand it to Cyp; he stuck it out
there four years, although anyone who had half a brain
could tell it would drive somebody like him crazy.

Cyprian was always talking about how much he needed
to be alone, but he always wanted a gang around him.
Someone to talk to. No, someone to listen to him. Then
Cyprian decided he wanted to come back here to Orano.

For Charlotte's money, it was a lot better than Canada.
At least he had gas and electric. But you had to hand it
to Cyprian, he bought that Godforsaken place where his
family's house used to be, for the view of the mountains,
he said. Which was not like Cyprian. Protestants had nature, he used to say; Catholics have the word of God. He
was softening up in some ways. Everybody did as they
got older; you just got tired of all those fights. But in some
ways he never let up, and she loved him for that because
she never let up, either. But until she died, she would not
forgive him, and she stored that in her heart like a
seed with an elaborate outer covering, polished, many-
chambered, her one grievance: "Do not speak to me of
your sorrow. Your sorrow is nothing to mine."

Still, there was nobody like Cyp, which was why she
came up here every year. There was something between
them, between all of them. They were connected to something, they stood for something. They were not only
themselves, secretaries and schoolteachers, people who
took care of their mothers, ushers in movie theaters, the
lame ducks no man wanted. When all of them came together, they were something.

Which was why she brought Felicitas up here, although
she knew it was a queer thing to do to a fourteen-year-
old kid. She had come from a normal family; she knew
what normal kids did over the summer. Went to camp or
some goddamn thing. She sent Felicitas to C.Y.O. camp,
Camp St. Rita, one summer, and Felicitas raised holy
hell. Why should she throw good money after bad sending the kid someplace she hated? At least she was happy
up here with Cyprian. There was no sense putting a
square peg out to greener pastures. Felicitas was not an
ordinary kid, she wasn't like any of her cousins, so there
was no sense suggesting *that* for the summer.

At least here she was happy and they were together.
The two of them were oddballs and they fought like cats
and dogs, but they knew how to enjoy themselves. They
got along. They were close, even though Felicitas was her
father's daughter, up in her room reading Latin. And that
goddamn *Jane Eyre*. Felicitas must've read that book fifty
times. It was a good story. Charlotte liked it, and the
movie was terrific. Joan Fontaine. Just the right one to

play it. It was great the way sometimes they got the right
person to play a part. Most of the time they didn't. Why
they thought Vivien Leigh was right for Scarlett O'Hara
Charlotte would never know. But Joan Fontaine was just
right. She hoped Felicitas didn't think she was some kind
of Joan Fontaine.

Some people probably thought Charlotte wanted some
other kind of daughter. Especially her family. Some easier
kind of kid, someone interested in things Charlotte could
talk about. But they didn't understand. Felicitas was what
she wanted. She looked at the girl driving in the pickup
with the priest, whose head was out the window as he
cleared the hedge, and she thought quite simply, knowing she did not exaggerate. "For those two I would die."

Clare worried about the money. She thought that for once
in his life Cyprian shouldn't have to scrape. In that, she
was different from the others. She had never lacked
money, never had to worry about it. She had lived in a
world where her father's friends were Protestants, and
shared with these men and their children the expectation
of summer homes, linens ironed and embroidered by one
they paid and saw twice weekly. Mutual bonds, strong-
boxes, pictures not of the Sacred Heart but of muted
Raphael Madonnas brought from Italy. The Raphael
above the sideboard her father had brought from Rome
when he had traveled there for the company, ordering
Italian leathers. Her delicate mother, lace at her neck,
would write down on slips of paper she kept on her bedside table the orders for the meals of the week that
Bridget, the greenhorn cook, would cook. Bridget or the
latest girl from the old country the priest had found, some
of them remarkably dirty, some miraculous for color—
eyes blue, skin white, hair dark or honey-colored. Bridget
stayed with them ten years until she married some yahoo
of a laborer who wouldn't give her half of what she had
with the Learys—her own room, privacy, all the beautiful
linen.

Clare had a taste and an eye for quality, Cyprian said.
It was Clare he took with him to buy the vestments and
the chalices when old Harry Slade from Chicago gave
him the thousand dollars before he left for Canada. That

was a day to treasure, to hoard. She told none of the others, for it was she alone that he had asked for the strengths and talents she had been afraid he could not see. Bu. he had seen.

They went to Shaughnessy's on Thirty-third Street, next to St. Francis'. She could tell it made them nervous, someone in there as well dressed as she was. She had her green alliga or shoes on, she remembered, and the matching bag her father had given her. Actually, she had got the shoes to go with the bag; her father had brought her the bag before the war, but it was still in perfect condition in 1955. That was the kind of thing her father always gave her, well made, of the best materials. He had a respect for materials. He was a man of quality.

She had to talk Cyprian out of automatically buying the cheapest thing; he had that kind of panic reflex about money that everyone had who'd been brought up without enough of it. How she had loved walking through the aisles of beautiful cloth, yards of green silk, black vestments made up, the rose worn only twice in the year, on Gaudete and Laetare Sunday, the white lace albs. It was what she loved most in life and most valued: objects, perfectly crafted, for specific uses. In her own house she loved the little gold scissors used only for cutting grapes; in church she loved the pyx, used only to bring the Host to the dying; the corporal, on which the chalice rested. And she loved Cyprian for recognizing, when she brought the green chasubles to his attention, the most perfect watered silk, the fine, almost invisible gold cross. She loved him for saying "This one," for knowing the love of objects as she did.

She had loved the nuns in St. Scholastica's, her high school, for their beautiful white hands, the shape of their nails. the noiselessness of their feet in their excellent shoes on the wooden floors. And she had loved the ledger books they kept with their fine black pens with tips of gold. She loved their mathematics more than their Latin, longed to know where all that material to make their huge habits came from, who starched the white linen parts and what nun, sitting at a perfect desk wide as a room, paid bills so that these lovely women could eat the best food on what she guessed (but did not know, for no mere girls could ever see it, only the nuns and the priest who said mass for them) was beautiful china, rimmed with one thin, perfect line of gold.

She wanted that for herself, that convent life. She saw herself always the superior of her order: ordering things, paying for things, fingering the books, which blossomed under her stern and loving manipulations into carpets, linen, chairs and foreign missions, where the sisters preserved themselves from tropical diseases by wearing only white and eating only at their own formal table.

But her father had asked her to wait until after college, and she had, studying mathematics, coming home at night. doing problems in her bedroom, using the beautiful pen her father had bought her for confirmation, getting the highest grades, going to the sisters' college, knowing they knew she would be one of them soon and were delighted to have someone with her intellect and breeding. For, Sister Alphonsa confided to her, having her to tea in the parlor (since she knew Clare would be with them soon), most of the girls they got as postulants were frightfully common, and she wished they could be required to take elocution lessons before they were allowed out of the novitiate.

Clare had planned to enter the month after her college graduation, but her father died in March of her senior year, and Sister Alphonsa, acting on the advice of the superior, had let her know that they felt her place was with her dear mother, who was so delicate, rather than in the community. They led her to see that her entering would be an act of selfishness now, that God had demanded of her an extraordinary sacrifice, that God's ways were not ours. that God needed fine lay-women in the world.

The world was not what she wanted. The world was shabby and random, frayed and made of odds and ends. She wept, in silence, in despair, in the room that she loved best when she thought she was about to leave it, and was cheerful before her mother, who took to her bed, and entered her father's business, Leary and Kavanagh, manufacturers of fine leather goods, specializing in briefcases, and went to work in the office behind the beautiful, perfect store on Fifty-seventh Street between Park and Madison, which her father had opened just before the First World War.

It was then that she met Cyprian, just after she started working in the business. Sister Alphonsa had praised him, said he specialized in retreats for working women, suggested that Clare make one, for she was, Sister Alphonsa said, most in need of spiritual refreshment at this time. So she had gone to the convent of Our Lady of Sorrows and confessed that she was falling into the sin of hopelessness, that she suffered resentments, that she had great trouble in accepting the will of God. She had explained her situation and the priest invited her to talk to him in his office. And he had allowed her to talk. Never had there been a man like Cyprian to talk to, to let her weep without making her feel weakened, to appeal to her plain good sense, to remind her of the quality of her relationship with God; the excellence, the sureness, the solidity, the pure, tactile knowledge of the finest, the most beautiful, that would not be diminished by the wear, the brushes and the rapid, damning clips that were our lives.

Finally, after working in the business for a year, meeting with men—salesmen, accountants, men holding briefcases full of stuff for her to smell and touch and judge, to look at closely for hidden weaknesses— she knew that this was the world she was born for: to sit at the head of a table and dictate letters to a secretary older than her mother, to sit up nights over columns of numbers, eating sandwiches some young man had run for, smoking cigarettes she did not finish, so complete was her absorption in the black numbers before her.

After two years, she confessed to Father Cyprian that she was happy, with the gratitude of one who has been saved from drowning. For she could have drowned, could have lost, in the effort of simple breathing, her sense that life is more than simple breathing, could have become, like Muriel, like so many of the women who made the retreats, so many who gave up something to care for their mothers, pigeon-breasted, blind to fabric, frightened of scent and cigarettes, of men's hats, of rich foods and charge accounts, of lunch with strangers from across the country.

She was a woman who wore the best English tweeds,

blouses made to order, Italian shoes given as gifts by
grateful salesmen, perfume she bought so an ounce lasted
a year. She became—she knew she was not beautiful—a
handsome woman, a woman of quality. She had the defined, cutout look of a woman who handled money. Men
were fond of her, wanted to take her to lunch, but no one
had asked her to bed, nor did she yearn for the warmth
of men's caresses or the softening lines of a domestic life.
Both the life and the caresses seemed to her breathed
over, handled, enfeebling, and she treasured life most
when it seemed most distinguished and least blurred.
Once Cyprian had said to her, "I never worry about your
committing sins of impurity, even though you rub elbows
with all sorts of people, because I know you're too objective for that."

At first she was stung by the words, as she had been the
first time she had overheard someone referring to her as
plain, but she knew both were true. She was plain, she
was objective, and in fact those were what in her nature
she most treasured. She was plain and objective like stars
cut out on a perfectly black sky, like figures drawn in
black on perfectly white paper.

Cyprian thought of her differently than he did of the
other women. Because she had been born with money
and made more, he did not think her quite a woman. On
their visit the year before, twenty years after she had lost
her last regret about not having joined the convent, as
they sat examining the results of the soil samples he had
sent the county agent on her advice before he bought the
property, he had said, "You know, after all, you would
have hated it in a convent with all those women. You
think like a man."

She had not thought then to be hurt, for she knew what
he meant. He was a man who had spent his life listening
to women, guiding them through their doubts, their hyste-
rias, their day fears, their night terrors. Clare did not
doubt; she was not uncertain. She had a mind like his,
made of some durable and porous substance. Like him,
she was interested in everything. That was the miracle of
Cyprian—everything interested him. He was concerned,
like her, about the way things worked: the Federal Re-
serve Board, the process of galvanization. And it was to

Clare he came when he needed the money to go to Canada. It was she to whom he confided his shame at leaving the order he had entered at fifteen and lived in for thirty years. It was she to whom he said, quite simply, "Above all, I must get away. I am afraid I will lose my mind." And with the same simplicity, he said he needed money, he hadn't a cent. And she had stood up quietly, turned to the desk where she kept the checkbook and, with her back to him, written a check for two thousand dollars. He told her he would pay her back slowly. He had paid her, these fifteen years, four hundred dollars. He spoke of the debt each time they were alone. She had told no one of this, not even Charlotte. She had not told her mother.

So many of the women who gathered around Cyprian were the ones left to take care of their parents because they had not been chosen by men. But it was more than that. They accepted things as no one else would accept them anymore. Clare alone knew their differentness and accepted her own: the rest of them lived in a virginity far more radical than their intact physical states. They lived, unbelievably, among people like themselves. They made a living on their own kind. Muriel took in typing from priests; Elizabeth taught third grade and, with two other teachers, went to three-thirty mass every day at St. Jean's Church; Charlotte worked for Tom O'Brien, president of the Catholic Insurance Brokers' Guild, who would not sell insurance to divorcees; Mary Rose lived somehow above everything; even the prostitutes she talked to had some brush with the Church. But Clare lunched with men who stroked their secretaries' knees under tables. She hired girls, beautiful girls—she had to keep in her father's store a tone of elegance—who bled in her bathroom from botched abortions. She bought Spanish leathers from a fat Austrian who, she had been told, had a predilection for young boys.

She had no real friends among the people that she worked with, for she feared their incomprehension. She feared passing that point of intimacy after which someone would feel free to say, "I hope you don't mind my asking, but what is it with you?" Her virginity no one would believe; they preferred to think of her as having cleverly hidden something unspeakable, some practice that would

shock even the most casual of them. She did not want
them to now that she left the small, good restaurants she
favored to go home to her mother, who, preserving her invalid status as a trophy for having given birth to Clare,
had preserved as well a body with such modest expectations of health that it had remained virtually unchanged.
Her mother would perhaps outlive her. She did not want
them to know of her genteel conversations on her
mother's bed, of her mother's saying, after she had asked
Clare about her day, "Don't talk to me about the business. I never could bear to hear your father say a word
about the business. It makes my head ache."

And she did not want them to know about her daily
mass, how she knelt before a God she could see as a fine,
dull whiteness of absolute quality, without fray or flaw.

Her secretiveness made people fearful, and she had
heard more than one of the girls who worked for her say,
"She's as hard as nails, like all dykes." She did not want
anyone to know that she had never for one second wished
another human to have access to her body. If for no other
reason, she suspected that such knowledge would make
people think her easy to cheat.

And so, as different as she was from these women with
whom she spent her vacation, she was at her ease only
among them. Even knowing as she did that they lived in
a world as fragile and as insubstantial as a house of snow,
this was the world that was home to her. Felicitas she
loved as she loved no other. She had loved Felicitas' baby
hand grabbing onto her skirts as they crossed streets together; she loved the days when she had Felicitas in the
store, looking up from her book when Clare came out
from the back to take care of an important customer. She
loved their lunches at Longchamps, where they ate cream
puff after cream puff, pretending that Felicitas needed
practice learning to eat them properly, using only a fork.
She wanted for Felicitas a life of quality, a sure life. She
wished for Felicitas a life in which she need choose nothing that was not the best. In her will, she left the proceeds
of the sale of the business to Cyprian and Felicitas. She
had opened a trust fund for Felicitas when she was born.
Her education, Charlotte knew, was taken care of. Clare
had, in addition, after Cyprian had come to her in such

need, opened a savings account for him. There was twenty thousand dollars in it now. But she had kept the bankbook, and he did not know of the account's existence. Clare knew it had to be that way, for he knew no more of money than a child. Now she would give him the money so that he could build his house.

Mary Rose thought it was adorable, the way Cyp and Felicitas drove off together every morning after mass. She got a kick out of Felicitas. She was a funny little thing, a little monkey of a girl, but she was all girl and things interested her, they really did, that all the others didn't see. Mary Rose knew; she had nieces, and a lot of the girls that worked with her at the theater were, what, maybe sixteen.

The poor kid, it was a queer life for her, although she didn't seem unhappy. At first when she looked at Mary Rose, it used to make Mary Rose feel spooky. She had those spooky eyes, like Patty McCormack in *The Bad Seed*. Not that Mary Rose had seen it—it was on the condemned list—but she'd seen the posters: PROMISE YOU WILL NOT REVEAL THE ENDING. It scared her and she was an adult; what would it do to a teen-ager who came in? And she knew from experience it was teen-agers who flocked to see that kind of movie. Mary Rose had to usher at those movies now, even if they were on the condemned list, because you couldn't just say to a boss, "Look, I have to take two weeks off until you stop showing this movie." After all, two weeks was two weeks, and even though she was crazy about Joe Siegel, the manager, and he would give her the shirt off his back, still, he had to run a business, and it was that kind of thing that made people think Catholics were fishy. Which Mary Rose personally was against. Although one time she had a very interesting discussion about the Legion of Decency with Joe, and he admitted that he wished there was a Jewish Legion of Decency so he'd have an easy way of telling his kids what they should see and what they should back away from. He knew there was, "Excuse me, Mary Rose," he had said, a lot of crap on the market and it gave kids all kinds of ideas. The thing about Joe was, he was really a gentleman, so she didn't like to make a lot of trouble for him about not working at movies that were condemned.

Anyway, she didn't think Felicitas was like Patty Mc-Cormack in *The Bad Seed* anymore. It was just that the kid was a real thinker. In a way, she was kind of like a young Ann Blyth, like Ann Blyth when she was a teenager in those movies with Jane Withers. Now, Ann Blyth was somebody who gave Mary Rose a lot of hope. She'd been somebody who had kept the faith and stayed in the business. Married a doctor, too. It was true she hadn't done anything since *The Helen Morgan Story*, but that was by choice, because she wanted to spend time with her children, not because the studios didn't want her.

So many people in the business were divorced or up to something funny. Like Ingrid Bergman, whom Mary Rose loved. Didn't she look like a regular angel in *The Bells of St. Mary's?* She looked perfect in that habit, a perfect nun. Who would believe she'd run off on her husband and get in trouble with some Italian director and then just have a baby. She had to admit that disappointed her, although she didn't miss one Ingrid Bergman movie and she was all over herself when they got an Ingrid Bergman movie at the theater.

That was one of the things that made Mary Rose feel ashamed of herself. Muriel said she wouldn't go to any movies that had any divorced people in them. Mary Rose piped up that at that rate Muriel would never get to see a movie. And Muriel said, "So be it," which really made Mary Rose feel put in her place and thoroughly ashamed, so that the next day in confession she asked Cyprian if he thought it was a sin, her being an usher for condemned movies. She explained to him that she'd probably lose her job if she said no, and that at her age she didn't know where she'd get another job, and that a lot of movies weren't even hiring ushers anymore, and how in some ways Joe Siegel kept her on out of the goodness of his heart, and what would her mother do if she lost her job?

Cyprian said she should try as best as she could not to work at those times. Perhaps she could ask to take her vacation those days. And then right there in confession a terrible thought came to her: she hated the idea of taking her vacation in days, January maybe, or some crazy time,

instead of being able to come up to Orano with her friends
in the summer, where she could walk around and at least
get some good fresh air into her lungs. So then, being that
she was so resentful of Muriel for bringing the matter up
in the first place, she had to confess *that*. And then Cyprian had a great idea. He said that when a condemned
movie was playing, she should ask if she could work at
the candy counter. That way she wasn't really connecting
herself with the movie as such. That was the great thing
about Cyprian, smart as he was, he had a lot of common
sense.

That night in bed, she had thought of a really good
comeback she should have given Muriel: *Song of Berna-
dette* starred Jennifer Jones, and she was divorced. But
Mary Rose wasn't the type to hold a grudge or keep an
argument going. Life was too short, and this was her vacation, and she was crazy about all the girls, even Muriel,
who was really kind about taking Mary Rose on nature
walks and pointing out the wildflowers.

No, Felicitas was a funny kid, but she was good for a
laugh, too. The latest was, she asked Mary Rose for cigarettes, and Mary Rose gave them to her. After all, she'd
been smoking since she was fourteen. And she asked
Mary Rose if she would show her how to put on make-up.
Felicitas said she always poked herself in the eye with the
wand of the mascara. Mary Rose could see Felicitas was
just a regular kid. She got a big kick out of her, and she
got a big kick out of her and Cyprian going off like spies,
always looking like they had state secrets.

Felicitas liked movies, too, although the latest was this
television thing with doctors. But Felicitas had come into
the theater to see *West Side Story*. Joe let Mary Rose
bring Felicitas in without paying, and she sat in the back
of the theater with Mary Rose, the two of them bawling
their eyes out. She stayed for three shows, so she landed
up spending the night with Mary Rose and Mary Rose's
mother.

Mary Rose wondered what her mother was up to while
she was here in the country. One thing was, she didn't
have to worry about her mother being lonely; she had to
worry more about the cops coming by to pick up one of
her mother's friends. But she didn't really have to worry
about that, because the cops were friends of her mother's

too, unless they were one of this new breed they sent to college at night.

Mary Rose's mother really liked the horses and she liked a game of cards. It was all right, she had her pension and Mary Rose was working and her mother was very good about not betting over her head. So sometimes they were a little short toward the end of the month, but then some months they had money to burn. Which they did burn; any money her mother won they were not going to be old sticks about and pay bills. They had made the bargain that they would always go out on the town with the money. Night clubs were what her mother liked, particularly the Copa on a Saturday night. Luckily, Mary Rose knew the headwaiter from the old days, so he always squeezed them in. He got a big kick out of seeing Mrs. Costello at eighty-six dressed to the nines. And he liked to talk to Mary Rose about the old days.

It was hard to believe, standing in the middle of a church driveway in 1963, that thirty years ago she was a dancer in a night club. A lot of water had gone under the bridge, a lot of it because of Cyprian. God, she'd been in bad shape when she'd met him. He'd saved her life.

It was a terrible time. Now it was hard to remember that she hadn't known Burt was that way at the time. But God, she was, what, twenty years old when she met him?

They were trying out for a show together. Fred Astaire and his sister were in it. She was a real lady. He never got a partner like her again. Mary Rose thought Ginger Rogers was coarse.

She ought to have known, but she didn't because Burt seemed so sweet. He was really like a little boy and a lot more polite than anyone she'd ever gone out with. And religious, too. He never asked anything of her, not in that way, and that was a relief because most of the people she went out with, knowing she was in show business, thought she was loose, which she absolutely was not. One guy said what all the guys told each other was you never got anywhere with a girl who wore a miraculous medal, so she got herself a miraculous medal and wore it *outside*, even if it didn't look good with that particular outfit. Looking back on it, that was part of the problem with Burt. But who would have thought it was a problem that somebody acted like a gentleman and kept his hands to himself?

Even when he danced there was something serious about it. Even when he was clowning. At first after they were married, she thought he just didn't want to have sex with her because he was shy, but it would be okay when they were married for a while longer and he got used to her. There was no one she could talk to about it, and everyone kept making jokes about when was she going to get pregnant. She would lie in the bed at night, hearing the cars on the street, wishing she could be out there in one of those cars or walking, talking to anybody, in a drugstore, anywhere but there, lying on the bed knowing something was wrong.

At nights they were both working in the Astaire show, so she thought maybe the morning would be a good time. One morning she turned to him, took his head in her hands, kissed him as they had kissed while they were courting. And then it happened. He fell on top of her. He opened her legs. She knew that would happen, but he opened them like he hated them, like he wished they would break. And he did it to her before she was ready. She thought he would kiss her, but he was on top of her, bucking, hurting, wanting to hurt.

Then he got up and was sick in the bathroom. And then all the trouble began. He started writing her these crazy letters. He told her she had unleashed a devil, that he had tried to keep the devil locked up in his heart. He started drawing crazy pictures, pictures of she didn't know what, crazy-looking boys with big penises, and then he'd draw circles over the penises to try to block them out, and then she'd come upon them in one of the drawers or in the bread bin or something. That was after they had been married only two months. But then sometimes he was just nice and sweet and his old self, and they'd go for walks or for a soda at Whelan's after the show. They'd hold hands on the subway, and she was sure everything would go away. She loved him so much, they were going to be so happy.

Then he got worse and took knives to her. She still thought she couldn't tell anybody. Because she was his wife and she'd seen enough troubles come to marriages from the outside. She didn't even want to tell the parish priest. So she went to confession on the other side of the city, to someplace where the Paracletists were having a mission. That was how she met Cyprian.

Maybe it was being in the dark, or maybe it was being in a strange church, or maybe it was just Cyprian, but something happened the minute she heard his voice. "God bless you," he said like any other priest, but something happened. It was as if someone had pressed a spot inside her throat so sore that she'd lived with it because she hadn't dared to touch it. She began, "Bless me, Father, for I have sinned." But then she stopped and said, "Well, no, it's not exactly that I've sinned."

And then he did something perfectly wonderful in the dark. He laughed.

But she knew he was not laughing at her. She knew she could tell him everything. Something dropped, some hard thing, earth loosened, liquid ran through her veins. They felt sharp, electric, as if cold had surprised her, shocked her, making spaces through which colder air could travel. This was perfect freedom in the darkness with a man she could not see who could forgive her. And who had laughed. She had always thought God was someone who was always amused, amused at her, but not only at her. God stood at the head of a table, not a wooden table, but something temporary, set up only for the occasion. Heaven was everyone delighted to see everyone, everyone dressed up. And God was the most delighted.

So she could tell this man, whose face she could not see, whose voice she loved, that life was a nightmare. That she lived with someone who whispered when he thought she slept that he wished only for her death and who then would put his head in her lap and say, "Help me. Help me. Something is wrong in me." That she could not tell anyone, that she was frightened, she was afraid of dying, of being killed, that she had failed, that if she loved him enough or in the right way this would not have happened, that there must be something wrong with her that simply being her husband had done this to him.

And she said to the priest, "I don't know what to do."

And he said, "Of course you don't."

That was wonderful, for in some ways that had been

the most painful to her, that she did not know what to do, that she was, in the most important way, the only important way, a stupid person who didn't know what to do. She was afraid that being a wife meant you always knew what to do about your husband. And she did not know what to do.

And then this priest, whose name she did not know, invited her into the office in the rectory, the office with the pictures of the popes on the wall, Pius X, Leo XIII, Pius XI. Why were they all called Pius, she wondered. She knew she wouldn't have chosen that name if she were pope, and she certainly would have tried to talk any friend of hers out of it. The housekeeper showed her into the office and she waited for the priest. He came in from another door, a door to which she suspected women had no access.

How beautiful his color was, high red by high cheekbones, black hair, brown eyes that she thought could see everything. He had forgiven her, but those eyes were not forgiving; she could see forgiveness was something he had put on with his ordination. He was not born to it.

He was a tall man, a strong man. He could protect her, or any woman, from physical danger. She thought how good he would have been on stage. And she thought what she had thought a lot before but knew she must not think because it was probably sacrilegious, that the Church was kind of like the theater, that sometimes at mass she got the same thrill she did when she saw a really good play.

The priest sat down behind the desk and said, "We must think of something to help you."

She told him about Burt, his threats, his weeping, his desire to kill her, his desire to kill himself. Was he a Catholic, asked the priest. Where were his parents? He seemed pleased that Burt was a Catholic and his parents were in Jersey City. That was all he wanted to know. She could tell that was all he needed to know.

He asked if she would like him to come to her house and try to talk to her husband.

"Yes, please," she said.

And then she wept, because she knew this man would make something happen.

When she got home, Burt had filled the apartment with

lighted candles. He was saying the rosary out loud, but really loud, in a crazy way. It frightened her more than any of his threats. It frightened her more than his taking a knife to her. She hoped the priest would come soon. It was four o'clock. She remembered thinking that the earliest he would probably come was seven-thirty. That was what people meant when they said "night" or "evening."

She closed the bedroom door and sat there reading, hearing him outside shouting prayers. The doorbell rang at seven-fifteen. Burt answered it. He saw the priest but did not stop his praying. Mary Rose came out of the bedroom. The priest nodded to her. And then he turned to Burt and said, "I'm Father Cyprian. I want you to come with me."

And very simply, like the boy she had loved him for being, he went out the door. She had never seen him again.

Father Cyprian called her that night and said he had put him in Bellevue, that she would have to sign some papers, but not right now. Many of the doctors there were his friends.

She thanked him, but she was not grateful. Where had he put Burt without asking her? It was a hospital where no one she knew ever went. But she had not known what to do and he had helped her. She was no longer in danger of death.

Burt was declared insane. Mary Rose was represented in court by a lawyer who was a friend of Cyprian's. Cyprian went with her to Burt's parents, to her own parents, and explained. No one questioned him; everyone seemed grateful for his attention, grateful that a priest, and such a priest, not just a parish priest but a Paracletist, an order priest, had taken over.

While Cyprian was in New York, he visited Burt occasionally. He advised her never to go to the hospital herself; he said it was unnecessary and would disturb someone like her too deeply. She obeyed him.

Only once had she rebelled, when she had fallen in love with Billy Dole and had asked Cyprian if there was any way she could remarry. He told her that her marriage to Burt had been a lawful one; Burt had not been insane at the time of the marriage, and the marriage had been consummated. He reminded her of the words of Christ: "What therefore God hath joined together, let no man put asunder." And again: "For they shall be two in one flesh." "He said two," said Father Cyprian, "not three."

She had gotten angry. She was so seldom in her life angry that her anger stood out in her memory, rare and oddly valuable. She had said to Cyprian, "What do you know about the flesh? I'm tired of you running my life."

He had said nothing. And after a beat of silence like the silence before a rain, she fell to her knees before him and asked his forgiveness.

"There's nothing to forgive," he said. "You're only human. Everyone breaks down."

But he never broke down. And he never said to her, even in that moment of her unforgivable ingratitude, what he had a perfect right to say: "What would you do without my help?"

She could not imagine where she would be without him. Dead at the hands of a maniac or married outside the Church, her life ruined by guilt, one of those mothers who has to beg the parish priest to let her child make first communion with the others.

All those years he had not failed her. He had kept her on the path. He had reminded her of the love of God, which was beyond her understanding. He told her God had chosen her for a special trial and that she might be, without knowing it, simply through her example and her sacrifice, a channel of extraordinary graces. He reminded her of the joy she brought to her mother's life. He told her she was an edification to him. He told her that her friendship with Joe Siegel was not a sin as long as she knew there could be nothing between them until the day Burt died.

Her life would have been impossible without Cyprian. She watched him drive away in his red truck. She saw his dark head through the window and beside him, golden, the head of the child.

II

Felicitas waited for him to say something. Sometimes she would wait for miles. The trees passed them, the speed of their travel feathering the leaves so they seemed lighter, the dark summer greens of trees she could not name. She would wait for him to say something and she would feel her heart tight, like a bird's heart, because she wanted to please him, so full was she of honor to be where she was.

What was it on his face? He was not happy; he was not glad to see her. He was never glad. Even when he laughed he wasn't happy. He laughed a lot, but usually at someone. Even when she said something to be funny, something to make her mother laugh, or Clare, or Elizabeth, or Mary Rose, he would step back, as if he were stepping back into the shade to calculate the light. Sometimes she felt he was looking at her through one of those machines surveyors had, to get a better look at her. Or sometimes she could imagine him looking down at her through the sight of a rifle; she could imagine that in the eye of his mind there was a cross wire, and he struggled to center it in the middle of her body. Sometimes she imagined the cross wire, a blade that could slice her perfectly in two. She could imagine the top half of her body falling in one direction, the bottom in another, and he walking over in his cassock to look inside, pulling out some things, putting in others, all her organs now rectangular and dry. No blood, just rearrangement.

His hands on the wheel were always darker than the hands of anyone she knew, as if he were more exposed to sun. They were the hands that held the Body of Christ, curved now around the steering wheel. All the women spoke of what a comfort he was to them, but she could not see in those hands the promise of comfort. "Do more,

35

you can do more. Do more, for you must," those hands said to Felicitas, who loved them above all others.

He taught her things about building, things that no one she was friends w'th knew about. Now he was teaching her to use the power saw, even though her mother said, "For Christ's sake, Cyp, she could cut her whole goddamn hand off."

When Cyprian didn't listen to her mother like that, Felicitas felt two ways. First, she was excited at the power of not listening to her mother's voice. It thrilled her that one adult would defy another adult for her sake. Would defy *her mother*. But she was more like her mother than she was l'ke Cyprian. She was not a man. She had seen other men do that. She had seen that look on the fathers of her friends. It said, "In this world you are not important." It said, "I." It said, "Obey me only."

When Cyprian wanted her to do what her mother didn't want her to, she didn't know what to do. But she did what Cyprian told her. He was a priest. Chosen by God and anointed. No woman could be.

He taught her how to make cement. He had her lift buckets of it wet. Her mother said, "Cyp, what about her insides? She's a girl. You don't know about that kind of thing."

Father Cyprian said, "She is a girl and not a flower." And sometimes he said, "She's not the kind of girl a man will spend a lifetime taking care of." And he said, "She won't throw her life away on some man. She knows better. She has too much to do."

But when he said, "She is a girl and not a flower," Felicitas wept for all that she was not and would not be.

When he worked in cement, the gray got under his nails, clung to the reddish hairs and made his hands look ancient. Before mass, he cleaned his hands for half an hour. To make straight the way of the Lord.

"It is a great temptation to mistake nature for the God of nature," said Cypr an, s'gnaling left.

Felicitas was silent. She knew that there was nothing she was supposed to say.

"This beauty all around us modern man mistakes for God. Pantheism. Natural beauty is only a reflection of divine beauty. It has no meaning in itself. We love it only in that it is a foretaste of the beauty of God. It is a particularly American error, the love of nature for its own sake. Protestants, having no tradition, having put their faith only in the Bible, having ignored or repudiated the great beauty of apostolic succession, need some source and look to nature to find the truth about God. But nature is not like God; it is capricious, it is amoral, it does not partake of divine reason. It has nothing to teach us. It is only for the soul a temporary rest."

"Why did you move to the country, then?" asked Felicitas, knowing that for the moment she could ask him anything, as long as it was "in a genuine and humble spirit of inquiry."

"Because nature at least conforms to the natural law. The cities conform to nothing but their own rottenness."

"I like the city," said Felicitas.

"You'll grow out of that," said Father Cyprian. "You will come to realize the rottenness of the age into which you were born. John Kennedy, the television Catholic. Holding hands with communists. He was educated by communists. A man named Laski was his greatest inspiration. A man who hated God.

"Look at the Cuban missile crisis. It was his inability to understand the relentless nature of the communist conspiracy that led him into a crisis. A totally unnecessary crisis that plunged us to the brink of war."

Felicitas remembered that day at school. They assembled everyone in the auditorium, which had stained-glass windows like a church but with gates in front of them for protection against basketballs, volleyballs, spitballs; the parish stressed athletics, and there were orange rims of baskets at either end of the room. Sometimes mass was said here when the church became too full, and Felicitas would see the drama of the transubstantiation through holes of a basketball net.

That day everyone was festive because classes broke early at eleven. There was the Mediterranean release of sentences cut in half, books left open, problems unsolved, numbers meaningless and incomplete on blackboards, the excitement of the formation of a line and a march down to the auditorium in silence—for Catholic children could go nowhere but in silence, on a line. They fanned out into the empty room they would fill, rebellion always just below the surface. One villain blew the paper off a straw he had secreted; it flew up into the thick and dusty air, a daring slice, almost itself air, and fell down on the head of some third-grader, who popped it into his mouth. But no one noticed. The nuns were huddled together, whispering. It made the children whisper, and the whisper grew, untoward, unprecedented, as the alert nuns grew torpid in their worried knots and just for once forgot the danger of the whispering, the moving in one's seat that could result, God knew, in all the chaos of the world.

Sister Raymond Josephine, the pr ncipal, who wore orthopedic shoes, whose face had flattened from the pain of her sore feet, whose skin was waxy and who had over her thin upper lip a yellow, almost but not quite invisible mustache, stood on the stage where the Christmas play took place and the Holy Name Society minstrel show late in October. She tapped the microphone. Fel citas could tell from the way she tapped the microphone, miraculously without rage, that something had gone very wrong. And she would tell them; she was on that stage to let them know.

Felicitas looked around her, in case she died there. She tried to choose among her classmates the one she would like to die beside. She thought of the fat face of Khrushchev, the sh ning face of John F. Kennedy, the soft shoe of Nikita Khrushchev, the soft foreign shoe he banged on the table of the United Nations when he vowed to bury the Americans, the hard, expensive shoes of John F. Kennedy, the shoe with pinholes in the leather, wing tips they were called, which showed he was a man a girl was right to love. And she thought of dying w thout her mother, only a mile away in Mr. O'Brien's insurance office, of the dangerous air, dense with sharp hooks and fatal to the naked skin, air full of fire that no one could see. She saw herself walking the mile to reach her mother and arriving there in flames, her face gone and her arms two cinders.

"In the name of the Father and of the Son and of the Holy Ghost," said S ster Raymond Josephine. And then the Hail Mary. Announcements were always begun with a prayer. To remind us that all things came from God.

"Boys and girls, the President of the United States has announced a state of national emergency. The Russians have landed missiles on Cuba, which, as you know, has become a communist country, only ninety miles from our own shores."

Felicitas tried to calculate ninety miles. It was half the distance to Orano. The communists were half the distance from America that she was from Father Cyprian.

Sister Raymond Josephine announced a day of recollection. After lunch, all children would return not to school but to church, where they would spend the rest of the day assembled in prayer.

Felicitas regretted most of all, more than the Cubans or the Russians, more than dying in flames of fire, more than having to live under godless communism, that she had brought her lunch to school that day. If only she had decided to meet her mother at the office and had gone to lunch with her in the luncheonette, as she had done every day of her school life until seventh grade, when she decided she wanted to have lunch with her friends. Who were her friends now, that she would die with? She looked around at the scared faces and wondered that she had ever chosen Mary Ellen Manning or Janet Byrne or Eileen Corrigan over her mother even for one hour of her life, even to share sandwiches with in the dark, gray basement lunchroom, where they now would wait for bombs.

The children ate in silence. Even the eighth grade, Felicitas' class, the oldest, did not shout or talk about boys or singers. They prayed silently. Sister Imelda, the art nun, led the rosary while they ate.

In the schoolyard, all the jockeying for who would walk with whom, all the fierce, colored passion for proximity to those most loved, most imitated, melted away, and children held each other's hands like European children, like the pictures they had seen of victims they had thought remote and now were practicing to be.

At one o'clock, the sisters led them class by class across the street to church. Mary Ellen Manning tapped Felicitas, "Do you think this is what it said in the Fatima letter?"

"I don't know," said Felicitas.

"You know, I heard the pope fainted when he read it."

"Nobody knows that for sure," said Felicitas, who had been trained by Father Cyprian to beware of pious rumors.

"Maybe it said it was the end of the world in 1962," said Mary Ellen.

The end of the world. The children knelt in church, closer to one another in their pews than usual, and thought: *The end of the world. Planes, bombs, fire,* they thought, praying.

"St. Michael the archangel, defend us in battle, be our protection against the wickedness and snares of the devil." This was a prayer they said every day, at every mass, against the spread of communism.

The day of recollection began with benediction. Dressed in gold, his gold back to them, the pastor knelt. The organist began, *"O Salutaris Hostia."*

O Saving Victim. What did that mean? Nothing. Felicitas had known the Latin since she had been in school. Since before she had met Father Cyprian. She had always known those words, and always known those backs, those splendid golden backs turned toward her, backs of men as gods who made God come among his people. She could feel it, the presence of God. How could He end the earth in flame? Once He had done it, in water. Flame, then. Flame would come of God.

Her only prayer was, *Let me die beside my mother. Let me not die among strangers.*

She thought of her mother's buoyant flesh, the tautness of her freckled arms, her perfume, her white handkerchiefs with her initials monogrammed, "for the office," and her suits, her brooches, for she went to business, not like anybody's mother, and did not wear slippers in the house after she sent the children off, but went out with her child, to work, to the world, where people knew her. From the world she brought back money, stories, imitations and contempt for mothers of small children who complained about their easy lot. Felicitas wanted to die beside her mother, and she prayed, not to be spared disaster but to die where she belonged.

"Go your way, your faith has saved you." These were the words she thought with her eye upon the monstrance, in which Christ as bread was housed.

Once Father Cyprian said a German priest translated those words from the Greek: "Go your way, your faith has made you safe."

Felicitas prayed only for the safest of her mother's close proximity. And yet she felt once more upon them all God's presence, safety, majesty, the gold of benediction. The sun came down upon them, and the Flame would come, and over all God watched, the Eye inside the triangle, and brooded and drew back. He would not save them. He would bring them to Himself.

All the long afternoon the children prayed, as strangers, then as brothers, then as animals. For comfort. To be spared.

And now, driving in the truck, Felicitas thought that they had been spared because the Holy Spirit had inspired John F. Kennedy, who was not, as Father Cyprian had said, a fool.

"I think Kennedy's good," said Felicitas one year after the Bay of Pigs.

"That's why he was elected. Because the mind of the average voter is the mind of a fourteen-year-old girl."

Thus could he silence her. But he could not make her change her mind.

"Our age has put its trust in reason, and reason is a whore. She goes with anyone."

They passed cows on their right, nestled into their eating as if it were an occupation to give over life to. Martyrs to eating they were, and Felicitas thought of the sweet heaviness of such a life, dull and potent, and she smelled the smart flick of wild onion; the brash, corrective tang flicked against the calm life she had dreamed.

She asked, "Is it bad for their milk if they eat wild onion?"

"Who?" said Father Cyprian, who was thinking of that whore, the human reason.

"Those cows. Any cows."

"Three things are poisonous to cows—clover and alfalfa and wild onion. The first two kill, the third destroys the sweetness of the milk."

Clover, she thought, which was so beautiful, could make cows die. She wanted to remark on the deceptiveness of nature, poisonous berries that shone, men who

were beautiful but who could bring disaster, all that could
be taken in the body, bringing death. But she said nothing. He was talking about cows.

The smell of wild onion reminded her that he did not
think noticing smells was a good idea. Once he had punished her for it.

Once she had said, her head swimming with new grass,
the words for it coming to her tongue like quick, light fish,
meadowsweet, cowslip, peascod, baby's breath, looking at
him foolishly, for she was in love with the green atmosphere, "I think heaven will smell like this."

He gunned the engine, fierce with anger, his hands tight
around the wheel to punish her.

"In heaven there are no smells. No puppies and kittens.
No fur coats. I am sure that even you will be sufficiently
absorbed in the vision of God that you will not wish for
perfume."

Then he stopped the car in front of Myron Haber's
farm. Myron Haber had gone to school with him. He did
not call him Cyprian, the name he had been given in the
order, but Phil, his given name, the name people had
known him by before he left to join the Paracletists.

He said to Myron Haber, "I want to show this young
lady the difference in manures. She says she's interested
in perfumes."

Then they laughed, and Felicitas would always remember that laugh. In that laugh she was *the other*. She would
know always in that laugh what it was to be the outsider,
the woman among men, the black among whites, the child
among adults, the foreigner among natives. Always in her
life her outrage at injustice would bring back those men
laughing and the smells they made her smell.

Myron Haber's farm was filth and death and heaviness
in every limb that made no action possible. Myron Haber
let the windows blow out of his house. He let the trash pile
up before it. He let his dogs bite his children, let his children die of thirst, his sons go without shirts, his daughters
walk around in the old clothes of their brothers. He let his
wife lose all her teeth but three in back and two at the
bottom, where they did no good. She told Felicitas each
time she came that she could eat nothing solid. She pulled
Felicitas inside the house and whispered, "He won't buy

anything I can eat. Next time you come, bring baby food. Hide it under your shirt."

Myron Haber had old cars that piled and rusted under trees from which his children picked but never ate fruit. Felicitas believed that if she could one day learn not to hate the Habers, she would have found God. Cyprian would bring the Habers groceries, would take the children to the doctor's, would collect his old friend Myron from the jail or from the hospital or from some street in Orano where he had fallen nearly dead. He always brought Felicitas with him because he said that one of the paradoxes of God's love was that it could be found in the faces of the wretched. Because Christ said, "If you do unto these the least of my brethren, you do unto me."

Felicitas saw in the face of Myron Haber not the face of Christ but death and all that she preferred to die rather than recognize. Felicitas saw in that face the face of murder, the great pleasure of stopped breath. She knew that it was in her to kill Myron and his children and his wife, who longed for baby food. They were hate to her, not the Holy Spirit. They were all that was not God. She wished them death, a quick death, a quick transportation to a place where they would not inhabit flesh.

The beard on Myron Haber's face was gray, suggesting ruined meat. His mouth was perfectly evil and his eyes admitted no light. She could not imagine how he could see through those eyes. Myron Haber wished her harm. If he could, he would hurt her. And Father Cyprian had opened her up to this, would leave her with this man who she thought must be blind, so perfectly incapable of light were those dull eyes. He would leave her with Myron Haber to teach her something of the love of God.

"This is cow shit," said Father Cyprian, pulling a handful of brown dirt. "It has a warmer, meatier aroma."

"Chicken shit," he said, stooping for a yellow handful, "is a higher smell. More pungent, more bouquet."

"Take her out to the back, to the hogs, Phil," said Myron Haber, who could not stand up straight for laughing.

Cyprian took her hand. She could feel against her palms the dust of the manure liquifying into stinking mud. She could feel how the mud had traced the lines of his

palm. She followed him in fear. She could no more not
follow him than she could have refused a soldier at gun-
point. He was armed against her; he had weapons that
could kill.

The hog stood on his wicked feet, his eye half shut
with hate, with his complicity in punishing her crimes.

"Pig shit," he said, "is slimy and green, and among
connoisseurs, it is considered the most aromatic. This is
because pigs eat garbage, like the mind of modern man."

He pulled her over to the pigpen. She could feel her
stomach rise against her, something firm let go. She vom-
ited a clear brown pool against the pigpen, clear because
she had fasted for communion.

Silently, he covered her vomit with dirt. He wiped her
mouth with his own handkerchief. His arm around her,
he led her into the truck.

"I will not have you poisoned by the sentimental clap-
trap that passes for religion in this age. Christ and the
Virgin movie stars. The Passion just another cowpoke episode. Heaven a garden, the spiritual life a fireside chat
with Jesus. It is the spirit, Felicitas, the spirit that is life
eternal, not the smell of grasses."

She stared out at the grass and cried all the way home.
But told no one. And did not forgive. Vowed never to
forgive the force, the laughter.

Now, two years later, she had not forgiven. Sentimen-
tality? What did he mean by that that he so hated?

How could she understand it? He wanted for her a life
with God that had nothing to do with filthy Myron
Haber's farm but that was more like Myron Haber's farm
than like the smell of grasses. He wanted for her a love
that chose that farm before sweet fragrances.

Why? Because of what he had said, of what she had
been told of nature. Nature could trap. You could wander
among sweet grasses and not think of God. You could
mistake the grass for God, the fragrance. You could walk
in the early evening and see the white light with the iron-
colored light behind it. You could think that light was
God and not an emanation. You would not think that
Myron Haber's farm was God; you would search for God
to prove that life was not that farm, that sick disorder.
You would know that was not God; you would fly to God

from that, from that you would desire heaven. The grass could make you love the world, and Father Cyprian had said, in church and in the motel, holding a glass of whiskey, "You must hate the world and love God."

And you must not be womanish. It was womanish to say, "How sweet the grasses are." It was womanish to say the rosary during mass. It was womanish to carry pastel holy cards and stitched novena booklets bound with rubber bands. It was womanish to believe in happiness on earth, to be a Democrat, to care to be spoken to in a particular tone of voice, to dislike curses, whiskey and the smell of sweat. Vigil lights were womanish and spiritual chain letters, the *Catholic Digest,* the *Sacred Heart Messenger,* statues of the Infant of Prague that could be dressed in different colors for the different liturgical seasons.

The opposite of womanish was orthodox. The Passion of Christ was orthodox, the rosary said in private (it was most orthodox to prefer the sorrowful mysteries), the Stations of the Cross, devotion to the Holy Ghost, responding to the mass in Latin, litanies of the Blessed Virgin and the saints. Tower of ivory, house of gold, Ark of the Covenant, gate of heaven, morning star. To love these words was to know God. To love the smell of grasses was to be in error. Error has no rights, said Father Cyprian, explaining why it was that outside the Church there was no salvation.

There was in Father Cyprian nothing that was womanish. That made something in Felicitas' heart bend so that she valued more than anything in life that look in his eyes, the look that said, "You are the chosen one. Make straight the way of the Lord."

For the priesthood Cyprian had given over everything. For the priesthood, the signal honor, not of his singularity but of his estate, the order of Melchisedech, the honor he could share with no one in his family, who would now be honored to have him among them, not as son or brother but as he had been chosen. Whose sins he bound on earth were bound in heaven. And whose sins he loosed were loosed. He saw sometimes the perfect freedom of the absolution he could give. He saw the agonies of souls he could untie, a soul tied to the railroad tracks and he the hero in the nick of time. Death the train, inexorable, and yet we were, without it, nothing. He saw himself ungagging souls, souls that had been smothered, held prisoner by mustached villains. He could give them breath. He raised his hand. They were forgiven.

For this he had left his father and mother, entering forever the company of strangers. For this reason, when his brothers wrote him of his mother's death, he did not answer. He had written in reply to the letter saying she was dying, "Has she had the last sacraments?" His brother wrote back to say yes, of course, she had had extreme unction, but before she died she wished to have her sons around her bed.

He wrote to tell them it was sentimental. Privately he thought it was a Protestant invention. Sons around the table. Sons around the bed. He wrote his brothers to say that he would be united with his mother once again in heaven. He wrote to say that as long as he had ascertained that she had had the last rites, his responsibility as a son and as a priest were, to his satisfaction, now discharged. He wrote that he should be informed of her death but that he would stay where he was.

Besides, although he didn't mention it, he didn't have the money for the flight. He had at that time no regular income, having left the bishop of Charleston, South Carolina, in a disagreement that resulted from Cyprian's having, from the pulpit, forbidden the parishioners to use the sports facilities at the Y.M.C.A. under pain of mortal sin. When the news came of his mother's death, he had been six years relieved of his vows in the Paraclete order. He was dependent upon the charity of strangers, not a man among them except Frank, as penniless as he.

Clare had organized a subscription from the women who had over the years come to hear him preach, come to his confessional and his weekend retreats. Clare collected money and sent him each month a check for two hundred dollars, collected from eight women who waited for his New York visits like tame geese. Goose girls, he called them to himself. He could imagine them in their kerchiefs, colorless on early mornings, walking through colorful birds with murderous, sharp beaks. He could imagine them scattering grain; he could imagine their wooden shoes.

The priests he had left his parents for when the first Paracletist came up from Wilkes-Barre to preach a mission at their tiny church had betrayed him.

Father Adolphus spoke of the love of God, with the face of a saint. For many months Cyprian, who was then Philip, thought of the transparency of that face. He thought that was what the presence of God could do, make the face the substance of all sacred things—the transparent host, the candles, the flames themselves, consumed with light and fire. Which was God. In his own face, a farmer's son's face, he saw not that clear transparency but flesh, soil, earth, the animal he was. And he wished above all else to stand in those gold vestments, holding the monstrance in hands that were bound and sanctified. He wished to be anointed. He believed that the oil of anointment would seep into his flesh, catch fire and burn.

For this he left the farm that every year faced ruin and his brothers, who swam naked in the summer, whose round heads were shaved for lice, who wet the bed in winter. He wanted a face that was no face but a clear transparency. He would give over the flesh he lived in, the strong muscles of his back, so that his soul could show through the sharp, visible bones of his breast. To prove he was not flesh.

"Thou art a priest for ever, according to the order of Melchisedech . . . The Lord has sworn and he will not repent: thou art a priest forever . . . Without father, without mother, without genealogy, having neither beginning of days nor end of life, but likened unto the Son of God, continueth a priest for ever."

Those were Paul's words, Paul the chosen, struck down on the road, blinded; and his voice, on fire as his heart was, spoke of that great honor.

And the Old Testament words: "The priest shall dip his finger in the blood of the Victim for sin." Christ the Victim. The Saving Victim. Despised by men. "I am a worm and no man: the reproached of men, the outcast of the people." This David said, who danced before the Lord; and Peter, who denied and was the leader: "The stone which the builders rejected has become the cornerstone. And a stone of stumbling and a rock of scandal, to them who stumble at the word."

And this was his work, not among those who stumbled, but among those whom Peter called "a chosen generation, a kingly priesthood, a holy nation, a purchased people: that you may declare his virtues, who hath called you out of darkness into his marvellous light."

And of the whole sewer of the modern world, the great dark stink of it, only this remnant was left to him: women whose lives had gone bad in one way or another, who came to him in times of crisis. He was there, wearing the great distinction of his priesthood like a cloak cut big to hide the body.

They were perfectly faithful.

"And I will raise me up a faithful priest, who shall do according to my heart, and my soul; and I will build him a faithful house; and he shall walk all days before my anointed."

They had built him a faithful house. They sent him money every month of their lives. They had stood by him when he left his brothers, the priests he had left his home for.

How bitter those last days were. Days? They were years, in which he complained daily to the superior, "We are not living according to the rule."

The men were beginning to own cars in their own names if they were on the road and preaching. The founder had meant them to travel in poverty. How often Cyprian had come across a soul in need in a train station or sitting next to him on a bus. He was available; it was part of his ministry. A passenger among passengers. He was available for the salvation of their souls. To whom is a priest available in a car? Speeding down the murderous highway, anonymous in his black Chevrolet?

And in the monastery, the men no longer wore their habits. Chinos, that's what one of 'hem had said.

"What's that you're wearing, Father?" he had asked one of the young priests who sat on a bench in the garden reading a novel. *From Here to Eternity*. To think that someone should be allowed to bring such filthy hogwash inside monastery grounds. This boy had been in the war. The war had changed it all.

"Chinos, Cyp," said the young man, who did not put down his book to respond.

Cyprian had knocked the book out of his hand.

"Why are you out of the habit, Father?"

"I have permission of the superior, Father."

Enraged, Cyprian knocked on the huge dark door of the superior's office. The superior, Augustine Bass. He did not answer as everyone had answered to a knock when Cyprian was first in the order. *"Deo gratias,"* they used to say. "Yup," said Father Augustine Bass. When Cyprian opened the door, he saw the superior holding a golf club.

"Practicing my drive," said the superior.

"I beg your pardon, Father?" said Cyprian.

"What can I do for you, Cyprian?" said Father Augustine, putting down his golf club. Augustine did not like Cyprian, and Cyprian knew it. Augustine knew Cyprian had opposed his election, had favored the older, stricter man, Reginald. He had also heard Cyprian refer to him contemptuously as "the new breed." "Behold thou art lukewarm and I will vomit thee out of my mouth," Cyprian had once said of Augustine and his friends, who were trying to bring the order up-to-date. It had come to Augustine from more than one of the men that Cyprian had referred to him as "effeminate" and "womanish."

What, over the years, had they not differed on? There were the pictures of the Blessed Mother on the front of the mass cards: Cyprian wanted Giotto, and Augustine knew the public would not buy them but would have their masses said by the Franciscans, who would give them the Madonnas and the Sacred Hearts they liked. Cyprian objected to a woman's choir in the monastery parish church; he said it was not liturgical; he objected to their singing English hymns. Augustine stood up for the choir on the ground that it inspired feelings of togetherness among the women in the parish, who too often got no credit for their labors.

"Togetherness," Cyprian had said, walking out of the meeting in a rage. And here he was again, wearing the familiar face of his rage. "Togetherness is not found in canon law."

"Father," said Cyprian, refus'ng the seat Augustine had indicated, "one of the men is sitting in the garden in secular clothes reading a condemned book."

"Which one?" said Augustine, laughing as he opened his cigar box.

"Do you think it's amusing, Father Augustine, violation of the rule?"

"The rule may be interpreted by the superior. And I need not remind you, Father Cyprian, that I am the superior."

"Damn it, Augustine, the monastic life has no meaning if it's interchangeable with the life of the street."

"Cyprian, this is 1953."

"The year of our Lord, Father," said Cyprian, slamming the door of the superior's office.

After that, Cyprian had never been given any preaching assignments. He had never stepped into another pulpit as a Paracletist, except to say the six-thirty mass in the parish church. A mass filled w'th drunks and old women. He had been made to do manual labor while his brother priests, his brothers but inferior, he knew, in mind, took the retreats, preached the missions in the churches all around the country, reported back to him that pastors and parishioners had asked for him.

While he was fixing the toilets.

One day, the superior had called for him. When he opened the door, Augustine said, "Cyp, you're a farm boy. I hear you're a handy guy with tools, and these days, with the unions and all, you can't hire an honest workman for less than an arm and a leg. Well, you know, all the plumbing here is older than we are, and I was wondering if you could take it over as your special assignment until the summer."

"The plumbing?"

It was February.

"Yes."

"What about my Lenten assignments?"

"They will be given to some other man."

"Who?"

"That is not your province, Father. Your province is to obey your superior. According to the rule."

That late winter and spring he fixed the leaks, climbed

down the drains, replaced the washers and the ball-cock apparatuses. He had to work all day in workman's clothes. At night, he would change into his habit.

He prayed that winter for humility. He confessed each week the sin of spiritual pride. But his heart grew hard and bitter, and one day Raymond, the priest he had encountered in the garden, saw him replacing a lever on one of the toilets and said to him, "Out of habit, Father?"

And Cyprian's heart was filled with rage. He took his hand and made a fist of it, the hand that had held the Body of Christ. He knocked the young man down with a workman's punch and left him lying in the middle of the tools.

He confessed to his confessor what he believed to be a mortal sin. His confessor said he believed Cyprian incapable of sinning mortally. But he advised him to take a leave of absence. He told him that the archbishop of Tucson, a personal friend of his, was in desperate need of priests to cope with the great influx of Catholic population since the war. The bishop needed someone who could speak to the problems of both the more sophisticated Easterners and the simple Indians whose souls, too, were in his care. Father Reginald, Cyprian's confessor, said he thought Cyprian would be better away from the community. He should request to be secularized; he should request to be released from the Paracletists to be a secular priest under the bishop of Tucson.

In the confessional, Father Cyprian mourned for the early matins he had sung with his brother priests, for the silent meals in the refectory, for the debates about the spiritual life, about St. Thomas, for the rule, which he had left his parents for.

He wrote a letter asking permission to be secularized. Augustine Bass granted it and applied to Rome. Rome's answer took two months. In the meantime, Cyprian was instructed to go on working on the plumbing.

"I am a worm and no man." He prayed constantly, cleaning the drains of his brothers.

He told no one of his decision. The women would come out and make plans for a summer retreat, and he would say, "I'm afraid I'll be on the road this summer."

They thought he meant he would be on the mission cir-

cuit. Parishes in Pennsylvania, Maryland, Ohio, where
the Paracletists were strong. They d'd not know he would
no longer be Father Cyprian Leonard, O.H.P., but simply
Philip Leonard, a priest.

The day he was to leave the monastery, he called Clare
and Elizabeth. They took him to Charlotte's house, and
the next day they drove him to Grand Central Station.

He stayed in Tucson two years. Then he quarreled with
the bishop, who said he was bad for interfaith coopera-
tion. Interfaith. Outside the Church there is no salvation.
He would not let souls under his care risk eternal dam-
nation to swim with Methodists, eat hot dogs with Bap-
tists. He went to Sudbury and lived among the Indians,
who mined sulfur. But he found them too corrupt, con-
genitally dishonest, at once savage and pious, as ready to
slit his throat as to take communion from his hands. He
felt the first pull of rheumatism. He saw himself beginning to drink. He decided to come home to the diocese of
his birth. He asked to come under the jurisdiction of the
bishop of Anconia, who accepted his request. There was
no parish for him. He was glad; he did not think he could
work with the new men. He preferred to live alone.

"Watch out!" the child beside him cried. He had forgotten she was with him. He had forgotten where he was.
Now he saw her head strike the windshield. He did not
see blood. He prayed, "God, take me and not the child."

Felicitas cried out as her head struck the window. First
she felt nothing, then only the abstract sensation of deep
pressure at the thin base of her skull. She felt the bones in
her skull flower, saw blood flowers behind her eyes, then
maps, then buildings falling into one another and more
buildings, and at last, before she let herself fall back, the
bones around her eyes were branches budding, but they
would never come to bud, for the buds were tight and
were her eyes. She let herself lie back, she let herself fall
into Father Cyprian's arms. In the wash of perfect weakness, she allowed her eyes to open and she smiled, then
giggled. She could feel him holding her up. She was
swimming in dark water, but those arms would save her.
Then she allowed the lights to vanish. She was perfectly
happy.

If this child dies, then I will die, thought Cyprian, lifting Felicitas from the truck to the roadside. All the fierce urgency of love bloomed in his throat. He had left father and mother, but the child was his. In the sty of the world, she shone like diamonds for him. Girl of ice, never comfortable like other children, resisting kisses, riddles, covering herself from blandishments, preserving herself for something she could name in secret but would not. The smile she gave him now was foolish, was a child's. She giggled like a child. He wanted to slap her for being so unlike herself, for trying to deceive him as he held her by the road.

He had not seen the car. The man, a stranger, a salesman, shouted at him, and he answered, "Shut your mouth, the child is dying."

The man was silent. Cyprian got his cassock from the truck and put it on the shoulder of the road. He laid Felicitas on the grass that was half gravel. On his priestly dress. And he prayed, "I will accept any punishment if this child lives."

He knew he could not live under the weight of her death. He prayed for himself, for the child and then for her mother, whom he had not thought of till he heard the siren. The police would ask her name. Not his.

"Are you her father?" asked the policeman.

Without father, without mother, without descent.

"I'm a priest."

"Sorry, Father. This little girl a relative of yours?"

Without father, without mother, without genealogy.

"She's visiting me for the summer."

Then he wept, for the poverty of their connection. He had no claim to her; there was no name for what they were to each other. She would leave him, always. He could ask nothing of her; she was not his child.

"Take it easy, Father. She just had the wind knocked out of her. Probably a slight concussion. Nothing to worry about at her age."

He knelt then and prayed above her. It occurred to him that the policeman had probably never seen a priest weep. And he reproached himself, in his great joy at her deliverance from death, for crying like a woman.

The ambulance came. He rode beside her, cramped in

the back, and held her hands. When she opened her eyes, his face was close beside hers.

"Father," she said, conscious of the great honor of his presence. She kissed his hand. He had not let her down.

III

Charlotte had expected that Cyprian and Felicitas would not be right behind them, but all of them had been sitting in the motel for an hour and a half and no one with a bite of breakfast. Charlotte began to get aggravated. She knew what had happened. Cyprian had taken the kid out to the property again. Everybody thought it was crazy, him buying the land his family's house was on, all overgrown now, a mess, you couldn't walk ten feet, but that was Cyprian; he got an idea in his head.

He would take Felicitas out and talk to her about water tables and cinder blocks and God knew what, and there was Felicitas, taking things as seriously as an owl, writing things down in a goddamn notebook she carried around with her labeled "Father Cyprian's house and property."

She didn't know how Felicitas could pick up everything about all this country stuff. She'd never been outside Brooklyn except to go to camp, where she had such a fit that time. But now Charlotte found all this stuff in her room, books about building, *Popular Mechanics.* It looked like a goddamn boy's room. Except that Felicitas wasn't a tomboy. She was interested in boys, only she wanted them to come to *her;* she wasn't going to go ass-wiggling around town like the others. But she walked up and down in front of the Dohertys' house trying to trap the Doherty kid into talking to her. The Doherty kid was as stupid as a porcupine. And couldn't tell the nose in front of his face. Typical Felicitas. Always a day late and a dollar short.

Finally at ten o'clock everyone gave up and had breakfast, except for Charlotte, who waited in the motel. She intended to give both of them hell, but especially Felicitas, for thoughtlessness. Then Cyprian came in like a ghost and Charlotte's heart dropped.

"Where's Felicitas?" she asked, seeing him get out of the pickup alone.

"In the hospital. We had an accident."

Charlotte sat down on the motel driveway. She cried, rocking back and forth. She could feel the pebbles press into the backs of her thighs through her cotton summer dress. If her child died, then she would die.

"Get up, Charlotte, and compose yourself," said Cyprian.

"I won't. I'll stay here till doomsday," said Charlotte. It was the first time she had disobeyed Cyprian, her confessor, the one man living that she loved.

"The child is all right. She had a slight concussion."

"And you're tiptop. Not a goddamn scratch on you," Charlotte said, still sitting on the pebbles.

"The accident was my fault," said Cyprian, so low that Charlotte could hardly hear him.

She rose to her feet.

"I'll take you to the hospital," said Cyprian.

As they drove, Charlotte sat silent, hating Cyprian. Her child was ill. He had not called her. For three hours her child had been in the hospital without her. He had taken care of things, and everyone would say, "That's Cyprian, always there when you need him, a godsend in a crisis, takes the whole burden." But she knew why he had not called her. He wanted the child for himself.

When Felicitas awakened, the room blurred behind her eyes. She could see a blond nurse; she could see something round and pink and translucent form around the mouth of the girl in the bed next to her and she felt the live dash of emergency. For the first time since the accident, she felt awake. Then she saw the girl was in no danger; she was filing her nails and popping bubble gum.

"Whadja jump like that for?" asked the girl.

"I was confused," said Felicitas. "I was confused by your gum."

"This?" said the girl. She blew a bubble two-thirds the size of her head.

"Yes," said Felicitas with great formality, as if her confusion were reasonable. She did not like the girl and it was impossible that the girl would like her. For one thing, she was wearing white nail polish. Felicitas was willing to be flexible on certain issues, but on white nail polish she took a hard line. Besides, this girl was no older than she was, and she thought it was entirely inappropriate for a fourteen-year-old to be wearing nail polish. She looked down at her own blunt nails like a goodwife at a witch trial.

"What's your name?" asked the girl, chewing.

"Felicitas."

"What kind of a name is that?"

"It's just a regular name. A lot of people have it."

"I'll *bet*."

"Well, what's your name that's so great?" said Felicitas.

"Gidget."

"Gidget?"

"Yeah, like all those movies."

"I know *that*," said Felicitas. "I've seen them all. *Gidget, Gidget Goes Hawaiian, Gidget Goes to Rome.*"

"*Gidget Grows Up*," said Gidget knowingly.

"Yes, but no one's name is really Gidget. What were you christened?"

"What do you care?"

"I just want to know. You're the one who started on names."

"Adelaide."

"You think that's a regular name?"

"No, that's why I make everybody call me Gidget. At least I *knew* I didn't have a regular name and I tried to do something about it. And Adelaide's a lot more regular than yours."

"I like mine."

"You'd last around two minutes in my school with that name."

"It sounds like a very intelligent place."

"It doesn't have to be intelligent. It's fun. What are you, a brain?"

That was the word. That's what all the kids called her. But this girl didn't have to know that.

"I was almost kicked out of school for smoking," said Felicitas with the elegance of an amateur liar.

"Like fun. I can tell you never had a cigarette in your life."

Just as Felicitas was about to answer that she smoked two packs a day, a thin, tan boy walked in. His pants were black and much too tight, Felicitas thought. He walked as if he were riding a rocking horse.

"Ken-*eeee*," shouted Gidget.

Kenny sat down on the bed and without a word began kissing Gidget. Felicitas was frightened, frightened that someone would come in and either blame her for not stopping the performance or connect her with it. Then she was angry that they did what they did, not caring that she was two feet away from them. Then she was full of an obscure and cutting envy. She did not like this boy and she did not like Gidget. But she knew no boy would ever walk into her room and just like that begin to kiss her, not caring what anybody thought. For one moment she thought she would give up everything, her fine mind, her common sense, the love of her mother and her mother's friends, the honor of being Father Cyprian's chosen one, the great privilege of carrying out what they all stood for, simply to be Gidget and have a boyfriend in black pants that were too tight. But as she lost herself in the sick sleep she could not keep off, she knew it was impossible. She could not be like that. She would not want to. She could not be like anyone she knew.

Swimming up from sleep, she reached out and touched her mother. Her mother's flesh was so light it could hold her up. Her mother had no hair anywhere on her body and she never sweat. Her flesh seemed magic to Felicitas, clean and safe. She could rest her head anywhere on her mother's body and be held up. How proud she was to have a mother of such flesh, such suits and perfume, such white handkerchiefs and such perfect nails, unpolished but the perfect shape, the oval without effort. Her mother's hand was on her forehead now. She could open her eyes without fear.

"Gave your head quite a bunk," said Charlotte.

Bunk was their word for bump, a baby word they kept and used, misers who spent their treasure.

"I'm okay. Just sleepy."

With her mother's body near her, she could sleep. She would not now simply fall into some black, rootless hole, unrecognizable on her return, the depth transforming her to her worst hidden monsters. She had feared she would come up from those sleeps a skull, or bloody. She could come up eyeless or a devil; she could lose her tongue. But she was safe now, she could reach and touch her mother's skin, that skin like the inside of a melon or a peach. She touched her mother's arm and turned it over, running her fingers up and down the cool length of the inner arm from wrist to elbow. And once more she slept.

On her next waking, she saw Clare's face and Elizabeth's and, standing against the sink as if he was aware of how his maleness tipped the room, Father Cyprian. She could hear Mary Rose outside, making the nurse laugh. And in the chair near the door sat Muriel, silently praying the rosary. Her first thought upon waking was what Gidget would think of all these old ladies and a priest beside her bed for hours. She thought of the difference in the scenes: she surrounded by the love of no one under fifty, and Gidget in her bed, Kennys' skinny behind an inch beside her thigh, his hand only just keeping itself back from her high breast. She wanted to disown the people at her bed; she wanted to say, "I'm an orphan and these are the people at the orphanage. They have to be here. It has nothing to do with me."

But Cyprian stood and said, "How are you, dear?" and the weight of his words fell around her, a curtain of water, and shut out the world.

"Which one of these is your mom?"

"Guess," said Felicitas. Sleepiness always made her surly.

"Felicitas!" said her mother, shocked at the levity with which her daughter played with her life. *"I'm* her mother," Charlotte said, in a voice Felicitas liked because she saw it frightened Gidget.

When she woke up again, she could hear Clare talking to Gidget. She felt jealousy needle behind her eye and she sat up.

"Clare, isn't this picture awful?" said Felicitas, knowing that Gidget had selected it. Volunteers came around and changed the pictures daily.

If she could make fun of someone's bad taste with Clare, then that would be a shelter. Then Gidget would know she had no way in. Perhaps she could get Clare to speak out about white nail polish and the people who wore it.

"It's not bad for a hospital picture. It could be a lot worse," said Clare.

"This lady owns a shoe store," said Gidget. "I was asking her if she had any free samples. Like especially sling backs. Hint, hint."

Felicitas lay back on the pillows. Happiness was hers, and victory. She was being carried on the shoulders of a cheering crowd. Gidget had shown her crassness in a display so obvious that Felicitas could have done no better had she invented it herself. What Clare disliked most of all, what she had trained Felicitas to spot and censure, was vulgarity. It was impossible that Clare could ever be well disposed toward the girl after this.

"Gidget is just your age. She'll be going into ninth grade also," Clare said.

How could Clare go on being nice to her? It was manners, just good manners. Clare thought good manners were very important, Felicitas remembered, falling into a deep marsh of sleep.

Everyone had left a book or two for Felicitas. They knew she could not read much, but it was all that they could think of to give her. So they brought her what they thought she would enjoy.

They bought her books that were available in Orano. Muriel went first to the rack in the vestibule of St. Boniface Church, where Cyprian was filling in for the month of August. She brought Felicitas three pamphlets: "So You Think It's All Right to Go Steady?" "TV for Teens" and "St. Peggy of the Tennis Court." Felicitas was frightened of Muriel. She knew that Muriel did not like her. And so Felicitas had to read the pamphlets, because Muriel would ask her about them in front of Father Cyprian. She probably hoped Felicitas wouldn't read them so she could say to Father Cyprian, "I could have saved my money." Felicitas would not, as her mother would say, give her the satisfaction. She picked up the first pamphlet on the pile, "St. Peggy of the Tennis Court," by Owen Cavanagh, O.P.

You do not know St. Peggy, for her cause has not yet come before the Holy See. And there is good reason for that: St. Peggy is still living in Chicago, or St. Louis, or New York, or Montreal, or wherever pure Catholic girls love God with all their hearts. And I am writing this to remind you that God does not require any extraordinary outward signs of sanctity. God does not call everyone to be a Little Flower, achieving sanctity in the cloistered life of a Carmelite convent, nor does He ask of everyone a martyr's death. Not all saints are St. Catherines or St. Agathas. The great St. Elizabeth of Hungary reminds us that sanctity is by no means barred to someone of the married state. And the glorious St. Frances of Rome makes clear the Church's firm position that it is in fulfilling the duties of a wife and mother that most women will achieve sanctification.

But St. Peggy has not even reached that point in life when she must make the highest sacrifices known to womanhood. For when our story begins, Peggy is only seventeen years old.

If you asked any of her classmates whether they thought Peggy was a saint, they would look at you with surprise. "What, Peggy?" they would say. "A saint? Why, she's far too much fun."

For to her classmates, Peggy is the energetic editor of the *Rosarian*, the yearbook of Our Lady of the Rosary High School. They know that she goes out, not every Saturday night but a good number of them, with Jimmy Rice, captain of the basketball team at St. Joe's High across the city. And they know that Peggy is a crackerjack at almost any sport. As a matter of fact, their hopes for getting the diocesan cup for tennis this year rest on Peggy's willing shoulders. They forget, because Peggy does not make much of it, that she spends her Saturdays reading to the blind. And what they do not know is that Peggy gave up working with the children in Guardian Angel Orphanage because Sister Roberta confided to her that they had more girls that they could use at Guardian Angel but no one to read to the blind. Giving up the children whom she loved and who loved her was a keen disappointment to Peggy, but she knew it was more pleasing in the eyes of God to serve those souls most in need of serving.

Felicitas could not keep back sleep now. She hoped that when Muriel came that night she would find her asleep with the pamphlets on her stomach.

But Muriel did not come that night. She sent a message with Father Cyprian. She wanted to know how Felicitas liked the pamphlets she had bought her. When the women and Father Cyprian went home, Felicitas vowed, by God, that she would finish that goddamn pamphlet before Gidget turned the lights off.

Peggy's next opportunity for sanctity came at the senior prom, when she (1) refused to wear a strapless gown, (2) refused Jimmy Rice's marriage proposal, or made him promise he would wait until he'd spent a year at Notre Dame, and (3) left her prom corsage on Our Lady's altar in the convent.

But that was nothing. Tennis was the occasion for the severest test of Peggy's sanctity. In Our Lady of the Rosary school, there was a girl named Phyllis Corrado. She was the only child of her mother, a widow.

It had not escaped Peggy's notice that the girls just didn't seem to like Phyllis Corrado. And so Peggy would try to include Phyllis in some of her group's activities. She would shun all of Peggy's efforts, however. Peggy couldn't help thinking that Phyllis was her own worst enemy, which only made her feel more sorry for the girl. Peggy knew that Phyllis didn't have much money to buy fashionable clothes, but Phyllis ignored that priceless asset to any girl's attractiveness, however low her clothing budget—good grooming. It made Peggy feel sorry to see that Phyllis was not fastidious about her hair and nails.

Peggy was surprised that Phyllis went out for tennis

that year. But she was glad, too. She thought it was a
good sign. Whenever Peggy tried to encourage Phyllis,
her friendly, heartfelt comments were greeted only by
sullen rebuffs.

Peggy was too busy with the yearbook, with the
blind, with Jimmy and with her sister Helen's new baby
girl to give all to tennis that she would have liked to.
One night when she went down to the C.Y.O. tennis
courts, Mr. O'Brien, who gave out the towels, said, "We
haven't seen much of you, Peggy."

"Gosh, Mr. O'Brien, I've got an awful lot on my
mind. There's the yearbook and my sister's baby."

"And one James Rice?"

Peggy blushed. Mr. O'Brien was Jimmy's godfather.

"Lucky boy," said Mr. O'Brien.

"I don't know about that," said Peggy, crimson to the
roots of her hair.

"Your friend Phyllis has been here every night practicing."

"Phyllis Corrado?"

"Yup. She'll give you a run for your money."

"I hope *so*," said Peggy, walking jauntily into the
locker room.

Peggy was glad to see Phyllis; she was genuinely
fond of the girl. But Phyllis barely said hello. Peggy remembered how hard it must be for Phyllis, having to
work every night at the soda fountain just to make
ends meet. She thought of her own good mother and
father and whispered a silent prayer of thanksgiving.

When Peggy played against Phyllis, she saw how
hard the girl had worked. She knew that she was the
better player, but Phyllis' hard work had made her a
tough contender.

The day of the diocesan tryouts, Peggy had to play
Phyllis to see which one of them would represent Our
Lady of the Rosary at the finals. Only one girl could
go. Peggy breathed a quick prayer to Our Lady, as she
always did before a game.

Suddenly it came to her that God did not want her to
beat Phyllis. She thought of her parents and Jimmy and
her nice clothes and her dear own room that her folks
had let her decorate herself. And she thought how

much more she had than Phyllis. She decided she would let Phyllis win; she would let Phyllis represent Our Lady of the Rosary at the finals. She knew she would be letting the girls down, but she wasn't living her life for the girls; she was living it for God.

Felicitas threw the pamphlet on the floor. She thought that if Muriel wasn't around in the morning, she would discuss the pamphlet with Father Cyprian and ask him if he thought all that crap was really necessary. Then she would ask her mother and Elizabeth and Clare. She knew one thing, that Peggy was the kind of girl who made her puke. She would rather be herself than Peggy. Even if it meant she couldn't be a saint.

All day long Gidget watched television. She kept up with soap operas about doctors in the afternoons, and on Monday night she watched *Ben Casey,* a show about a surly doctor with a lot of dark hair on his chest, so much that he couldn't button the top buttons of his intern's blouse. On Thursday nights she watched *Dr. Kildare,* who buttoned the collar of his intern's blouse so tightly that he looked like a priest. That year everyone wore intern's blouses. You could tell their allegiance to the star they loved by the way they buttoned their blouses at the neck.

"Who are you for, Kildare or Casey?" asked Gidget one day.

"Kildare," said Felicitas, trying to sound offhand, trying to pretend she had seen either show before she had come under Gidget's tutelage.

"You would," said Gidget.

"Would what?"

"Like Kildare."

"A lot of people do."

"A lot of people who like saps. I like my men tough and sexy. Like Kenny."

Gidget could regularly silence Felicitas by these suggestions of her expertise.

"I don't know, I guess I like men who are nicer than that," said Felicitas.

Gidget snorted.

Felicitas was glad she could pretend to be asleep. When Gidget's parents came to visit her, Felicitas could read.

They usually came in the morning, when Felicitas often did not have visitors.

Both Gidget's parents were small and blond. For a brief, disloyal and remarkably intense moment. Felicitas wished for two matched parents, small and blond, looking like anybody. But Felicitas could tell that Gidget's parents had nothing to say to her; she saw that they were frightened of their child. Mr. Harrison spoke to his daughter mostly about food, the food in the hospital, the food he had most recently eaten.

"Gidget, we get you outa here, the first thing we do is take you to that new smorgasbord on Route 42. The shrimp are, no exaggeration, that big."

And he would make a space between his thumbs and forefingers that could accommodate, Felicitas thought, the head of a newborn.

"And the craziness of it is you pay the same if you eat one or fifty."

Gidget's reply was that she hated whatever food her father happened to mention.

"What I'd give my eyeteeth for in this dump is a milk shake and some French fries."

Gidget's mother seemed able to converse with her daughter only on the subject of Kenny.

"Oh, Ma, you don't even know him. He happens to be a very refined person once you get to know him."

Meanwhile, Felicitas was reading *Quartet in Heaven,* a book about women saints by Sheila Kaye-Smith. She was so tired of reading accounts of the Little Flower's life that she thought she would go mad if she read one more word about picking up straight pins in silence for the love of God. And she had promised herself that she would not read any more about Latin Americans who had visions. So the only two of the quartet who interested her were St. Catherine of Genoa, who was active during the Black Plague, and a nineteenth-century American named Cornelia Connolly.

Cornelia, an Episcopalian herself, had married an Episcopalian clergyman. They were the toast of ante-bellum Natchez, Mississippi, until they decided to convert to Catholicism. Then her husband decided he wanted to become a Catholic priest. But the only way he could become a priest was for Cornelia to become a nun. She didn't want to do this because she had three children whom she didn't want to give up. But she didn't want to displease her husband, so she became a nun in Rome, where he became a priest. He celebrated his first mass in his wife's convent and gave their daughter her first holy communion.

Everything went all right until Cornelia was transferred to England, where she became a great success at starting schools for wealthy Catholic girls. Then her husband decided he had made a mistake; they should get married again and go back to being Episcopalians. When Cornelia refused, he took her to court, claiming that the papists had hypnotized them both. But even the bigoted English supported her, and she died victorious in her convent.

Felicitas saw no reason for anyone to want to get this woman canonized. She thought Cornelia had an astonishing lack of backbone. And she thought she was a lousy mother. But what put her off most was Cornelia's prayer for increased suffering in her life, after which her youngest child died in torment "after being pushed by a playful dog into a vat of boiling sugar."

Felicitas thought it was one thing to pray for trials and quite another to have your child caramelized in front of you. It was just that kind of thing that shook her faith. But Father Cyprian had given her the book. He told her it was by a highly educated, highly intellectual English Catholic convert. She was married to a fine English Catholic convert, a gentleman, a playwright.

Father Cyprian had a real thing about English converts, Felicitas thought. He was always giving her books by "highly educated Englishwomen." The pictures on the back would always be of women in terrible glasses whose blouses looked four sizes too big for them. Felicitas decided there were some things she didn't have to listen to Father Cyprian about. Highly educated English converts were at the top of the list.

The doctor said Felicitas could go home in one more day. He looked at the pile of books on the table beside her bed.

"How many days have you been here, Felicitas? Only

four? That's quite a bit of reading matter for a young lady."

"I like to read," said Felicitas, terrified that he would read the titles of the books and Gidget would hear them. Up to that time, she had been too self-absorbed to notice Felicitas' books.

"Well, don't read too much. Get a lot of sleep. And besides, how many books does a girl your age need to read?"

"Some people need a lot," said Gidget.

"What about you, young lady? I'll bet your boyfriends don't even give you a chance to turn the page."

Gidget giggled. The doctor patted her cheek.

At that moment, Felicitas would have been perfectly happy if the two of them had been devoured by flames. She would have liked to lie in her half (the uncharred half) of a burning room, reading the book Elizabeth had given her, while Gidget and the doctor went up in a puff of technicolor smoke.

She loved the book Elizabeth had given her. Elizabeth had stayed behind after all the others left the room. She handed Felicitas a package wrapped in gold paper, slipping it under the sheets as if it were illicit. Her look was the look of a guilty child, torn between his knowledge of the crime and his pleasure in committing it.

"I suppose Father Cyprian wouldn't think this is a very spiritual book, but I think it's the most wonderful book in the world," Elizabeth said.

Then she ran out of the room as if she were afraid the book would explode behind her. Felicitas opened the package and looked at the title: *Pride and Prejudice*.

Felicitas began the book because she loved Elizabeth and because it was the one book on her table that wasn't about Catholics. But then she realized that she had found the book she wanted most to live in. She wanted to be like Elizabeth Bennet, full of the right answers, never looking foolish. She thought that if Elizabeth Bennet were in the bed next to Gidget, Gidget would be sorry. She wished she would find the right sentence that would make Gidget see the bottomless depths of her inferiority. She thought that Elizabeth Bennet could. But she could not, because it meant too much to her that Gidget like her. In her dreams she heard Gidget saying, "I didn't know you were such a neat person." At the same time, from the bottom of her heart she hated the blonde creature in the bed beside her.

She hated her most of all because Gidget had made her betray the people she most loved.

Gidget had said, "Isn't it just the biggest pain, having all those people hanging over you all the time?"

Felicitas thought how perfectly easy it would be to let herself be absorbed into the warm, sweet world Gidget inhabited. The temptation was like the desire to stop walking in the cold, to put down the load of groceries one was carrying to the poor and to enter the nearest pizza parlor and start playing the jukebox while across town the widow and her orphans starved.

Felicitas could taste the savor of Gidget's praise; she hungered for it as for salt. The hunger lifted the back of her tongue, and she thought that they would never know what she would say of them.

She melted the hard, sharp image of Father Cyprian and her mother and her mother's friends until it clouded and then muddied, like a tablet that dissolved in water and, invisible, lost both taste and shape. She turned to Gidget, who was filing her white nails.

"It's the biggest drag in the world," she said.

"Then why do you put up with it?" asked Gidget. "I wouldn't put up with it."

Felicitas' mind was racing with the quick brilliance of deceit. "Because my mom says if I come on vacation with her every year, she'll get me a car on my sixteenth birthday."

There was a terrible moment of silence in which Gidget said nothing and the images of Cyprian and the women once again took on their hardness and once more lodged in the front of her brain. Then Gidget said, "I guess it's worth it. I guess that's what I would do."

Felicitas felt a moment of pure pleasure, a confection of joy fantastic as a Versailles cake. But it hardened in her mouth and grew granular and acid. That night she cried. She thought of Peter warming his hands by the fire, denying to the servant girl his knowledge of the Lord. For his denial, Peter asked that he be crucified upside down, as he was not worthy to share the manner of death of Him he had betrayed.

And in the dark hospital room, Felicitas lay hearing Gidget's regular, ignorant breath and knew she would never forgive her. Felicitas had begun that day reading *The Seven Storey Mountain,* Cyprian's latest gift, and she determined that the life she wanted for herself was the life that Thomas Merton chose, a life so purified that it stood out against the sky, a fir ice-covered. She thought if she could aspire to a life so perfect, she would find God, a pool of perfect coldness, still, a sweetness plumb and fathomless that burnt her flesh.

And then that afternoon, to get the praise of someone she despised, she betrayed everything she loved.

She cried in her strange metal bed. The light outside the window shone in, comfortless, accusing, not the eye of God suggesting mercy, but the unforgiving and undifferentiating beam that knew and would not cover her clear act of cowardice and shame.

How could she be like Thomas Merton? How could God come to her in silence and in burning when she worked to gain the favor of a fool? She could not sleep. She thought of Merton's childhood, of his artist parents, of his nights of girls and whiskey. He had never had to work for money. And she knew that, being who she was, a girl whose people could not pay her way, she could not walk through Europe, she could not go to night clubs full of jazz and cigarettes and could not be received by silent priests in white wool who would wake at three to sing and work till sundown.

She was female. She did not have money. And she hated nuns. What's more, she lied to get a fool to like her.

How, then, would God find her? How could she live cold and silent, purified like Thomas Merton, being who she was? She lay in darkness and prayed for that still pool of perfect coldness which that night was God.

They brought two cars to take her home: Clare's Oldsmobile and Cyprian's red pickup. Felicitas said good-by to Gidget with the vengeful edge of a lord who has sold his patrimony to a manufacturer of artificial limbs.

She was enraged that Father Cyprian gave Gidget a

farewell blessing; she counted the number of seconds he left his hands on Gidget's head. And Mary Rose said she would send Gidget a postcard of New York, and then Clare took her shoe size. Only Charlotte remained unfriendly, and so Felicitas chose to reward her mother. She asked to ride back with her mother, in case she felt dizzy on the way.

Charlotte was silent for a moment with the honor of being chosen by her child. But she said, "Father Cyprian wanted you to ride in the truck with him. To break the curse."

But Father Cyprian had laid his hands on Gidget's head and said to her, "I hope you'll be well soon, dear."

He had said "dear" to Gidget. Felicitas would not ride with him in the truck.

He turned to Felicitas and said, "Don't you feel safe with me anymore?"

He needed her now; he needed the assurance of her safety. He had chosen her. He was a man, and men were cursed with a terrible emptiness. A terrible loneliness they could not speak of. So deep, so ragged was the loneliness in him that she could no more refuse it than forget her name.

She took his hand. He opened the door of the truck for her and, treasuring her weakness, gave his arm for her safe passage. It was quite unnecessary, but the luxury of his support made her head light.

"Did you profit from your stay in the hospital?" asked Father Cyprian, driving more slowly than usual.

"How could I with that idiot in the room?"

Cyprian put his hand on Felicitas' leg to make her silent. "Felicitas, that child is dying."

"Gidget?"

"In a year she'll be dead. She has something called Hodgkin's disease."

Felicitas knew what was expected: he would have liked her to burst into tears. But she was not sorry Gidget was dying.

"She didn't act like she was dying," said Felicitas with sullen logic.

"It takes a lot of courage, don't you think? Dying in bebop? Keeping up that front?"

So he admired her. Perhaps, because she was dying, he admired Gidget more than he did Felicitas. She knew that she was supposed to be sorry that someone her own age was dying. But she was jealous of that death, for it had won his admiration. And she would not forgive Gidget. Because of Gidget she had betrayed her own to a fool.

Felicitas stared straight ahead of her. Cyprian assumed that she was shattered by the news of a young girl's death. But the image of Gidget's blonde head lodged itself behind the heavy bones around Felicitas' eyes. Her head ached now with jealousy and rage.

She was glad the girl was dying. She would have liked to die like that. She knew that was the thing that made everybody love you. No one could think up a better trick for love than dying young.

But when Gidget was dead, they would forget her: Cyprian and Elizabeth and Clare and Mary Rose. But they would not forget Felicitas. On her their hope depended. She would live when they had died. When they were silent, she would have a tongue; when they were bodiless, her legs would walk above them.

They required her. It was her life they needed. How could they fail to love her best? She was the only one.

IV

Muriel knew she had got the wrong things for Felicitas to read. The error had bitten at her heart. It marked her failure as a woman: she did not know the right gift for a child. Spinsterish, it marked her as a woman who had not known men. When she was eighteen, teaching herself typing from a book her mother had sent for, she imagined herself in the kitchen surrounded by the children of the neighborhood, flicking her apron in half-serious dismissal, saying, "Shoo now, I have work to do," but keeping them away for only half an hour, so deeply did they need the comfort of her presence, the quiet understanding their natural mothers were too busy for, the luxury of sweets she hid around her mother's house for them.

But it had not been so. What was it in her? Did she give off some sharp scent that frightened children? Was it the touch of her fingers that they hated? What was it that her flesh said that made them shudder? She would always make mistakes. For the children of her sister she baked cookies with coconut, which they would not eat. Finally one said, "The taste of coconut makes me afraid."

They thought that she would poison them. She should have known: children do not like coconut or sharp cheese or bloody meat. They do like chocolate and white bread. Children want simple food, food neither dry nor moist. And she would serve them lima beans, salad with mayonnaise, liver or kidneys, canned purple plums. All the food she ate they thought would make them die. When her nieces and nephews stayed with her, their parents snuck them out at night for hot dogs.

With Felicitas she had tried hard. But Felicitas had always been against her. It was not a natural indifference, such as her nephews and her nieces had. It was a studied perverseness. The child was stubborn; her heart was hard. Muriel had talked to Cyprian about it. Cyprian had said, "Children are not dependable. There is a kind of beauty of soul, a complexity of mind and spirit, to which children have no access."

He had understood her sorrow once again. He had understood the gross injustice of her lot: never to be loved when she was loving. But she did not love Felicitas, not in the natural way, although she wished, in Christian love, the salvation of the child's soul.

But Cyprian loved the child naturally. He would die for the child.

He would not die for her, for Muriel, who loved him with the pure, hard fire of a single devotion. None of them could love him as she did, for they loved others, were connected and encumbered by the love of other human beings. She was not. She had brushed out with fire all the root connections of her life; she had kept clean for him and God, a sanctuary perfect in its stillness, in the proportion of exaltation, high with love, empty of all but love, where love was housed and cooled and kindled. How could the child do that? Half beast, filled up with food and movies and the trash of this cheap age.

He said, "She will be the comfort of our old age." He said, "She will embody what we stand for in the world when we are dead."

He loved the child above all others. When she left him to go back to school, Muriel could see his body heave with grief; he would shiver and look around for sweaters; he would say, "There's a chill, there's a draft, there's a wind somewhere." When the autumn was perfect, flame-colored, the blue sky brilliant and remote, the sun hard and potent as in summer. But he shivered and he asked for sweaters, which Muriel bought him in September, which, when she returned to visit in the spring, he had lost.

He had spoken to her about the reading matter she had brought Felicitas in the hospital. The pamphlets, he said, were sentimental. They exalted the American heresy that God could be found through athletics. They encouraged, he said, an Elks Club spirituality. They ignored the truth that we must hate the world to love God.

He said that Muriel should consult him before she gave Felicitas anything to read, particularly anything of a religious nature. As her spiritual director, he was responsible for the development of her soul, particularly at her impressionable age. And she had, said Father Cyprian, an extraordinary soul, perhaps the most extraordinary he had ever known.

That was what he had said of her, Muriel. An extraordinary soul. And now he said it of the child.

The child was a beast and a thief. She stole what she had no need of. She hoarded and she wasted. And Muriel, hungering in the flame of her great love, prayed not to hate, prayed for the soothing love of God that swallowed spite and envy and the brute sins she was subject to, the sins she would cut out, like shards of glass imbedded in the flesh. She prayed for the soothing balm of love so that she, too, would love the child.

"I believe she enjoyed the things I gave her to read," said Muriel.

Cyprian patted Muriel on the arm. "In the end, that kind of transitory pleasure is not the most important."

But Muriel wanted, above all, to have given Felicitas that kind of transitory pleasure. She imagined the child in bed, reading secretly after lights out, grateful to Muriel, secretly wishing to be like her. She imagined that it was Felicitas' shyness that had stopped her from complimenting Muriel on her gift.

She turned to Charlotte. "Felicitas never thanked me for the pamphlets. Do you think she enjoyed them?"

Charlotte caught Clare's eye in the mirror. Muriel saw that she and Clare were trying not to laugh. Hate was in her heart then; they were all against her.

"I think she got a big kick out of them, Muriel," said Charlotte.

They were mocking her. I am mocked and scorned, despised of men, thought Muriel. She turned her hate into prayer. She was alone, it was night, it was the Garden. She was entirely abandoned.

"She didn't say anything to me about them. I didn't know if she'd ever read them."

"I'm sure she will say something," said Elizabeth. "Felicitas is always absent-minded, and I think the head injury has scattered her thoughts. But she will say something, I'm sure."

When hell freezes over, thought Charlotte. She had told her to thank Muriel; she knew that Muriel always wanted her pound of flesh. But Felicitas had said, "They were complete crap. I won't thank anyone for giving me crap to read."

Maybe if Elizabeth asked her, Felicitas would say something. But she wouldn't take any bets on it. Not with that kid. She said she wouldn't lie to make people happy. She had said it as a tiny child and had stuck to it. Charlotte thought maybe she should be grateful, at least the kid was not a liar. But it made life hard. You had to grease the wheels. God knew you had to in the business world, which was full of pains in the ass like Muriel. In key positions with a lot of pull. Felicitas would never have to go out into the business world, but she wished Felicitas would thank Muriel just to keep the goddamn peace.

Felicitas would never go to business. Nor would she have a man to care for her. For both lives flexibility was needed, the ability to bend, and Felicitas—Charlotte could see it every time the kid walked down the road— had that straight spine, no waist, a hard, tight body that would not bend for man or company; she would not take back what she said. She was the kind of person who could lead an army. She was bound to be an old maid. Which was okay with Charlotte, most of her friends were, and it was better than being tied to some old fart who wore you out and wanted you to thank him for it. Sometimes she could see, though, in her daughter that if she fell in love with somebody, it would be all over. Even the way she carried on about the Doherty boy, which was ridiculous, since he was eighteen and it didn't get her anyplace. But she took it all so goddamn seriously. And Charlotte wanted to say to her, "Hold back, hold part of yourself back." But that was the kind of thing you didn't listen to until you were too old and had been through the goddamn mill yourself anyway.

What would become of her daughter? Nothing ordinary. Charlotte hadn't brought her up for that. What had she brought her up for? Frank had had a real program in mind for Felicitas: she would be a journalist or a professor of philosophy. She would be a politician and lobby for Catholic causes.

But what did she want for Felicitas? All her life she had worked too hard to think about what she wanted.

Thank God Felicitas had her father's brains and wouldn't need any man to support her. And wouldn't need to kiss ass for a buck. Not that she had; Charlotte could congratulate herself that she had never kissed anyone's ass. And thank God for Mr. O'Brien (every day she prayed for him at mass). They worked together like a charm. Ever since he had had that sore on his tongue and she went into his office and found him sitting at his desk trembling, convinced he was dying of cancer. That was because his brother had just died of cancer. He was terrified.

She brought in Lourdes water and made him drink it and told him to go to daily mass. And he said, "Will you go for me?" And she said, "I go anyway. But I'll offer my mass up for you." Within a month he was right as rain. And since then, for twenty-four years, he'd do anything for her. Which was, she knew, unusual in a boss. But he was a gentleman from the old school. Every day she thanked God for her boss.

But Felicitas would be a boss, she wouldn't have one. She knew that whatever Felicitas did, she'd knock everybody on their ass. Provided she didn't get up on her high horse too often. Charlotte hoped that prayer would make Felicitas humble.

Cyprian would keep her straight. God knew what Cyprian wanted for Felicitas, but he was keeping a close eye on her, which was a load off Charlotte's mind.

Elizabeth was afraid that Cyprian would find out she had given Felicitas Jane Austen and would be angry. She was a coward; if he raised his voice to her, she would simply disappear. His words would strike her head and she would crumble, insubstantial as she knew herself to be. She looked around her in the car. Everyone around her was a solid, Muriel and Clare and Mary Rose. And Charlotte—how Charlotte inhabited space; a clear-cut habitation, a pure tenantry. But Elizabeth saw how she herself was: a vapor, vaporous. She could disappear; she was ready any moment to become invisible. It was a coward's talent, a thief's trick, an exile's coloration. To have neither bulk nor color was her skill.

She knew what Cyprian thought about reading literature for its own sake. Harmless, he had said in the confessional, but finally a waste of time. The writers of England were not Catholic; they may have had a natural genius, but they were not inspired by the Holy Ghost. Even Shakespeare, for all his greatness, could do nothing for the salvation of even one soul.

In confession, praying for attentiveness, Elizabeth heard in her mind songs from *Twelfth Night*. She was listening to Cyprian; she trusted him with the salvation of her soul, but in the back of her mind she heard, wicked and charming,

O mistress mine! where are you roaming?

Cyprian was right. It would not lead to the salvation of
her soul.

"What shall I do, since I do love it?" she asked, kneeling in the dark.

"Read it, if you must, for recreation, but know the
strict limits of its value. It is not a deeply spiritual vision;
it cannot be, for it was written in an unsanctified age."

For the rain it raineth every day.

She prayed for the voice to be silent. So undependable
was her mind that she could not keep out songs when she
was being given vital spiritual counsel, counsel that was
sacramental in its character, for it took place in the great
sacrament of penance.

In her mind, she heard a lute. And then,

I am slain by a fair cruel maid.

When she was a young girl, she had changed the words
to "I am slain by a fair cruel swain."

The more she heard the music, the more certain she
was that she must work to give it up or to admit that its
importance was minor.

She did not even mention Jane Austen in the confessional. She did not dare to; Jane Austen's vision was not,
she knew, deeply spiritual. The world of the spirit was
cold and exalted; there was no furniture or conversation;
no jokes or wordplay. The dark night of the spirit she
dreaded as she dreaded walks on cliffs whose drop was
obvious. It was, she knew, her cowardice that made her
wish she was Anne Elliot in *Persuasion,* visiting, doing
good in ordinary corporal ways, obedient, grown pale with
resignation and lost love. But where was God in that?
And where was God in Mr. Bennet making fun of his
poor stupid wife?

How Elizabeth loved Mr. Bennet and Anne Elliot and
Fanny and Elinor and Emma. Where was God in that?
Was it in the shape, the curve of it, the rhythm, the pro-

portion of the houses and the walks? God was Lear, radiant with understanding. At the end of all these works was rest: the truth that made a place of perfect quiet. God was the silence made by poetry; the shelter after words but made by words; the green world full of jokes.

She knew she felt this all because her character was insubstantial. And she would not say to Cyprian, "I think you're wrong. In these words I will look for my salvation."

Charlotte would have. Charlotte would have said, "Get off your high horse, Cyp."

And Cyprian would have shouted at Charlotte.

And Charlotte would have shouted back.

And she, Elizabeth, would have become invisible.

She was a coward. She would not contradict Cyprian; he was her confessor. Neither would she give up reading what she loved. He had not quite forbidden her. He had encouraged her to see these things as unimportant. But this she could not do.

He told her to spend more time reading Dante, the great poet of the Catholic vision, the great spokesman of the age when men knew that they lived for God. But Dante bored her. She was not interested in such brute punishments, such a detailed and unforgiving God spending his days imagining just tortures. And the *Paradiso* made her fall asleep. That was not heaven, that abstract and airy stratosphere. The proportions were too large. She had no mind for exaltation, which she knew was a result of the puniness of her spiritual life.

She confessed to Father Cyprian that Dante did not please her. She asked if she could turn her attention to Chaucer, who was Catholic and who had visited the pope. Cyprian agreed. She read her Chaucer guiltily, for the wrong reasons. It helped her in her spiritual life. She saw God on the roads and in the taverns. She went on reading Jane Austen, as she had to every night or else she could not sleep.

She wanted that world for Felicitas. Perhaps she simply wanted someone she could talk to of the passion of her life. When she had come into Felicitas' room, Felicitas had grabbed her hand and said, "That was the best book I ever read."

Elizabeth lowered her voice. "It isn't very spiritual," she whispered.

"It's perfect."

Felicitas, however, thought that Darcy was not good enough for her friend Lizzie Bennet. They had heated conversations and whispered while the others went to lunch.

"She would not be an easy woman to be married to," whispered Elizabeth, fearfully looking over her shoulder.

"Yeah, but he's got a stick up his ass. Even to the end."

"No, he's a man of great firmness. But not, I think, inflexible," said Elizabeth under her breath.

Suddenly Felicitas began to laugh. "Elizabeth, we don't have to whisper like this. It isn't porno."

Elizabeth laughed too. "But don't tell the others. I don't think Father Cyprian would approve."

"He doesn't know everything," said Felicitas. "He's not God."

Then Cyprian appeared at the door. Felicitas hid the book under the sheet. Elizabeth ran out of the room, blushing and terrified.

"Say hello to Mr. Collins if you see him," said Felicitas over Father Cyprian's head.

Elizabeth giggled. This would be their private joke. She loved private jokes. It was shameful, but it was the truth. Which is why she loved Charlotte and Felicitas: they were always tapping each other, saying things under their breath and using code words. This was heaven to her, insubstantial as she was. Heaven was a private joke.

Clare was afraid that riding in the pickup would be bad for Felicitas' head. Sometimes she thought she was the only one whose feet touched the real earth. It was she who had spoken to the doctor about Felicitas' concussion, she who had been given the prescriptions, the advice. She was the one who asked, "How much should she be reading? Will it hurt her eyes?" The rest of them fought over what she did read or, like sweet Elizabeth, brought contraband.

It was important that Felicitas learn about the land, for it was she who would inherit the property Clare had bought the property in her name and in Cyprian's. No-

body worried about what would happen to Cyprian when
he got too old to knock around from parish to parish, five
dollars here, a mass for someone's dead, twenty for a
weekend while the pastor went to visit his old aunt. Cyprian hadn't had a cent when he left the Paracletists; he
hadn't a cent now. She couldn't bear to see him wait six
months till he had said enough masses to buy cement or
drill bits. He would never ask, so it was up to her to guess
at what he needed for the house, the property. She had to
look and listen and give him only limited sums for particular purchases. "The scandal of the particular." That is
what some theologians called the Incarnation. She had
heard that once in college. It was nonsense to her.

It was the particular, that which must be searched out,
differentiated and then husbanded. The great care that
was needed to preserve the fine and the beautiful was a
cause she could give her life for. She was in all things in
her life a merchant, searching foreign markets for the one
perfect bolt of cloth among the yards of flawed goods, the
one gold bell in a hill of brass shoes, the diamond in the
bowl of colored glass.

She wanted to give Felicitas some sense of balance,
wanted her to see the different grasses, the stones, in cloth
so fine each stitch shone, in smooth wood and fragrant
leather. She worried that without her, Felicitas would fly
out of the world.

She had made Felicitas her heir. Having bought the
property for Cyprian in her own name, she wanted to
keep it in the right hands. She did not want blood relatives making claims on it. She had left everything to Felicitas: the business and the property.

But Felicitas was barely out of childhood, and Clare
saw the strains and hopes that pressed her down and
made her so hostile to the foolish dying girl who shared
her room. There would be no place in the world where
Felicitas could exist with the clarity, the piquancy, she
lived in here on her vacations.

Perhaps it would be best for Felicitas to learn a solitary
expertise, to live away from the city, where she would be
made to dress well and defer. Clare had promised Felicitas she would pay for her education. She would encourage
her to study agriculture.

How glad Cyprian would be to have Felicitas beside him to reclaim the land. She could see fields green with early lettuce and a pantry stocked for winter and a bowl of warmish milk beside the sink. She would suggest this plan; she had always been able to talk quite straightforwardly to Felicitas. She would look into agricultural colleges. There was one at Cornell; someone's nephew had once gone there.

Mary Rose couldn't get over the fact that the girl in the other bed was dying. It really shook her up. If God was love, why did that kind of thing have to happen? She was a cute girl, just fourteen. She was a snot to Felicitas, but Mary Rose could see that she was just jealous of all the attention Felicitas was getting, all the people by the bed watching out for her, asking the nurses things, bringing her stuff to read. Mary Rose had smuggled in candy bars; it was the only thing she could think of to bring that seemed like fun. But there that poor kid was, dying, and Mary Rose couldn't explain it to herself.

It was like when Joe's wife died of cancer. She'd been sick for over a year. Lots of times Mary Rose would open up the theater for Joe if he couldn't get away, and he would say to her, "Now, tell me, Mary Rose, with your religion, what's it all about? She was a good woman, a perfect wife and mother, the best. Why should she have to suffer like that?"

Mary Rose knew that with non-Catholics you couldn't say, "It's God's will." It was the kind of thing they didn't like about Catholics, that kind of answer. They thought it meant you had no feelings. But what else could she say? What she did say ended up being stupid, as usual. She should have kept her mouth shut and asked Cyprian and then told Joe what Cyprian had said. But no, she had to open her trap.

"How do you know, Joe? Maybe her death saved her from something worse. Maybe she would've started fooling around with another man."

Then Joe began to cry. "I'd rather have her fool around with a hundred men and still have her with me."

Mary Rose was getting desperate. Desperation always

made her talkative. "Well, maybe she would've become a drunk or a dope fiend."

Joe shook his head. "Anything is better than death. I would still love her, even if she became a drunk or a dope fiend."

Mary Rose felt she had to bring him some comfort. "You see, Joe, I believe you'll see her in heaven."

"I thought you people didn't believe Jews went to heaven."

He was right. Jews weren't baptized, so they went to limbo with the babies who died before baptism. But she couldn't say to Joe, "You'll see your wife in limbo." So she told him a white lie about heaven. "I think everyone who's good goes to heaven."

Then Joe kissed her on the cheek. "There's a lot of things about your religion that I don't understand. For instance, your husband. Here's a guy you lived with maybe a coupla months. You haven't seen him, what is it, thirty years? He's never coming out of the hospital and you've never been able to get married. You're a beautiful girl, Mary Rose, and you're the best-natured one I ever came across. It's a shame you had to let life pass you by."

"I did all right, Joe. I've had a lot of laughs."

"But, you see, to me, Mary Rose, and I'm speaking now as a Jewish person, you should have had a husband and children."

"Well, I never met anyone I wanted to marry."

"What about Billy Dole? He broke his heart for you."

"He married someone else."

"On the rebound."

"Some broken heart."

Joe took her out for late supper every Thursday night now. And he said, "What harm could it do, two old coots like us getting married? I'm sixty, you're sixty-two, we're a couple of old coots and the best of friends."

But she kept telling him she couldn't marry until her husband died. And he kept saying, "Okay, kid, I'm not going anywhere."

She asked Cyprian if he thought it was an occasion of sin, her having supper with Joe. And he said no, Joe was a decent fellow and she was entitled to a little pleasure in life. And Joe was crazy about her mother. Sometimes he took her mother to the track.

But she confessed to Cyprian that sometimes she found it hard to understand why that had happened to Burt and why she had had to stay married to him.

Cyprian told her that the will of God was the magnificent mystery at the center of the Christian life. He told her to remember that the cross was at the heart of everything; we were not put on earth to be happy, we were put on earth to know, love and serve God and to be happy with Him forever in heaven. He told her that this life was nothing, that she must remember that the reward of living the Christian life, of bending the human will to the will of the Father, was an eternity of splendor face-to-face with God.

Joe said that for Jews you went to Abraham's bosom. That sounded comfortable to her. Simply to rest, not to have to struggle to be cheerful when you felt like hell.

Joe said he kind of believed in reincarnation, like that movie where Dick Powell came back as a dog. But that didn't appeal to Mary Rose. Life was great, but it took a lot out of you. What she wanted was to give it over, to be waited on, to wait for things to happen. Most of the time now she was tired, even when she was having a good time.

She thought of Felicitas, with all the years ahead of her. She'd have a hard time bending to anything. It was one thing Cyprian telling Mary Rose to bend, she was the type, but Felicitas wasn't. She worried for her. Everybody wanted something out of her. Mary Rose wanted her to have a good time, to take it easy. She hoped they'd let her be herself.

She saw Felicitas' head in the pickup. She and Cyprian had not stopped talking since they got into the truck. Maybe that just was Felicitas' way. Maybe this was where she belonged. She seemed happy. Maybe that was all you could ask nowadays.

Cyprian asked Felicitas for her thoughts on the books he had given her in the hospital.

She would not lie to him. But she could weigh the testimony in his favor.

"I thought *The Seven Storey Mountain* was terrific. I really like him, Thomas Merton. But I still think it's a lot easier to become a monk if you've spent the first thirty years of your life running around Europe and New York."

"It wasn't the first part I wanted you to concentrate on. It was the part after his conversion, the spirituality."

"I wish I could be like that one day myself."

"It's a life's work, the attainment of that level of spirituality. And much more difficult in the world than in the cloister. Particularly in this stinking age."

Felicitas thought of the white wool habits, the chanting on cold mornings, the dark chill of a prayerful house.

"Perhaps I should become a contemplative."

Cyprian felt a little thrill of panic. Never to see her face again. "I think your vocation is outside the cloister. Your temperament is, like my own, too independent for community life. You would suffer in a religious community, as I did."

"Thomas Merton didn't. He said the pressures of community life were good for your humility, putting up with everyone's quirks."

Cyprian's hands tightened on the wheel. "You couldn't even put up with the poor girl in the bed beside you who was dying."

"Gidget wouldn't be in the cloister."

"A convent or a monastery is full of all sorts."

"Not like her. Not idiots."

"Believe me, Felicitas, the religious life attracts more than its fair share of idiots. To say nothing of jackasses and lamebrains. Fine distinctions, but they need to be kept."

"What about knuckleheads and birdbrains?"

"Birdbrains abound. Also the variety called *Cervellus pius,* peabrain. A species noted for its toughness and its plentitude."

"What about *Battus in Bellfrius* and *Rockus in Headus?*"

"They abound. They abound."

"Well, what should ah do with mah *lahf?*" asked Felicitas, doing her Scarlett O'Hara. She put one hand on her forehead and pretended to fan herself with the other.

"Whah, sugar," Cyprian mocked back, "ain't nothin'
for you to do but stay right heah. We got protection heah
from the idiots in the atmosphere. Also vultures, jackals
and mad dogs. Ah got a plot of land heah, and in front
of it ah have posted a sign: IDIOTS BEWARE. We have not
had a visitation recently."

She loved it when he did accents. She loved him to do
Italian barbers. Irish cops, Germans who owned delica-
tessens. And she loved, above all, going with him to the
property.

He turned in the direction of the land. He signaled to
the other car that they should go back to the motel. Clare
waved and continued on the highway.

"I have something to show you," he said. "Something
I discovered since you've been hurt."

In the two months he had owned the land, Cyprian had
cleared half the undergrowth. Now you could walk to the
old foundation easily. Now you could see, without ob-
struction, the three mountains. It was afternoon now, and
the hills were blue. The trees swayed and the weeds
deepened with color, the white milkweed and the orange
tiger lily. There was one weed she could not name that at
this hour sent out a dark odor that enclosed the land with
an odd urban suggestion of corruption and high style.

Cyprian walked slowly to accommodate to her injury.
He walked past the old foundation, a hundred feet to the
left, lifted some old boards and beckoned to her.

"Just stand here on this spot and tell me what you see,"
he said.

She moved behind him. He was standing at the edge of
a great hole.

"Look down and tell me," he said. He was as excited
as a child.

She looked down. Shadows disappeared into the hole.
She focused in the darkness. Then she could see two
shapes, hers and Cyprian's, in the water. Her heart lifted.
She could see herself and him.

"Water," she said. "You found the old well!"

She knew how he had worried about that, the expense
of digging a new well, the worry if the old one was not
found.

"The one good thing the bastards did who owned this

property was to keep the well boarded up. But it was so overgrown I couldn't find it."

"Is the water good?" she asked. She had been reading about wells, knowing he was worried.

He pulled a rope. At the end of the rope was a bucket. He reached into the bucket and cupped his hands, then brought his hands up to her face. She bent her head and drank.

The water was cold and clear. She rejoiced, as if she had been years wandering in the desert, as if she were Moses, striking twice.

"It's wonderful," she said.

He drank the rest of the water from his hands.

"You'll never get water like that in the city," he said.

"Never," she cried in the ecstasy of this new wealth. "It's a miracle the water isn't brackish."

"A miracle," he said. His fingers were still wet.

He took his thumb and on her forehead made a cross. "I sign you in the name of the Father and of the Son and of the Holy Ghost. There," he said, "you are signed and sealed in the water of this land."

He kissed the top of her head. She put her arms around him. She let her head stay for a moment on his chest.

She was perfectly happy. She would never leave him.

PART II

1969-1970

I

On St. Patrick's Day of 1969, Felicitas had an interview at Barnard College. That day, everyone on the subway was wearing green. Men who never dreamed of ornament as a possible diversion wore green shirts and ties and hats; women in all other ways conventionally adorned sported on their cheeks green painted shamrocks. Jocose, heavy girls whose natures were political wore KISS ME, I'M IRISH buttons on their large breasts and on their pocketbook straps buttons that said, AMERICA, LOVE IT OR LEAVE IT, or HATE COPS? NEXT TIME YOU'RE IN TROUBLE CALL A HIPPIE.

Felicitas had begun college at St. Anne's, a small school ten minutes from her home, which was run by the sisters of St. James. Clare had gone there, and Elizabeth had a friend, Sister Matilda, in the English department. Felicitas won a scholarship. Clare's idea that she might go to Cornell was quickly dropped. When the time came, there was no question that she must attend a Catholic college. She decided that she would study classics.

But after 1968 she could not study classics at St. Anne's. Before the middle of the 1960's, before the Second Vatican Council, many Catholic girls, often unremarkable as students, majored in Latin. They had studied it in Catholic high school and they simply went on. It was the language of the Church, and for a pious girl who was neither scientific nor imaginative, it was a respectable course. But in 1963 Latin ceased to be the language of the Church as it expressed itself to the laity. In 1968, Felicitas' sophomore year, she was the only classics major in the college. In November of that year, Father Donovan, who taught Greek and Latin, had a heart attack. It was decided that he would not be replaced. He advised Felicitas to transfer to Columbia rather than to Fordham. A Dominican, he preferred to see her educated by pagans than by Jesuits.

At Barnard on St. Patrick's Day, no one was wearing green. The secretary to the registrar wore a yellow woolen mini-dress, blue patterned stockings and flat strapped shoes like a little girl's. She sent Felicitas to the chairman of the classics department. Felicitas walked up a formal staircase past girls who all looked perfect to her in their jeans and sweaters. St. Anne's still had a dress code. She felt foolish in her red wool jumper and black pumps; she felt vulnerable. All the girls, she could see, were learned and sexy, with two parents each who sent them packages from Oregon or Texas full of homemade jellies and knit slippers. Or else they came from the Upper East Side and had one foreign parent who could give advice on contraceptives and perfume. She never went to the classics department. When she got to the top of the staircase, she walked purposefully down the hall, pretending to squint at room numbers, went down the staircase at the other end of the corridor, out the door and down into the subway.

All the way home, she thought of the perfect curve of Greek sentences, of the peace of translating Boethius. She decided she could not give it up. Of course she would have to go somewhere to study. But she could not go to school with those girls. She decided she would go to the Columbia School of General Studies, the proletarian arm of the university, with secretaries who worked for their degrees at night, with insurance men who wanted other languages.

It took her two full weeks to get the courage to go back to 116th Street. This time she got off on the other side of the street from Barnard. It was early April and the treetops overhanging College Walk were granular with yellow buds. On this side of the street, professors who looked as if they could be spies carried briefcases into the library and did not lift their eyes. Someone's wife and babies played on the steps. Young men dressed like Indians or soldiers swaggered past. There were young women, too, but their extraordinariness was muted: they might work as waitresses; they could do their own typing. She loved the statues and the fountains green with age, the lawns that nineteenth-century Germans might have walked on and the tired faces, only half as beautiful as those across the street.

At General Studies, she was sent to the office of Professor Oblonsky, who was to serve as her adviser. Serge Oblonsky was a White Russian, a medievalist who taught Latin for his supper. He was almost preternaturally untidy; Felicitas could see that he would spend half his life looking for things that were under other things, searching for laundry tickets, opera tickets, driver's licenses, insurance policies. All the time he was greeting her, he was looking for her application. He gave off an odor that would have seemed unsanitary were it not so bookish. The office smelled of wet leather and dust, of carbon paper and milk about to go bad. Felicitas did not dislike the smell because she knew that no one in a Catholic college would have been allowed to have an office like this: some nun would have seen to it, throwing out perhaps a half a century's research wrapped in old newspaper, for the love of Our Lord.

"Ah, I see you are a Roman Catholic student," said Professor Oblonsky, working his bottle-shaped nose.

Felicitas said nothing; there was nothing, she believed, to say.

"That means your handwriting will be legible, that you will know your grammar but have the sense of poetry of an opossum."

Felicitas had gone to school with girls like that; it injured her to be mistaken for one of them. She suddenly saw herself: small and bosomless, with glasses and high heels. She could see how he must think of her. But she would not let anyone mistake her nature in so facile and so radical a way. She stood up so that he would be sure to see her over the piles of paper on his desk.

"I write legibly because I see no virtue in disorder. I know my grammar; there is nothing to be gained from ignorance. But I have lain awake in anguish over the fate of Dido; I have wept in mourning for her. I wonder if you can say the same."

He was silent for a moment.

"Are your parents both American?" he asked, looking in his pocket for a pen.

"My parents have nothing to do with it. I am who I am."

"Spoken like a burning bush. I will call you that. Not Miss Taylor, but Miss *Ignes Flamens*. Miss Burning Bush."

Felicitas flushed with pleasure. Nothing would be difficult here. Professor Oblonsky would like her more than any other student. He would value her and tease her; he would weep, she could see now, at her graduation.

"I am glad to see there are still young ladies who can blush," he said.

They planned her program for the fall. She would be studying with him the historians Tacitus and Herodotus and the poet Catullus. Father Donovan had not thought Catullus appropriate for young women. She would begin Greek; she would study Byzantine art and Renaissance history. She walked out of the college gates, her heart high with her prospects.

That summer, she spent only one week in Orano. The sight of Muriel inflamed her into frenzy; she was tired of Elizabeth's fears and Father Cyprian's rage, which all the women spent their days placating, Mary Rose with jokes, Clare with reason. And she was tired of her mother saying, "For Christ's sake, keep your mouth shut about the war in front of Cyprian."

She had been against the war since 1966. In November of that year, Kevin Doyle, who had lived next door to her all her life, was brought home dead.

She had played with Kevin constantly until they started school. But with the first weeks of their first term, it was clear that there could be nothing between them. Felicitas was smart and Kevin was not. Dumb, slow, backward, were the adjectives applied to him, as if his brain were another lumbering body that he dragged behind his literal flesh. In their extreme youth, Kevin had been kind to her, and many times during the first six grades of school she would have liked to help him. But it was not possible; the gulf was never bridgeable. They never spoke to each other, although their homes were fifty feet apart. With every report card, the nuns gave Felicitas holy pictures, moony, transfixed portraits of young girls on cloud banks who carried meaningful symbolic objects, palms or lyres, arrows, lambs or wheels. And Kevin would accept his report card from the pastor or the principal and return to his seat in silence, beyond shame and notice.

His life changed when he became old enough to work on machines. The news spread fast: he could fix anyone's radio, he could repair clocks and electric mixers. And then he began on cars. From that day forward, he was treasured, he was honored. His school-day shame was trivial; he became suddenly older than his classmates, his muscles thickened, even the hair on his head lost its adolescent fineness and became adult. Girls from unknown areas of town, from public school, girls with tight sweaters and ankle bracelets, appeared in the driveway, and he drove away with them, too young for a legitimate driver's license but magically beyond the law, in one of his many salvaged cars.

In April of 1966, he turned eighteen and enlisted in the army. Within six months, he had been sent to Vietnam, killed and sent back home.

The news of his death shocked Felicitas as no other death had shocked her, because of his age, his deftness and her history of unkindness. She thought of *his* kindness, fixing their radiators, starting Clare's car on cold nights. She regretted as she regretted nothing else, for she was still young, her hierarchical silences, the neglectful tilt of her head as she walked past his desk after her blackboard triumphs. She mourned him first from vanity, because she valued mourning and felt she had a talent for it, and she valued the idea of death he had at once brought close and rendered foreign: he was her age; he had died in Asia. But then she mourned him sincerely. She remembered the bland, comforting lunches they had shared before they started school, the secrets he had told her: he was frightened of the cellar; the smell of his grandmother's breath made him cry. And finally she stood beside his grave and mourned him, child to child.

At the funeral, she was the only one who wept. His parents and the V.F.W. and the American Legion and Father McCarthy spoke of his death as if it was no loss but victory, a trophy, an award. Over the grave, Father

McCarthy did not read the simple psalms of burial; he substituted texts from Jeremiah:

> I have set thee this day over the nations, and over kingdoms, to root up and to pull down, and to waste and to destroy, and to build and to plant . . .

> For behold I have made thee this day a fortified city and a pillar of iron and a wall of brass, over all the land . . .

> And they shall fight against thee and shall not prevail: for I am with thee, saith the Lord.

Mrs. Doyle's face was hard with angry pride. She said she would not miss her son; it was an honor to lose him —he had died to prove something. Mr. Doyle said he would rather see his son dead than a draft dodger. No one said, "This boy's death is a terrible loss, nothing can make up for it." They said, "It was right that he should die."

She went home after the funeral and wrote a letter to the Women's Strike for Peace. "Please send me any information you have, including bibliographies," she wrote. All summer long, she read about the war. The books she read led her to other books. By the time September came and she had started at St. Anne's, she had vowed that she would never put her weight behind this effort, which was wicked and deceitful, evil, brutal and forgetful. Which was death.

She looked at the sad, patient faces of the Vietnamese in the newspaper, and at the satisfied faces of the generals. She thought of Father Cyprian and Myron Haber that day at the farm when they had made her smell things. She called back the memory of weakness and injustice, and she vowed to die before she would give support to any people who supported this great humiliating instrument of death.

In September of 1967, in great secrecy, she bought a railroad ticket to Washington so that she could go on the Pentagon march. She was entirely alone. There was no one she knew who could possibly accompany her. She envied and resented the heartiness of her fellow passengers, large Protestant families with red cheeks and good teeth who said "Gosh darn it" and offered her nuts and cookies from the paper sacks they carried. She did not want the food; she did not want to sing "We Shall Overcome." She wanted to read the book she had bought in the store at Penn Station, *Vietnam*, by Mary McCarthy. She had been warned against Mary McCarthy for years. Ever since *The Group*, nuns had shaken their heads and breathed her name as a warning to the better students. "What good do all those brains do her? Four husbands and writing filth," they said. It was a comfort to have that book with her; she felt accompanied by a daring older sister whom defiance had made glamorous.

She was silent when she got to Washington as her fellow marchers shouted, "Hey, hey, LBJ, how many kids did you kill today?" She was silent on the green lawn of the Lincoln Memorial. In silence she read the advice on what to do in case of tear gas, and in silence she took the train back to Penn Station and the subway to her house, where, walking home, she met four boys, her neighbors, who sat all day in the candy store and waited to be drafted. She was afraid that through some primitive virile prescience they would know where she had been. She was afraid they would beat her up. She had known them all their lives; she knew it was not impossible. She knew the hatred in their hearts against long-haired boys and girls in blue jeans and senators who stood against the President. They said, "Look at them, you can't tell the girls from the boys," and in their minds' eyes they saw bloody fists, mouths with teeth broken, heads cracking on the pavement, heavy boots and dirty woolen jackets. When they smiled at her, she could see the bully's thin mouth, strong teeth and watchful eyes. If they knew she had been marching against the war, they would be tempted to terrify her, to teach her a lesson. If they did not hurt her physically, it would be only because their mothers knew her mother, because they retained a primitive regard for female weakness and thought of her as an orphan because her father was dead.

Father Cyprian was like them. He wanted to punish her, but she could never fear him as she feared the boys who waited on the corner. He had raised her to argue with him; now he demanded her silence. But she had not been trained to silence, so they argued always now. They could not speak two sentences without fighting about the war. When the terrible thing happened, they had had a fight about Daniel Berrigan. Cyprian had called him "a snot-nosed limelighter," and Felicitas had said, "He is the only hero in the Church."

Cyprian had stood up then and banged his fist on the table, making the wine jump out of the glasses and spill like blood. He said, "How dare you speak to me like that?"

Felicitas also stood up. It was a foolish move; she was half his size and he bulked above her.

"I speak the truth," she said.

"You have no humility," he shouted. "You have been corrupted by this proud and lying age."

"I was not brought up to be humble. I was brought up to speak the truth."

"You are a scandal to us all," he said.

She walked out of the house she had helped him to build. She had wheeled barrowsful of concrete for the wall; she had carried ladders. The sky was full of stars, clustered and milky above the roof she had repaired with him. She knew the road so well she could have walked it under a pitch-dark sky. She wept, in anger and in fear. He could not speak so to her, like Jehovah on the mountain. He was not correct. Yet he had made her bend beneath the righteousness of his tone. He could make her feel deprived of shelter. Now, walking down the road, away from him, she felt utterly impoverished. She shivered with the moderate cold; she was childishly frightened. Every bush contained a murderer that he could save her from.

But she would not recant. She was right and he was not. She would not say otherwise, even if it meant this hunger and this terror. This enduring chill.

She heard steps on the road behind her. Clare called, "Will you wait for me? I can't keep up in these shoes."

Felicitas stopped, although she did not want the comfort of Clare's reason. But it was kind of her to come out of the house like that. It was dangerous for her.

Clare took a Kleenex out of her jacket pocket and handed it to Felicitas.

"I've never known anyone like you for Kleenex and flashlights," said Felicitas.

"It's my place in the company," said Clare and lit a cigarette.

"I know what you think," Felicitas said. "You think I should have been quiet."

"I think life is easier if one proceeds with tact and caution."

"*He* doesn't. He thinks he can say anything."

"He is himself."

"And I am myself."

"Then these things are bound to happen."

They walked on in silence. The flashlight made a perfect lunar circle at their feet.

"What should I do now?" asked Felicitas.

"Go back and go quietly to bed."

Felicitas did. No one spoke to her. Even her mother was silent. She slept the sleep of the recent convict, the new thief.

In the morning, it was Muriel who came to waken her. "Father had a slight heart attack during the night. Of course, no one blames you."

Felicitas felt the integrity of pure hate. The woman hated her, and she hated the woman.

She ran up the stairs in her bare feet.

"It's a little late now for concern," Muriel called after her.

Father Cyprian was sitting at the table. The doctor was just driving away in his car. How had she slept through it all?

"How are you, Father?" she asked, taking his hand and chafing it. She forgot that he might still be angry.

"I've been sentenced to a long life, if I can control my food and temper. I will not give up liquor or argument. Sugar and fats I relinquish; they are an infant's luxury."

His face was gray. His day's beard made him an old man. She did not want to be near him.

She stayed four more days, weeding the garden while he rested in bed. Then she said she had to leave early to get ready for school. No one questioned her.

Cyprian had built his house on the old foundation of the house he was brought up in. It was a one-story cinder-block building, long and narrow and, Felicitas now saw, jail-like. Three hundred yards to the right, Muriel had had a house built. It was more human than Cyprian's, a three-story wood-frame house with picture windows, and Cyprian spent an uneven amount of time there, depending upon his moods. Muriel was now so dry that any suggestion of scandal was absurd. The townspeople thought them brother and sister. They kept to themselves in the winter; in the summer the house was full of other company.

Riding home on the bus from Orano, Felicitas felt exhausted. She slept through the high, considered greens of western New York State, slept past Binghamton and woke in New Jersey on the stretch that overlooked the sulfurous ruin of the gas companies. Burnt, burnt out. If everything in life were like that, she thought, who would go on living? Who would live life in bankruptcy, she wondered, when suicide, an act rich in imagination, lay so easily to hand.

The lives of the women she loved were bankrupt. She was tired of their efforts to live the lives of bankrupts, making do with God and each other, purchasing the icon of a man, a tyrant, who had won their veneration not through honorableness but through fear, who stood out on the landscape not for his distinction but because it was a desert. Bare and dry, they struggled with their bankrupt soil, their love was water, shelter. And their love, she thought, was the manure around the roots, the lie they lived so that he would not have to see the truth: without their shelter, he would wither; left out in the air, he would be struck down.

Why did they need it so, a man to lie to? Why did they need his force, his rancor, his advice on the spiritual life that suggested they would not reach heaven without him? Why did they take his advice about their earthly lives, he who was always mistaken, always counseling silence, forbearance, humility, while he raged and cursed the fools who banished him to a cinder-block house and the love of women?

She, too, had done it, for he had the trick of making a woman believe his love was honor, his love was distinction, his love was the trial by fire of fine gold. She had listened to the catalog of her sins—not sins, he said, but imperfections. She was proud, she was stiff-necked, she was ungrateful, she was sentimental. She could not fight against the stinkpot of her age.

But she had tried to fight against it, refusing dates, high heels, rum and Cokes, team sports, love songs, finally, by the time she was out of high school, even ordinary friendship, so sure was she of the honor of the isolate, the danger of contamination, of dulling her fine edge.

There was no one near her age who loved her. She watched in envy clusters, pairs, mixed groups of four. She sometimes followed couples blocks out of her way, dogging them in her good old-fashioned shoes, in love with their connection. She swooned sometimes over the linked hands of strangers, over friends whose touch was easy on each other's shoulders. And she huddled wet and frozen in her segregation, loved by the generation of her parents whose hope she was.

It exhausted her now. It never used to. When she believed she stood outside the multitude because of honor, she trained like an athlete, like a messenger preparing to run with the good news of truth. But now she perceived that the women had forgotten themselves, forgotten what they stood for. Now they stood for Cyprian, they stood around him, because he was a man and wounded. It was an act of female instinct, and she would not give her life for an instinctive act. She would not give up the comradeship of fellows to be the youngest of the brood hens circled around the dying cock whose struts they reverenced. She would not do it.

As the bus entered the rank darkness of the Lincoln Tunnel, she vowed to change her life.

She would begin by not being the favorite student of Professor Oblonsky; that would be too easy, and change required what was difficult. She knew she ought to change her course of study. But she could not bear to. She would not give up the prospect of Greek. Father Donovan had had his heart attack before he had been able to do more than take her through the alphabet. On her own, she had gone through the present tense and was able to make up infantile sentences. It was her great desire to read *Antigone,* the *Oresteia.* She would not give that up for chums, for company. But she could give up her course on Renaissance history for one on modern political theory.

II

The tenth day of September, she went to Columbia to register. It was her first day of belonging, her first day with a definite place to go, and it made the trees look different to her. They were hers now. In paying her fees, she had won the right to look at them familiarly. The vivid trees gave her courage, and no one looked at her as if she were peculiar. She stood on lines an hour long, entranced with happiness. She held her IBM cards like talismans. Perhaps she would have friends now, perhaps one of these faces, for the moment unattached to meaning, would be the face of her dear friend. Some people looked odd, some were foreign, some were even dirty. They did not exhibit the energetic cleanliness or desperate lack of fashion of the Catholic girls who had heretofore shared her education. She smiled for her I.D. photograph, then laughed to see her own face. It was the face of elation; it was a face that looked unserious; it could have been anybody's face.

Charlotte hoped Felicitas would be all right up there. She was personally against non-Catholic education, and Cyprian had kicked up a terrible fuss, which only made Felicitas get her back up and be more determined. Cyprian could be a real horse's ass with Felicitas, particularly in the last couple of years. He was really out of touch, living up there with goddamn Muriel, the two of them talking all night about how terrible the world was. Of course the world was terrible, but what the hell were you going to do about it? Unless you wanted to live up there like them and get old before your time.

That was what one of Charlotte's aunts said about Felicitas: "She's old before her time." It always frightened Charlotte, making the walls of her heart feel thin and vulnerable. Perhaps she had robbed her daughter of a childhood. Perhaps she had been a thief. So she had let her go to Columbia, if that was what she wanted. It was too late now anyway; if she was going to go off the track, she was going to go off. She had a lot of background behind her.

Charlotte talked to the girls and they thought it was a good thing, all in all. Mary Rose said she thought Mel Ferrer had gone to Columbia, and he was a very good actor and married to Audrey Hepburn. Elizabeth said Felicitas should have the pleasure of knowing Greek; it was one of her greatest regrets that she had not learned it. Clare said if Felicitas was going to do any real good in the world, she'd have to learn to mix with different kinds of people.

So that was that. The world was crazy, it was dangerous and Charlotte knew that she was opening her child's world to more danger. But she had opened her to danger in giving her birth. She asked Felicitas if she wanted Clare to meet her for lunch, just the first day.

Felicitas loved Clare, but she did not want a tasteful lunch at some small foreign restaurant on that day. She wanted to eat in the cafeteria. She thought of what that meal would be: a hamburger and macaroni salad. There was no room for Clare in a world of meals like that. "No," she told her mother, "I'll have lunch up there alone."

"Clare's a brain, she speaks their language, she can help you."

"Mother, *no*," Felicitas said, as if Charlotte were a dog about to tip over the garbage.

"All right," said Charlotte angrily. "You know best. You've got all the goddamn answers. Go your own way."

Felicitas chose to hear her mother's words as a blessing. She kept the words and ignored the tone.

"If I know all the answers, what are the questions?" she said, pinching her mother's arm.

"Don't pinch. You know what Mrs. Gambarino says. Pinching is the number-one cause of cancer in the United States."

They did imitations of Mrs. Gambarino, who lived up the block and had theories for every disease. Then they went to bed. Charlotte prayed in silence for her daughter's safety. She knew that all the children of God were saved. But they were not safe.

Felicitas sat in the last seat of the row nearest the door in the room where Modern Political Theory met. She was deeply grateful that she did not seem to look particularly out of the ordinary. There was a serious, workmanlike aspect to the students. The sheen of privilege did not transform the texture of their skins, did not stream from them like the rays of light from the palms of the Virgin. She was prepared to believe them brilliant but not desirable. They would not wreck her peace.

Then a man walked in the door and the classroom took on an agreeable hush. At first, she thought he must be one of the students; it was quite beyond her experience to assume that a professor would be dressed in blue jeans, chukka boots and a work shirt opened to reveal an unprofessional amount of disappointingly hairless chest. Over his shoulder he carried a green cloth sack, which he threw onto the front desk from what seemed halfway across the room. It landed with a thud that moved Felicitas to anger. The classroom was a place of quiet and decorum; it was a sanctuary, not unlike a church. What could he be up to? She ran her fingers over the image of Alma Mater embossed on her new notebook.

He sat on the desk and ran his hand over his mouth as if the prospect of speech was distasteful.

"I know what you all expect: a magical mystery tour of politics beginning with Aristotle and ending with Dean Rusk. Well, I'll tell you right now, if that's what you expect, you've come to the wrong place. I've walked that road and it's a dead end."

He was the handsomest man she had ever seen. The highest point of his cheekbones, the part of his face above where she imagined his beard stopped, was burnished as if he had polished and buffed it like a perfect apple. He

reminded her of a fine piece of furniture. She had learned
from Clare how to judge furniture. She thought of Clare
now. What would she have done? Would she have left,
outraged by his bad manners, or would she have been
entranced by the presence of real beauty?

He sat on the desk again, unbuttoned his cuff buttons
and rolled his sleeves to just below the elbow. Felicitas
wondered if he had calculated just how much forearm he
would expose. She understood for the first time how men
felt about women: his rolling up of his shirt-sleeves was
one of the most riveting spectacles she had ever witnessed;
she could not have stopped looking if someone had ordered her to. She was reminded of the taste of lime.

"I'm a political scientist. You might say I've spent my
life trying to figure out man the political animal. You
might call me the pornographer of the body politic."

One of the older women laughed. Felicitas looked out
the window. She wished he would be silent. The foolishness of his utterances almost took away the impact of his
beauty. But no, it could not, for there he was, whatever
he was saying, radiant with beauty, running his hands
through his thick hair, settling on everyone alike his fine
blue gaze. Was there sadness there? She wanted to think
so. But she thought all men looked sad, unless they looked
uninteresting.

"It seems to me, and it is not my idea, of course, but
the great St. Herbert's, whose name I will invoke . . ."
He went to the board and wrote the word "MARCUSE" in
capital letters. Felicitas imagined the muscles of his back
that made his arms move.

"We have come to the point where the technology we
thought would free us has enslaved us. It is reason that
has done this, reason divorced from desire. There are no
greater examples of this than Vietnam and nuclear prolif-
eration, both the work of man cut off from nature, the
work of man subverting his life-giving desires and being
twisted into having artificial desires that require the death
and enslavement of others. I will not teach the philosophy
of enslavement; I will not enshrine the methodology of
death. I will not spend our time together walking in the
minefield of rationalists and pessimists. I want to teach

you the groundwork for the future. We will read together
those thinkers who bring life, not death."

He wrote on the board next to Marcuse, "ROUSSEAU,
MILL, ENGELS, MARX."

Felicitas copied the names down in a trance. She could
barely hear what he said, could barely see what he was
writing, could barely remember having heard those names
before. Her pen and the process of writing seemed strange
to her. She could not stop staring at his back. She could
not stop repeating his name: Robert Cavendish, Robert
Cavendish. This is desire, she thought, staring; this is
what they mean.

In Greek class, Felicitas was translating the *Apology* of
Plato. For as long as she could remember, she had wanted
to read Plato in Greek. But now the beautiful face of
Robert Cavendish eclipsed it, muddying the cold transparent water that was her mind when she was translating,
coloring it, making it by turns turbulent and brackish. In
her mind was not the clear blue of the sky above the students of Socrates but the polished, rose-colored face of
that man, ripe-textured, delicious, she imagined, to the
tongue.

In Professor Oblonsky's class she could not concentrate
on the satiric poetry of Horace. She wished it were the
second half of the course, in which they would be reading
Catullus. She got Professor Oblonsky's jokes but did not
laugh at them. Her mind was on Professor Cavendish and
the colorful revolution he planned, where only the wicked
would bleed and that let blood would be salutary.

He began the course by talking about Rousseau. She
could see the difference between the way he taught and
the way Catholics taught. There was nothing second-rate
about his knowledge, it was not scratched from the hard
earth of immigrant labor, the money for it had not been
hoarded, did not represent cream cut out of coffee, mar-
garine instead of butter, no new dresses for the girls, a
mother ironing the shirts of strangers. She could tell by
the way he spoke about Rousseau that his learning had
been granted him in leisure. And there was no hint of
apology for learning, no shadowboxing with invisible old
neighbors, no fear of sins of pride or loss of spiritual pur-

ity in exchange for what he knew. He told them about Harvard in the fifties. "Uptight bullshit," he called it. He kept announcing his fear of his own prejudice. He spoke about "the myth of objectivity," which used to be his god.

"There is no such thing as objectivity," he warned his students, who, born poorer, copied down each word he said. "There is no learning of real value without passion." And then, worried that he had been too objective, "Objectivity is bullshit. I was frozen to death by the passionless rhetoric of my training."

As he spoke about the cold of objectivity, Felicitas felt cheated. Never for one moment in her education had knowledge been presented to her coolly, for its own sake, all sides of the matter granted equal weight. That kind of objectivity seemed to her blessed, as if ideas were beautiful and valued for themselves, not for their use. Robert Cavendish had been taught by men who had not felt endangered. They gave him ideas like good cloth, and he had not, Felicitas felt, the sense to value them. Yet they were his to trample, like the tweed jacket he rolled into a ball and shoved into his green cloth sack.

And now he wanted the hot, twisted world of villains and great heroes. The world she was trying to leave. He said his learning had been cold. The heat of hers had come from the hot flesh of martyrs, and it stank of burning. She envied him his cool Octobers with high-minded scholars who were thin and blue-veined and whose flesh was calm.

"You're not talking much about school," Charlotte said. "Aren't you happy?"

"Of course," said Felicitas, who spent her hours wrapped in a dark cloak of helpless longing and mute rage.

"How's the Greek?"

"It's fine. We're doing Plato."

"You're very big on Plato, right?"

"Of course."

"What does Cyprian think of Plato?"

"Cyprian thinks you should learn Greek to read the fathers of the Church. He thinks that learning before Christ is beside the point."

"He has a point."

"He does not. It's an asinine opinion."

"Well, what the hell did they have to tell us? They didn't know their ass from a hole in the ground. All those gods and screwing everybody."

"Mother, I can't talk to you about this. Ask Elizabeth. She has the patience to explain it."

"And what do you think Father Cyprian would say if he knew you were reading books by Karl Marx?"

"Mother, it happens to be very important in the history of political thought."

"Get thee behind me, Satan," said Charlotte. "Thanks a lot but no thanks."

Felicitas made an exasperated clicking sound.

"I thought you were going to Columbia to study Greek. Karl Marx is certainly the hell not Greek."

"I have to take electives," said Felicitas. "I have to do this."

"Electives my ass," said her mother. "You're all het up about the goddamn war. That's why you took it. You'll get yourself into trouble, young lady. Mark my words."

"Oh, Mother, we're *in* trouble. Everyone alive now is in trouble."

"That's the goddamn truth," said Charlotte.

"We can hardly speak of our history without tears of shame," Robert Cavendish had said. She imagined tears coursing down his beautiful face, pure tears of fellow feeling. He understood suffering; she knew that now. The flesh of the Vietnamese was to him like the flesh of his own children, he had said. She tried to imagine his children. That meant he must have a wife. Perhaps he was unhappily married. She imagined him weeping. She imagined what her mother would say to a man like Robert Cavendish: "Dry up, don't be a sap." But she was not like her mother. She knew his suffering was genuine. She would be his comforter. She would dry his tears with her hair.

"I think I'll let my hair grow really long," she said to her mother.

"Forget it," Charlotte said. "You're not the type."

Elizabeth asked Felicitas if she might meet her at Columbia for dinner, if Felicitas could perhaps show her the li-

brary. Felicitas suggested that Elizabeth meet her on the
third floor at one of the tables on the right side of the
catalog room.

Shyly Elizabeth walked up the steps. This was real
learning, what she had always wanted. The hints she had
had of it at normal school were almost worse than nothing. Shakespeare and Dickens and Swift abridged, Chaucer and Cervantes in translation. Always in terms of how
to teach them to children, never for themselves. And all
the hours of her education spent in cutting colored circles, sticking bits of wood together, learning songs. When
what she wanted was this, all this around her, these silent, serious people who knew what they were doing.

She turned right into the catalog room. How wonderful everyone looked there, bent over something (she was
sure that all the books here must be wonderful) with their
European-looking heads and pencils. The air was muted
and all actions took on a beautiful heaviness. She saw
Felicitas across the room, her small head quite at home
here. And Elizabeth thanked God that Felicitas was finally where she belonged, in this wonderful room, translating Greek.

Elizabeth imagined what she would do here if she were
Felicitas' age. First she would research a book on Jane
Austen. *Friendship in Jane Austen* it would be called. Perhaps someone had already written that topic. She hoped
not. In her dream no one had. Then she would learn
Anglo-Saxon. She would read *The Seafarer* in the original.
She would write a book about forgiveness, she thought,
touching lightly the green leather of the tables. But she
would choose above all, like Felicitas, to be studying Greek.

Felicitas was not reading Greek when Elizabeth came
up to her. Elizabeth felt a piercing disappointment. She
was reading a perfectly ordinary English book.

They walked to a student cafeteria. Elizabeth could not
believe the noise. How could these children come from
studying, from reading their wonderful books, to this din?
She squinted, as if the light were too bright. In fact, it was
nearly dark in the room. One would have trouble reading

here, which was what she imagined students wanted to do over dinner.

"What's the matter?" asked Felicitas, seeing Elizabeth's pained face.

"It's the noise. Dreadful."

"The music?"

"If you call it that. How can anyone think?"

"Everyone thinks all the time. They come here to hang out."

"To what?"

"Hang out. Relax."

"It hardly seems relaxing."

"Well, it is. You have to take my word for it."

In the cafeteria with Elizabeth, Felicitas felt far closer to her fellow students than she ever had before. She saw that she was far more like them than she was like Elizabeth, and that was a great comfort. She felt as if she knew all these people, as if she could introduce Elizabeth to any of them, whereas before she had sat among them a stranger, her high heels and jumper making her not one of them. But Elizabeth was wearing a small velvet hat and black kid gloves. Felicitas could see herself for the first time in blue jeans. She would wear them, she decided, when the weather changed.

"What are you working on?" Elizabeth asked as they sat at a table.

"Rousseau. I have to do this report for Political Theory."

"On what?"

"Rousseau's criteria for the moral life."

"I didn't think he had any."

"Oh, Elizabeth, that's just the Church's party line. He was a very serious moralist."

In fact, the purpose of Felicitas' report was to prove that there was no basis for his moral judgments, that they were weak and muddle-headed and dangerous to the polis. She wanted to do very well so that Professor Cavendish would notice her.

"Rousseau believed in the heart," said Felicitas.

"Everybody believes in the heart, don't they?" said Elizabeth.

Felicitas snorted. "What about Cyprian?"

"Oh, Felicitas, he loves you so much he can hardly bear it."

"He doesn't know anything about love."

"None of us knows much."

Felicitas thought of Robert Cavendish. He knew about love.

"Anyway," said Felicitas, "I'm enjoying this course immensely."

"Politics?"

"Yes."

"I've never been very interested in politics."

"Neither were the good Germans. That's what Hitler counted on."

Elizabeth blushed. "What shall we have to eat?" she asked. She felt like weeping. She had thought the evening would be extraordinary; they would walk among the edifying buildings and talk about the books they loved as the first autumn chill surrounded them.

On the line for the hot foods, Elizabeth said, "The library is wonderful."

"You could get a card, you know. You just pay a fee."

"Oh, no," said Elizabeth.

"Why?"

"Well, I don't belong. I'd be intruding."

"On the books?"

"On the people who belong there."

"Elizabeth, you seem to feel there's something wrong in getting what you want."

"Perhaps I do. Perhaps it's foolish."

"No perhaps about it," said Felicitas, reaching under an infrared lamp for French fries. Tomorrow she would buy blue jeans and wear them.

Elizabeth vowed that she would not come again unless Felicitas seemed most especially to want her to. She looked around her at the trays of food, choosing a dish of grapefruit sections and a piece of whole-wheat bread. Felicitas asked the cashier for butter and threw it on Elizabeth's tray, her eyes searching the cluttered tables for the people who would be her friends.

Felicitas did not look up at the others in the classroom once while she was reading her paper. She was conscious of a great heat in her face, and the heat made her feel fragile. When she stopped reading, she looked up to see Robert Cavendish walking toward her. He was applauding as he walked.

"Very good, Miss Felicitas Taylor. Very good. Entirely wrong but passionately wrong. There's something to that. Not everything, but it's a start."

The class stirred mutinously in their seats. Professor Cavendish was addressing her only. He was looking into her eyes. There was a hint of opalescence in his; she thought that when he got old, he would probably have cataracts. But his eyes were so beautiful and she had desired his gaze for so long that she began to cry. Humiliated, as if she had soiled herself, she stood in front of the class weeping.

"See you Friday, then, for more Rousseau," said Robert Cavendish, standing in front of Felicitas to render her invisible to her classmates. She felt his gesture was an extraordinary act of mercy, as if he had placed his body between her and gunfire. She knew he would think she was crying because he had said she was wrong. She did not want him to think that, but she could not tell him the truth, that she was weeping with desire.

But he did not ask her why she was crying. And she could tell he did not want to make her stop.

"Go on, cry," he said. "It's beautiful to see tears in the classroom. There are too few tears in the classroom, too little laughter. The classroom is a cold place. People leave their bodies and their hearts outside."

He took a handkerchief from his back pocket, held it up to her eyes and blotted the tears. Then he took a corner of it, licked it, and wiped her cheeks. The ink from her manuscript had come off onto her hands and then onto her cheeks when she had rubbed her eyes.

Her legs began to tremble and she felt she must sit down. He gave her his handkerchief.

"Give your nose a good blow," he said.

She blew her nose and laughed through the handkerchief. Then she began to cry again.

"You're a very passionate little girl, do you know that?"

She rolled his handkerchief into a ball and stuffed it into her pocketbook.

"I've soiled your handkerchief," she said. "I'll have to bring it home and give it back to you on Friday."

"And I will have to take you out to lunch."

She walked beside him down the steps of Hamilton Hall. Her body was made of strings that quivered, now with pleasure, now with terror. When he touched her arm to open the heavy door for her, she was afraid and hopeful that his fingers had left a mark on her clothing, like the shroud of Turin or Veronica's veil. She felt the burning of her flesh beneath his fingers, which had rested there for no more than an instant. And when, after a second, he took his hand away, she felt the strongest deprivation of her life.

He took her to the dining room of one of the dormitories. It was a dark, serious room where flirtatious girls sat on mahogany window seats and smoked cigarettes. Felicitas felt small here, damp and colorless, as if she were dressed in wet wool and visibly prone to earaches.

She stood behind him on the line, trembling with her own good fortune. To be with him by herself! It was a luxury she had dreamed of but never expected. She began to weep again.

"What's the matter?" he asked.

"I don't know."

"Are you about to get your period or something?"

She had never in her life heard a man speak of menstruation. Even her family doctor never mentioned it. But Robert Cavendish spoke about it in the perfectly utilitarian way that woman did, defining it as a nuisance, a distraction, one more drag and pull, expected but yet odd enough to note. She thought that he must know a lot about women to be able to speak like that. He wasn't like other people; he could speak about things without being embarrassed. She decided she would speak as if she were that sort of person too.

"I'm not sure when my period is due," she said.

"Don't you keep track?"

"No."

"So you don't know if you're late or not?"

"Look, can we talk about something else?" she asked,

fearing that she was displaying her unquestionable virginity.

"All right, but there's no sense being uptight about it. It's a perfectly natural function. It's really quite beautiful. I wish I could do it, be in touch with a natural cycle like that."

Felicitas was looking through the salads, pretending to search for peaches and cottage cheese so she would not have to answer him.

"I'll bet you think that's crazy," he said.

"No," said Felicitas. "Just ignorant."

She could have killed herself for speaking out like that. That was the trouble with her. She could never hold her tongue. She had been told and told.

But he was not angry with her. He put back his head and laughed, exposing his neck, which was strong and surprisingly rose-colored.

"I don't think anybody's ever called me ignorant before," he said. "Perhaps you have a great deal to teach me. Yes, I think perhaps you do."

Felicitas blushed and was rendered immobile. He put his arm around her to lead her through the line. For one moment she leaned against him, then moved away, outraged by her own presumption.

He held her chair for her. Never, she thought, had anyone performed an act so gallant, so perfectly desirable. This was what she had missed in life. Living as she lived, she had had no access to the life she saw in movies, to the gestures she had read about. And she was tired of it, the spare desert landscape she was trained to favor, her appointed meal of bone and water, her bespoke garment, tailored and unvaried, whose distinction lay not in its color but in its cut. Excellence had been defined for her as monochrome, but beside Robert Cavendish she felt herself grow colorful. Her cheeks lost their evenness, gave over being whey-colored. She could hear her mother saying, "You're always so goddamn pale. I wish you'd take vitamins." Her mother knew it was useless to suggest that Felicitas take the sun. That was one of Father Cyprian's great targets for scorn: people who lay in the sun, people who waited for color. Never for an hour had she lain beside an ocean or even, like some girls on her block, held a metal pie plate under her chin as a reflector. And her hands showed it, serious hands, governess hands; the sad pink nails, she thought, of the good student.

"Where did you learn to think?" he asked, breaking his bread before she had opened her napkin.

Terror shot into her face. She would not tell him what her life was like, for to let him know would be to lose him. He did not have to know the oddness of her history. She could, if she were careful, make him think her usual, make him think her worthy of regard, not as a curiosity but as herself, an object neither feared nor foreign but familiar, worthy of plain love.

"I've always read a good deal," she said. She took the memory of Father Cyprian and laid it out, crushed it, pressed it into a hard ball and hurled it to the back of her dark mind. Like a dog, she kicked sand over it, covered it with earth and made it silent. Then she turned to this man. She would give up everything she was or had been if he would only talk to her, if he would only find her worthy of attention and regard.

"You must have been unhappy to have done all that reading instead of living."

So that was how he thought of her, timid, frightened, shivering before her books.

"Reading is living," she said. "The dead don't read."

"A wise virgin. You'd never be caught without oil in your lamp."

"I'd never spend the night waiting for someone else's bridegroom."

He laughed. She was triumphant; she had made him laugh. Perhaps now he would talk to her, not out of charity but because she could amuse him.

He took her hand again. "You know, you're really a fascinating little thing."

She wanted to but would not bridle. Rochester had called Jane Eyre "a little thing." And she had won him, over the florid and well-dressed company of his equals.

He did not move his hand away. Felicitas looked straight into his eyes, a look of pure, new love, naked and uncolored. She squeezed his hand tentatively, as if she were selecting an orange. She feared that he would leave her now, run off in horror or in pity, and she would be there alone. But he looked back at her and smiled.

"I think you should drop my class."

She moved her hand away. She had so shocked him that he did not want to see her, even in a classroom. It was too great a punishment.

"But why?" she said. "Why should I drop your class?"

"Because I'm hoping to become your lover. And it will be much easier if I don't have to give you a grade at the end of the term."

Felicitas' relief was so great that she laughed. Her heart, her head had no weight. She was all delight.

"Why are you laughing?" he asked. "Is the idea of being my lover so amusing?"

She stopped, shocked that he should think she laughed at him. She looked at him and said, her heart lodged firmly in the center of her chest again, "It would be the greatest honor in the world."

He took her hand and kissed it, and they sat, holding each other's hands, in the artificial light of a basement room.

After class on Friday, Robert walked immediately to Felicitas' desk.

"I'm through for the week now," he said. "And I'm in the mood to celebrate. Let's go over to the West End and settle down to some serious drinking."

She was conscious of the envy of her classmates. She let it fall over her shoulders like a rich fur cloak.

"I want to know all about you," Robert said, covering her hands with his, which were cold from his frosted beer mug.

"Oh, no," she said flirtatiously, for she was in terror. "Today I get to hear about you."

He leaned back against the booth. She could tell that his own history was a topic he was prepared to be expansive about.

"Let's just say that I was thirty-five goddamn years old before I did one thing I wanted to do. Privilege. God, how I hate it. My whole life stank of privilege. Exeter. Amherst. Harvard. God almighty, all those Easter holidays in Nassau, all those summers on the Vineyard. What did they ever get me but more privilege? What did they ever make me but unbending and scared shitless of anything I couldn't control? I fucked my wife once a week from duty. Christ, in the prime of my life, I fucked as if I were paying a debt."

Felicitas nodded soberly, yet casually, as if this were the kind of conversation she was used to hearing. Perhaps that was how people were: you asked people about themselves and they told you about their sex lives. Why shouldn't they? All her life she had lived among virgins and widows. She knew nothing about life.

"I mean," he said, "I didn't know what women wanted because I was completely out of touch with the feminine side of myself. Now I wish I had been born a woman. A black woman. You know who I wish I had been born?"

"Who?"

"Billie Holiday. There was a woman who knew things."

"I believe she was very unhappy," said Felicitas.

"Of course, because she lived in this fucked-up culture. God, how I wish I'd been born Third World."

Felicitas wanted to tell him that a majority of the world's population would have loved to have been born *him*. But she kept silent. She did not want to ruin what was going to be the most important experience of her life with her sharp, terrible tongue.

"I mean, look at the guys in my department. Cripples, they're all cripples. Stooped in their prime from carrying the weight of a rotten carcass. Western civilization. It breaks their backs and they don't even know it. Thank God the world changed while I was young enough to enjoy it."

He looked at her empty glass. "How about another?"

"I'd love one," she said. She was looking forward to watching him walk...

He was back in a minute and began talking before he sat down. "My marriage was another joke. A tragic joke. But all jokes are tragic if you look at them."

"Thank you for the drink," Felicitas said.

"Sure," he said. "Don't you think all jokes are tragic?"

"Yes," she said, knowing that was what he wanted.

"Do you know what my wife said when I told her I was leaving her? 'What about our families?' she said. She didn't care about me. She cared about the house in Nantucket that our parents shared. Never in the history of the world have there been four in-laws so fond of one another. They still share the house; they spend all summer talking about what a bastard I am. All she cared about was Thanksgiving and her great-grandmother's table. The minute I left, she moved back in with her parents in Connecticut. Which just goes to show you what she really wanted all the time. Now she's married to someone as uptight as she is. Which is fine for her, but it bothers me about the kids. They live on the Upper East Side, so at least I can keep an eye on them. I put Blair in a free school this year; I told Sybil I'd hold back the child support if I couldn't oversee her education."

The word "oversee" made Felicitas think of *Uncle Tom's Cabin.*

"No, I really worry about the kids being so repressed. This summer I took them to the country, to a place a friend of mine has. He used to be a lawyer, but now he's a rock producer."

"A rock producer?" Felicitas asked, picturing boulders growing in neat rows.

"You know, he does records. I thought it would be great to get the kids out of the city for a while. But my kids were too uptight to handle it. This guy, my friend has three kids, and they were all used to swimming naked. But my daughter snuck into town and bought a bathing suit. Eleven years old. I told her she was beautiful, that bodies were beautiful. But I'm afraid it's too late for her to hear me."

"Perhaps it's a difficult age," Felicitas said. She was looking at the dark hair on his forearms.

"No, I was the same way until a few years ago. Until I met Yarrow."

Fear shot into Felicitas' heart.

"Yarrow was incredible. She brought me to life. She was the only woman I ever met who was genuinely not possessive. She was in my Intro class, just like you. At first I was so fucked up I couldn't pick up on the fact that she was offering herself to me. She said, 'Why don't I fuck you instead of doing a paper?' I was shocked. It took me a long time to realize that fucking is a political act."

In what sense? Felicitas wanted to ask. But she didn't want to hear the answer.

"Yarrow has her shit incredibly together. She lives on the Coast most of the time. Comes in every now and again, you never know when. I wish my kids could spend more time around her. She's incredibly unrepressed."

Felicitas was staring miserably into her glass.

"My God, I've spent the whole time talking about myself. You've barely said a thing."

"It's all right," she said. "You're much more interesting than I am."

"I'm going to show you exactly how interesting you are," he said. "I'm going to bring you to life.

"I have the feeling you've really got it," he said, "a first-rate mind, by which I mean a passionate mind. I don't have it, I know that now."

"Oh, you do, you do," she said, taking his hand. "Everything about you is first-rate."

"I haven't written a goddamn thing that's worth anything."

"But I'm sure you will now," she said.

"No, I have to concentrate on living now. My training is all wrong for what I believe in. It's too late for me. But it's not for you. I really think, given the right kind of direction, you might do something extraordinary. You just can't separate your mind from your body or your feelings. Your mind's in great shape; we just have to liberate those emotions of yours."

She thought of Cyprian and his scorn for the emotions. Robert was right; she had been repressed. How lucky she was to have found him, so she could change before it was too late.

Clare had heard the reluctance in Felicitas' acceptance of her luncheon invitation. But she had accepted, and so Clare waited for her, had been waiting forty minutes now at a noontime table that was hard to come by. She wore a gray suit whose wool was so fine that it showed a hint of lilac in the threads. She liked to wear variations of one shade; as she grew older she rejected, as she believed all women would be wise to do, bright colors. Formerly she would have worn, for example, a silk scarf of some vivid shade. But now she wore a lilac chiffon at her throat. It made her eyes grayer and the whiteness of her skin pearl white.

She could not bear the fashions this year: women dressed like Indians or five-year-olds, their long hair dirty and unstyled, their legs exposed or covered to the ground. There was no care for cut or fabric. She was aware that dressed as she was, she would embarrass Felicitas on the Columbia campus, which was why Felicitas had been quick to say she would meet Clare downtown.

Felicitas entered the dark restaurant as if she thought the patrons were armed against her. Frowning—she had always been famous for her frowns, Clare thought—she searched among the tables for the right one. Clare was used to Felicitas' frowns, but this one was different—she did not stop frowning when she saw Clare. And Clare understood that Felicitas was not glad to be with her, for the first time was not glad to see her face. A little thrill of fear struck, like a lit match, below one of her ribs.

"I'm late," Felicitas said, her voice a challenge.

"It's all right. You look worried."

"I'm not worried."

"Then preoccupied."

"Maybe I am."

"About what?"

"There's a war going on, you know. I think a lot about the war."

"You've always thought a lot about the war. This is something else."

"I don't have to tell you everything. You think that if you just sound reasonable enough, I'll tell you everything. Reason isn't everything."

Clare was on the point of saying, a reflex from freshman theology, "There's faith," but said instead, "Why don't you see what looks good to eat?"

Felicitas opened the menu and frowned at it. "It's incredibly expensive."

"It doesn't matter."

"You could feed a family of five in Spanish Harlem on what we'll spend."

"Felicitas, if you don't want to have lunch here or with me, you're free to leave."

Clare saw the child whom she had loved since birth look at her with a childish, disappointed hatred. She had stolen from Felicitas the privilege of rejection. Now, if Felicitas left, it would be because Clare had suggested it. She felt herself by far the strongest of all the women, and she was, of course, the one Felicitas should rail against.

Felicitas began to cry. "It's just that I can't stand places like this," she sobbed. "All these people in their expensive clothes getting rich off the war."

Clare knew that Felicitas' rage had nothing to do with Southeast Asia.

"Shall we just get a hot dog? Or a rain check?"

"I think I'll just go. I'm sorry, Clare, I just feel too weird to be with anybody."

That was what they all said now, "I feel too weird." All the young people said it, as if an unsettled mind absolved them from the rules of human discourse. But she would let Felicitas go, out of weakness or out of love she was not sure which.

"Maybe next week," said Clare, kissing Felicitas' warm cheek.

"Sure," Felicitas said, looking as if she'd memorized the exits.

She took the train back uptown. She wondered what Robert would think of Clare. It made her laugh to think of him among those women: he would have no way of placing them, nothing he could use in his life as a point of reference.

He would find Clare, at first, a type more familiar to him than the others. He would think her spinsterish and cool; she would make him think of Massachusetts or some cold New England state. Already she felt angry, imagining his misjudgment. On the train she defended Clare to Robert Cavendish, who would not listen, even in her dreams.

That afternoon, she went into the registrar's office to arrange to drop Robert's course. It was so easy; nothing in a Catholic college would have been so easy. She simply had to fill out her name and the course's number and give the paper to a woman, who dropped it in a wooden box. She felt that by signing her name she had done something momentous. Handing the paper to the secretary, she felt as if she were voting for a pope. She expected a puff of white smoke; she feared a puff of black: the eye of God, seeing her sign away her virginity, might send a warning, a visible sign, a gold cross in the sky, a burning tower.

She realized that she had nothing she could wear to bed that would not betray an innocence so radical as to deflect all possible desire. She went into the first store she saw on Amsterdam Avenue. All the clothes looked so insubstantial it seemed incomprehensible that they would survive even a first wearing. Clare had trained her to look for what would last. These unlined polyesters with quarter-inch hems shocked her at first, then seemed, in their very lack of permanence, generous and joyful. They would give her the air of spontaneity so foreign to her; they would suggest she wore what pleased her at the moment, that she dressed for the fun of it.

She did not know if one were allowed to try on night-gowns, but she thought she'd better not ask the salesgirl, who clearly *did* know. Her skirt was so short that when she bent down you could see her panties, which said WHOOPEE across her buttocks. Felicitas wondered if Robert would like that girl, those underpants. If he did, would she have to wear them? She did not know what would please the man who would be her lover, but she divined that what would please him was not natural to *her*. She would have to learn it, as she had learned the Greek alphabet, stumbling over strange shapes and sounds, discovering a way of looking at the world different from the one she had been born to but suggesting riches she would not have thought of.

She selected a short black nightgown with stiff lace around the neck and hem. Never in her life had she considered wearing anything like it. Women alone wear pastel night clothes, she thought; women who do not believe in sex. She brought the nightgown to the blond salesgirl. It was twelve dollars. She had twelve fifty with her. Now she could not have lunch. That pleased her, knowing that the gown would cost her something more than money. Now she would be able to associate the sense of love with the sense of hunger, which was, she thought, the proper combination.

She decided to stop by Robert's office to tell him she had dropped his course. He was sitting at his desk across from a woman in the class, someone Felicitas would never have thought of sitting next to. She looked so stupid that Felicitas was afraid her stupidity might be catching, like ringworm. She was a secretary. She had long Fu Manchu nails and she always wore pants and boots, a sweater and no bra. Felicitas could see the shape of her breasts as she walked. Now she wondered if the woman wore underpants. There she was, laughing with Robert. She had thrown the blue book of her midterm at him.

"Oh, Professor, how do you expect me to know all that?" she said. "It's practically my first course in the whole world."

All her life, Felicitas had envied girls who could throw things playfully. She was sure that if she threw a blue book at someone, it would glance off just the right vertebra and paralyze him for life or render him idiotic. Now all the passion of her soul went into envying that girl, who must also be able to untie ties, knock hats off and steal food from a man's plate. Robert was laughing with her. Felicitas stood silently in the doorway. She pretended she was Christina Rossetti. "When I am dead, my dearest," went through her head as she looked at the girl's crossed legs. She was perfectly silent for three minutes and a half before he noticed her.

"Felicitas," he said, looking up and smiling. "I didn't see you there."

The other girl looked out the window.

"I just came to tell you I've dropped your course," Felicitas said.

He looked surprised. "But why? You were doing so well. You were sure to get an A."

All the firmness left her body, all her bones grew flexible and liquid; she wanted to sit down on the floor and weep. She had been willing to give him her life and he had forgotten he had asked her. She must leave now and never see him again. She had made a terrible, a humiliating mistake. She must never see him again.

She walked away before that girl could see her

anguished face. Her good shoes made a desperate sound
on the rubber floor of the corridor. She was a fool; she
had presumed a man like that could love her. Her cheeks
burned. She thought she would be ill. She would stay in
bed a week with a fever. Her throat would close;
her breathing would come hard. She stepped into the air.
The branches were black against the clear, forced blue of
the sky as she walked toward the library. She could not
bear to go home now. She would sit among books, where
she belonged, among the other sad and careful girls, in
love with languages, since no one alive loved them.

"Felicitas."

She turned around. He was running down the path behind her.

"Thank God I caught up with you," Robert said. "I'm
so sorry. Can you forgive me? I don't know what I could
have been thinking of. That chick is so stupid she's a complete mind fuck."

Now he was here, she could afford the luxury of anger.
Of course he was distracted. He was distracted looking at
that girl's breasts.

"It's of no consequence," she said, staring above him at
the branches.

"Oh, baby, you must think I'm an incredible shit."

He put his arm around her the way city editors
put their arms around cub reporters in movies when they
were trying to talk them into something.

"Will you give me another chance? Heh? For old times'
sake."

"There are no old times. I hardly know you."

"Well, then, for the sake of our someday having many
old times to look back on."

Pleasure was a liquid; it rushed up the veins and
warmed the foolish blood. Now she was happy. He held
her chin between his fingers; he was looking in her eyes.

"Okay," she said.

"Okay what?"

"I forgive you."

He put both his arms around her. "People can only
really forgive each other with their bodies."

She let her head rest against him for a moment. She
was so happy it exhausted her.

He lifted her face and kissed her, and she thought, I will remember this all my life. She tried to memorize the branches and the buildings and the sky. Her lips were sore from biting them; his were buoyant, soft. She had not imagined a man's mouth to have such a texture. She was swimming with happiness; she would have been glad to die.

"Shit," he said.

She pulled away from him. What had she done wrong? She thought she could at least kiss. Had he, at this preliminary stage, already found her wanting?

"What have I done?"

"Oh, baby, it's not you, you're perfect. It's just that I really want to be with you tonight and I can't."

She moved away from him. It was that girl, that idiot, that secretary.

"I see," she said.

"No, you don't. My daughter's in a Halloween play tonight and I promised I'd be there."

She felt a new fear, the fear of the unseemly. She should not have been kissing a man with an eleven-year-old daughter.

"I don't suppose I could talk you into going with me?" he said.

He could have talked her into beetling over cliffs. But she wondered whether it would be a proper thing to do: to see the daughter of her lover playing a witch or a gypsy or the autumn wind.

"Is it a good thing to do?" she asked.

"In the Aristotelian sense? Or in the sense of Rousseau's common good?"

"I mean good for us," she said, more simply than she meant to.

"You are my friend. I'd like to share my daughter with you."

Felicitas said she would go. It occurred to her that "share" was a peculiar verb to have "daughter" as its object. She wondered if the girl would hate her. She thought if she were the girl, she would.

She walked back to Robert's office with him to pick up his books and stuff them in his green bag.

"You know, there was a time when I was too fucked up to carry a bag like this," he said. "I thought it was too unprofessional or too effeminate or something. Then I thought to myself, 'Probably everyone in history you admire would have carried a bag like this.' "

"What do you mean?" she asked.

"I mean, you could divide historical figures by who would carry a bag like this on the Columbia campus in 1969 and who would carry a briefcase."

"So you think that Rousseau would carry a bag like yours."

"Right. And Metternich would carry a briefcase. One of those big, hard, square ones."

"With the clips."

"Right. And Aristotle would have a slim attaché case, soft leather. Whereas Blake would carry a bag like mine."

"Blake wouldn't carry a bag at all. And what about Spinoza? You see, it's not that clear-cut."

"I see Spinoza as a green-bag man myself. A bag full of lenses. Like this."

He imitated Spinoza walking down College Walk. He limped and squinted and wrote things down on his hand. Felicitas laughed.

"Oh, baby, it's so great to hear you laugh. You don't laugh enough."

"It's just that I'm so happy," she said.

He kissed her while they were waiting for the light.

Robert's daughter went to school a few blocks from Columbia, so they walked together, and in the cool evening he allowed her to take his arm. She felt treasured. She was a medieval queen; her clothes were of immense value. She wanted to cover him with kisses, she wanted to be embracing him even as she walked beside him. His hands were cold. He had no gloves, so she took hers off to be with him.

They went into a brownstone which had in its front window the sign THE DRED SCOTT SCHOOL. Felicitas had not been in a grad school since she had left her own. She expected familiar smells: souring milk, chalk dust, damp coats and the high, bitter smell of children's anxiety. She expected cutouts of pumpkins and witches, but instead there were peace symbols. And the play was not, as she had expected, some makeshift holiday performance chosen for the maximum number of speaking parts. The children were doing *Marat Sade*.

"How old are the children here?" asked Felicitas, looking at the program.

"Blair's one of the oldest. They go from six to twelve."

"Isn't *Marat Sade* a bit sophisticated for them?"

"Look," he said impatiently, "these kids live in a madhouse. Contemporary America is a madhouse. It's a play they can directly relate to. Children are never too young for revolutionary conciousness. This school is one of the few that realize it."

Too in love to argue, she gazed at the audience. None of them looked as if they could be anybody's parents. With their long hair and jeans and their sexy, dangerous boots, they looked as if they had never been buffed down by domestic life. Even the older fathers suggested gunrunners, the mothers mediums or experts in germ warfare. She thought she was the only one there tame enough to be a parent.

It was a relief to Felicitas that when the curtain went up, the performances were as bad as those in any gradeschool play. She was afraid the children, in a nightmare of precocity, might actually have known their lines and moved across the stage as if they were not paralyzed by fear. But the prompter had to shout out half the lines of the Marquis de Sade, an elegant twelve-year-old, covered with shame now for his indolence.

Robert's daughter played Charlotte Corday. Her long brown hair fell around her shoulders. In the white nightgown, which was her only costume, she looked fully grown. Her bare legs were straight but sexual. Her eyes, made up to look mad, were not the eyes of a child.

The play took over three hours. There was no intermission. All that time she sat in the dark and watched the profile of her beloved. She desired more than anything to touch him. But they were at his daughter's school. She could see that he had forgotten her. He was thinking of his daughter.

She wondered whether he would introduce her to the other parents. She walked beside him, smiling, wearing the face of the reasonable accomplice whose partner, all dash and verve, leaves her the job of public innocence.

But Robert seemed not to know any of them. He took Felicitas' hand and pulled her backstage. His daughter was standing with the children who must be her friends. They were kissing one another in their make-up, delighted with their false selves.

Blair ran to her father when she saw him. She looked right past Felicitas, who had dropped back, imagining that the girl would prefer not to see her. He did not introduce her to his daughter. In a moment, one of Blair's friends pulled her away, and she was gone.

"Ready?" asked Robert, taking her hand again. She wondered how he could turn from his daughter to her with such a remarkable lack of transition. She wondered if that meant he did not really desire her. She could not imagine having turned away from him to speak to anyone in her family or turning from them to speak to him without a break so obvious it would suggest a drop in temperature, a change of season.

Robert's apartment was on the corner of 110th Street and Amsterdam Avenue. A block lower, on Broadway, Spanish grocers displayed foreign-looking vegetables—red bananas, unfamiliar beans. Old women walked, stupefied by being out at night; young boys who looked as if they would kill them for their umbrellas helped them kindly across streets. Broadway was dangerous and frantic. The drugstore stayed open until one o'clock, and you could find almost anything to eat all night. But one block up, the presence of both the Cathedral of St. John the Divine and St. Luke's Hospital made the area less playful. The street was darker there, the buildings taller, quieter. It seemed at once more menacing and safer. You could be killed there, that was obvious, but it would be a subtler procedure, more anonymous, in better taste.

Felicitas had never been in a man's apartment; she had never been in the apartment of anyone less than twenty years older than herself whom she had not known all her life.

Having naturally assumed that the apartment would be

empty, she was surprised to see lights on and to hear music.

"What's happening?" Robert called out, as if he was not at his own door.

At the sound of his voice, two women came down the hall. The rooms of the apartment gave off a central corridor, so Felicitas at first saw nothing. Then she heard a quiet tinkling of bells. For a moment she expected some small animal. But it was a woman walking toward her, her hair long and flowing, barefoot, wearing a dress that seemed to be made of gauze. Beside her was another barefoot woman, wearing jeans and a sweat shirt.

"Iris, Sally," said Robert, "I want you to meet Felicitas."

"Hey," said Iris.

Sally nodded.

Felicitas nodded at them both.

"You guys into tea?" asked Iris.

"Great," said Robert.

Felicitas trailed up the hall behind them almost immobilized with misery. Who were these women and why were they here now?

"Iris and Sally and I share the apartment. And Sally's little boy, Mao."

Who was the father of Mao, Felicitas wanted to ask.

"The thing is," said Robert, "I rip off the system, but I'm not going to get hung up in all this privilege crap, all this capitalist privacy stuff. It's such a Western hang-up."

"In Red China, all the babies sleep in the same crib," said Iris.

"Surely not all of them," Felicitas said, imagining a crib the size of Montana.

"I mean, you know, all the ones who are, like, in the same town or something," Iris said.

Felicitas looked around the living room. It was a large room which faced another building; she could see that even at noon the room would be dark. There was a red poster that said, in white letters that looked as if they had been torn from newspapers, LA LUTTE CONTINUE. Completely covering one wall was a dartboard, six feet in diameter, made of the face of Henry Kissinger. Andy Warhol's "Marilyn Monroe" was on another wall, and next to that a color photograph of Mao. None of the furniture was more than eight inches off the floor.

"Sit down, you look uncomfortable," said Sally ungraciously.

"I'm fine," said Felicitas. She was standing in the middle of the room.

Robert went into what Felicitas suspected was his bedroom and came out with a plastic bag and a small cardboard envelope.

"Yippee, grass time," said Iris, bringing in a teapot and four cups.

"Something very important is going to happen to Felicitas tonight," he said, "and I think we should celebrate."

"Like what?" asked Sally.

Robert reached over and pulled Felicitas toward him. "I hope Felicitas will remember tonight as the most beautiful night of her life," he said.

Felicitas could think only of the nuns' saying that the happiest day of anyone's life should be the day of his first communion. They had said nothing about the happiest night, however. Felicitas was so mortified by Robert's publicizing what she thought was an event of great intimacy that she felt paralyzed. She allowed Robert to pull he down to the floor, where she sat in a circle with the two other women.

Robert rolled the joint and lit it, inhaling deeply with his eyes closed. She had never seen him with his eyes closed before. He looked like a Renaissance angel, she thought, strong and manly, his fine head supported by a neck that was at once virile and elegant.

He passed the joint to her. She knew she had to pretend to have done this before. She took the joint as if it were a cigarette, took two short puffs and passed it to Sally, who sat next to her.

"You've never smoked before?" asked Sally.

"Sure I have," said Felicitas.

"Well, you've never been stoned before, doing it that way."

"I get stoned very easily." Felicitas said.

Sally turned away from her. She took—reproachfully,

it seemed to Felicitas—a very long drag and held it in her lungs for minutes.

"Good shit," she said to Robert.

"Mertz brought it in from the Coast."

The three of them began laughing.

"He have a chick with him?"

"Dynamite," said Robert. "Hair down to her ass, leather pants. Incredible."

The three of them laughed again. Felicitas thought she should begin pretending to be stoned. She started to sway and smile vaguely, focusing on the picture of Mao. But she thought she should be quiet, since she didn't know what people said when they were stoned. She tried to make herself look like the people in *Newsweek* articles about drug abuse.

Robert turned the record player on. It was a sitar. She was glad she recognized it and glad of its atonality. She could absorb herself in its strangeness, which they might interpret as some sort of drug-induced attentiveness.

The four of them sat in a circle, passing the joint between them, swaying, smiling, Iris making flowing gestures, Sally lying on the floor and staring at the ceiling.

Iris got up and disappeared into another room. She came back with a yellow chrysanthemum. To Felicitas' intense surprise, she handed her the flower.

"I hope it's real beautiful for you," she said.

Felicitas wanted to run. She thought that perhaps even Robert was not worth all this embarrassment. But then she thought, embarrassment is an unworthy emotion. The great are not embarrassed. She wanted Robert with all her heart. If this made her stop wanting him, she was not worthy of him.

"Thank you," she said, able to take the flower but not to touch the girl.

Robert took her and brought her into his room. Now she was alone; now she trembled. Now she was doing something that would bring her to the center of the world. As she walked into his room, she could have died of gratitude. He was bringing her into life, he was allowing her an act as great as any she had read about. Before that moment she had believed her life would always be covert, that she would always be watchful, hungry, an émigré in some strange city where she looked with longing at the windows of strangers. Now she was becoming part of something. She received the inclusion as a blessing. When he touched her hair, she bowed her head in gratitude. In touching her, he made her human, like the children in *Hansel and Gretel,* cursed into frozen positions, freed to their own flesh by the touch of their own kind.

He turned the light on in his room. He rubbed her temples, as if she had complained of headache. He traced the shape of her lips with his fingertips. He brought her to the bed.

After it was finished, she lay still, her arms slack, her palms down on the brown sheet. But she did not feel transformed. A great tenderness for him in his silence and exhaustion overcame her, but it was not unlike other tendernesses she had known. She felt no new sensation, neither grief nor transport. It was pleasant lying beside him. But she had not been lifted above herself. And it surprised her, rather.

She wondered who would be the first to move. She did not mind his being there, but she sensed the need for a change in posture. She moved her right leg slightly at the knee. He lifted himself up on one arm.

"How was it for you?" he asked.

"Very nice."

"That's all?"

"It was wonderful, Robert. Thank you very much."

"It'll get even better," he said, turning off the lights. He yawned obtrusively.

"We'll talk tomorrow," he said, getting under the covers.

It occurred to her that he expected her to spend the night. She felt a thrill of panic. Her mother, of course, expected her as well.

She would have to call her mother, she would have to lie. In constructing that lie, the faces of everyone she loved ringed her. She could feel, collecting at the base of her skull, the shocked or worried faces of Clare, Elizabeth, Muriel and Mary Rose, and in the center the stern face of Father Cyprian, blue black with judgment.

"And where the hell are you?" asked Charlotte when

she heard her daughter's voice on the telephone. The rocking challenge roused Felicitas to defense.

"*Mother*, I'm having a big exam tomorrow, and this girl in my class and I were studying, and it got late, and now she's invited me to stay."

"Stay where?" Charlotte asked suspiciously.

"On 110th Street. In her apartment."

"You could have called."

She heard her mother's voice sink with relief. Her mother only wanted an answer. She did not want to fight, she did not care particularly if the answer was true or even plausible.

"I'll see you at suppertime tomorrow," Felicitas said. "I'm sorry if I made you worry."

"As long as you're all right."

She hung up the phone with a sense of disappointment. It had been too easy. She had never lied before, and it had come so naturally, so without effort. She wondered if it meant she had no nature that tonight she had done two important things quite different from the things she had done all her life, and they did not seem difficult or strange.

She got into bed beside Robert. He was naked, so she took her nightgown off. She wanted to embrace him, but she did not want to wake him. She took his hand and held it. They were both lying on their backs. They slept so, hand in hand, like children in a wood, asleep because they have no prospects.

She slept lightly. In the dark room where sunrise brought no change in atmosphere, where morning meant only a slight lift of visible weight, she woke often. At first, she thought she had fallen asleep in the movies. The gray light seemed to flicker and the closeness of another body made her think she was in a public place. She felt a stickiness between her legs and secondarily her own nakedness. She did not move; unused to sleeping with anyone, she had no idea what would wake someone.

When he did wake, it was sudden and without transition. When he saw her, she could tell he did not quite know who she was. She was not hurt by his confusion. She thought that if she had slept the night through, she, too, would be puzzled. There was so much strangeness in it; surely he must feel that too.

"Good morning," she said, hoping to relieve the strangeness.

"Ssh," he said. "I hate people who are polite in the morning."

She tried to think of something rude to say, if that was what he wanted.

He got up and went outside to the bathroom. She was shocked to see he had not put his bathrobe on. She supposed she should get dressed.

Just to the left of Robert's bed was a large old-fashioned mirror on a stand. Shyly, Felicitas looked at her own reflection.

She was looking now for transformation. But she did not, as almost any other girl would have done, cherish the familiar secret shape her body made in an empty room. She had never spent time in front of a mirror. Her face had long since ceased suggesting promise. It had been five years since she had accepted, with an even heart, the almost entirely round shape of her face, her eyes that she thought one day would seem Oriental but were only small and quizzical, her squat, bulb-shaped nose, her thin mouth that never looked pleased but, to her, always either hungry or dissatisfied. Why should any man love her, having the face she had? She had no beauty, and she knew what beauty bought, had always known, although abstractly, for never in her life had anyone suggested that beauty would be her portion. Even as a child she had been valued for her sense. She had been dressed for ease of movement, and her mother, whose real genius lay in never longing for what did not seem accessible, never tried to prettify her. Clearly Charlotte had thought the only kind thing to do was to keep attention from her daughter's fleshy nature, not to raise false hopes. Felicitas felt the honor, then, of Robert's love, the perfect gift of it, the bestowed treasure, the pure act of grace.

He came into the room abstracted, bearish in his difficult slow movement. Seeing her naked seemed to rouse him. He stood behind her and reached around to cover her breasts.

"All right, sweet one?" he asked.

She was overcome with his caring. He watched himself run his hands over the front of her body.

"You were right to be admiring yourself," he said, watching himself as he covered the top of her head with small, dry kisses.

She colored. How he had misunderstood her! How foolish he must think her, deceived about her charms like an aging Southern spinster. Nothing was worse than that: not to have beauty and not to know it.

"I wasn't admiring myself," she said. "I was just standing here."

"I wasn't criticizing, I was praising. You should learn to hear the difference. And besides, there's a lot to admire," he said, leading her over to the bed.

He made love to her again, quickly, almost silently. She smiled, not for the pleasure but for the honor.

"I'll bet you're hungry," he said later. "What about breakfast?"

"That would be fine. Thank you very much."

In the kitchen, little Mao, who looked around two, was about to unscrew the lid of the large jar of Granola.

"Cut it out," said Sally, her voice bourgeois with impatience.

She pretended to be absorbed in her child so she would not have to greet Robert and Felicitas.

"Hey, beautiful," said Robert, embracing her as she sponged the counter.

"Sleep well?" she said, never looking up.

"Great."

"I've got to take Mao to day care," she said. She carried the child out of the room. Felicitas had never heard him make a sound. Not liking Sally, she decided that his quietness was evidence of deep disturbance.

Robert squeezed oranges and poured Granola into Chinese bowls. He lit the burner under the kettle and asked what kind of tea she wanted. She had no idea what he meant.

"Milk and sugar," she said.

"No white sugar in this house," he said, so sharply that she knew she had misspoken, although she did not know why.

"Anything, then, thank you."

"How about Red Zinger?"

"Fine." She had no idea what she would actually be served.

Over breakfast, he spoke about Marcuse, about the poisoning aspect of Western culture. Her mind wandered. She was blissfully happy simply to be where she could hear his voice. She was so overcome with his beauty that it made her daring. She wanted to touch him. She wanted to touch the rough hair of his knuckles with the flats of her fingertips. She wanted to kiss his thick gray-black hair. She decided she would do it, she would lay her dry, rather tired lips on all the textures that she loved.

This made him desire her again. This time, the love-making was slow, and so it interested her more. She knew she was not responding as she should; there was no sensation like what she had known as pleasure. She believed she would learn, though. Something in Robert would inspire her to learn. She believed she was getting better at it. There were no other faces in her brain now and she did not have to struggle to be attentive.

This time, she, too, was tired afterwards. She looked at the clock, aware that he was dropping off to sleep again. It was ten thirty-five. If she did not hurry, she would miss Latin at eleven. Fortunately she had prepared a passage of the *Satires* two days ago. Before everything happened.

She got out of bed and gathered up her clothes.

"Where are you going?" he asked from the bed.

"I have a class."

"Come on, this is a special day. Cut it. Be here with me."

He sat up, the bottom half of his body covered by a sheet. He held his arms out to her. She was overcome with pleasure that he wanted her.

He held her this time as he slept. She lay with her head against his chest. When she breathed, the fine hairs fluttered. She thought she would always remember that, the hairs of his chest fluttering from her breath. She slept, not moving. She was sure she would not dream.

At twelve o'clock, the clock radio switched on. She was startled to be awakened by a strange voice. She could not remember where she was. He picked his watch up off the floor and looked at it.

"Jesus," he said, "I've got to move."

"Where are you going?"

"I've got a one o'clock class."

That was the class she had taken with him.

For a moment, she was deeply disappointed. Then she realized that of course it was more important for him to go to his class than for her to go to hers. Twenty people depended on his presence. She thought of her classmates, waiting for the passage she had been assigned to translate. But it was nothing compared to the students who waited for him.

"Come on, honey, I have to let you out," he said. "You might as well go now because I've got to rush and I'll be no fun."

She dressed quickly, not looking at her clothes. She wished she could have a shower.

"When will we see each other again?" she asked, putting on her shoes carefully so she would not have to look at him.

"Whenever we want to," he said, combing his hair in front of the mirror.

She wanted to leave quickly so he would not see her need. He walked her down the dark corridor, but she could tell he was not thinking of her.

"I'll see you soon," she said, kissing his cheek.

"Right," he said, closing the door behind her.

III

She had always known, from the moment she considered being Robert's lover, that she would want him more than he wanted her. It seemed to her natural. It was as easy to accept as any other natural fact, like gravity or the heat of the sun. One lived with such facts. One might be interested in their causes, but it was folly to pretend that one could do anything but bend to them. Robert, being who he was, was infinitely more desirable than she. It was not just his beauty, although everything followed from that. It was the way he took on life, the way he was desired. Everyone she had known before him, she could now see, was a coward or a pauper. He was daring; he was profligate; he would, despite the words of Jesus—for there was nothing of meekness in him—inherit the earth. He strode, he took in air, he colored everything he touched. Of course she would want him more than he wanted her.

Why, then, was it so painful, since she had always understood? She walked down the stairs of his building, cold with shame that she wanted him so badly. Perhaps another kind of woman, beautiful, imaginative, courageous, could arouse in him the hunger he aroused in her. She hoped that if he found someone as wonderful as he, she would joyfully give him over to her. But she could not imagine any woman like him. Part of his majesty was that he was a man, with a man's bodily strength, never having had to question the propriety of his inheritance. No woman could be as sure as he, as simple. Part of his greatness was in his simplicity. He could be simple because he was not afraid.

But she was afraid, frightened of the gift she had dared to take, frightened of the loss she knew would follow. For he would never love her as she loved him. He didn't have to.

She could not bear, just yet, the thought of going home. What she had once seen as the comfort of the house now saddened her: the disorder, the dark clutter, the unloved surfaces covered with the greeting cards that people sent her mother at all seasons. There would be Halloween cards now and the Thanksgiving wishes of the thoughtful early. If she looked at all of it right now, it would make her see the oddness of her past more clearly than she wanted to.

She decided to visit Mary Rose at the theater. Mary Rose had said, "Anytime, Joe'll always let me off. You know him. He's a pushover."

It had been years since she had gone there. The theater was on Forty-third Street and Broadway, and what used

to suggest Tin-Pan Alley now suggested all she did not
want to associate with sex. It had nothing to do, she
knew, with her and Robert and what they had done together. She wished she had not had to see all those grotesque breasts and buttocks, coming as she did from
Robert for the first time. It made her feel panic. Was that
the world she had taken on, was that what she was part
of now? In loving the touch of Robert's hand, was it her
duty to know about anonymous desire, longings that sickened her, couplings based on hate or torture? Robert
would say, she knew, that everything of the body was innocent. She would have to learn that. He had learned it
because he was not afraid of things. And she would have
to extend her range of beauty to include the world that
most human beings, she now saw, inhabited.

Nevertheless, she was shocked to see that the theater
where Mary Rose worked was showing *I Am Curious
(Yellow)*. It was utterly incongruous to see Mary Rose,
with her permanent and her navy-blue dress, a polka-dot
handkerchief fixed like a fan in the breast pocket, selling
tickets for a pornographic film.

"One, please," said Felicitas. It was their old joke. Felicitas would surprise Mary Rose, who would then say,
"Get in here, you old skeezix." And she would go into the
booth with Mary Rose until the line diminished to the
size that Joe could handle.

But now Mary Rose was not entranced to see her. Her
first words were not words of greeting but "Don't let your
mother know about the picture." Joe seemed uneasy too.
He hugged Felicitas and let Mary Rose go to lunch, as if
he did not want Felicitas to be near the theater.

They went to Schrafft's on Thirty-eighth Street. Felicitas
had never eaten anywhere but in a Schrafft's with Mary
Rose. Mary Rose liked to be loyal because Schrafft's had
always hired Irish girls just over from the other side.

"You won't tell your mother about the picture, will
you?" she asked. "Especially as it puts a bad light on Joe.
He has to take what they send him."

Felicitas was annoyed with Mary Rose's agitation. Here
it was, everything that Robert hated: fear, respectability,
a narrow moral sense that thrived on blushes and false
names. She was tired of it, too tired to sympathize.

"Mary Rose, don't carry on. It isn't so bad. Sex isn't the worst thing in the world, you know."

Mary Rose thought it was kind of Felicitas to make her feel better.

"I haven't seen it," she said, "but Joe says it's a scandal. What can he do, though? He's got to take what they send."

"Nobody has to do what they don't think is right."

Felicitas reminded Mary Rose of Muriel, sitting there like that, so sure she was right.

"But I don't think it's bad," said Felicitas. "It just shows people enjoying themselves."

"In sinful ways."

"Pleasure isn't sinful."

Mary Rose hated to argue. "What'll you have for lunch?"

"A hamburger."

Mary Rose ordered for the two of them.

"Aren't you tired of having a life with no pleasure?" asked Felicitas.

"I have a good time, honey. Don't worry about me."

"Your body doesn't have a good time."

"What it never had it doesn't miss."

Felicitas felt relentless. She wanted Mary Rose to show her anger; she wanted to make her say that her life had been ruined and that it was all Cyprian's fault. If she could make Mary Rose admit that, if she could make her stop lying to herself, she would feel joyous. She would have done something worthwhile. She would have helped another human being to be free, just as Robert was helping her. She sat forward in her chair like a rookie cop.

"What about you and Joe, aren't you frustrated?"

Mary Rose blushed. "Eat your lunch, honey. Don't worry about Joe and me. We're the best of pals."

"Pals," said Felicitas in disgust.

She ate in silence while Mary Rose told stories about her ninety-year-old mother and her bookie friends. Always the same stories, the cops at the door, her mother hiding crooks behind the Sacred Heart altar. Felicitas could no longer laugh at them. The jokes seemed desperate, a tap dance on a chain gang. She would not laugh at Mary Rose.

"Don't tell your mother or the other girls," said Mary Rose, dropping Felicitas at the subway.

"Why would I tell them? I don't care that much," said Felicitas.

Mary Rose thought it was nice of Felicitas to make light of it. She'd always thought Felicitas was kind.

When Felicitas walked into the kitchen of her house, her mother was at the stove. The sight of Charlotte's back, broad in her floral blouse, the sash of her apron, the solid, shapely contours of her legs in their high heels, even the rose flesh color of her stockings, set up such a longing in Felicitas that she wanted to run to her mother, to lay her head on her mother's breast and say, "Put your arms around me. Let me sleep in your bed tonight. Tell me something funny."

But her mother's face was not welcoming.

"Twice in a row," she said. "Two dinners shot to hell with your thoughtlessness."

She was late again, and this time for no reason. She had stopped at the luncheonette to have a coffee and read *Newsweek* for the latest pictures of the war, walked the long way home, then realized she had left her handbag in the luncheonette. It had taken her an hour and a half to walk the eight blocks from the subway to the house.

"I'm sorry. I lost my pocketbook. I couldn't just leave it, could I?"

"Dinner will be worthless. You might as well not eat it. Don't waste your time."

Felicitas knew that her mother did not cook meals in which delicate timing was an issue. She made stews and soups on Sunday that would last the first half of the week. All her dishes were based on ground beef, except for Sunday's, which was celebrated with a chicken breast or a chop. Felicitas did not understand why her mother's food tasted so good. It did not deserve to, all things considered, slapped together and reheated. But she had never had a dull meal in her mother's house. Her mother's cooking never varied. She had not tried a new recipe, she boasted, since the first week of her marriage. What she hated were the girls in the office who were always clipping recipes from magazines—chicken with peaches, mock apple pie —and then talking about them during lunch. For Charlotte's money, it was a goddamn waste of time. She thought most people spent at least three times as long thinking about food as they ought to.

"Look at these noodles," Charlotte said, "stuck together like I don't know what."

"Oh, Ma, they'll come unstuck when the chili goes on top of them, and besides, what does it matter?"

"Come over here, let me see you," her mother said.

Felicitas was terrified. Her mother *knew*.

"Stick out your tongue," her mother said.

Felicitas did as she was told. Then her mother pulled the skin under her eye to expose the rim behind the lower lashes. Charlotte thought that you could tell if someone was going to get a cold if the color of that rim was pink rather than red.

"You look pale," her mother said. "You're not getting enough sleep. How was your exam?"

"Fine."

"School is important, but don't risk your health. I read where college kids are the second most common group for ulcers."

"Who's the first?"

"Executives with incomes over fifty grand."

They both laughed. They loved surveys taken for no reason, statistics compiled for their own sakes. They liked visualizing people writing numbers in columns a mile long.

"You just want me to be sick so you'll know what to do with me," Felicitas said.

"Please. I never went in for bedside manner. I'm not the type."

Felicitas thought of her mother's uneasy ministrations during her childhood sickness. Her mother would wake early to give her medicine. She would leave bottles of juice beside the bed and pills in cups with notes taped on them. She would move the television into Felicitas' bedroom. Then she would go to work. She would call her daughter every hour. She came home for lunch. Sickness had no overlay of pleasure for Felicitas. It was solitary, tiresome. It made her mother fractious. She was rarely sick.

That night, she ate her dinner in a state of abstraction, sitting across from her mother but thinking of Robert, longing to be with him, deeply ashamed of her longing. Since she could not talk to her mother about Robert, she had nothing to say.

"I have another test tomorrow," she said as soon as she had finished eating, so she could disappear into her room.

"I'll do the dishes. You go to work," said Charlotte, kissing her daughter's forehead to check for fever.

In her room, Felicitas lay on her back and looked at the ceiling. She conjured his face, his eyes, the rosy color of his throat. She thought that if she did not see him again, the rest of her life would be spent in terrible emptiness. She had to hear his voice again. Even the shame of needing him and having him know was more bearable than silence. She decided she would phone him.

"How are you?" he said easily.

"Fine."

"I thought of you all day today. I wondered what you were feeling."

"I was feeling fine," she said.

He had thought of her. Perhaps she could say it then. Her heart was beating very fast.

"I was hoping we could see each other again."

"Of course we will."

"Do you know when?"

"Whenever we want.'"

"Will it be soon?"

He laughed. "You're incredibly structured."

She laughed, to make it sound as if she knew her fault and thought it funny.

"Look" he said, "come on up to the apartment tomorrow night around supper. Mostly every night there are a lot of friends around to share a meal. If I'm not hung up somewhere, I'll be there. Otherwise you can just meet the other people. You already know Sally and Iris. I want you to know them better. They're very together chicks. Very free."

"I'd like to get to know them," Felicitas lied.

"Great, then come tomorrow night."

"I hope to see you," she said, trying to keep her voice casual.

"Great," said Robert.

She was unprepared for Greek class once again. She had been unable to concentrate, thinking of Robert.

After class, Professor Gifford asked to speak to her.

Julia Gifford was beautiful in a way Felicitas thought of as belonging only to Protestants. She was tall and large-boned, in her middle thirties, and her hair was nearly white. She clipped it to the back of her head with a series of bone hairpins. Felicitas wondered if she knew Robert and what she thought of him.

"Miss Taylor, you confuse me," Julia Gifford said.

Felicitas blushed.

"In the beginning of term, your work was extraordinary, and now you've fallen way behind. Have you been feeling well?"

"I'm undergoing some tests," Felicitas said. She was fond of Professor Gifford, and she did not want to lie to her and say that she was ill. But it was, she believed, the nature of her life now to be undergoing tests.

Professor Gifford lowered her eyes, imagining untimely death.

"Please let me know if I can be of help," she said.

More than anything, Felicitas wished someone could be of help. But not Professor Gifford, who, Felicitas could see, had never needed anything.

At six-thirty, Felicitas stepped into the foyer of Robert's building and pressed the buzzer with his name on it. Instantly the bell was pressed from upstairs to let her in. She wanted to tell Robert that he must wait to find out who it was before he pressed the buzzer. It could be anyone, someone to kill him, someone who would tie him up and sprinkle gasoline on newspapers around the room and light them. She wanted to embrace him and tell him he was vulnerable, being beautiful and highly visible. He was vulnerable to any danger in the world. By the time she got to the door of his apartment, she was overwhelmed by all that he was prey to. She would not have been surprised to come upon him lying in a pool of blood.

Having borne all this, she was disturbed to see Robert's door open, to hear music coming from it, to hear the laughter of women in the hall. Of course, he had said his friends would be there. She would meet his friends. Perhaps some of them would like her. Perhaps one of them, an older woman, a colleague, would say, "Robert, she's the best thing that's ever happened to you." Or an older man would say, "Robert, you're a lucky man." Then she would convince him to send his daughter to another school.

A golden retriever with a red bandanna tied around its neck came out of Robert's apartment and peed against the banister. It sniffed Felicitas and went back in. She followed.

Songs that she had heard before were playing on the stereo. She heard Mick Jagger's voice and Robert's singing

Under my thumb, the girl who once had me down.
Under my thumb, the girl who pushed me around.

He was dancing by himself, holding a plate of food. None of the other people in the room were looking at him.

She had bought herself a pair of jeans. And so, standing in the doorway, she did not look as improbable as she had two days before in her wool jumper. She did not like the way the girls dressed in gauzy blouses or T-shirts, so she bought a sweater just like Robert's. She bought chukka boots like his as well. She wondered if he noticed, when he turned around and saw her, that they were dressed identically.

He said nothing, merely came over to her and took her by the waist, still dancing. He wanted her to dance. She could not move as he did, and she knew how foolish people looked when they were dancing badly. She was still holding her pocketbook. She did not want to dance with him. But she could do nothing else, because it was a room of strangers and she had nowhere to go.

"Loosen your ass, honey," he said. "It's all in the ass."

She put her arms around his neck and pretended to dance slowly.

"Who's this one?" she heard someone say.

"One of Robert's rescuees. He believes in mercy fucking."

That was Sally's voice. She opened her eyes. Rage inspired her. She listened to the music and swayed her upper torso in time to it.

"That's better, baby," Robert said into her ear. "It's just like fucking—it takes practice."

"Hey, Felicitas," said Iris, coming behind them with a bowl of rice. "It's nice you came. You'll have to meet everyone."

Felicitas realized how desperate she was. If she was glad to see Iris, she must be nearly dead.

Iris took her hand and led her around the room as if she were blind or idiotic.

"You know Sally, and these are Richard and Brad, the guys downstairs. And these are their dogs, Ho, Che and Jesus."

She looked past Sally. Nothing in life, no ideal, moral or religious or imaginative, would move her to forgive the words she had heard.

"Sit down," said one of the men sitting to the right of Sally. Felicitas could tell that his physical ideal was derived from the image of one of the minor prophets. He had small, round, reddish eyes; his fingernails curved like birds' claws and were yellow gray with nicotine and dirt. His roommate sat across from him, his legs crossed, drumming on his knees. He was one of those tall, thick boys who is instantly recognized in any city of the world as American. He wore a bandanna at his throat, exactly like the dog's, and she imagined he did not comb his hair to offset his obvious and impossible good health. This was a boy brought up on milk and steak. Twenty years ago, he would have been putting on shows in his father's barn. Now he wore a Che Guevara sweat shirt. But she thought it could as easily have been the Nordic head of Knute Rockne emblazoned there, or the head of Trigger, or of Rin-Tin-Tin.

Iris brought Felicitas a bowl of rice. She whispered, "They are all into macrobiotics, especially Robert. They all think meat's bad karma. But I know it's not. I had a vision."

"Don't start giving her that shit about meat being good karma, Iris," said the minor prophet. "It has nothing to do with visions. Meat makes you feel fucked up. Meat has more class implications than any other food."

"Hey, we should do an article on that," said the blond boy. "I mean, how Americans would compromise anything to buy their kids red meat. Which they don't even need."

"Which is actually harmful," said the prophet.

"I think what's harmful is the kind of vibes you attach to meat, not the meat itself," said Iris, looking hopefully at Felicitas for confirmation.

"Don't try to talk to her about any ideas," said Sally. "Don't even try. Believe me, I live with the chick, and you could go bugshit. You might as well talk to my kid."

"It's just that you're into linear thinking and I'm not," said Iris.

"Nobody's into linear thinking," said the blond boy angrily. "It's just that class implications stare you in the face."

"What class are you, new girl?" said the prophet to Felicitas.

She knew what they expected her to say, that she was middle class and proud of it. She knew they thought that they were workers. But she had grown up in a neighborhood of workers and they were nothing like these two. The only romance of the working class was to get out of it. She wanted to tell them that the workers would do anything for color TV sets, that they were capable of acts of kindness as single souls, but together they were frightened, grasping, that their dreams were all of vengeance and escape. She wanted to talk to them about force and necessity, about the faces of the men at six o'clock. But these were Robert's friends, so she said instead, "I'm a student. That complicates questions of class. Economically, I'm lower than the workers. But that means nothing, really."

"It's the only thing that means a fucking thing," said the blond boy. "That's why the workers and the students are the only hope, a coalition. We're both ripped off."

"Felicitas is a classicist. Say 'ripped off' for us in Latin," Sally said.

"You're an incredible bitch, you know that?" said the prophet in a way that made Felicitas see that they had once been lovers but no longer were. But this was not a room in which it was possible to cross the floor in order to avoid embarrassment.

"How come you're into that stuff?" he asked, turning to Felicitas.

"It's beautiful," she said, grateful that he had, for reasons however spurious, defended her.

" 'Beauty' is a very class-loaded term. I mean, you think that stuff's beautiful and the Puerto Ricans think those statues that bleed from the eyes are beautiful. What's the difference? I mean, how do you tell?"

Order, harmony, radiance, she wanted to say, but knew that in this room it was impossible.

"I guess I mean it's beautiful to me. And it makes me happy to do it. I don't think anything I learn in the university will help the revolution. But I like to think I would give up studying Greek if it would help the North Vietnamese."

Robert came up behind her and laughed.

"This is the universe she lives in. She thinks an angel will come up to her and say, 'If you give up Greek, we'll save a village.' But she'd do it, wouldn't you. Even though it's the thing you love best in the world. It *is* the thing you love best, isn't it?" he asked, sitting behind her and drawing her into the V of his open legs.

To lean against him gave her so much pleasure that she felt invisible. Nothing mattered; this was life, was the one essential, to feel his chin on the top of her head, to feel his arm around her.

"Robert, she said nothing she could learn at the university would help the revolution. I thought she took your course," said Sally in the tone of hate she used whenever Felicitas was the subject. "So much for working within the system."

Robert laughed. "Felicitas is waiting for the revolution in men's hearts. She's waiting for the Second Coming."

"No, I'm not," she said.

They all laughed. Robert pretended to cuff her. He threw her off balance and tickled her.

"You should get her to write for the paper," he said to the two men. "She writes a clearer prose than any student I've had in this place in ten years. She has a truly passionate mind, really unusual. As a matter of fact, I think the three women in this room could be at the vanguard of the new movement. Felicitas the head, Sally the hands and Iris the heart."

The mystical body of Christ, Felicitas thought, but said nothing.

"The revolution's got to be in the hands of women," Robert said, "extraordinary women who've achieved a balance. Like these three."

The three of them lowered their eyes, flushed with pleasure, rendered speechless by Robert's words.

"Are you into writing?" the blond boy asked Felicitas. "I mean for our paper. Maybe you know it. It's called *Sub Rosa*, after Rosa Luxemburg."

The face of Rosa Luxemburg flashed into her mind. That was the face she wanted for herself: brilliant, needing no one, all that was not essential burnt away by a mind at once precise and practical, always on the edge of being brutal or unjust.

"I'd like that," she said.

"We'll talk tomorrow," he said.

"This is really great, Felicitas," said Robert. "This is really great."

She leaned back against his chest. She was perfectly happy. She had pleased him.

They sat in a circle on the floor, discussing the best way to reach the workers. Sally said that the only way to do that was to work beside them. Felicitas did not want to think so, but it seemed the most sensible thing she had heard since coming into the apartment.

"I think you're right, Sally," Felicitas said. It took all the moral courage she possessed to say it.

Sally ignored her and looked straight at Robert. "I've applied for a job at Lenox Hill Hospital as a nurse's aide."

Robert was staring at the ceiling. He was drumming songs out on Felicitas' head. Sally could see he had not heard her. Her eyes darkened with anger, like a landscape regularly losing light.

"That's a typical fucked-up analysis of the problem," said the prophet. "You are incapable of seeing things in anything but bourgeois terms. Why don't you invite your old nanny to lunch? I'm sure your parents could still get in touch with her. You could have a nice chat."

"Fuck off," said Sally. "The really oppressed workers are in the hospitals, cleaning up other people's shit for a dollar twenty-five an hour. Why aren't they on welfare? That's oppression, it isn't anything else. I mean, those doctors are making a hundred grand a year."

And getting ulcers, Felicitas could hear her mother say. She must silence the voice of her mother.

"There are collectives in Detroit that have cells in the Ford plant and the GM plant. They know what they're doing. They have some organization, some theoretical base. What do you have?" asked David, the prophet.

"I have a theoretical base," said Sally.

"Bullshit. Your mind never left Tenafly."

"And you're obsessed because they wouldn't let your father into the country club. That's your theoretical base."

"In terms of theory, you're all out of it," said Robert, pulling out of his trance. "I mean, you have to take into account the whole impact of technology, the way it seduces the workers so they don't know what they want. No one in America can even fuck properly, they're all so fucked over by machines. All they want is more machines."

"So what do you do about it?" Sally asked.

"Beats me," said Robert, "but I do know that the revolution has to be a revolution of consciousness. Maybe we should put mescaline in all the water coolers in the GM plant. I don't know. But I know you're not going to get anywhere with that simplistic Marxist model, which is nineteenth century in form. There's got to be a contemporary matrix, a whole new analysis. Combining Marx and Freud and a whole bunch of other shit."

"Isn't that what Marcuse's doing?" asked Felicitas.

Robert sat up and looked at her sourly. "Well, he's making a start," he said, moving away from her.

Felicitas was frightened by his movement. "Perhaps you'll complete Marcuse's work," she said eagerly.

"Oh, it's all bullshit," Robert said. "Who the fuck cares about print anymore? It's that the whole environment has got to become more erotic. People have to own their sexuality and not have it owned by GM."

"How will that happen?" asked Felicitas.

Robert put his hand on her breast. "Come inside," he said. "I'll show you."

While he was making love to her, she could think only of the voices of the people in the living room. Of course they knew where she and Robert were and what they were doing. What was going on in all their minds? Had there been any break in the conversation about revolutionary cells in General Motors? She ran her fingers through Robert's thick hair.

"You're so beautiful. You're the most beautiful man who ever lived," she said, kissing his shoulder.

"Do I make you happy?"

"I've never been so happy in my life. I think I've never really been happy at all before."

"That's what I want," he said. "I want to make you happy."

They slept together in each other's arms. When she woke, she could see it was one-thirty in the morning. She sat up, horrified, and Robert's head, dislodged from where it rested on her shoulder, fell with a humiliating drop onto the pillow. She should have been home three hours ago. She was afraid her mother had sent the police after her. She got dressed quickly, convinced that any moment the police, all friends of her mother, would be arriving. In her mind she heard the punishing stomp of heavy boots, she saw Cossacks, gangsters, masters of violation, who would come in the night, uncovering the innocent as they slept.

But she was not innocent. If they came here, they would have come to the right place. She was guilty of the crimes they had imagined. She knew she must make Robert dress immediately. The police would be there any minute. If they were both dressed, nothing could be proved.

She shook him with the panic of the publicly accused.

"Get up, Robert, get up," she said, turning on the light so it would shine into his face.

"What the hell's the problem?" he said, covering his eyes.

"It's after one o'clock. I was supposed to be home by ten. My mother will be sending the police here."

Robert sat up. "She knows you're here?"

"No."

"Then how the fuck are the police going to find you? Jesus Christ, you're paranoid."

Felicitas sat down on the bed.

"I have to call her. She'll be frantic."

"Tell her you're staying with a friend. Stay here."

"I have to go home."

"At this hour? You'll be killed on the subway."

"Would you take me home?"

"Forget it, baby. You work it out. I'm not going to aid and abet your oppression."

"I am not oppressed."

"You're shaking. You're shaking like a little slave." He stood up and put on his pants. "Use the phone if you want to. I'm getting out of here."

She dialed her mother. Only when she heard the ringing of the telephone was she sure that she had lost him. Her heart became enlarged; she felt that she had sickened, aged. Because of fear, she had lost what was most beautiful, most perfect, most desirable in life.

She let the phone ring fifteen times. Her mother did not answer. When Felicitas had not come home, Charlotte had called Elizabeth. She could not bear to be alone.

All the signs had come together, as if she were a prophet putting bones and feathers into meaningful fresh shapes, new combinations, making up the form of revelation that had always been there, uninterpretable. She was losing her daughter.

Only now she saw the terrible true weight of what she had accepted as plain thoughtlessness and simple disobedience. And it occurred to her that her daughter now was too old to be accused of disobedience. The word was inappropriate. It was as if she were opening her daughter's mouth to look for milk teeth.

That night the weight of all she had done pressed on her, all she had not given her one child, her only child. Her own mother had had ten and none of them had left her. None of them had stayed away past midnight, out and wandering on the streets or sitting in the houses of strangers, so struck with the conversation of strangers they did not care whom they hurt.

What had happened? There had been all her brothers and sisters laughing, singing at the table, marrying, bringing home trophies. And now she sat alone in an apartment, at a table covered by a plastic tablecloth with patterns of fruit and pitchers, and waited for her daughter, who was lost to her, was somewhere, frightened or hysterical. Or having fun.

She tried to put her daughter in a roomful of people her own age. Her difficulty told her something. She could see Felicitas only among elders, the child in the temple amazing the scribes with learning.

And Jesus advanced in wisdom and age and grace with God and men.

It comforted her to think that Christ had done the same thing to His parents had Felicitas was doing now to her. She thought of the Virgin Mary wandering through Jerusalem in terror, up streets where dark men shouted prices and held things in front of her face.

A lost child: of all fears the most rooted, the most physical, the mind's pictures quicker and more injuring than the imagination of any other disaster.

It was midnight and her child was not at home. She saw her crushed beneath the wheels of cars, flattened under subway trains. She was a natural victim, with her child's body and her absent-mindedness. She saw her child reflected in a killer's eye, a rapist or a simple thief grown desperate with recognition.

Or perhaps she was having a good time.

She saw her daughter in the party scenes of movies, her head back, laughing, the room filled with smoke and blondes who were paid to be there. But she could not give features to the other faces in the room. Only the faces of movie stars would come, dangerous men with hard mouths: John Garfield, Richard Widmark.

She saw her daughter in a hospital, her head covered with bandages, looking up at the triangular faces of nurses who stood above her, speaking incomprehensible languages.

She thought of the Virgin Mary wandering through Jerusalem, looking for her child among thieves. Then she thought of Felicitas in a college classroom, entrancing the professors at midnight by teaching them Catholic truths. She imagined herself walking in among them, saying to her daughter, "Where the hell have you been all this time?" and a distinguished man, a German, saying, "You must forgif us. Vee haf lost track of de time. Your daughter is a girl of great, great gifts." And Felicitas saying, "Oh, Ma, you're such a worrywart."

Then she saw her daughter in the arms of a seducer who would kill her in the morning to stop her tongue. She saw her daughter bleeding in a bed, wearing the black nightgown Charlotte had found in her drawer.

It was twenty after midnight and her child was lost to her. She thought of all she had not done. In all the years, never a friend to sleep over. Even as a child, Felicitas, frightened by other children, wept and begged to be let in the house. When Charlotte ordered her to stay outdoors, she would see Felicitas, huddled, miserable, outside the magic circle. How she hated the other children and blamed them and wished to punish them.

What should she have done? Whose fault was it? Cyprian said Felicitas was meant for higher things, and her great genius would bear fruit and must be nourished, not by the games of children but by listening to the truth.

Charlotte thought that that was wrong. But with Cyprian, Felicitas grew strong and flourished; with Charlotte's friends, Felicitas was funny, clever. She was at home. What did you do with a child who did not like children?

But now her child was lost to her.

Felicitas could not be dead. God could not be so cruel.

He had been cruel to other mothers. Why should he spare her? She was not extraordinary.

But Felicitas was. She prayed, "Protect this child, whom You have made unusual."

All the care of bringing a child to twenty years of age. The terrible waste of a death then. All children were gifted; at twenty all were promising.

She prayed, "Protect this child. Take her under the shadow of Your wing."

But still she saw her dead, or bleeding. She stood up and shook herself like a horse. She walked over to the telephone.

Elizabeth answered, miraculously wakeful.

"Felicitas isn't home," Charlotte said. "It's making me nuts being all alone here."

"I'll come," said Elizabeth.

"Take a taxi," said Charlotte.

"I don't have the cash and everything's closed. I'll just take the train."

Charlotte was filled with a flood of love: her friend would take a subway, would ride in the murderous night to be with her. Because the child was lost.

Charlotte waited forty minutes, then walked to the subway stop to meet Elizabeth. It was one-fifteen. The women did not embrace or touch each other. They walked silently in the November night.

At the corner of the street where Charlotte lived, she turned to Elizabeth and asked, "Do you think I've done wrong by her? Do you think I've been bad for her?"

"How do you ever know?" said Elizabeth, thinking of her son, dead before the age of reason.

Felicitas sat on Robert's bed, shivering, imagining her mother dead, the victim of armed men who had killed her for her portable TV. And for the rest of her life, she would have to live with the knowledge that at the moment of her mother's stabbing, she had been in the bed of a lover.

Robert walked into the room and turned the light on. He had lost all patience with her. "Why are you sitting in the dark?"

"I don't know."

"Did you get your mother?"

"No."

"Well, maybe she's out on the town."

"She doesn't do that sort of thing."

"No, but *you* do. You're a bad girl."

"I'm worried about her, Robert."

"Try her again, for God's sake."

Felicitas picked up the phone and dialed. On the second ring, her mother answered. The rage in her voice made Felicitas furious; it buried her fear entirely.

"I'm not coming home tonight, Mother."

"Where are you?"

"At a friend's."

"Who?"

"You don't know them."

"Fine," said her mother. "Maybe when you get home you'll find your belongings on the street."

Her mother slammed the phone down with a force that rang with punishment.

"You see, it wasn't that hard," said Robert. "Come in now and talk to everybody. Get rid of those bad vibrations. Change is hard, it's really hard. You have to get rid of bad emotional reactions and zero in on the pure ones. You have to be able to tell emotional repression from real love, which is always freeing."

"I have so much to learn," she said, embracing him.

"Most of us do, in this fucked-up culture," he said.

In the kitchen of Charlotte's apartment, Elizabeth burned her hand on the kettle trying to make tea.

"Put butter on it," Charlotte said absently.

Elizabeth felt crushed. She thought herself incapable of the most elementary consolation. She could not even make tea without causing problems.

Charlotte sat down and put her head into her hands. Elizabeth saw her shoulders heave with sobs, but they lasted only a moment.

"Why did I do that? Why am I such a bitch? Why do I always do that kind of thing? Why do I sound like a bitch when I want to tell the kid I'm glad she's safe?"

For the first time in their friendship, Elizabeth saw Charlotte in need.

"Felicitas knows what you mean," Elizabeth said.

"She used to."

"Do you want to go to bed now? Now you know she's all right?"

"Who the hell could sleep? Let's play some cards."

Charlotte loved cards and had taught Elizabeth canasta. It was the only card game Elizabeth knew. Her strategy was always the same: she hoarded her cards so that she would be able to pick up the pack. Occasionally she won with a dazzling score, but usually Charlotte ruined her by going out early, quickly, and leaving Elizabeth with a handful of riches, all turned to debts.

Charlotte dealt and Elizabeth dealt, then Charlotte dealt again. Elizabeth watched the sky go grayish white, then fill like a globe of blood and lighten, then absorb itself in blue. They sat at the kitchen table playing cards until it was time to dress for work.

Felicitas went into the living room with Robert. Her eyes were sore with shame and anxiety; she imagined herself a small night animal, punished by headlights into blindness or a foolish suicide. All that she felt for her mother pressed upon her, all the danger of that love, the fear inseparable from it, the force of that protection and enclosure, the great weight of safety given, the provisions of survival, of tenderness, the gifts, the spells, the medicines, the blankets, the good shoes, the parting of her hair, the blows, the threats not spoken, but always palpable: "One day I may no longer love you. Then you will be entirely alone."

She looked at the people in Robert's living room and wondered if they had been subject to such fears. In their circle, still talking about the workers, they might look tired, slothful, angry, dishonest, treacherous or muddled, but they did not look afraid. She loved them for that, she loved them with the great love that a circle of unknown human faces can inspire, faces that we suspect possess all those virtues that we lack. She wondered, with a rush of hopefulness, if they could help her, if they would take her in, if she could be for the first time warmed and nourished by a circle of people more or less like herself.

Iris moved over and made room for Felicitas. "Parent shit can be very heavy," she said.

Felicitas was grateful for Iris' kindness, but a good heart in the body of a fool had never meant much to her. She thought of Iris and her visions. In one vision, she confided to Felicitas, she had been told to change her name from Jane Cox to Iris Earthperson. What comfort could she bring? She would be equally comforting to murderers or men who planted bombs in schools.

"Even I'm a little fucked up about my parents. I can't go home without a jacket and tie," said Robert.

"I never go home," said Sally.

These words terrified Felicitas.

"Sometimes you have to not go home," said Brad. "When I go home, I'm really fucked over for, like, a month afterwards maybe. They seduce you. They seduce you with their food and their cars. It's hard to get that shit out of your system when you let yourself get into it for a while."

"That's why your politics have to be so solid," said Richard. "You've got to be willing to sacrifice your family for a principle. I have to be willing to say I'd let the Panthers burn my parents' house down."

"With them in it?" asked Felicitas.

"If it became necessary," he said. "The thing is, they hang around your neck with all their expectations. Like in high school I was good in math, so my old man's always asking me how I'm doing in math. Do I want to go to graduate school in math? When I haven't been into that abstract bullshit in years. But he gets this hopeful look on his face and I tell him I'm thinking about it. It's just that I can't stand that hopeful look."

"It's harder for Felicitas," Robert said. "Her mother's expectations are overwhelming. It's a terrible burden."

As always when he seemed to understand her, she was deeply grateful. He seemed even more a miracle; his sympathies more vivid than ordinary people's, more valuable.

"That's really hard," said Brad. "It's like my father really wants me to take over the business; he says he can't stand for it to go out of the family, it's been in the family for four generations, and, like, I have this responsibility."

"Well, my family thinks I have a responsibility not only to them and to their ancestors but to the future generations. I'm supposed to bear the truth; I'm supposed to let my light shine before men," Felicitas said, snapping her fingers and waving her arms.

They laughed. Then she was sickened by her own betrayal. She had opened up to strangers the most precious, the most hidden treasure. She had given it away so they would like her. She had squandered her gold, burnt up the oil of her lamp.

She shut her mind off. She was tired, tired of the way she lived and the way they wanted her to live. She had lived all her life between extremes of honor and humiliation. She did not want to be frightened; she did not want to be alone. She wanted these people to like her. She wanted to have friends.

That year, November ended a baffled torpor. Resentments rose that had been buried for three seasons. The skirts of secretaries and the trousers of account executives rode up their legs with the dry static the new cold had brought; people gave each other small electric shocks with every handshake, inflicting a surprising pain where they had meant a neutral greeting. Women's heels struck pavements with unworldly, primitive rings, like hammer blows intending to strike fire. That year, the women's skirts were short again, and the long, exposed legs of heedless girls reddened at bus stops; the golden hair of their recklessly uncovered heads grew dull in the Puritan light of the first days of that December. It was in those days that Felicitas decided she must leave her mother's house.

It was only there, she realized, that she could not be happy. She was happy with her new friends, happy in their apartment, happy in Robert's bed, happy in the library looking up statistics on the literacy rate in Cuba before the revolution for her article in *Sub Rosa*. She was happy doing dishes early in the morning while the others slept, happy even doing the papers for Iris' course in early childhood education. Iris was taking courses at Manhattan Community College so she could be qualified to work in day-care centers, but she said writing papers was too fucking linear, she couldn't get into it, and she didn't see what it had to do with loving kids. Felicitas saw that Iris was perfect for the work she wanted to do. Having the mind of a three-year-old herself, she was not bored with young children; she was simply taller than the children and had better manual coordination.

She was certainly wonderful with little Mao, far better than Sally, his mother. Felicitas had never imagined that anyone who had gone through the physical bearing of a child could be so abstract in the care of it. She asked Robert what he thought, and from his answers she realized that he was only marginally aware of the presence of a child in his home.

Felicitas and Sally hated each other, but the hatred was clear and in its way respectful. Felicitas could see in Sally her own moral passion and the cruelty that she knew she, too, was capable of, an almost instinctive cruelty, the automatic reflex of the absolutist, always on guard for violations. They barely spoke to each other. When they realized, as they often did, that they were on the same side in an argument, they would give up the point to the opponent and begin some practical task, sometimes rising at the same moment to empty ashtrays or take plates off the floor.

But even Sally did not say she thought Felicitas should stay in her mother's house, although she knew it meant that Felicitas would be living in Robert's apartment if she left her mother's. She did not object, but the others were enthusiastic when Robert made the suggestion one night while everyone was eating. The guys downstairs suggested that she could crash with them, since she was such a big help on the paper. But Robert said no, she should stay with him and Iris and Sally; it was more like a family, and Felicitas needed a lot of support right now. Not that she was weak, but she needed support. Iris said that was great because Felicitas happened to be saving her life at the moment, helping her with all the school shit. Robert said everyone should be really supportive of Felicitas because if she went back home, she'd be lost forever. They all said they loved her and she was doing a great thing. She told them she would tell her mother after Christmas.

IV

Clare drove badly on the morning of December 24, worried about Felicitas and Cyprian, what they would do to each other this time, what they would say. She picked up Elizabeth first. Elizabeth's unreadiness was even more pronounced than usual, and Clare knew this meant that Elizabeth was frightened.

"I'm not sure I'm looking forward to this," said Clare after she had let Elizabeth into the apartment with her spare key to get the blue bag and the keys that Elizabeth had forgotten. All of Elizabeth's friends and most of the local merchants had copies of the keys to Elizabeth's apartment, since all of them had, on occasion, calmed her, called the police, the locksmith, the building superintendent, and then begged her to give them keys so that it would not happen again.

"What's gotten into Felicitas? She's like someone I don't know," said Elizabeth.

"What's happened to the world?" said Clare, noticing as she turned the corner a girl wearing a coat made of different patches of dyed leather.

"Do you think it was the Council?" asked Elizabeth.

Clare thought once more of the extreme parochialism of her friends. "Most people have never even heard of the Council. It's just that people are getting sloppy. They don't feel they have to be careful anymore."

"Felicitas isn't sloppy."

"No, she's furious."

"At what?" asked Elizabeth.

"At all of us."

"What have we done?" Elizabeth's tone put the question at the furthest remove from the rhetorical.

Clare looked at Elizabeth. "Perhaps we've stolen her youth."

A car honked its horn in desperate rage. Clare had turned the corner without looking, barely missing the front grille of a red Dodge. Elizabeth was shocked at this near brush with danger. In all the years that Clare had driven her, she had never come so close.

Felicitas knew that the women would be late. But she waited until a few minutes before the time that Clare had mentioned to call Robert. What she did not want was to sit with her coat on, looking out the window after she had stopped hearing his voice.

"Good luck, love," he said. "Remember, it's life or death."

"What will you do on Christmas, Robert?" Felicitas asked, imagining him with his children, imagining him in the apartment, the revolutionary posters covered with cutouts of snowmen and elves.

"Get stoned," said Robert. "I've treated myself to some really good hash for Christmas."

She imagined that he said that out of grief and despair, and she thought how gallant he was. He was not diminished by ordinary disappointments; he was not brought low.

When Clare and Elizabeth arrived, Felicitas helped Clare rearrange the packages in the trunk. She worked in silence, looking forward to sitting in the back seat with her eyes closed, dreaming of Robert as they drove up the West Side Highway.

"What do you think Muriel put up this year?" asked Charlotte. "Pickled what?"

"What was it last year?" said Clare. "Oh, yes, pears. Pickled pears."

"Typical," said Charlotte.

"And cauliflower," said Elizabeth, "and then all the tomatoes she doesn't know what to do with."

"God knows what it does to Cyprian's stomach," Charlotte said. "It can't be good for him, with that history of ulcers."

"Do you know who are the prime targets for ulcers?" Felicitas asked.

Charlotte laughed. Her laughs were full of the little snores that indicate pleasure. She wiped her eye with the side of her hand. Simultaneously she and Felicitas said, "Executives with an income of over fifty thousand dollars."

"It's all true," Clare said. "You don't know. You don't know what you're spared."

"Excuse me," said Charlotte, "but I'd rather have fifty grand and puke every day than my salary and guts like the broad side of a barn."

"You would not, Charlotte, and you know it," Clare said.

"Nobody's made me any offers," said Charlotte. "Besides, in that bracket you're probably paid to keep your mouth shut, which lets me out."

They stopped at a lookout point in the Catskills to have lunch. It was a point of pride with them that they never had to eat in highway restaurants. Charlotte was responsible for the food. For every trip, she brought ham-and-

cheese sandwiches on pumpernickel bread and a thermos
of whiskey sours. She had done this as long as Felicitas
could remember, and Felicitas had always, like the
others, had a cocktail with her lunch. Years ago, Clare
had acquired small plastic trays that snapped into the
window grooves. They snapped their trays in and Charlotte passed the sandwiches. After everyone had been
given a sandwich, she poured the drinks.

"Hits the spot, doesn't it?" she said.

"I don't know how you do it, Charlotte," said Elizabeth. "I never get a drink as good as this one in any restaurant."

"It's the company," said Charlotte. "And being in the
outdoors."

"Ma, we're in a car with all the windows closed," said
Felicitas.

"You can see out, can't you?" said Charlotte, pretending to cuff her daughter.

This drop to the Hudson River was probably the only
natural scene that Charlotte looked at from one year's end
to the next. She felt the pride of ownership. Like a home-
steader pacing his land, she rolled down the car window.

"I'm crazy about that water," she said.

They ate and drank in silence for a while. Then Clare
said, "Just when *did* Muriel become such a crackerjack
cook? She never cooked while her mother was alive."

"She took a course," Elizabeth said. "In night school
after her mother died."

"Why does that burn me up so much?" asked Charlotte.

Because you're jealous, thought Felicitas. Sally's face
came to her mind and the tightness in her neck when she
saw her accomplishing any domestic act with proficiency
in front of Robert. She did not want Robert in the car
now; she pushed his face out the window. She wanted to
enjoy, as she always did, looking at the Hudson and
drinking whiskey sours.

"It burns you up because some people are born pains
in the ass," said Felicitas. "They can't even lift a finger
without being irritating."

"Poor Cyprian," said Clare. "Think of having to live
with that old stick day in and day out."

"Nobody made him," said Charlotte, crushing a paper bag.

"I think she's good to him," said Elizabeth. "I think she looks after him well. He needs that."

Felicitas looked at the faces of her mother and her mother's friends. She thought those faces showed no need. She could not imagine in those faces the sheer need she lived in, a need so pure that she sometimes felt that her skin had failed, that if she touched her cheek, it would begin bleeding. And she thought of the hair on Robert's knuckles and his wrists, of his beautiful feet and shoulders. That she could do this separated her from the other women, that she could long so for a body, that she could need the body of another who would never love her, who might be at this moment in bed with someone else.

She was sure he was in bed with Sally. She was sure that on Christmas they would both get stoned and go to bed from boredom, leaving Mao and Iris to look at the tree. And when she got back, perhaps he would not want her. She knew she had made a mistake. She should never have made this trip; she should never have gone away.

As they drove up the road that led to Cyprian's house, the four of them shared one last thought, brilliant in its daring: "Perhaps it's not too late to turn back."

But duty and memory pressed them up the hill. Clare shifted into second gear, and the break in the motor's rhythm, that small second of reluctance, gave them hope that perhaps the car would turn around and send them speeding, like cartoon mice in a toy jeep, over the horizon. The four of them laughed when Charlotte said, "Well, here we are," at the exact spot where she always said it: in front of the ruined house of the Prendergasts, where children stood outside the door and stared in any weather.

Cyprian came out to greet them. The high, painful flood of love pressed behind the ribs where Felicitas had, since childhood, thought her heart to be. He was wearing a workman's coat, dark blue, and a dark woolen sailor's hat. He was becoming an old man.

"You made it," he said, leaning on the car.

She wanted to spring out to him, as she did when she

was little, to collide through the sheer eager force of pleasure with the fabric of his coat, to take his hand, to feel his hand on her head, a blessing and an honor and a shelter. And she wanted to say, "There is no one like you. I will never love anyone as I love you."

But he would not meet her eye. "How are you, dear?" he said in the neutral voice he would have used for one of the Prendergast children.

So she would not embrace him. Loss appeared, as if someone had built a house of ice, clear and solid and immovable, beside their feet. She could see that he no longer loved her. For one incident of doubt, she had lost him, as Moses had lost the vision of the Promised Land. Well, good, she was well rid of such a love. He did not love her. She would go back to her friends.

She unloaded the car in silence. "Will you snap out of it?" said Charlotte. "Don't wreck everybody's Christmas."

"Tell *him* that," said Felicitas.

"It's up to you," her mother said. "You're younger. You're a girl."

"I'm sick of it. I wish we hadn't come."

"Well, we did. So make the best of it."

"I'm sick of making the best of it."

"That's life, kid, making the best of it."

"Not for everybody," said Felicitas. She was thinking of Robert as she carried all the bags into the house.

Cyprian walked around the house, trying to bring himself under control. He pretended to be getting firewood, but Muriel had done that. Early that morning he had heard her slamming the door, dropping the logs into the basket, banging the cat's dish on the cement steps. He could hear her from his bed inside his house a hundred feet away. She did nothing quietly, nothing easily. Her movements were all juts and accusations. He had always imagined that women moved more gracefully than men, with large, curved movements of the arm and slow, cupped movements of the hand. He imagined Christ being served by Martha. Had she had that rushed uneasiness that all these women had? Of course not. Even her discontent was simple: she was jealous of her sister; she wanted help in the kitchen.

What had happened to women? He thought of his mother, her poor dropped breasts behind her apron, the thinness of her wedding ring, which was almost invisible on her soft fingers. Nobody looked like that now. They poured their bodies into hard skeletal garments that gave them breasts and buttocks as rigid and fortified as battleships.

And they could not be quiet. Surely his mother had been quiet. Surely the Mother of God had stillness in her heart.

But even the ones who seemed quiet, even the ones who seemed simple, Elizabeth and Mary Rose, for instance, were full of secret questions, secret murmurings. In none of them had he found that warm stream that he expected in the souls of women.

He had not expected that from Felicitas. He had expected from her the better part that Christ had chosen for Mary. He never thought she should be trained to cook and sew and care for children. He thought she should be trained to listen, then to write what she had heard or speak it formally to strangers, who would be the more impressed at such authority from such a girl.

But what had she become? Full of anger, full of argument, as convinced in her opinions as any of the smart alecks he had had to talk to in the parishes. He knew it had not always been so. He remembered her in the truck beside him, listening, looking out the windows. He had been amazed by her questions. At twelve she had a better mind than most priests. He remembered her after the accident, the sweetness in her face, so sweet that he had feared that she was dying.

What was there on that face now? Darkness, anger and impatience. The lust for the last word. She had become— he could tell—a materialist. It had coarsened her features; it had dulled her eyes. Each day she lost more of the spirit. She thought she was concerned for the poor, but it was a loss of faith.

"If Christ wanted to feed the poor, He could feed the world on three loaves of bread," he said to her.

"Why doesn't He?"

The anger in her voice, the arrogance. No use. The arguments were bitter. She no longer loved him.

And those who loved him had grown old and loved him now because they had grown used to it, loved him because they might as well.

Felicitas, who did not need to love him, no longer thought it was worth the trouble.

He wanted the luxury of simple prayer: "Make the child love me once again." But God knew, and he knew better than to pray for such a thing. If Felicitas no longer loved him, perhaps God was telling him that human love was empty, that he must save his love for God alone. Who would not disappoint him.

His failure as a priest was that he expected too much from people. Then in disappointment he railed against them. Man had been turned away. The love of God could not engender disappointment. Perhaps God was telling him that he must divest himself of human love. He must empty himself.

He saw the top of Felicitas' head through the window. He would not let himself weep.

Muriel watched Felicitas reading while the other set the table. That was the kind of thing her mother always let her get away with. Muriel did not like to see the others in her kitchen; she wished they had not come. And if they had to come, she did not see why they had to stay there. They could have stayed in a motel, they always had before, and the motels were better now. They had those little kitchens; you didn't have to eat out.

All her life she had dreamed of having her own house, and only now, now that her mother was dead and she was over sixty-five, had she got it. Everything connected with it was a pleasure to her. Before she had left Philadelphia, she took cooking and sewing. She was the oldest in the classes by thirty-five years, except for the men, who tried to talk to her, being nearer her age. But she found out that they were there because they were divorced, and she preferred not to talk to them. She knew that in the eyes of the Church, divorce itself was not a sin, only remarriage, but nevertheless it was the kind of thing she did not feel quite right about.

The girls who took the classes did it all for marriage. Many were engaged and made a point of taking their rings off when they washed dishes and asking people to make sure they remembered to put them on again. The others, Muriel could see, believed that all this effort would increase their marriageability. At least three times during the course of the semester, one of the heavy women wearing ski pants would say, "The way to a man's heart is through his stomach." They would say this to one of their identical-looking friends or to one of the men, who would then look as if he had been exposed to rifle fire.

Muriel did not like cooking, but she knew that Cyprian was particular about food. She much preferred sewing. She loved the measuring, the checking, the bolts of material, the thimbles and the wonderful specialized scissors. But it was agony for her to choose the fabric for the curtains of her new house; for months she thought she had made a mistake. Perhaps she had chosen a print too obviously maidenish: small green flowers on a darker background. She saw the way Clare took the material between her fingers and said nothing. Well, she had not had Clare's advantages. In the end, she loved her curtains because she had chosen them and made them and because if they were a mistake, it was nobody's business. It was nobody's house but hers.

Cyprian said nothing about the house most of the time. Only occasionally he would say, "You've made a real little nest here."

When he said that, she thought she would die of pleasure. And she thought how lucky she was. After all these years, she had what she wanted. It was very often now that she thanked God, not, as before, for what she had been spared—great sickness or starvation or violent assault. Now her thanksgiving came freely, like light or water. Now she was grateful for what she had.

It was wrong of her, she knew, to hate their coming. But having waited so long, she did not like to share. She did not like to see Charlotte, with her fleshy body that took up all the kitchen space, heating things at the stove. She did not like to see Elizabeth hesitantly putting knives down and then spoons beside them at the table. And she did not like Felicitas reading the *U.S. News and World Report*, sitting in that most unladylike way, her legs crossed, one foot on the other knee, saying, "These people should be shot."

It was for just one more day. Today was almost over. On the morning of the twenty-sixth they would be gone. Then her house would be restored to her.

Cyprian walked into the house, carrying logs.

"I brought some in this morning," said Muriel.

"Well, I've brought some more," he said impatiently, making the basket overfull.

"Supper in about ten minutes. We brought up real Italian ravioli. In the deli near our house, they make it up for you and pack it in these tin trays, so you just stick it in the oven," Charlotte said.

"I haven't had Italian food in years," said Cyprian.

"Yes, you did, Father," said Muriel. "Remember, I made that spaghetti."

"Well, this stuff is really great. You couldn't get any better, not even if you cooked it yourself," said Charlotte.

"Do you ever make that kind of thing yourself, Charlotte?" asked Muriel.

"The way I work, who the hell has time?"

They sat themselves around the table. Cyprian sat at the head and opposite him Muriel, who held the silver salt shaker as if she was afraid someone would steal it. Felicitas did not want to sit next to Father Cyprian, but she could not bear the thought of being next to Muriel. She took her seat across from her mother, between Cyprian and Clare.

Throughout dinner, Felicitas was silent. Charlotte brought up the topic of folk masses. "I'm sorry," she said, "I just don't happen to think a guitar is a liturgical instrument. And those kids up there, the girls with the skirts up around their asses and the goddamn long hair on both of them, so it's a good thing the skirts are short or you wouldn't be able to tell the girls from the boys."

"They object, the new breed, to the amount it would cost to get an organ for a church. A thousand dollars, they say. You could feed the poor with that. Then twenty of them go out and buy guitars. But *that* money could not have been used to feed the poor," Cyprian said.

Felicitas watched Cyprian eating. He always ate anxiously, as if he were afraid his food was going to be taken away from him.

"It's that the music is so dull, so repetitive." said Elizabeth.

"Well, let's face it, a lot of the hymns those old bags in those choirs used to belt out were no prizes," Charlotte said.

"They're trying to keep the young people in church," said Clare. "That's the thinking behind it."

"The young people don't need the Church. They're achieving salvation on peace marches," said Cyprian.

The weight of the conversation, the predictability of everyone's position, pressed down on Felicitas' stomach as if a wrestler were kneeling there. But she did not want to fight. Six months ago, she would have struck out. Now she saw that it was useless, and the prospect of the effort merely bored her. She no longer cared enough, she thought, to ruffle the smooth surface of the lake they rowed on in their shabby rented boat. After coffee, she excused herself. She said she had to work on a paper for school.

"A paper on what?" asked Cyprian.

"Herodotus," she lied. She had to pick someone neutral enough that Cyprian would not try to get her into an argument, to use her paper topic as a proof of the corruption of her education. No one, she thought, could use Herodotus as a field for righteous indignation. Cyprian would have to let her go.

"You warm enough in there?" her mother asked.

"It's fine," she said.

"I'll put some coffee on for you later when you want a break," said Charlotte.

Felicitas closed the door behind her. She sat at the desk in her room reading Emma Goldman; she was writing an article about her for the paper. But beside her on the desk, she kept a copy of Herodotus, in case anybody tried to take her by surprise.

She tried to read the book, but she could think only of Robert. She wanted to be with him, to be with her friends, who were not always trying to provoke her to a fight, who did not watch her every gesture as if they were looking for symptoms of a terminal disease. She wanted

Robert to be holding her, to be telling her she was fine the way she was now, that she did not have to change any more.

In the living room, they were extremely quiet. It was a clear relief to them that Felicitas had gone into the other room. Muriel passed around brandy. Their quietness was fearful; the dull gray sky outside seemed to warn them that whatever they said would probably cause trouble. After a while, they all took books and sat in different corners of the room. Everyone was to be silent. No one wanted to fight.

The next morning, everyone awoke with a pall of singular betrayal hanging over him. The assumption that they should feel joyous settled in their stomachs like a meal of dough. Charlotte in particular, knowing that it was Felicitas who had caused it, felt the weight of responsibility. She would have to tell jokes, sing, play cards, keep people's glasses filled, anything, so that the silence could not reveal to these people who loved one another their deep misery at being there together on that day.

Of course it was a mistake to have come, but after that whole episode in the summer, they all felt they had to. Felicitas was so goddamn stubborn; she *would* let Cyprian have a heart attack before she would give in to him. But Muriel was an ass to say that lousy thing: "Nobody blames you." Well, nobody did, except her. Cyprian could always have a heart attack anytime; he was the type. He didn't need Felicitas to provoke him; anything could do it—the price of nails or nuns in mini-skirts. Felicitas just happened to be there at the wrong time. Which was just that kid's luck.

Charlotte put her bathrobe on and walked into the kitchen.

Clare was sitting with a cup of coffee in front of her, looking at a copy of *Time*.

"All they have is instant," she said to Charlotte.

"I guess she missed that class in cooking school."

"Merry Christmas," said Clare, toasting her.

"Please," said Charlotte. "Don't make me laugh."

When Elizabeth heard them in the kitchen, she awakened. Hers was the darkest room in the house. She had to turn the lights on to get dressed; she did not feel comfortable going outside her room in a bathrobe.

Charlotte handed her the cup of coffee she had made for herself.

"When do you think we'll be leaving?" she asked the other two.

Clare and Charlotte laughed.

"You're one for the books, you know?" said Charlotte.

"Maybe we should leave right now," said Clare. "We could pretend we were kidnapped."

"If only we could get that pain in the ass out of here," said Charlotte. "She's the one who wrecks everything. God knows what it does to Cyp's mind, having to listen to her gas every night."

Suddenly Muriel was at the window.

"You think she heard?" whispered Charlotte.

"God knows what she hears," said Clare.

"Where's she been?"

"In the chapel, making a visit."

"Maybe she could pray for a percolator," Charlotte said. "I'll work on the coffee beans myself. I'm at a much less advanced state of spirituality."

Muriel heard them laughing as she turned the knob. She was sure they were laughing at her. Tomorrow they would be gone. There was just today to get through.

"What time does Father plan on saying mass?" Elizabeth asked Muriel.

"We always have it at nine o'clock."

"I'd better wake Felicitas," said Charlotte.

"She never wakes up of her own accord, does she?" said Muriel.

"She works very hard in college," said Charlotte. "It's more exhausting than physical labor. Mental exhaustion, it's called."

"There was another name for it in my day," said Muriel. "When I was that age, I couldn't wait to be up in the morning."

"To do what?" asked Charlotte.

"To get to mass," said Muriel.

"Now there are later masses," Charlotte said. "Evening ones. Seven o'clock at night, in our church."

"And half the attendance of the old morning masses."

"Not in our church," Charlotte lied. "Three priests give out communion every night. Sometimes it takes them fifteen minutes."

"It must be a very unusual parish," Muriel said.

"Yeah, well, there are a lot of unusual things around," said Charlotte.

"I'll go wake Felicitas," Clare said. She thought that of all of them, she could give Felicitas the most realistic sense of how she should behave so that the day would not destroy them all.

She pulled back the curtains in Felicitas' room. Disapprovingly, she held the material between her thumb and third finger. Why did none of them care about these things, she wondered. Why did they take pride in the poverty of the physical world they inhabited when, in fact, they spent more on these things than they should have? It was not that they bought what was less expensive, it was that they did not care for what was beautiful.

"What time is it?" Felicitas asked.

"Eight-ten. Mass is at nine, so it's time for you to get ready."

"Oh, God, I wish I could sleep," said Felicitas, even as she was throwing the covers off and sitting up. "What I would really like is to sleep until it's time to go home."

"It won't be so hard," Clare said. "There'll be mass and breakfast and then you and I can go for a walk."

"Cyprian will want to come," Felicitas said sullenly.

"Not anymore. The cold bothers him terribly now."

Felicitas thought that that was one more weapon he could use against her: his age and his infirmity.

"Then there'll be the presents," Clare went on. "And then supper. And then another walk. Then we can go to bed."

"I might as well stay here, then," Felicitas said.

Clare laughed and sat down on the bed beside her.

"This isn't much fun for you, is it? I suppose it's never been."

"It used to be," Felicitas said. "But now I just don't want to be around him. I'm tired of everyone deferring and keeping quiet and thinking up jokes. Why should he demand all that? Why should he get it?"

"Because he's extraordinary, and he's suffered, and he's helped us all. You didn't know him when he was younger. He was never rushed; he always listened. He always had time. There weren't many who did; not many men will listen to women."

"It was an ego trip for him," Felicitas said.

Clare shook her head. It was such a grave, somber movement that Felicitas was ashamed of what she had said.

"Our lives would have been poor and dull without him."

They are poor and dull now, Felicitas wanted to say. But not to Clare, who sat beside her like the queen of a defeated country.

"Clare, I don't want to live like that. I can't stand it anymore. I have to have something more than what all of you have."

"Maybe you'll get it," said Clare, fingering the bedspread.

"I want to move out of my mother's house," Felicitas said. "I want to live in an apartment near school with friends, people my own age. They really like me. We really have a good time."

Clare felt a thrill of fear. Felicitas wanted her help in escaping. She felt like a kidnapper on the victim's side. That was what they had done to Felicitas: she had been the victim of a kidnapping. They had stolen her and hidden her from her own kind. They had convinced her that outside their thieves' hut there were murderous animals. They had made her believe she was safe only with them.

"It might be a good idea," Clare said. "It's a long trip from Brooklyn."

"And it won't cost much money," Felicitas said. She did not want to tell Clare that Robert would charge her no rent. She did not want Clare to know about Robert.

"Do you want me to talk to your mother for you?" Clare asked.

"No, I'll do it tomorrow. In the car. Just be on my side."

"I'm on your side," Clare said.

Felicitas embraced her. For a moment she wanted to

tell Clare everything. Then she remembered that you could never tell them anything about sex.

"Do me one favor," Clare said. "No arguments today."

"I promise," said Felicitas. "Oh, shit, I have no skirt to wear to mass."

"It doesn't matter," Clare said. "You know that's not the kind of thing he cares about."

"It's hard to tell. It's hard to keep it all straight."

"Externals never concern him."

No, Felicitas thought, he's interested only in souls. She would have preferred that he be angry about uncovered heads. The area of his concern would have been less private, less vulnerable. She shivered. The house was too cold. She thought of Robert's apartment, where it was always warm enough for summer dresses.

The five women walked the hundred yards from Muriel's house to Cyprian's in single file. In the gray light of that dry Christmas, Cyprian's house looked to Felicitas like the cell of the condemned man. She knew why he had made his choices of design and material. It was in the interests of economy and austerity. But now she saw that he had built it to look like a prison.

They walked, still single file, into the chapel, which was the room to the left of the kitchen. Cyprian had bought most of his ecclesiastical furniture from parishes that had changed their décor in the spirit of the Council. But the prie-dieu he had bought from St. Joseph's Church, which had suffered a minor fire. The wood on the front was singed, and the leather gave off an acrid scent that filled the chapel with a damaged, bitter smell.

He came out of his bedroom wearing his white vestments. He stood in front of the altar, his back to them, saying the mass in Latin. The bishop of Rochester had given him a dispensation to say a private Latin mass. So he could turn his back on them, Felicitas thought, so he could say his foreign prayers, not for them but for God.

Walking out behind them, she saw them all as old. Even Clare, even her mother, walked more slowly than they used to. Were they beginning to stoop or was it their winter clothing? From the back, they looked nothing like her friends.

Charlotte's presents were all ordered from one of the several mail-order catalogs that she received. These catalogs specialized in joke gifts or in gadgets. Some of the joke gifts were too obscene for her consideration: ice trays that made cubes in the form of Jayne Mansfield's upper torso, telescopes that left a black ring around the eye when the patsy looked through it at a picture of a naked woman. Many of the items were musical or motorized versions of ordinary household items, designed to make the homemaker's life speedier or more lyrical. And there were tools to render foods into exact imaginative shapes: knives that made radish rosettes, presses to make perfectly round hamburgers. Many of the joke items had to do with the bathroom, and in these Charlotte indulged. All of her friends had toilet paper on a musical toilet roll that played "How Dry I Am."

Charlotte hated to shop, and these catalogs allowed her, from her home, to select for her friends gifts that she felt were both useful and memorable. It was this combination that was important to her. She couldn't bear the idea of her presents lying on the top shelf closet, unremembered and unused.

From other, more sober, mail-order firms, she got her presents for Elizabeth and Clare, which, having met once with great success, were repeated yearly. For Elizabeth she ordered stationery imprinted with her name and address; Clare she enrolled in the Cheese-of-the-Month Club. She sent Mary Rose and her mother a box of assorted salamis. She gave her daughter money. Each year, she increased the amount of the check by ten dollars. This year, she gave Felicitas a check for two hundred dollars. Charlotte was happy with this arrangement; she found it difficult to understand her daughter's wants. She could not buy her books, and she imagined Felicitas to have no other real desires.

Cyprian came into Muriel's house dressed once more in his work pants and sweater. He sat down at the table. Four women rushed to give him coffee. Even Clare rushed, Felicitas noted unhappily as she sat beside him at the table.

"How's the well holding up?" Felicitas asked him.

"Fine."

"No pipes frozen this winter?"

"Not yet. But there's a long way to go."

There was nothing more for them to say to each other. Charlotte saw the silence and, fearing it, raised her voice. "There's nothing like a Latin mass. I always say," she said.

"English is not a spiritual language," Cyprian said. "It's the language of merchants."

He ate his breakfast quickly. Clare and Elizabeth were making piles of presents. Felicitas wondered why there was no Christmas tree. Perhaps it was because one of them, Muriel or Cyprian, did not think it sufficiently liturgical.

"When I was small, we opened our presents at midnight on Christmas Eve," said Elizabeth, anxious to help by making conversation.

"Is that a Southern custom?" asked Muriel.

"My family was not really Southern in the way people think of it," Elizabeth said. "We were from New Orleans, whose culture is really more French."

Muriel felt rebuked by her answer. "Well, I wouldn't know," she said. "I've only visited two states in my life."

"You could travel now, now that you are more free."

"I'm content where I am," said Muriel, seeing that they were trying to oust her with ideas of travel and, when she had left, take her place.

"I would love to see France or Italy," said Elizabeth.

"Maybe we'll go," said Clare. "Why don't we all go to Rome?"

"Oh, no," said Elizabeth.

" 'Oh, no' why?" asked Felicitas.

"It's terribly far away," said Elizabeth.

"That's the point, Elizabeth," Felicitas said impatiently.

"Who'll open the first present?" asked Clare quickly.

"Father, of course," Muriel said.

Clare dropped a gift into Cyprian's lap. It was from Charlotte. Felicitas went into the kitchen to get a Kleenex. When she came out, Cyprian was pointing a gun at her. She screamed.

"Come here," he said. "I want to see if you trust me."

She came over to him. She was not sure that she was not in danger, but there was nothing else for her to do.

"Kneel down," he said.

She knelt before him. He put the gun to her head and pulled the trigger. A little jet of flame appeared at the top of the gun.

"It's a lighter," Charlotte said, as if to assure her daughter.

Felicitas felt humiliated by her own obedience. She would have been happier if Cyprian had shot her. Robert was right—it was a fight to the death.

Cyprian sat, crossing his legs, playing with his lighter, pulling the trigger, making the flame appear and disappear.

"It's a very handsome gift, Charlotte," he said.

"And it's not the kind of thing that will get lost," Charlotte said. "You know the way lighters are always getting lost. This way, you leave it on the coffee table and you always know where it is, you always have a light."

Clare passed a box to Muriel; it was from Charlotte as well. On the cover of the box was a picture of a man in tails with a towel over his arm and above his head lettering that read SILENT BUTLER

"It's one of those little vacuums for the table. It sweeps up the crumbs," Charlotte said.

"Thank you," said Muriel, putting the box under her chair. She felt the gift as a rebuke. She didn't know what Charlotte could mean by it. She always cleaned the crumbs up instantly; she never let them fall to the floor.

Elizabeth had bought handkerchiefs for everyone but Cyprian and Felicitas. For Cyprian, she had bought an edition of *The Consolation of Philosophy*, bound in green leather with a frontispiece that was a treasure. For Felicitas, she had chosen the *Theaetetus*, bound in red, with marbled endpapers.

Felicitas embraced her. It was the first time in a year that Elizabeth had felt she was anything but an annoyance to Felicitas. Cyprian fingered his book. Tears came to his eyes. They all saw them but let him pretend to blow his nose. It was the word "consolation" that made him weep. He feared he was beyond that, that he could not be consoled.

The turkey was underdone. When Cyprian cut into the skin, blood showed through and pink, wet flesh. He held the first slice up on the end of the fork, looked at it and then put it on the platter, silently.

Shame covered Muriel's body. "It isn't cooked," she said. "We can't eat it."

"Just shove it back in the oven. It's not like it's wrecked for good, it just isn't cooked enough," said Charlotte.

"It will be inedible," Muriel said. "It will be too tough."

"Let's open the champagne," Clare said. "By the time we finish it, the turkey will be ready."

How had it happened? Muriel had read the directions in the cookbook; she had even copied them down on an index card to make sure she had gotten it right. She suspected foul play; she suspected someone had turned the oven down to make her look foolish. It must have been Felicitas. She must have changed the oven temperature.

The champagne gave them all a headache. By the time Muriel had taken the turkey out of the oven, the Brussels sprouts had wrinkled up like the tips of a swimmer's fingers, the cream sauce had congealed on the onions and the glaze on the carrots stuck to the serving dish and had to be scraped off with a knife. Everyone's excessive praise was only a reproach to Muriel. She knew what they were thinking as they sawed and sawed their slices of meat. They were happy she had failed; she could see that. It had made their Christmas.

She wished they had a television. Then they wouldn't have had to make conversation. They sat in their distant chairs, reading, feigning yawns. Felicitas got up "to work." An hour later Clare said, "I hope we can make an early start."

"How early?" asked Cyprian.

"Eight or so."

"We want to beat the rush hour," said Charlotte.

"That's right, you might meet up with Prendergast's tractor. There could be a terrible bottleneck," said Cyprian. All the women laughed.

"What time will you want mass, then?" Muriel asked.

"Is seven possible?" Clare asked Cyprian.

"It's fine," he said.

"Normally we have it at nine," Muriel said.

"We want to get an early start," Clare said.

Inside her small room, Felicitas lay awake, lively with anxiety and fear. Tomorrow she would tell her mother she was moving out. In honor of their leaving, Cyprian said mass in sixteen minutes. By seven-twenty they were in the car. By the time they got onto the highway, they were weeping.

"Was it always like that?" asked Elizabeth.

"It couldn't have been," said Clare.

"It's her. She ruins everything," said Charlotte.

"Why do you always blame her?" Felicitas asked.

"Since when have you been such a big fan of Muriel's?" asked her mother.

"I can't stand her," Felicitas said. "You know that. But it's not just her. It's all of you."

"He's so unhappy," said Elizabeth.

"He's unhappy because he's turned everyone against him with his tyrannizing," said Felicitas.

"He hasn't turned us against him," Charlotte said.

"That's because you like to be tyrannized."

There was a silence in the car, as if they expected to be overtaken by secret police. The silence encouraged Felicitas.

"Look at you, all of you, you're no different than she is. You just hang on him and wait on him, hoping he'll say something nice to you. And when's the last time he even said anything decent to you? When's the last time he said one word of praise to anybody?"

"You don't know everything," said Charlotte.

"Well, he never says anything decent to me," said Felicitas.

"He adores you," said Clare.

"That's not enough," Felicitas said sulkily.

"What the hell do you want?" asked Charlotte.

"I want him to like me," said Felicitas.

"Oh, crap, Felicitas," said Charlotte. "Mr. Kowalski at the delicatessen *likes* you. Cyprian would die for you."

"But he won't let me live," said Felicitas.

"Don't get dramatic," said her mother. "What the hell do you want out of life, anyway?"

"I just want an ordinary life. I want to have friends. I want to do normal things."

"You used to have friends," said Elizabeth.

"In eighth grade," said Felicitas. "That was the last time I had friends."

"What happened to them?" Clare asked.

"I don't know, they bored me," said Felicitas.

"So whose fault is that?" asked Charlotte.

"But I have friends now," said Felicitas. "Interesting people. They want me to move in with them."

"Fine," said her mother. "Beautiful. You have no home, you have to move in with strangers."

"Slow down, Charlotte," said Clare. "I think Felicitas has a point."

"You know nothing about it," said Charlotte. "You have no children."

Silence invaded the air like an enemy plane; it buzzed inside the confines of the car. Charlotte was notorious for her temper; no one wanted to rouse her. She would say terrible things. She would be sorry later, but in a mood like this, they all knew, she could say anything.

After ten miles of silence, Elizabeth put her hand on Charlotte's shoulder. "I think it would be a nice thing for her, living with other students. It's a great pleasure to study with friends."

Charlotte met Elizabeth's gaze in the rear-view mirror. It was a fierce eye that attached to hers, but Elizabeth would not retract her stare.

"I suppose you all cooked this up so you could gang up on me," Charlotte said.

"Not Elizabeth," said Felicitas.

Elizabeth felt jealousy needle through her. Felicitas had confided in Clare but not in her.

"And you," said Charlotte to Clare, "you should have known better. You've felt the rough side of my tongue."

"And lived to tell the tale," said Clare.

"So this is it," said Charlotte. "Moving into an apartment."

Felicitas put her arms around her mother and kissed the top of her head. "Oh, Mommy, thank you, thank you."

"Thank me when you're combing roaches out of your

hair. That neighborhood. God knows what it's infested with."

"Combing roaches out of her hair?" said Clare incredulously. "Charlotte, where do you think these things up?"

"A fertile imagination," Charlotte said. "I inherit it from my daughter."

As soon as Clare and Elizabeth left, Felicitas rushed into her mother's bedroom to phone Robert.

"Robert, I can do it," she said. "My mother said I can move."

"That's great, honey," he said. He sounded distracted.

"Is anyone else there?" she asked.

"Just some friends from the Coast."

"When will we do it? When will I move in?"

"Whenever you want," he said. He seemed to have walked away from the telephone.

"Robert?" she said, trying to call him back.

"That's great, honey," he said. "We'll see each other real soon."

"When?"

"Whenever you want."

She hung the phone up in despair. He was with another woman. This was the sort of thing she was going to have to learn not to mind.

The next day, she woke early. If she was not going to fail her courses, she would have to spend this week making up all the work she had missed all term. She feared that perhaps this was a sign that her love for Robert was inferior; perhaps if she truly loved him, she would be glad to fail her courses for him. But she could not do that. She would see as much of him as she could. And she would move in with him in three weeks, when she had finished the last of her finals.

She knew she had disappointed her professors. In Latin, she had relied on her natural fluency and gotten by, but she had not progressed. In Greek, her showing had been only tolerable. She had missed more classes in Renaissance art than she had attended, but she would do all right, because the professor had published a book which said everything he had said in his lectures. For the first time in her life, she would not do brilliantly. That said something for her love, but perhaps not enough, not enough for Robert to notice, not enough for him to value.

The morning passed in the greenish light of the library reading room. At one o'clock, she went to the delicatessen and bought a loaf of brown bread and some muenster cheese to bring to the apartment for her lunch and the lunch of anyone around. The upstairs buzzer rang the instant after she had pressed the downstairs one. She hoped that when she moved in, she could convince everyone not to ring upstairs until whoever it was downstairs had announced himself.

Robert answered the door in his coat. "Oh, sweetheart, I have to run. Dentist appointment. Walk me a few blocks?"

He pulled her by the hand and they ran to 113th Street and Riverside Drive. She was incredibly happy to be with him, running hand in hand in the cold.

"Robert," she said. "I thought I'd move in after finals."

"Great," he said. "Just at the beginning of the new semester. That'll make two beginnings."

"Will you be able to help me move my things?"

"No problem."

"I'll see you before that, though, won't I?"

"Of course you will," he said, stepping into the dentist's building. She watched him run through the foyer. He had never even buttoned his coat.

For three weeks, Felicitas slept four hours a night, ate ten small meals a day, all standing, did not wash her hair. At the end of this time she had taken and passed all her finals. For two days, she simply slept. Her mother would awaken her by telephone late in the afternoon. She would walk down to the candy store for coffee and an English muffin at three o'clock. This was her breakfast. An hour later, she would come home and cook supper. At night she and her mother watched television and played cards. They said nothing about Felicitas' moving out. After another two days, she began to pack her things. Only after this was done and there were no more Felicitas' clothes in the closet did they talk about the move.

"When's the big day?" asked Charlotte.

"Saturday. My friends borrowed a van."

"That's nice," Charlotte said.

Felicitas thought that "That's nice" was the most uncharacteristic sentence her mother had ever uttered. She feared that she had ended her mother's life if she could now speak sentences like that. But it had to be. She thought of Cyprian, stroking his book and weeping, holding the toy lighter to her head. She had to get away. It would be best for everyone.

Normally on Saturdays Charlotte slept until eleven. It was her one luxury, her one habit that could be called by anybody a vice, and she guarded it with a fierce, proprietorial intensity, a sheik who watched jealously the youngest, the only real beloved of his harem. Having worked five days a week, fifty weeks a year, all the years of her life since she was eighteen, having raised a child alone, she lived most of her life against a backdrop of fatigue it was not possible to acknowledge.

Nothing tempted her from her weekend sleep; fine days washed over her, parades, out-of-town visitors. But that Saturday she woke at eight. She went down to the bakery and bought buns and doughnuts for Felicitas' friends. She didn't want them to think Felicitas had a peculiar family. It was important that she keep her friends now; she was getting older.

They had said they would be there at nine but did not arrive until noon.

That was, Felicitas thought, one of the big differences between her friends and her mother's. Even Elizabeth, who never achieved it, thought punctuality was important. If they failed to arrive when they said they would, they apologized. Felicitas knew that Robert and the others would not think it necessary.

And they would not eat the food her mother had bought. She knew what they would say about the cheese buns and the turnovers, the doughnuts stacked on the flowered plate: they would say it was bad, all of it bad. Iris would say it was bad karma. Sally would say it had no nutritive value. Richard would say it was a capitalist plot to make the workers weak so that they'd be in bad shape when the revolution came. Brad would say nothing, since his parents had brought him up not to talk about food. And Robert would probably handle everything and then put it back on the plate, which would offend her mother most of all.

Charlotte kept asking if "the girls" had enough pots and pans, enough covered dishes. Felicitas had mentioned only Iris and Sally, and her mother had not thought to question further. It had not occurred to her that an unmarried woman might occupy the same piece of real estate as a man. In the end, Charlotte packed two cartons' worth of kitchen equipment, including two gadgets she had been saving as surprise gifts: a Veg-a-Matic and a musical lazy Susan. She also packed eight cans of tuna fish and three jars of peanut butter. "Quick protein," she kept saying.

"Mom, I'm not going to Mount Everest," Felicitas said.

"Says who?" Charlotte answered.

The truck pulled up with everyone in it wearing jeans and work shirts. When Felicitas saw Robert walking up the path, her heart beat with a surprisingly painful irregularity. She had not thought of that before: he would be inside her house.

Robert shook Charlotte's hand and introduced himself. "I'm sorry we're late. I've never been to Brooklyn."

"Well, I've never been to the Empire State Building," said Charlotte. "That's the way it is in New York."

"We should probably start loading the stuff right now," Felicitas said, terrified that, although she had warned them to be circumspect, someone would say something revealing.

Felicitas owned very little except books. She was not the kind of girl to whom people gave things for her bedroom. She had no knickknacks and few clothes. She left her pictures, Holbein's "Sir Thomas More" and a blond Filippo Lippi, on the wall. It seemed rude to her to remove them.

In ten minutes, everything she owned was loaded in the van.

"How about a coffee break?" asked Charlotte.

"We're not really into coffee," Iris said.

"What about tea? Or milk?" She turned to Richard and

Brad. "I know boys usually like milk. My brothers used to drink a quart of milk a day when they were your age."

"What kind of teas do you have?" asked Richard.

"Whatever's on sale at A & P. Ann Page, I think they call it; it's their own brand."

"No, I mean, do you have any herb teas?"

Charlotte wrinkled her nose. "You've come to the wrong place, babe."

Robert laughed. "Why don't we all have some tea and some of these delicious-looking pastries?" he said.

"That's what they're there for," Charlotte said. "Help yourself, you kids. Don't hold back. I really appreciate all the help you're giving my daughter."

"We really love her," Iris said.

"I didn't think you knew her that long," said Charlotte. Robert laughed.

"You really go for those cheese buns, don't you?" Charlotte said, passing him the plate.

"I do, Mrs. Taylor," Robert said. "They're first-rate."

"Did you ever see Tyrone Power? The movie star, I mean," said Charlotte.

"Isn't he usually in those swashbuckling movies?" Robert asked.

"Now, you mustn't mix him up with Errol Flynn," said Charlotte.

"He was in *The Sun Also Rises*," said Felicitas, anxious at every word exchanged between Robert and her mother.

"Yes, I think I have seen that," said Robert.

"Well, anyway, you remind me of him," said Charlotte. "Are you by any chance Irish?"

"Maybe somewhere along the line. But I'm sorry to say I'm Anglo-Saxon as far as anyone remembers."

"Don't be sorry," said Charlotte. "Don't apologize. Everybody apologizes for what they are. Nobody's satisfied."

"That's really true," said Iris.

Charlotte looked at her suspiciously. "Are you one of the girls in the apartment?"

"Yes," Felicitas answered quickly. "Iris and Sally."

"How do you girls handle cooking?" Charlotte asked.

"We share," said Iris.

"Iris is much better than I am," said Sally. "But we eat very well. Very healthily."

"Yeah, but does it taste good? Healthy isn't everything. If it doesn't taste good, nobody will eat it, healthy or not," Charlotte said.

"We eat very well," Sally repeated primly.

"I think we'd better get on our way," Felicitas said, looking nervously at Robert.

Charlotte stood up quickly and said, "Call me when you get settled."

Felicitas was afraid to look at her mother. She didn't want to cry in front of everyone, in front of Robert. And Charlotte didn't want to cry in front of Felicitas' new friends. So they did not embrace. Felicitas waved at her mother without looking at her.

At the window, Charlotte watched the van drive down the road. She picked up the plates and started washing them. She cried into the sink. She tried to think what mothers did when their children went off to war. She hoped she had done the right thing. Before she had finished the dishes, the phone rang.

"How was it?" asked Clare.

"They're all nice kids. One of them is older. I think he's a professor. Felicitas is gaga over him."

"Are they going together?"

"How would I know? I'm the last person she tells anything these days." . .

"What's he like?"

"Tyrone Power. Too handsome for his own good. A real charm boy."

"It's no crime to be handsome," Clare said.

"Handsome is as handsome does," said Charlotte.

"Why don't we go out tonight?" Clare said. "I'll stop and get Elizabeth."

"Let's go to the movies. I have to get my mind off this crap."

"We all do," Clare said. "We've all got to learn to live without her."

Charlotte felt herself beginning to cry. "Someone's at the door," she lied. "I'll see you tonight."

She walked into Felicitas' room, lay down on her bed and covered herself with the quilt that Clare had given

Felicitas for her twelfth birthday. She realized that she was very tired. She had missed her sleep.

Robert drove badly over the Brooklyn Bridge. He was not used to paying attention to cars; he kept turning his head to talk.

"I like your mother," he said to Felicitas. "She's a real peasant."

Felicitas turned to him for the first time in anger.

"That's right, Robert. My grandfather would have been plowing your grandfather's fields."

"Don't get uptight," said Iris. "Robert doesn't say peasant as a put-down."

"If there's anything I hate it's the bourgeoisie," said Robert.

"You're not bourgeois, you're aristocracy," Felicitas said.

"That's a very bourgeois analysis," said Richard from the back of the van.

"I'm not bourgeois, I'm working class," said Felicitas.

"Everyone loves the working class," said Robert, "even Marx. 'Everybody loves the workers, why don't they love me?' " he sang to the tune of "I've Been Working on the Railroad."

Felicitas stiffened. The others in the back were laughing. She remembered the laughter of Myron Haber that day on his awful farm when Cyprian made her smell the different manures.

"Relax," said Robert. "Don't get uptight. I know this is a big thing for you, but it's really exciting, you know? You're your own person for the first time."

Felicitas had a vision of herself in a clown suit, being shot out of a cannon. She began to laugh.

"That's better," Robert said, leaning over to kiss her, missing by a foot the truck in the next lane.

After the last box had been set down, Iris said she would make tea. They sat around for almost an hour, drinking tea, smoking joints and cigarettes, talking about Angela Davis and the fates of the prisoners. Throughout all this, Felicitas was impatient. She wanted to be alone in her new room, she wanted to unpack the things that she had always lived with but had lived with in the room that had been hers since childhood, a room she had not chosen. Still, she had to act as if she were interested in their talk. She was grateful to them for so much: for opening their home to her, for helping her move in. She loved their generosity, their ease. They did not make it seem as if her presence were anything that intruded, so she must not act as if their presence in their own home were intruding upon her. It was her home too now, but she felt compelled to be modest in this assumption of new property.

She knew they valued the communal above the private. Old models of monastic life came to her: monks arguing in Latin about the proper balance between prayer and work. She knew where she had always stood: with the pale ones, alone in their cells while the crops withered and fraternal relations disintegrated. But perhaps this had always been her problem. Yes, she was sure that was it. It was not generous, this hunger for solitude. It probably led to war.

She was going to try to be better at communal life. But when they had finished and begun to leave and she had washed the cups and teapot and had walked into her room for the first time by herself, she felt a wonderful gray airiness between her ribs, as if the hot, wet flesh between them was being cleansed and refreshed. She unpacked her books and put them in a new order on the shelves. Formerly they had been merely alphabetically arranged; now she shelved them alphabetically by subject. This seemed to her an emblem of real change. She put on her dresser the small red jewelry box that held the few good pieces Clare had given her, which she never wore but liked owning. Next to the box, she put the green-bound *Theaetetus* that had been Elizabeth's Christmas present. In the drawer of the small table next to her bed she hid a picture of her mother. She unpacked her sheets and made her bed. Then she realized she had forgotten her quilt. She felt ill with disappointment. Her first night would not be perfect. But perhaps she would spend the night in Robert's bed. She told herself she could not think that way. She must carefully excise such expectations. What would happen would happen. If he wanted her, she was here, and when he didn't, she had her own room and all the other people to talk to. It was perfect. And she could get her quilt next weekend. She had told her mother she would come home on weekends, at least for the first month or so.

That semester, she registered for a literature course called "The Novel of the Modern City," a history course on the French Revolution, a sociology course on the black family, and a course on the Latin satirists, for which she would not have to work. She had decided that she would not continue Greek.

At registration, she lied and said she had lost her I.D. She wanted a new one; she wanted to present a new face. She was disappointed when she got her new card to discover that the picture was nearly identical to the one she had had taken in September. She looked no older, no more sage or complicated. She did not understand how that could be; in the last four months she had learned the only important things in her life.

Theoretically, everyone in the apartment took turns cooking. But Iris was willing to barter cooking for almost anything: typing, research for her papers, the loan of a blouse. And so most often Iris cooked for the others, who were on vegetarian diets, meals she did not eat herself.

Felicitas had never cooked. She went to the library and discovered that it was possible to borrow cookbooks for a month. She read them late at night on the nights when Robert didn't want her. It was difficult to imagine which of the recipes she read were possible to cook for these people. There was so much they wouldn't eat! The recipes she found that did seem right always contained a term or two that baffled her to the point of despair—roux or fumet —or a direction that demanded that she beat egg whites until they were firm but not stiff. When it was her first turn to cook, she asked Iris to do it for her. She was happy to oblige; Felicitas had agreed to write her English paper.

The first week, Robert asked for her every night. By the second week, he had grown less ardent. For one thing, he had begun teaching again and was busier, and for another, she had gone home to her mother's on the weekend, after he had told her he thought she should not.

When she returned to the apartment, stunned and weakened from the effort of sustained deceit, he had not spoken to her. She told herself that he must be preparing his classes; if they were going to live together, she would have to learn to understand what might seem like inattention but was, in fact, only the space he needed to accomplish his work, the privacy that someone of his generous temperament required simply to sustain a life.

The Tuesday after she had gone home, he invited her into his room after dinner. When he took his clothes off, he was not erect. She wondered what she had done wrong. She allowed him to guide her hand, and finally he seemed ready to penetrate her. But his orgasm was a half-hearted shudder, and she wished she were alone in her room.

"Have I done something to make you unhappy?" she asked when he had put his pants on and lit a joint.

"Never ask that," he said. "If you don't know what you've done, it's better not to ask."

Tears of failure came to her eyes and she covered her face with a pillow. He pulled it away.

"What's the matter now?" he asked.

"I so want to make you happy."

"You always act like you're waiting for something, waiting for something more to happen. It spooks me," he said.

"I'm not waiting for anything, Robert."

"Good," he said. "You have to learn to live more in the here and now."

"I'm trying."

"You look at life as a big term paper," he said. "Diligence is a passé virtue, like loyalty to the king. You have to try to be more spontaneous."

"One can't try to be more spontaneous. That's a contradiction," she said.

"You'll die a casuist," said Robert, "but at least you won't die a virgin."

"I'm grateful for that," she said.

"Don't be grateful. Just enjoy yourself."

"I am, Robert."

"That's good," he said. "You know I only want you to be happy."

"I've never been happier in my life," she said, wondering if it were true. He lay down on the bed again. She embraced him and pressed his head onto her shoulder, as if the weight of it would press out all uncertainty. In a moment, he was asleep. But she was wakeful. She went into her own room to read. She didn't want to disturb him and she didn't want to lie beside him, watchful. He would think she was waiting for something to happen. It was a vice of hers, this watchfulness, and one should learn, she thought, to keep one's vices private. It was a new vice in the catalog. Even the Church had not yet got around to it.

When Felicitas opened the door, she heard a voice that sounded sickeningly familiar. Walking up the corridor, she prayed with the perfect concentration of the desperate: "Sweet Jesus, when I get to the living room, let her not be there."

But there she was: Mary Rose, sitting on the Indian pillow under the picture of Che, and Joe Siegel on the floor across the room.

Mary Rose was talking to Iris. They were talking about cats. *Now* they were talking about cats, but God only knew what Iris had said already. She was incapable of deceit, not through any strength of character but because she lacked the intellectual apparatus either to invent or to sustain it. She parlayed this fallibility into a virtue and made it an emblem of the age of Aquarius, yet unborn. When everybody got their shit together, Iris reckoned, nobody would need to lie. She would be ready for it and ahead of the game because she wouldn't have all that bad karma to get rid of. The implication was, of course, that others would be up to their necks in bad karma from countless lifetimes of inferior existences.

The idea that Felicitas would lie to her mother was incomprehensible to Iris, whose own mother, three times married now, rode cross-country in a van selling hand-made jewelry. Iris said that Felicitas' mother was a very kind and far-out lady, and she would never lie to her or to any of her friends.

"How long have you been here?" Felicitas asked Mary Rose and Joe. She realized she was not being very welcoming, but then, she did not welcome them. All the years of kindness made her feel some sense of duty. She remembered that Dante had put bad hosts in the Ninth Circle. She kissed Mary Rose and offered tea to her and Joe.

"Iris is just after making it," said Mary Rose.

That was a good sign. They couldn't have been in the apartment long. Iris always offered tea to guests immediately upon their arrival. And part of the time, she would have had to be in the kitchen.

"I told them you wouldn't be long. I told them dinner was always at six when you cooked it. And I knew it was Robert's early day, so you'd be here early," said Iris.

"Is Robert here yet?" asked Felicitas as Custer might have asked about the Indians.

"He's in his room," said Iris.

She decided that bravado was her only hope; it was, as a tone, asexual as well as deflecting. "So you haven't met Robert," she said, putting her head back.

"No, we haven't seen any boys," said Mary Rose. She might have been playing Judy Garland's kind but addled mother in a movie set in a small town.

"Listen, honey, we were going to take you out to dinner, but since your friends are all here waiting for you, why don't we just order a batch of pizzas?" Joe said. His tone was kindly, but Felicitas could tell by the way he looked at her that he had gotten the drift of their living arrangements.

"Wow, that would be really far out," said Iris.

"Thank you, Joe," said Felicitas.

"We'll call up first, and then you and I'll go get them, okay, honey?"

Joe always called Felicitas "honey" because he had a lot of trouble with her name. Most non-Catholics did, particularly if they were over forty and had at least one parent not born in the United States.

As if responding to the news of food, Richard and Brad came into the apartment and then Sally, dragging Mao, who cried every day at this time from hunger and fatigue and from the premonition that the sun was setting.

"These are Felicitas' friends, and they're going to get us pizzas for dinner," Iris said.

Felicitas hoped they would have sense enough not to

light joints in front of Joe and Mary Rose; she was relying on Richard's paranoia. They sat down in the circle they habitually made. Brad, never able entirely to forget the manners he had been taught at the school he refused to name, asked Joe what he did for a living.

"Movies," Joe said.

"Are you a director?"

Joe and Mary Rose laughed.

"Joe Siegel de Mille," said Mary Rose, "and his cast of thousands."

"No, seriously," said Joe, "I manage a movie theater downtown. Whenever you kids want, stop by and I'll give you a free pass."

"That's dynamite," said Iris. "Lately, I'm into going to the movies in the afternoon, but I'm afraid of weirdos. You probably don't have a lot of weirdos."

"We have our share. But if anybody bothered you, I'd handle it," said Joe.

Robert came into the living room. He had been sleeping, and he looked as if he was prepared to be unpleasant.

"Robert, these are friends of my mother's," said Felicitas.

He nodded. "We have any of that iced tea?"

Sally, Iris and Felicitas rose at the same instant and ran anxiously into the kitchen. Sally was there first, and she walked triumphantly into the living room carrying iced tea in a mug.

Robert drank it without thanking her.

"My three o'clock class was an incredible bummer. Bunch of tight asses. Tight-ass kids, my God," he said.

"Are you a teacher?" Mary Rose asked, looking up at Robert in astonishment.

"That's what they tell me," he said. "So what do you think of Felicitas' new home?"

"It's very spacious," said Mary Rose.

Joe looked at his watch. "Come on, honey, let's get those pizzas," he said.

Felicitas got Joe's coat and her own. She could tell Joe wanted to talk to her; she had never seen him look so serious. He was trying, she guessed, to assume the face of Andy Hardy's father, to have mastered, by the time they hit the streets, a stern but understanding countenance. But actually he looked more like a dog whose bone has been put somewhere out of its reach.

"Your friends seem very nice," he said.

"They are nice. They're very kind to me. We have good times together."

"Good times aren't everything," said Joe. "I know, at your age they seem to be. But they're not; you learn that as you grow older. Particularly for a girl."

"Why should girls be different?"

"They have to bear the children."

"I don't want children."

"That's what you think. That's what my Rochelle thought at your age. And look at her. I'm a grandfather three times in five years."

"I'm nothing like Rochelle," Felicitas said, picturing the bouncy, obedient daughter whom she could never remember seeing wearing anything except a cheerleader's skirt or a skating outfit.

"You all think you're not like anybody at your age. Then you find out you are."

They walked silently. The air was heavy with Joe's reluctantly adopted sense of duty. All her life, men Joe's age had thought they had lost the main access to generational wisdom, as though she lived in some dark age ruled by mother goddesses who thought the sun came up because a rooster crowed.

"Does your mother know about all this?" asked Joe.

"All what?" Felicitas asked in a tone she hoped sounded defiant.

"This teacher. Living right there with you."

"She's met Robert."

"And she knows where he lives?"

Panic washed over Felicitas like a bath of acid. "She doesn't have to know," she said.

"How do you think you're going to keep it from her?"

"She won't come to the apartment. She never comes into the city."

"And what if she does?"

"I'll tell her something. I'll tell her his electricity went out and he had to stay in the spare room for a while."

"I never thought you'd lie to your mother. You were so close."

"Maybe I have to. Maybe I have to do a lot of things you didn't think I'd do. You or anybody. Maybe I'm not what everybody thinks I am."

"Honey, you don't have to talk to me like that. I'm not trying to make you feel bad. It's just that I'm a man. I know what men are like. They don't want what they can get easily. Rochelle used to think I was an old fuddy-duddy, but she listened, out of respect. Now she tells me she's glad she listened, she's glad she waited till she married Frank."

"I'm not going to get married. There's no one for me to marry."

"You mustn't think like that. You're an attractive girl."

"That's not the point. I wasn't brought up to get married. I wasn't brought up for an ordinary life."

"You were brought up for *this?*"

"I was brought up to do what I believe in."

Joe kissed the top of her head. "This is none of my business. Only think about what I said."

"You won't say anything to my mother, though?"

"I'm not like that."

"What about Mary Rose?"

"Mary Rose wouldn't believe anything was going on even if you told her. Particularly not about you. She'd never believe anything bad about you."

"So you think what I'm doing is bad?"

"It isn't good," he said, walking into Nino's Pizza Parlor. They had ordered six pies, two with anchovies, two mushroom and two plain. She had told him it would be far too much, but he said, "Better too much than too little." They carried the pizzas home, three each. All the way home she envied Rochelle Siegel, married in Larchmont to Frank Helpern, a periodontist. She must have walked like this with her father all her life, talking about marriage, ordering too much food. Throughout the meal, Robert was sullen and quiet. Felicitas knew that he could have been charming to Joe and Mary Rose if he had wanted to be. He had been charming to her mother. But he sat in the middle of the circle looking up sourly at every comment, so that everyone soon felt that conversation was unseemly. Joe and Mary Rose sat close to each other in a silence more distinct than the shared silence of the others. Mary Rose looked like a good little girl playing a doll in a Christmas pageant in her pillbox hat with her two spots of rouge. She had said nothing after Robert snapped at her when she asked if anyone had ever told him he looked like Tyrone Power.

As soon as it was feasible, Joe looked at his watch and made an elaborate show of tiredness. He yawned and stretched and said he didn't know what got into him these days, he couldn't seem to get enough shut-eye.

He had trouble rising from the position he was in, sitting cross-legged on the floor. Mary Rose gave him her hand. Her pocketbook knocked him in the face and he sat down again, putting his handkerchief to his eye. Then Mary Rose sat down on the floor beside him. Felicitas was afraid they were going to stay all night, unable to figure out a way to get up off the floor with grace. She went over and stood behind them. Robert walked to the window. Sally went into the kitchen.

"Heave-ho," Joe said, bracing himself against Mary Rose. This time he made it to his feet.

Iris said, "So I can come down to the theater anytime in the day or anything?"

"Sure thing," said Joe.

"That is really far out. Like I always have someplace to go."

"You too, honey," Joe said to Felicitas.

Mary Rose stuck five dollars in Felicitas' jeans pocket when they said good-by. She always acted as if she were passing counterfeit when she gave Felicitas money, as though it was crucial that no one should know of the transaction.

"Don't be a stranger, now," she said.

Felicitas had never known Mary Rose to be so quiet. She was sure that Mary Rose knew everything, that Joe misunderstood her and mistook her kindness for a simpler kind of innocence. She wanted to run after them, but this was her home now; she belonged here. She touched the walls as she walked up the corridor. The Jimi Hendrix poster had fallen to the floor, but she didn't feel like putting it back up. It was always falling. She was worried about Robert. She was afraid that he was ill or that she had done something that displeased him.

Sally and Iris were spilling the Creative Playthings blocks onto the living room floor for Mao. Robert was still standing at the window, his arms on the crossbar, his head resting on his arms in a posture that suggested the bleak moment before a difficult resignation. He could have been Aeneas about to leave Troy, she thought; he could have been General MacArthur. As she walked up behind him, she felt herself ennobled by his posture: she was a nurse in the First World War; she was Calpurnia, beloved wife of Caesar.

"You okay?" she asked, resting her cheek on his back.

He shrugged.

"Do you want to make love?" It was the first time *she* had suggested sex to *him*. She was not desirous herself, but she had heard that when men were distressed, sex was a comfort.

He sighed as he went into the bedroom, sighed as he took his pants off, sighed untying his shoes. She took his shoes off for him, and his sweater, and his shirt. She laid him on the bed and put his head on her breast. She felt for his penis. It was not erect. He put her hand away.

"I don't think things are working out," he said.

She felt her flesh grow coarse and harden, then become a rind around her bones. It pressed on the soft pulp of the organs that made blood and carried it, it pulled the thin wires that brought signals, that made news travel to her fragile brain. Those awful words: he was not happy with her.

"What have I done wrong?" she asked.

"Nothing. That question is typical. As if you were a bad little girl in convent school waiting for punishment. You're always waiting for something."

"Everybody's always waiting for something," she said, squeezing words out of her closing throat.

"No, they're not, goddamn it. Everybody is not always fucking deferring gratification like you, trying to please everybody—me, your mother, your mother's friends, God."

She was silent. She lay back on the bed and bit the insides of her cheeks. He would hate her to cry.

"It's just not working," he said. "Your conditioning's too strong. I can't overcome it. You just don't fit in."

"Just tell me what I'm doing that you don't like and I'll change it," she said, trying to sound businesslike, as if they were two architects discussing blueprints.

"It's your whole fucking gestalt. It's the things you trail, going back to your mother's all the time, bringing those people here."

"I didn't bring them. They just came."

"They wouldn't come if you made it clear they weren't welcome."

"But I've known them all my life."

"A lot of Jews knew a lot of Nazis all their lives."

She wanted to tell him it was a false analogy, but she was silent.

"That's not all," he said. "Your whole approach to our relationship is incredibly bourgeois. I keep feeling you're into some kind of weird marriage-fantasy trip."

"I never said or did anything to give you that idea."

"You didn't have to. I could tell."

"Tell from what?"

"The way you're always waiting for me. Sitting in that room, waiting."

"I'm reading."

He threw his shirt down on the floor. "You are deliberately not hearing me. I can't speak to you if you won't hear me."

"I'm listening, Robert."

"Look, the root problem is monogamy. It's hanging you up and it's hanging me up sexually. I think you should be fucking other people."

She closed her eyes. He wanted to give her away. He wanted someone else to have her. She looked at his naked body. She had never imagined herself making love to someone else. This was the body she had taken up sex for. She wasn't interested in sex for its own sake, in some random flash of dots and zigzags in the brain that could arrange itself into the form of anyone, the face of anyone. She laid her head on his arm. She would do anything if she could just be with him some of the time.

"You really think it's for the best?" she asked.

"I really do, honey. Your possessiveness trip is really hanging me up."

She put her arms around him and they kissed.

"You know, I think the guys downstairs are turned on to you. Particularly Richard."

She didn't want to think about that now; she wanted him to go on kissing her. But it would make him happy for her to agree. She wanted to make him happy. She wanted him to be able to make love.

"Okay," she said.

"I think it would be a really healthy thing for both of us," he said.

She brought his head down to her breast.

"I really want you to want it," he said. "You know that. I really want you to want it."

"You want me to want *it*, but you don't want me to want *you*."

"What, sweetheart?"

"Nothing." She wanted him so much that she cried out, a cry of longing he could not but misunderstand.

Charlotte lived alone now for the first time in her life. She was fifty-eight years old and she had never had her evenings to herself. When Felicitas was little, first in school, Charlotte ironed every evening, listening to radio serials: *Johnny Dollar, The Romance of Helen Trent.* She did not want people to think that because she was a working mother, her child was neglected. Felicitas wore a white blouse underneath the blue wool jumper of her uniform. Charlotte had bought two of them and each night she ironed one. Later, when Felicitas was older and had homework, Charlotte did not listen to the radio. She watched the top of her daughter's serious head, watched her work so hard at writing that she broke the points of her pencils, watched her take her ruler and draw margins at the right side of each page, watched her look up at the ceiling for the answers to the sums she could not add, the words she could not spell.

Charlotte was perfectly happy then, alone with her small daughter in the living room. She could read when she felt Felicitas in the apartment. As long as she could sense in some near room the even rhythm of her daugh-

ter's breath, her mind could follow through the pages of
print the fates of heroines, the tracks of killers, the intelligence of private eyes or fragile English ladies. But now,
with Felicitas away, she could not concentrate. The apartment was too big. She was always cold. She had taken to
wearing sweaters, which was not like her. She had always
been the one to open windows, to unpack electric fans in
early May, to put on cotton while her colleagues lan-
guished in their sweaty wools. But she was cold now; she
was distracted; she thought all the time about her daughter. When she saw her every day, she hardly ever thought
of her.

Felicitas phoned every night at seven. She came home
on Saturdays and went back Sunday nights. That was terrible, walking her to the subway, slipping tokens in her
pocket, waiting to cry until the train was gone. It was
ridiculous, the child was ten miles away; if anything went
wrong she would know instantly.

She knew Felicitas did not want her to visit the apartment, and she would not go. She had brought her child
up oddly, had deprived her of the company of sisters and
brothers by her own late age in marrying, had allowed—
perhaps she had even encouraged, knowing it would keep
her closer—all her daughter's eccentricities. Now that Felicitas was older, she had to become like other people.
Whether or not she got married, she had to learn to get
along with people better than she did. To roll with the
punches. To bend in the wind. Charlotte saw herself as a
wall in front of which her child, her tree, had flourished.
With Charlotte near, Felicitas did not have to bend in the
wind. She could not be knocked down, there was a wall
behind her. But she knew her child had to grow, had to
grow unprotected, needed exposure, needed loss of shelter. She had to leave her alone.

She hoped Felicitas' new friends were nice. She hoped
they wouldn't take advantage of her. She hoped Felicitas
knew how to handle herself with boys. She had never
spoken of these things to Felicitas; she hadn't thought Felicitas was interested. It was too late now. There was no
sense in thinking of it.

Brad and Richard never locked their door. It was a political act, they said, to leave a door unlocked in New York City. They said they trusted The People not to steal anything they didn't need. It seemed to Felicitas a point in favor of the proposition that they had nothing worth stealing. They came upstairs to listen to Sally's record player; they used Robert's typewriter and Iris' electric juicer; they allowed the three dogs access to the entire building. Since the dogs were not housebroken, this caused no small amount of ill will among the tenants. But in time, since they were New Yorkers and for the most part connected with a university, they gave up their complaints.

Felicitas found the dogs a great comfort. She was lonelier than she had ever been before. She spent all of her evenings in her room, unwilling to go to the library in case Robert should come home while she was gone. But now Robert was rarely home in the evenings, and she sat in her room trying to read, unable to concentrate, her ear strained for footsteps in the corridor. He was right; she was waiting for him.

The dogs were a diversion. She would call one of them on the bed with her, usually Ho, because he was the quietest, and he would lie against her as she read. She could concentrate with the dog's back against her. She sensed the constant rhythm of rich lungs in the warm mass beside her, she could feel the quick, intelligent heart against her hand and the stupid, heraldic head that housed the stuff that made him run in his light sleep. With the dogs she felt what she almost never felt in that apartment: safe.

She began smuggling them dog food. She knew the brown rice, beans, eggs and cottage cheese that they were fed could never satisfy them. It was a radical misunderstanding of their nature to involve them in vegetarianism, particularly as a political gesture; this was one of the few political positions she was sure of.

She saw how giving the dogs meat made them calmer. She decided she would try to housebreak them, and she got several dog-training books out of the library, which all agreed that at their age (they were three), it was ten times as difficult to housebreak them as it would have been in puppyhood. But she was determined to succeed.

The first step, according to all the books, was to feed

them at regular times. She told both Brad and Richard that she wanted to try to housebreak the dogs, so she would be responsible for their feeding. She did not tell them she was feeding the dogs meat. Each day at eight, eleven, four, six and ten o'clock, she walked the dogs. At first, it was difficult. They would become entangled in one another's leads and in Felicitas' legs. But she was astonished at how quickly they learned to walk well together. In ten days the walks ceased to be a trial. In two weeks, the dogs were housebroken.

Richard and particularly Brad were happy that she had succeeded. It wasn't that they were against housebreaking, they said; they just weren't into dealing with it.

The dogs were a good excuse for Felicitas to go downstairs to Brad and Richard's apartment. On the day she decided to do what Robert wanted, she bought a pound of hamburger. She fed the three dogs secretly in her room, then took them downstairs on their leashes. She knew Richard was home alone.

"Hi," she said, standing at the door of Richard's room. "I brought the dogs back."

"Want some tea?" he asked.

"Okay."

She walked behind him into the kitchen, wondering how she would convince him to go to bed with her. How thin he was, compared to Robert, how unadventurous his shoulders, how cowardly the thin bones of his chest. It seemed as wrong as anything she could imagine to be having sex with anyone other than Robert. She had given up virginity, not just the membrane that was hidden and therefore abstract but the imagination of herself as solitary, unregarded, unapproached, for Robert—not for the act of sex or for the sake of entering the world most of her kind inhabited. Perhaps Robert was right; perhaps her fantasies were matrimonial. But she had always known that Robert wasn't hers and she had not expected that to change. What she could not contemplate was giving herself up to another in a way that seemed to her so radical.

Perhaps that was her mistake, perhaps there was nothing very radical or very significant about sex. Perhaps mature people, people of experience and understanding, knew what she did not know, that it didn't have to do

with love or even with seeing the person again. Perhaps it
had to do with what Robert was always talking about:
living in the present. His idea was that sexual possessiveness was based on the concept of property, the desire to
own, which was really the desire to exclude. Of course
that was wrong. Owning, exclusion, such things led to
force, to war, to steel on flesh, to ruined villages. She did
not want such a life for herself; it was not moral.

But what she felt when she saw Robert walking down
the hall, what she felt even for his clothes or samples of
his handwriting, she could not feel for anybody else. She
could try not to mind his having other women. She understood that she was neither good nor wise nor beautiful
enough to satisfy him. Robert was extraordinary; he required many women to fulfill his many sides. She was not
extraordinary; she was merely odd. She was content to
have him occasionally. The partial attentions of Robert
were far more valuable than the full attentions of an ordinary man.

Richard was not remarkable, either. He was intelligent
in a bleak, partisan way, but he wore his sense of natural
impoverishment like a coat passed down by a dead
brother. He was not beautiful. He was not easily beloved.
In that way he was like herself. She wished that she was
not seducing him out of a sense of duty, to please the man
for whom desire shot through the body she would give
away because he asked her to.

She had not thought of herself as a seducer. The last
time she had imagined herself initiating a sexual act, she
had been thirteen and had tried to get Joey Doherty to
kiss her. She read in *Seventeen* magazine that if you
looked at a boy's mouth, he would know you wanted him
to kiss you. Joey had moved to Long Island before she
had been able to try it. She would try it now on Richard.

"Why are you looking at my mouth like that?" Richard
asked defensively. "Is it my mustache? Are you thinking
it's taking me a hell of a long time to grow a mustache?
Don't you think I know that?"

She was suddenly sorry for him. It was the first time she
had seen the vulnerability of males. Her pity made it easy
to go on. "I wasn't thinking anything like that," she said.
"I was thinking it would be nice if you kissed me."

He came toward her with what was, to her, a startling immediacy, and he kissed her with an ardor that surprised her.

"I've always really liked you," he said shyly, but his hand was underneath her blouse.

That was what Robert had said, that Richard liked her. Perhaps Robert was right about everything. Perhaps it would work out really well for everybody.

Richard undressed her solicitously. He removed her clothes the way she removed Robert's. Then she saw: he wanted her the way she wanted Robert. It made her inexpressibly sad. She knew what he was feeling, and she did not want to make anybody feel that way.

He was a careful lover. He ran his fingers down her body, he looked out and listened for her pleasure. Every time she touched him, he said, "Thank you." And she knew why. He was not beautiful.

Every inch of Robert's body was smooth, curved and elegant. Richard's poor bones jutted in sad, inappropriate places; his arms were thin and almost hairless; she could have measured the space between his breasts with one of her hands. His penis looked distressingly adult against his childish legs. But he kissed her with sweetness and with fire, he touched her in imaginative places. In spite of herself, or perhaps because she so wanted to, she began to enjoy what he was doing to her.

His approach to orgasm was unrhythmic and uneven. She was not sure, but she thought she heard him whispering, "Fidel Castro, Fidel Castro."

"Is it okay?" he asked desperately.

"Sure," she said.

"Okay, then," he said.

She had never seen anybody move so fast; she had never heard anyone make so much noise.

"Did you come?" he asked, smiling down on her with a look she could almost call foolish, it was so pleased.

"No," she said.

"I'm sorry," he said. "I came too soon."

"That's all right."

"No, it isn't. I'm really trying to overcome that fault. I went to a doctor about it. He gave me some very good advice. I'm much better now."

•

"What did he say?"

"He said that when I felt I couldn't last any longer, I should think of something very serious, very important."

"What do you think about?"

"I think about Fidel Castro. Sometimes when I'm in real trouble, I repeat his name. It's very helpful."

"Like a patron saint," she said.

"What?"

"Catholics are always taught to pray to a special saint in times of danger. Usually not in this context, though."

"Well, Fidel is a kind of saint to me," he said.

Felicitas thought it was unfortunate that none of her new friends got her jokes. Perhaps it was because they weren't Catholic.

She spent the day at Richard's, and he asked if she would spend the night. He cooked four meals for her: he had studied Chinese cooking, and four times he brought into the bedroom beautiful plates of vegetables, leafy, steamy greens that were crisp and intact, surprisingly unlike the chow mein she and her mother ordered on Friday nights from Tim Chan's Oriental Palace.

He made love to her over and over, and he told her she was lovely, that she made him happy, that he was almost never happy but with her he was, that it was very easy to be with her, that she was very kind.

"I don't think I'm particularly kind. Not compared to people I know who are really kind."

She was thinking of Elizabeth and Mary Rose.

"Compared to most of the people I know, you're really kind," he said, "which is rare in a smart person."

"What do you mean by 'kind'?"

"Most of the women I know practically throw you out of bed if they don't have an orgasm."

"That's what you mean by *kind?*"

"Well, you're always very nice about it."

"It's just that I don't care that much about orgasms."

He looked terribly disappointed.

"But I really like sleeping with you, Richard. You're a very good, a very thoughtful lover."

"I suppose I'm not as good as Robert."

"In many ways," she said, "you're a great deal better."

He fell upon her and kissed her joyfully. He wanted her again. She saw how easy it was to make men happy.

Before they went to sleep that night, Richard talked for an hour about the Panther murders and the series the newspaper was going to do about them. When he was finished talking, he kissed her and instantly fell asleep. She lay awake all night, thinking of men shot in their beds, the sounds of police feet, the walls above Fred Hampton's bed, destroyed by blood and bullets. She could imagine the terror, the pure physical outrage of being shot in the safety of sleep. She knew she could be killed in her bed, here with Richard. Her mother was safe; Father Cyprian and all the women slept in safety. She was in danger.

When she went back to the apartment upstairs the next morning, she could hear the sound of Sally's radio through the closed door of her room, but no one else appeared to be home.

She went into the living room to get *The New York Times*, which Robert left each morning on the painted orange crate that was the coffee table. Next to the paper was a black candle, which had dripped and stuck itself to the wood, and an ashtray full of cigarette butts and roaches.

She looked at the front page of the paper. They were there again, the tortured, patient faces in their military caps, the slight bodies. Beside them the Americans looked like mastodons. Their weight itself was a threat, their fairness and their health.

She walked around the living room, unable to sit still. She had been unfaithful. She had lost her virtue. To be Robert's lover was a pure act, an act of courage, like joining the Spanish Republican Army. But she had thought that act itself would comprise her sexual identity. Now she was the lover of someone else.

Poor Richard. She thought of how he sat in this room, churlishly arguing, waiting to hear the slightest breach of dogma, to spot the smallest apparition of the bourgeois spirit. He sat on his thin bones, arguing, arguing about the poor. It was because he thought himself one of them. He was poor in spirit, his interior life in rags and tatters. Interior life. No one would know what she meant by that. But she imagined inside Richard a homunculus, always undernourished.

She had made him happy by pretending to desire him. She had made him happy by appreciating his sweetness, a sweetness she appreciated all the more because she did not desire him. She had deceived him. Nothing she had said was in itself deceitful, but she was in his bed to please Robert. And she had pleased Richard by doing it. Should she tell him why she was there? No. She liked him now. He was kind to her. She had begun to fear it was not her nature to be pleasing. He reassured her.

But it was not what she wanted. She wanted Robert, Robert's pleasure, Robert's kindness, the hidden core of sweetness he would show her that he would show no one else. In becoming Richard's lover, she had lost herself. She did not know who she was. When she was Robert's lover, her identity was safe, clear in its singularity and its determination. But she did not want to hurt Richard; she did not want to be the kind of person who caused pain.

She realized she had been walking around in circles when she heard Sally's footsteps in the corridor.

"Are you all right?" asked Sally. She always addressed Felicitas as if speaking to her was against her better judgment.

"Yes, thank you," said Felicitas as she imagined Mme. de Rênal spoke to Mlle. de Mole on the way home from Julien Sorel's funeral.

"Helene's here," she said.

"Who's Helene?"

"From the Coast. The rest of us are supposed to go jump in the lake now," Sally said.

The innocence of her diction surprised Felicitas. It made her for the first time seem vulnerable.

"What's she like?" asked Felicitas.

"Perfect. She's black, she teaches at Berkeley, she's unbelievable-looking and she isn't needy."

"You mean not like us," Felicitas said. She didn't know where she got the courage to speak to Sally in that tone.

Sally laughed. "I didn't know I was so obvious."

"You're not. I'm the one who's obvious."

"I've had more practice. It's my fourth year around here."

"When do you graduate?" asked Felicitas.

Sally laughed again. "I would like to like you. You're no fool."

Felicitas bowed to her.

"But it's impossible for me to like anyone who goes to bed with Robert."

"I feel the same way."

"Well, we'll all have a sabbatical. None of us will get near him while Helene's here."

They sat down on the floor. At the same moment, they began to cry.

"I don't know what I'm doing here," said Sally, weeping. "I should know better."

"Why don't you leave?"

"Why don't you?"

"I just got here."

Sally shook her head. "I mean it. You should get out. It's poison."

"Why do you stay if it's poison?"

"He's the father of my child. He's the only man I've ever been to bed with."

Felicitas felt jealousy like a hot stone under her tongue. She envied Sally her fidelity, her maternity, the accouterments of an honorable wife.

"Nobody knows about this," said Sally. "I trust you to keep my confidence. If Robert ever found out, it would be the end of everything."

Felicitas was silent.

"You see, I know the trouble with him—he's very easily bored. I knew the way to keep him was to keep going away. So every few months I go to my sister's in Colorado. Robert thinks I'm fucking my way across the country and I just breeze in when I'm in the mood."

"Does he know he's Mao's father?"

"No."

She envied Sally's cleverness, she whose instinct was to be obedient, not prudent. Robert had told her to go to bed with Richard and she had simply obeyed. She had gone downstairs the moment he had told her what he wanted. Sally had been prudent, intelligent, had been able to move herself to another part of the country. Felicitas had imagined she would die if she were separated from Robert. No one ever dies of love, she thought.

"I admire you," said Felicitas.

"Don't," said Sally. "Desperation makes you clever."

"I slept with Richard because Robert wanted me to."

"Poor Richard," Sally said.

They thought of Richard in his hungry skin.

"That's why he hates me," Sally said. "I went down to seduce him after Robert told me to, but then I chickened out. I don't blame him for hating me. I hate myself."

"You have your child," Felicitas said illogically.

"I have no maternal passion," Sally said. "I'm only interested in Robert."

Felicitas was chilled. "Everyone loves their children," she said.

"Oh, I want him to survive. I don't want him to get sick or be stupid. But his presence alters nothing in my life. I can only be absorbed in one person. I will keep my child alive, I will be fond of him. But I would die for Robert before I would die for him."

"That kind of thing doesn't happen," said Felicitas. "Dying for somebody."

"No, but it means something, who you think you'd do it for."

"I wish we could be friends," Felicitas said.

"We can't," said Sally, "but I understand you."

"That's something," said Felicitas.

Sally shrugged. "Not a hell of a lot."

When she came home from class, she saw the woman in the living room. For a moment, her looks took Felicitas' breath away. Nearly six feet tall, she had a dangerous Afro that made her invulnerable. She wore a leather mini-skirt and aqua suede boots. Felicitas had never seen anyone as good-looking. She was as beautiful as the women in magazines.

With every step into the living room, Felicitas grew an inch shorter, her eyes became smaller, her hair duller and greasier. By the time she reached the center of the room, she saw herself four feet tall, perfectly flat-chested, with eyes the color and size of olive pits and hair that stuck to her skull like the skin of a zoo-bound seal. The woman did not look at her.

"This is Felicitas," Robert said, "a very serious little girl. *Une jeune fille bien élevée.*"

"That kind of hierarchical bullshit turns me off," said Helene, and she walked into the bedroom to get her bag. She looked at Felicitas with contempt.

"I don't get it, the three of you staying here like this. That's the problem with you white girls, you don't have enough shit in your own life. You have to come begging for it."

"You stayed here last night," Felicitas said with all the false hauteur she could muster.

"It's a place to stay for one night on your way to the airport," said Helene, turning away.

Robert hung his head like a six-year-old accused of breaking a garage window with a baseball. He held Helene's cape for her. She strode down the hall like departing royalty, trailing some wonderful fragrance. It must be musk, Felicitas thought in desolation.

When the door shut, she saw that Iris and Sally were standing there. The three women looked at one another stupidly.

"Let's get drunk," said Sally.

"Let's get drunk and stoned at the same time," said Iris.

Felicitas went into the kitchen and brought out the gallon jug of wine. Sally was rolling joints for each of them. They slumped on the floor, leaning against the couch, silently imbibing.

"Let's watch the TV with the sound off. That always cheers me up," said Iris.

They sat and watched the blue image in the dark.

"We look like we're waiting for shock treatments," Felicitas said.

Sally lay on her back and laughed.

"I don't get it," Iris said.

"Never mind, baby," said Sally.

An hour later, they were all asleep in front of the silent, flickering eye that watched them at the same time that it showed them Walter Cronkite, understanding but let down by what he saw.

Felicitas didn't remember putting herself to bed, but she woke up there at seven the next morning. All the lights were on in the living room and the TV still flickered. Robert was sitting at the table sullenly looking into a cup. He raised his head as she walked by him.

"What's up?" he asked.

"I slept with Richard," she said quickly.

"Good for you."

"I thought that was what you wanted."

"What I really want I can't have," he said.

"Well, I just thought I'd tell you."

"Look, would you please split? I need to be alone right now."

She turned and walked down the dark corridor. He wanted her to go away. Sally was right, you had to go away in order to keep him. It reminded her of the report of a general in Vietnam: we had to destroy the village in order to save it.

She walked downstairs to Richard's apartment. When she saw his face, she started crying. He was so glad to see her, and he was not the man she loved.

"What's wrong?" he asked. "Do you want tea? Do you want to take the dogs for a walk?"

"Okay."

"Okay what?"

"Let's walk the dogs. I'm sure all this drinking of tea can't be entirely good for us."

He leashed the dogs and tried to walk down the stairs with the three of them and hold Felicitas' hand at the same time. The impossible and clumsy aspects of the gesture made her wish once more that she could love him.

"Do you want to talk about anything?" he asked.

She shook her head. It was impossible that she should speak to the lover who desired her about the lover who did not.

"Do you want me to make you some food?"

She suddenly saw what Richard was meant to be—somebody's Jewish father. How had he gone so far off the track, talking about bombing the Pentagon when he should have been paying the orthodontist's bills?

"You're very sweet," she said. "In the most traditional sense. I hope you don't mind my saying that."

"I don't get that many compliments. I can't afford to be picky."

She took his arm. She would go to bed with him that afternoon in gratitude, kindness for kindness.

At six o'clock, she got out of bed and took the train to Brooklyn, to her mother's house.

Charlotte watched her daughter cry. She had come home at six forty-five and had spent the rest of the evening crying in her room.

Charlotte had tried to say comforting things like "Anything I can do?" "How about going to the deli with me?" "Want to play some cards?" But those were the wrong things and she knew it. She could only sit in the kitchen, playing games of solitaire and listening to her girl, who lay in a deep misery she could not touch. She couldn't touch it because she had no experience in these things. It had to be that professor. What did Charlotte Taylor know about things like that? She had met Frank when she was fifteen and waited for him for twenty years. But in those years, she had not been involved with any other man. So she had nothing to say to her daughter, she could not help her child.

Felicitas' face was sore from weeping. She did not know where she belonged. Not here: her mother would be horrified, would banish her if she knew what she had done. This was only a temporary hideout where she could collect her thoughts. She was homeless. Se saw herself in some minor European city in 1930, moving from boardinghouse to boardinghouse, where no one spoke her language and her room smelled of the previous night's dinner all day long.

She wanted a life, a purposeful, solitary life, of translation and reflection, where she could write aphorisms like a Russian, all in the form of the infinitive: "To drink tea is not to hew wood." "To live a life is not to cross a field." She wanted to learn Russian; she wanted to live in silence. But how could she live such a life? She would have to learn to support herself. She couldn't live with Robert and she couldn't live with her mother. She imagined herself one of those thin women with obscure and genteel work that paid her nothing, living in rooms with someone else's furniture, accused by another woman down the hall of stealing the soap.

Charlotte knocked on the door. "I'm going to hit the hay," she said.

"Okay," Felicitas said, almost silently.

"I was thinking maybe you'd better sleep in the bed with me. I've turned the heat off in your room and it's chilly."

Felicitas sobbed.

"Come on, bean," said Charlotte.

They got into the old hard bed with the metal headboard and the horsehair mattress that had been Charlotte's mother's. Charlotte lay down, said good night, kissed her daughter and turned her back to her. Felicitas slipped in behind her mother like a spoon. Exhausted from a day of crying, she fell instantly asleep. Charlotte lay awake and thought of mothers who killed the men who hurt their daughters. Only she did not know who to kill and why she had to kill him. And her child was not a child.

V

Felicitas' period was ten days late. Until the tenth day, she had not begun to worry. After that her days were structured around trips to the bathroom to check for the beautiful red spot that would be her salvation. She wondered if some waggish Renaissance poet had not begun a sonnet "O blessed blood." She prayed, and she knew it was a primitive, untrustworthy prayer, which God, if He were a person of quality, would ignore. Nevertheless she prayed. There was nothing else to do.

After three days, her checking techniques grew sophisticated. First, she wrapped toilet paper around her middle finger and pressed against her cervix. Then she discovered

Q-Tips, which were longer than her finger and more supple. She went through a box and a half in two days, closing her eyes with each insertion, hoping that when she opened them she would be holding a cotton swab turned pink at the tip.

She couldn't be pregnant. It was not the sort of thing that happened. She had douched after every sexual encounter. She had read in a magazine advertisement that douching was a safe, inexpensive form of birth control that required no doctor's examination, no prescription, that the wife could purchase it herself in any drugstore. She bought the douche because of the wording of that last clause: if they were polite enough to refer to all their customers as wives, they had to be a trustworthy firm.

She couldn't be pregnant. She was just tense. All this trouble, with Robert, with Richard, had made her nervous, had thrown off her natural hormonal balance. She couldn't possibly be pregnant; she was not that kind of person. She would just have to relax.

Robert had stopped speaking to her entirely. He had stopped speaking to all of them. It was clear he wanted them out.

One day when she came home there was a note from Sally. It was addressed to no one, merely taped to the refrigerator: "Split for the Coast. *Ciao*. Sally."

Felicitas knew what it had cost Sally to sound so offhand, so deracinated. She understood Sally: she was one of those obsessed, tortured creatures who had been taught patience by her desperation. She had a deep, accomplished cunning, she was a kind of witch. She could change shapes as easily as keep them. She had fused her identity with the object of her passion so long ago that it cost her nothing to transform herself in ways most radical to her. To hide her passion was a grief, a cost, but she had the discipline of an anchorite. It was the same fixation that drove men into the desert to starve and thirst and fix their minds upon one object. Love, they called it. Sally called it love. It was not love, it was the hunger to be utterly absorbed. Felicitas could understand that, but it was not in her nature to achieve it. She knew that to win Robert, she must keep away from him, she must hold herself back. But the sight of him caused a dreadful hunger to rise in her. It drove her so that she had to touch him, to speak to him. But he did not want to speak to her.

"Don't you have anywhere to go? Don't you have anything to do?" he would say. Or, when he was angrier, "Can't you go somewhere else? Do you have to sit around here waiting? What are you always waiting for? If you're waiting for me to love you, stop it. I don't love you. Stop waiting."

And when he spoke to her, the damage spread. Her throat, her chest felt irradiated with some substance that made fire and acid. She had nowhere to go. She could not go downstairs to Richard. His kindness made her feel like a murderer. She could not go home. She walked around the streets.

She tried to catch the eyes of the old women, the mad women who hid their hair in hats because they could not bear to touch it. She saw their legs, failed and tormented, and their feet in the shoes of someone dead before them, saw their belongings in paper sacks, their houses, their endowments, paper, plastic, famished cloth. Still the instinct to hoard was in them. Women lost that last, she thought. They would wander, but they could not wander unencumbered. In despair, the men who were their counterparts set off with whiskey and what they wore. But the women collected, they held on. They wandered because some man lost interest. These were not the women whose men beat them; these were ruined by neglect. And so they left the house the man had left, carrying what they could, leaving some things. They were not clever; they did not hold back; they held on.

She thought of Sally, wandering as well. She thought of all the women who had left their mothers for a man.

Her period was now six weeks overdue. She would have to see a doctor. She chose a name out of the phone book, looking in the Yellow Pages under G for gynecologist, then discovering she had to look under P for physician and then search the subheadings. She tried to find a hopeful name and settled on Hershcel Morgenstern. Morgenstern meant morning star; it was a good sign.

Increasingly, she lived in a world of portents: if the

faucet stopped dripping, she was not pregnant; if the
phone rang an even number of times, she was. And there
were those familiar trips to the bathroom to check herself
with Q-Tips. She forced herself to wait ten minutes between bathroom visits. But there was never anything to
be seen and her despair grew. What if I am, she would
say to herself, unnecessarily flushing the toilet, and then
always by the time she had reached the door, It isn't possible, it can't be.

But she had to see a doctor. Perhaps she was not pregnant but really ill. She lay in bed at night with a vision of
herself in white, tubes in her nose and arms and Robert's
face above her, stricken and regretful. What she would
have chosen for herself was a major illness. She would
like an invalid's life: long sleeps and simple foods and
friends who visited with flowers and jigsaw puzzles and
huge nineteenth-century books. She remembered the last,
the only time she had been in the hospital. It was the accident when Father Cyprian had not seen the other car
and she had hit her head. She remembered how Cyprian
had looked at her when he held her after the accident.
Never had she felt so loved, never had she been so treasured as when she opened her eyes and he could see she
was alive. Perhaps if she were really ill, she would see
Robert's face looking that way. Perhaps, opening her eyes
from anesthesia, she would see his face. He would be saying, "Thank God you're alive. I'll make everything up to
you."

She phoned the doctor, hoping she was terminally ill.
The nurse said she was lucky; there had been a cancella-
tion and she could come the next morning at ten o'clock.

Dr. Morgenstern was connected with Columbia Presby-
terian Hospital, and his office was in one of the large
buildings in the medical complex. She took the elevator
to the twenty-second floor. After she had given the receptionist her name, she looked out of the window at the city,
clear and accessible as a child's drawing of a city, spread-
ing out beneath her in a grounding of thin blue.

She waited in the paper dress the nurse had told her to
put on for the doctor. Her blood pressure was taken and
she was left alone. She had never been to a gynecologist
before, but she was not afraid. It was possible that she

was seriously ill. She had a right to be there; she could be dying.

Dr. Morgenstern walked into the room. He was aston- ishingly handsome, with crisp gray hair, a blue chalk- stripe suit. He left his white doctor's jacket open. She understood that he did not want to hide such beautiful tailoring. His stethoscope hung around his neck like an elegant, sophisticated charm that was all the rage in some place people went to ski in winter.

"What can I do for you, Miss Taylor?" he asked in a middle-European accent.

"My period is six weeks late."

"When was the last time you had sexual intercourse?"

"A few weeks ago."

"You have regular sexual contacts?"

"I suppose."

"Yes or no?"

"Yes," she said, and thought, "How odd, I'm a person who has regular sexual contacts."

He stuck his gloved hand up inside her. "And what will your boyfriend say when you tell him he is going to be a father?"

She sat up, pushing the doctor away with the force of her quick movement.

"That's impossible," she said.

"It is not only not impossible, it is a fact."

She lay back on the table and covered her face with the sheet that she had laid her head on.

"I can't have a baby," she said. She felt nauseated; the top of her head was in flames. It was not possible. She could not have something inside her that would one day be a child. That was not who she was. She thought of her mother, of her mother's face. "In trouble"—that was her mother's phrase for what had happened. And she saw her mother's anger and shame and Father Cyprian's anger and shame and his cold satisfaction that she had come to a bad end, as he had predicted.

"I can't have a baby," she said.

He was silent a minute.

"Perhaps it would be possible. We could check you into the hospital here if you could get a psychiatrist to say you were crazy. This is called a therapeutic abortion."

"I'm not crazy," she said. "I just don't want to have a baby."

"Do you go to a psychiatrist?"

"Of course not," Felicitas said indignantly. "I'm a perfectly normal person."

He wrote something on a piece of paper.

"If you can find a psychiatrist to swear that if you had a baby you would lose your mind, you can come back and I can put you in the hospital."

"How much would it cost?"

"Two thousand dollars."

She began to cry. "Where would I get two thousand dollars?"

He handed her a piece of paper. "I am afraid, Miss Taylor, there is nothing I can do for you. Please take this to the receptionist."

He left her alone in the room. She got dressed and gave the nurse the piece of paper, which was her bill. She paid in cash.

"Don't you want a receipt?" the receptionist called after her.

"No, thank you, you can keep it," said Felicitas, wishing to sound polite.

She walked the fifty blocks from 168th Street to the apartment, unbelieving, trying to catch her face in store windows, putting herself in profile. She looked no different to herself. Her face, always to her slightly comic, was still there. She always knew why people looked at her and wanted to laugh. She understood her face; she had always understood it. And her face was no different. So perhaps she wasn't pregnant.

The doctor had said she was, but they weren't always right. He had sent her urine specimen to the lab. Perhaps it would come back negative, and she would meet his embarrassed, sorry gaze with a serene punctiliousness. "Everyone makes mistakes," she would say to the haughty doctor, and his face would go sorrowful as he told her she was seriously ill.

But he had said there was no doubt of it, he could tell by the inside of her, the shape, the color. After all these years he ought to know, he had said. And she had never seen the inside of herself, so she did not know, he told her.

But she would not believe him. She saw her mother's face, the face of Father Cyprian, weeping, angry and betrayed. She had betrayed them all. They had placed their trust in her. And she had done this thing.

Perhaps they would never have to know about it. People had abortions. You were always reading in the *Daily News* about abortion rings some Irish cop had broken. And people wrote about them in novels.

Who could help her? If Sally hadn't left, she could have asked her. But as it was, of all the people she knew, she could not think of anyone to help her. She knew so few people: her mother and the women, Father Cyprian, Robert and Iris, Richard and Brad. She could not go to Robert or to Richard. It was clear to her that she had forfeited her right to the protection of paternity. Who would protect what he was not sure was his? Who would help a woman who was pregnant if he did not know that it was his seed, his act, his blood, that had put her in that condition?"

She was going to have a baby and she could not name its father. She felt her body fill with a dark shame, a shame she knew to be both ancient and profound. She was no longer herself; she was a pregnant woman. All the hard, skeletal edges of her personality, all the training that had made her mind a vessel that shone gold and silver, all the struggles of her character, all her concerns for history and for the shocking time she lived in, disappeared and she was one thing only: a pregnant woman with a child whose father was unknown.

She opened the apartment door. Iris was standing in the hall as if she had been waiting. When she saw Felicitas in tears, her face, which reduced itself to four quite clear expressions—fear, joy, sorrow and surprise—clouded over with a pure concern.

"Hey, what is it? Something's wrong, right?"

Felicitas shook her head.

"I'll bet there is something wrong or you wouldn't be all upset. Me, I'm always all upset, but you're not usually, so it must be something."

"It's okay, Iris, I'm okay," Felicitas said as firmly as she could.

"You're not pregnant or anything?"

A shock of terror ran through Felicitas. So it was visible. Everyone could tell.

"How do you know?"

"I go through your things a lot when you're not home. I fold your clothes in your drawers—you just roll them up—and I look at your books. So, like, I knew you were only using that crazy douche, and you were bound to get into trouble."

"Why didn't you say something?"

"I didn't want you to think I was prying."

'But you *were* prying."

"Yeah, but I didn't feel like I had a right to act on the information I got that way."

Felicitas was silent.

"Look, are you real upset?" Iris asked.

Felicitas began to cry again. Iris put her arm around her. "Go ahead and cry," she said. "It's good for you."

It was such a simple suggestion, such an old suggestion, that it touched her. She allowed herself to be pillowed on Iris. She saw no reason not to, for a while. But then she straightened up; she did not want to be crying in the arms of someone she did not take seriously, someone she had called a fool. It felt like theft to take her comfort.

"I know where you can get an abortion," Iris said.

"How?"

"I went. It's not so terrible. Then it's all over."

Felicitas saw her mother weeping with shame and then Father Cyprian's rigid, angry face.

"Can you help me, Iris?"

"Sure. You helped me out with my term papers."

Felicitas laughed. "Tit for tat."

"What does that mean?"

"It's something my mother says."

"You're really close to your mother."

Felicitas thought of her mother's warm, embracing arms, of the beautiful smell of her handkerchiefs. If she had a baby, her mother would never want to see her again and she would blame herself. For the rest of her life, Charlotte would consider herself a failure.

"That's why I have to have an abortion," Felicitas said.

"I'll help you. I know lots of people who have gone to this guy. But first I want to try this herbal stuff on you. The Indians use it to bring on abortion. I've kept it around. I thought it might come in handy."

"Okay," said Felicitas, "but give me that number."

"Sure," said Iris, "but first I'll make this brew. It might do the trick. And it's also a relaxant."

Felicitas sat down in the kitchen. Iris came back with a pouch of brownish powder. It had a vivid, potent, damaging smell. Perhaps it would work. She'd try anything. Tonight she would drink a bottle of gin as well.

Iris gave her the liquid in a white cracked mug, and Felicitas drank it as quickly as she could.

"Now go lie down," said Iris. "You never know, something might happen any minute. Those Indians."

She went into her room and opened her copy of *Pride and Prejudice*. "It is a fact universally acknowledged, that a single man in possession of a good fortune must be in want of a wife."

She closed her eyes and wept for all the parts of life that were closed to her forever now, since she was who she was and what had happened had happened to her.

It was a warm, unearthly day. The unseasonable weather and the darkness of the morning made her feel doomed. Yes, you are right to feel doom, she told herself, looking at the late hour on the clock's face. It is not a trick of atmosphere or weather, it is the nature of your life.

Now she was one of those girls whose fates, when she had heard of them or read about them, were distant, foreign, menacing but remote, almost fantastical, like the threat of chemical warfare or the return of Hitler. What happened to these girls? They were sent off to homes run by marginal, indefinite orders of nuns whose mission was to run houses where the girls gave birth in secret, where their babies were taken from them or kept from them, where births were met by no joy but by tears of anguish or a dull, unforgiving silence. And what did they come to, these creatures without husbands, without futures, with known histories that their time away had bleached of glamour? The dark and obscure births of these girls' babies were in no way connected to sex in the minds of those who thought of them; they were connected with punishment. So far away was pleasure from all the events that followed it that the births became almost miraculous, almost virgin births. dark where the Virgin's had been filled with light, all stain where hers had been immaculate.

Perhaps the doctor had made a mistake. She made herself a cup of coffee and called his office. But there was no mistake. The test was positive; she was going to have a child.

She would not have a child if she could never name its father. The unfixedness of the paternity of the child made her feel free to be rid of it. If it had no father, it was not really a baby. She knocked on Iris' door.

"What's new?" said Iris.

"The test came out positive."

"And that Indian stuff didn't work?"

"It didn't even make me feel sick."

"I wrote you the number of the abortion place. It's okay, real clean. It costs five hundred dollars."

"Oh," Felicitas said, taking the piece of paper with a phone number on it that Iris handed her.

"Do you have the money?"

"I have half of it," said Felicitas, thinking of the two hundred dollars her mother had given her for Christmas.

"What about Robert? He could give you some money."

"I don't want Robert to know. I don't know if it's his, and I don't want him to have anything to do with it."

Iris paused a minute. "I could lend you some money. My father sends me money all the time, and most of the time I don't even spend it."

"Thank you," said Felicitas. "I'd be very grateful."

"Only I think you should tell Robert. It's half his fault."

The pressure, the great darkness of the past days had pushed Robert from her mind entirely. She could no longer imagine herself as anyone interested in the attentions, the embraces of some man. It was an interest she had grown out of and she knew it to be finished, as one knows one has finished with the fear of horses or a taste for bubble gum. It had been an odd disease, her adoption of sexual interest, but it was over now. She would never be that person again. Now she was a person who had to have an abortion. After that, she did not know who she would be.

She waited until after lunch to call the number. The woman on the phone was businesslike and cheerful. Felicitas didn't know what she had expected—a disaster voice, a foreign voice—but she did not expect to hear a voice indistinguishable from the voice of Dr. Morgenstern's nurse.

"How far along are you?" asked the woman.

"Ten weeks."

"That's fine. That's nice and early. Just stand in front of the Loewey's movie theater at 242nd Street and Broadway the day after tomorrow at nine in the morning."

"That's all?"

"That's all, except you have to bring the money in small bills in an envelope."

"Why an envelope?"

"It makes it easy for us," the woman said. "You can bring a friend, but he can't come with you all the way."

"It doesn't matter," said Felicitas. She knew she would go alone.

It was only one o'clock and she had to get through the next forty hours. She couldn't bear to go to her classes. She decided she would go to movies until she was tired, and then she would sleep. She saw *Casablanca* at the Thalia at two and waited for the other half of the feature, *Smiles of a Summer Night*. At seven, she went to an East Side theater to see *M*A*S*H*, at nine she came back across town to see *The Owl and the Pussycat*. No one was home when she returned at eleven. She fell asleep quietly and slept deeply and well.

In the morning, Iris had to wake her at eleven-thirty. She brought Felicitas tea and toast in bed.

"I got the money out of the bank for you," she said, handing Felicitas an envelope.

"That's three hundred dollars," said Felicitas. "I only need two."

"I wanted you to have a little extra. In case something

comes up. Like in case you have to have a taxi or something."

"A hundred dollars for a taxi?"

"Well, in case something comes up."

"Thank you, I'll pay you back soon."

"It's okay," said Iris. "Usually I can't think of anything to do with the money my father sends me, except buy dope. I mean, Robert doesn't make me pay rent."

The name of Robert made them silent.

"We should do something weird today, you know, to get your mind off things. Something we wouldn't usually do."

"Like what?"

"I don't know, get stoned."

"Iris, you do that every day."

"Well, let's go to the thrift shop."

"What thrift shop?"

"There's this crazy lady I know, Russian or something, German maybe. She has this thrift shop on Ninety-third Street. Sometimes you can get real beautiful stuff there. Like my beaded evening bag and the silver mirror."

"I do like those things," said Felicitas.

"Well, let's go there, then. It's a really crazy place. Sometimes it takes up a whole day."

Felicitas walked beside Iris, enjoying the feeling of being a bad child, an imaginative child, playing hooky to spend the day with circus dancers. She rejected her own incessant, relentless seriousness, which she must have been born with. She had heard in her mind for as long as she could remember a voice that told her, "Everything you do matters too much." As a child, it had made her bored with other children, whom she had thought trivial and irresponsible and vague. As a young adolescent, she had had brief seasonal friendships, but they quickly paled and by the time she was in high school, she was happy again only in her old obsessions. The death of John Kennedy had made her even more sober. She had not come out of her serious inner life again until she met Robert.

But today she was playing in a more complete way than she had ever done, even as a child. She was grateful to Iris for having suggested this diversion—obviously she could never have thought of it herself and she saw her gratitude as one child's to another. It was a new emotion for her. As a child she had been grateful to no other child.

Iris chattered all the way to Ninety-third Street.

"Mrs. Markowitz was in a concentration camp. She kind of talks a lot, but I let her, and she likes me, and she gives me a lot of far-out stuff."

"Does she talk about being in a concentration camp?"

"No, she talks about being in Berlin in the twenties and being rich and having a lot of boyfriends."

"That must be wonderful," said Felicitas, who was romantic about middle-European women who had clearly sexual pasts followed by vaguely political ones.

"Yeah, except she's real lonely and tries to get me to stay for supper and go to movies and stuff."

"Do you ever?"

"Well, sometimes, but it's kind of creepy. I mean, her food's always a little moldy or old or something, and after a while she makes me feel a little weird."

Iris turned the handle on the door of a shop called the Treasure Chest. It was a dark hovel of incredible disorder, and the smell of age and rejection was heavy in the brown air.

"Yes, hello," said a foreign voice from the back of the store.

"Hi, Mrs. Markowitz," Iris shouted. "It's me. I brought my friend Felicitas. She's got to have an abortion tomorrow, so we're trying to think of ways to cheer ourselves up."

"Ah, my God," shouted the still-disembodied voice, "you poor thing. Terrible things men do to us. Myself, I had four abortions in Berlin—1922, 1924, two in 1927. There was a man, a foot doctor, what do you call them?"

"Podiatrist," shouted Felicitas to the voice in the back, "or chiropodist. I'm not sure which is more correct."

"Well, anyway, this man, this podiatrist, he would do abortions for you. Very clean, very nice. At one point, he wanted to marry me. But after all that between us, I couldn't see it."

"Got anything new that's good, Mrs. Markowitz?" shouted Iris.

The woman appeared, barely five feet tall, in velvet shoes, wearing a black wool dress, a yellow jewel at her neck and a russet turban. "I got something beautiful that would fit your friend," she said. "A real Chanel suit. 1945, maybe. Too small for you, Iris. American girls are so big. Too big, I think. You're a little one, like me," she said, pinching Felicitas' cheek.

Felicitas did not like the woman touching her. Was this what they were like in Berlin in the twenties? She had imagined tortured, passionate women, disdainful and exacting, tall and slender and high-strung. Not someone like Mrs. Markowitz. But perhaps this was what age did to passionate women.

"Try these on, too," said Iris, bringing a pair of classic black pumps. "I'm going to try on this long dress, this red satin strapless one, and these clear plastic shoes."

"Go on, darling, you know where," said Mrs. Markowitz.

Iris led the way to two curtained booths. She gave Felicitas the clothes she had selected for her.

"Try them on, they're real far out," she said.

Felicitas put the clothes on without looking. She felt as if she had walked into a hypnotist's parlor. She would be unable here to refuse to do anything that anyone suggested.

The suit's silk lining felt luxurious and wicked on her skin. Never had a garment fit her better. She felt queer. Perhaps she was wearing the clothes of someone dead. She went outside to look at herself in the mirror.

She was astonished at the way she looked. For the first time in her life, she looked like an adult. It was unfortunate the clothes were out of date, for it made them less sober, and these were serious clothes. They were moral clothes. They were the first clothes she had ever worn that expressed, she felt, her inner nature. But now she could not wear them in the street without being comic, even perhaps ridiculous.

"How are they?" Iris asked, still in her booth.

"I like them. How are yours?"

"Really far out." She opened the curtain. She did not look serious at all. Felicitas laughed.

"I really like it," Iris said. "I'm going to buy it."

"Where will you wear it?"

"Oh, around. I don't know. Someday I might be into wearing it all the time. Wait a minute," she said to Felicitas. In a second she was back, handing her a hat, a stiff arc of green feathers. "Try it on," she said.

"As my mother would say, 'It's a real outfit,'" Felicitas said. She had to pretend not to take seriously her own reflection. She and Iris stood next to each other, giggling at themselves in the mirror.

"How are my darlings today?" asked Mrs. Markowitz.

"Great," said Iris. "How much for all this stuff?"

"Twenty dollars, sweetheart."

"We'll take it. I'll treat," said Iris.

"Oh, Iris, you've spent so much money on me already."

"This is for fun," she said. "Let's go somewhere fancy and have a drink. You know, like somewhere from a forties movie. What place is there like that?"

"I don't know. The Stork Club?"

"Yeah," said Iris, dancing around, "let's go to the Stork Club."

They paid Mrs. Markowitz and ran laughing out of the store.

"Let's take a taxi," said Iris. "In the movies they were always taking taxis."

"Okay," said Felicitas, too disbalanced to refuse anything.

"The Stork Club," said Iris to the driver. They laughed the fifty blocks downtown. When they got there, the doorman bowed and let them in. They sat down seriously at the bar.

"What should we have to drink?" asked Iris.

"Martinis," said Felicitas, who had seen more movies than Iris. "Two martinis, very dry," she said to the bartender.

He said nothing, serving them silently, as if he served people like them every day.

"How do you feel? About the abortion and all?" asked Iris.

Felicitas was shocked to realize that it had been three hours since she had thought about it.

"Well, it's a very terrible thing," she said.

"I'm sorry I brought it up. Let's not think about it. Let's get drunk. In the movies women got drunk at the Stork Club, right? Even classy ones. Like Bette Davis and Joan Crawford."

"Yes, but they were never pregnant."

"Well, pretend you're not. Let's pretend our husbands both got killed in the war."

Felicitas laughed. She crossed her legs and looked at her shoes. "Do you think it made people different, wearing shoes like this and the men wearing hats all the time?"

"Probably they were a lot more uptight," said Iris.

"Do you think they were happier?"

"My parents weren't happy. And they wore clothes like these. My mother tried to kill herself in 1946."

"That's terrible."

"She tried to do it again when I was seven. I came into the bathroom and found her lying with her wrists bleeding into the sink."

"Poor Iris," said Felicitas, thinking of her own mother, who was never sick, never even got colds.

"It's no wonder I'm fucked up," said Iris, staring fishily into her drink.

"You're a good person, Iris, you have a good heart."

"Yeah, but I'm not very together."

"Yeah, a lot of people who are together aren't very nice."

"You're nice and you're together," said Iris almost resentfully.

"I used to be," said Felicitas and began crying into her drink. The two of them cried into their drinks, then ordered two more so they could go on crying into them. After they had finished four martinis and had talked and wept in their anachronistic clothes until they were beginning to be bored with drunken revelation, they staggered to the door, teetering on their unaccustomed high heels. The doorman got them a taxi, as someone like him had gotten taxis for the women Dorothy Parker wrote about. And that was how they felt riding home, falling asleep in their false clothes. They fell into two purely drunken sleeps in which they dreamed themselves misused, unkindly handled by men in hats who did not pay for taxis.

Felicitas awoke at six with a dry mouth and an aching head. It took her a few minutes to remember that this was the day of her abortion.

She thought she should take a bath, so she ran the water in the old discolored tub, where rust stains made a henna-colored path down the white porcelain wall from tap to drain. She helped herself to Iris' bubble bath and stayed in the tub for forty minutes, letting the water out as it grew cold, letting new hot water in until her fingertips were wrinkled and sweat broke out on her upper lip. She was too miserable to focus her mind on anything. For the first time she lay in the bath without wishing it was a place where one could comfortably read a book.

She thought of wearing her Chanel suit, but she was afraid they would think her too odd and turn her away. She dressed in one of the jumpers and turtlenecks she had worn habitually before she met Robert.

At seven-thirty she was ready to leave. Iris had said she would go with her, but she looked so vulnerable and so unhealthy in her sleep that Felicitas did not want to wake her. Besides, she was afraid that if Iris came along, she would say something indiscreet.

When she got out of the subway at 242nd Street, she saw the movie theater instantly. There were two people, a man and a woman, standing in front of it, and she could tell by their uneasy posture that they were waiting for the same person she was, the unknown person who would take them to the unknown place. It had the elements of a bad spy drama, the furtive looks, the secret destinations. She wanted to say something to the couple. But there was nothing for her to say.

They were in their thirties, skinny, with brutalized thin hair that she wore in a ponytail and he wore greased close to his head. They both wore black raincoats and they both smoked unfiltered cigarettes that they threw down, still lit and still unfinished, on the sidewalk at their feet. Felicitas could tell which butts were the woman's because they were stained by the orange of her lipstick. She was sure that lipstick had some edible, tropical name: Hawaiian Melon, Mango Moon.

A black car drove up and a man also wearing a black raincoat got out. He was plump and enterprising-looking, his mien was vaguely and peripherally medical; he might have sold elastic stockings or dental supplies.

"You here about the operation?" he asked.

For the first time, Felicitas regretted being alone. But

who would she have wanted with her? It would have been pitiable to have brought a female companion, and there was no man she could in honor ask.

"Things are a little held up there, so we'll have to kill some time," said the driver. "We'll go into this coffee shop for a while. Only you girls shouldn't drink anything but seltzer."

"Fuck that, I'm dying for a cup of coffee," said the woman in the ponytail.

"Okay, it's your funeral," said the driver.

"Watch your language," said the man.

In the coffee shop, the couple sat next to each other and Felicitas sat next to the driver. Abruptly the woman looked at Felicitas and asked, "You married?"

Felicitas had been silent for so many hours that she found it difficult to speak. "No," she said.

"We're married," said the woman, "but not to each other."

The couple laughed. This was obviously one of the emblems of their courtship. Felicitas laughed, too. It made her feel less lonely

"You ever been pregnant, you ever done this before?" asked the woman.

"No," said Felicitas.

"Well, don't worry about it. It's not as bad as they tell you. It's not as bad as having a baby."

"Thank you," said Felicitas, trying not to cry.

"You're just a baby yourself," the woman said. "It's a goddamn shame. What'd the guy do, run out on you when he found out?"

"No," said Felicitas, "He's out of the country."

"Always something," said the woman. "I'll keep an eye on you. I'll go first. You'll see, it isn't so bad."

"Drink up, girls," said the driver. "I think they're about ready for us."

He drove back on some of the streets they had just driven. Felicitas wondered if the idea of the coffee shop was simply a device to keep them from memorizing the route.

The driver stopped the car in front of a prosperous-looking apartment building and showed them to apartment number 5 on the second floor. In the living room there were three woman, sitting on orange chairs, in various stages of distress. Felicitas was surprised to see how middle class the setting was: the domesticated furniture, the well-dressed clients. She wondered what she had expected—gangsters' molls and farmers's daughters, wracked and syphilitic-mad *chanteuses?*

The woman in the ponytail let herself down heavily into one of the chairs. Felicitas took the chair beside her. One woman who was wearing a navy-blue pants suit and was obviously used to being a hostess smiled a practiced smile and said hello to the two newcomers. Felicitas expected her to produce a plate of canapés.

This was not the kind of room where anything had ever been laid down in haste or carelessness. Like all waiting rooms, it had not been genuinely inhabited; it had the look more legitimate medical ante-chambers had of restless and resentful tenancies. Felicitas knew—and it was a relief—that she would not stick her hand between the cushions of the chair she sat on and discover rumpled Kleenex or lost coins. Every day, when the day's business was done, someone went through this room to make sure there was not a scrap of evidence left behind. They had to be ready for police, who might come at any time with dogs and searchlights, clubs and ropes. The police could walk into this room and bring them all to jail. Every woman sitting there could give birth in half a year or more inside the dark and septic walls of a prison infirmary.

The driver, who had disappeared into a back room, now entered the waiting room. He clapped his hands jovially, like an M.C. at a provincial magic show.

"Okay, ladies," he said and sat behind the desk. "Why don't you just come up here one at a time and take care of the formalities before Dr. Rodriguez speaks to you individually? Now, who was here first?"

The woman in the blue pants suit walked over to him.

"Do you have your envelope?"

She gave it to him, smiling once again her gracious smile.

He counted the money and smiled back at her.

"Next?"

A thin woman whose hair was several shades of blond,

whose skin looked permanently damaged by some ailment, clearly nervous in its origin, came forward and handed the driver her envelope without having to be asked.

The third woman did not have her money in an envelope. Her hair was held back ineffectively by a clip; one strand of it kept falling forward and she kept brushing it back. Felicitas was sure she had not even made a stab at birth control; she found her the most sympathetic person in the room. She had a clear, translucent skin that suggested that when she spoke, it would be with some kind of accent. But she also looked as if she might not speak at all.

Next at the desk was the woman whom Felicitas had arrived with. She swaggered to the desk with a bravado that none of the others had been able to match. The driver gave her the same smile he had given the others. Nothing moved him, neither fear nor grace nor dash. She supposed she liked him for that. How awful it would have been had he had favorites.

Felicitas was the youngest in the group by at least ten years. She thought it was appropriate that she should, for that reason, go last. It made her seem less brash and less demanding. Her generation was always being criticized for those attitudes lately. She was glad to be doing her part to dispel that bad image. She was glad to be able to be polite.

After the driver had collected Felicitas' envelope and given her the smile, he disappeared into the back room once again and came out, this time with a small, depressed Hispanic man who wore his medical whites with the solemnity of a French first communion child before the First World War.

"This is Dr. Rodriguez," said the driver. "He was a very prominent doctor in his own country, but he has a lot of trouble learning English. He's bad at languages, which is why he's able to help you ladies out today."

The woman in the blue pants suit made a sympathetic clucking noise.

"Dr. Rodriguez would like you to write the date of your last period on a piece of paper. I'll collect them."

The women fished in their handbags for paper and

pencil, quickly wrote the numbers and folded the papers in the same spirit. But nothing could have been less playful than the doctor's face as he looked at the slips of paper, shaking his head at each with genuine grief, as if not one had come up with the combination of numbers he needed to mark his deliverance. He signaled to the driver.

"You were first, I think," the driver said to the woman in the blue pants suit. She stood up and walked graciously and efficiently to the back room. She *would* be first, Felicitas said to herself with annoyance, then regretted her failure of solidarity.

"This the first for all of you?" asked the woman who had come in the car with Felicitas.

"First abortion. But five kids. I'm not about to do it again. No way. My husband had a conniption fit," said the woman with several shades of blond hair.

"I have one child," said the woman with the interesting complexion, "but I'm divorced."

"I should be divorced," said Felicitas' companion, "but I'm biding my time." She cocked her head at Felicitas. "This little one's brand new at it."

The women looked at Felicitas with sympathy.

"I swear I don't know why we go through it. I'm going to tell that guy in there to sew it up while he's at it," said the blond woman.

The woman in the ponytail, Felicitas' friend, laughed loudly. Felicitas looked at the pale woman with concern; her face registered the alarm Felicitas felt.

"Do you think he's really a doctor?" she asked Felicitas.

"Don't ask," said the blonde.

"He's sober and he's clean, which is more than you can say for a lot of doctors," said the woman in the ponytail. "Count your blessings."

They had exhausted their conversation and had begun to look around the room for diversion. The blond woman had brought needlepoint: she began threading a needle with yellow thread. Felicitas' friend picked up a copy of *Reader's Digest* from the coffee table. The pale woman looked out the window, but she did it with such an air of custom that Felicitas was sure she would have been doing it at this hour of the morning whatever her situation, wherever she was.

In twenty minutes, the woman in the pants suit came out. The doctor showed her to the cot, where she lay and covered herself with a white blanket.

"You rest ten minutes," he said in heavily·accented English and bowed before he went inside again. The blond woman stood up and followed him.

"How was it?" asked the woman with the ponytail.

"Not as bad as I thought," said the woman in the pants suit, who looked as if she had combed her hair before coming out. "And the relief is worth it."

They grew silent so that she could sleep. The pale woman at the window began wringing her hands.

That was a gesture that Felicitas could not allow herself: the formal and accustomed signal of despair, the public and historical acknowledgment, the rhythmic and habitual acceptance of helplessness, of supplication in defeat. But, of course, the situation was desperate. They must not think of it. They had all said that to themselves: "We must not think of it." Except this woman, pale and sheltered, who was looking out of the window, obviously for some man to give her hope. The others had given up hope and had grown inventive: they made rude jokes; they carried needlepoint. No man would save them. They were beyond all that; perhaps they no longer wanted it.

Another half-hour went by. The woman in the pants suit was taken outside by the driver; the blond woman came out from the back room and took her place on the cot. The pale woman moved away from the window and walked toward the back room. She tried to get Felicitas' eye, but Felicitas would not look up at her. She knew it was a negligence she would regret for the rest of her life, but she could not afford to ally herself with the one weak person in the room, the one woman who waited for outside rescue, the one poor soul. The doctor closed the door. Inside the room, the woman could be heard weeping.

Felicitas stared at the door, but it revealed no activity, and in a second she gave up the expectation that the woman would come running out, that the silence would be broken by a cry, a scream, a bloody rush.

"That one's nervous as a cat," said the woman in the ponytail.

Felicitas did not know what to say, so absorbed was she in her own betrayal of the woman.

"What about you?"

Felicitas shrugged. "I'm trying not to think about it."

"That's easy for me. I never think about anything. That's what I'm doing here."

Felicitas laughed.

"So, you go to school or what?"

"College," said Felicitas.

"I want my kids to go to college. Think they will?"

"Sure," said Felicitas.

"They're smart kids. Especially the oldest. Takes after his father. A lot of good it did him, though. I'm no better, I'm a bitch. What can you do these days? They take kids in college without money?"

"They could go to the City University. Or they could get a scholarship."

"You have to be awful smart to get a scholarship. I don't know if they're that smart. I mean, they're smart enough, but I don't know if they're that smart."

"I have a scholarship."

"But you're real smart. I can tell. So how'd you get yourself into this mess? Don't tell me, it doesn't take brains." She looked at the door. "It's taking her longer than the others."

"I hope she's all right," said Felicitas.

"She's all right. That type always is," said the woman. The blonde on the cot snorted.

Five minutes later, the woman did come out the door, radiant, saying she didn't need to lie down.

"You lie down," said the doctor, "till I come back."

"Okay," she said flirtatiously.

"Ready for me?" the woman in the ponytail asked.

"Ready as we'll ever be," said the driver.

"Keep an eye on my purse," she said to Felicitas, winking.

Now Felicitas was all alone in the room except for the pale woman on the couch. No one had spoken while lying on the couch; perhaps they were in too much pain. Felicitas did not want to ask the pale woman if she was in pain. She did not want to know what was going to happen to her. She tried to read her book, *Labor Elites*. It was very dull. But she was far behind in her courses. She could still do well if she worked very hard for the rest of the term. She felt that if she could get good grades this time, it would make up for her having become pregnant. She couldn't bear to upset her mother with bad grades: that was why she was here, so people wouldn't be upset. That was why she was waiting for the woman in the ponytail to come out, so she could go in and have everything all over with.

The door opened quickly. The woman in the ponytail came into the room, not walking like the others but leaning heavily on the driver's arm. He pulled her to the door. There was blood on the floor where she walked.

"I have to lie down," she begged the driver.

He went on pulling her to the door.

"You have to get out of here, miss, that's what you have to do. I'll take you to your friend. He's on the corner, waiting. He'll know what to do with you. He'll take you to the hospital. They'll take care of you. We can't have you in here."

"Please let me lie down," she said.

"Come on, lady, don't waste time," he said, dragging her to the door, which he banged shut.

The pale woman seemed to have fallen asleep. Dr. Rodriguez appeared at the door, looking tortured by grief.

"Complications," he said. "Not good."

"Will she be all right?" asked Felicitas.

He shrugged and turned his palms up to the air, as if he was about to make some kind of folk statement about the weather.

"Come on, miss, next," he said.

Someone had made a footprint in the blood that had come from the woman's body. The print had repeated itself to the door. Felicitas stared, trying to discover if it was the woman stepping in her own blood or the driver, pulling her so that she could not be incriminating evidence.

The pale woman asleep on the cot was lying with her mouth open, her hands folded over her breast. And then Felicitas saw it: all the dead women, hacked and bled, eyes closed in a violent death because they preferred to die rather than to give birth. She saw the woman in the ponytail left by the driver in the parking lot alone, the man who came with her frantic, searching while she died, thinking it was his fault.

And she could see herself there, dying in the back of a movie theater, in the ladies' room in the subway. She could feel herself losing her life. She could see herself exposed in a room where the green walls closed down on her and her eyes closed and she bled her life out because the womb *was* full of blood, and fragile. She looked at the poor sad doctor.

"I'm sorry," she said. "I've changed my mind."

She turned and ran out the door, ran out of the building and onto the street. For a moment she felt relief. She had escaped death, she was alive, she was moving, she was not in pain. And then the truth of what she had done came to her clearly. She would have to have a baby now.

The apartment was completely empty. She took all the things out of her drawers and closet and put them into the two suitcases that belonged, really, to Clare. She left what she thought she could not carry easily: her quilt, her winter coat, her pictures.

She walked down the stairs. She could hear the dogs whimpering in Richard and Brad's apartment. She opened the door. The dogs had not been let out in days. They cried with pleasure and relief to see her. They jumped and ran in circles. Anger flooded her: her first just anger in some time. It was a cleansing and energizing force. She took the leash from the hook where it hung beside the door, hooked the dogs together and with some difficulty balanced her two suitcases and the three dogs. She went to the corner and hailed a cab.

"Can you take me to Brooklyn? Will you take these dogs?"

"Sure, if we can get past the demonstrators." The driver pointed up Broadway.

She heard a distant roar of voices, deep and faint as voices at sea. A band of marchers walked down Broadway. She could not see the signs they held, and so radical had been the isolation of her last few days that she had no idea what the march was about. She asked the driver.

"We've invaded Cambodia," he said.

She put her head down on the rich fur of the dogs' warm necks. She wept, for herself, for the world, for human helplessness. She was helpless before history; she was helpless before the condition of her own body. She wondered if she should stop the cab and join the marchers.

But there was no place for her among them. She was going to have a child.

PART III

1977

Felicitas

It was because of the bats that I decided to marry.

The attic of our house was infested with bats. The smell filtered down, until even we—who for our own good had learned to ignore disasters until it was too late to ignore them any longer—admitted that something had to be done. The smell cut into our lives; there were days when nothing was free of it. And yet we carefully avoided mentioning anything, out of some fairy-tale logic, for we knew that the first to speak would have to be the first to act. Cyprian was in the hospital. We were afraid he was dying. We were alone; we were women. We decided to be silent. Except my daughter Linda. Daily, not less than three times a day for a week, she would say, "Something stinks in here." It was not I who taught her this diction, but her friends. And so I vowed not to discourage it, vowed even to adopt it. She is an only child, born and reared in odd circumstances; I worry endlessly that she will not have friends.

"Nothing really stinks," I would say to her in that careful, charmless tone we use when we are lying to our children.

But I couldn't keep it up. And because I was Linda's mother, and Linda was the only one talking about the stink, I was the one who acted. And then everyone felt free to speak.

"It's some kind of dead animal. But it's that smell that smells too much like fruit to be an animal," said Elizabeth.

"Not an animal," said Muriel. "It smells like some kind of gas."

"Mustard gas," said my mother. "Mustard gas was yellow. People were good for nothing after that. Just one

241

whiff and they turned into vegetables. Nobody ever talks about the First World War. Even now, the veterans' hospitals are full of them."

"I wish we could find its exact location," said Clare.

"That's the trouble with this house," said Muriel. "Always something. I've never had this kind of trouble with my house."

"Let's look for it," said Linda. "It will be quite interesting."

Linda is not the sort of child who expects the worst. If she sees mud, she does not, as I did, imagine quicksand. Thunder is simply thunder, not the vision of the house burnt down or blown away. A tree is not a trap to break your neck in. She is mine, but not mine. When I catch her in unreasoned fear, my kind of fear, I clap my hand over her mouth, as if she were being impertinent or blasphemous. So she is the kind of child who thinks that looking for the invisible odor that has taken over our lives would be "quite interesting."

Quite interesting. These are my words. I try to replace them with words of her friends. I listen hard to the speech of her playmates; I spend days mastering their tics and fashions.

"Tough," I say. "It'll be a tough thing to do. Looking for the trouble in the attic."

"Tough as a moose and twice as loose," says Linda, imitating Cheryl, sister of her friend Linda Morrissey.

"Tough as a moose and twice as hairy," I say, imitating Cheryl's friend Cathy, who at twelve has a thirty-six-inch bust.

We open the attic door. And discover them. Bats. They fly around us. I hear their wings cut air. I recognize the sound: it is fear, the unfamiliar. I can see their black wings through the blacker air. I can see their brown mouse faces disappearing. Those black wings, those disappearing faces are all I fear. At the same time, they are a comfort. We are safe: it is only animals. However nightmarish they are, at least we have not imagined them. And they are better than a killing gas. We needn't fear the consequences of our ordinary actions. We needn't fear the lighting of a match, the banging of the oven door. It is animals, and ones that we have heard of. It's only bats, I say to the women downstairs.

"They're weird," says Linda. "Yucky," she lies. She is delighted.

"Mothballs," says Cyprian when I tell him, in the hospital.

Cyprian is right; I read about bats in the library and I call the County Extension Service. But he is glad to have thought of a solution that will make me go to the hardware store, that will require the help of Leo Byrne. Leo Byrne is the man I will marry, but I didn't know that until the episode of the bats. He had asked me to marry him a year before, but I refused him. We went on with our lives with no unease, without even a noticeable change of manners.

Leo's movements are slow, and I am not sure he isn't stupid. Even now, preparing to be his wife, having snuck into the folding bed in his trailer for eighteen months, having done business with him for seven years, I don't know whether or not he is stupid. Oh, I know he is: there is deep down in him a perfect misconception of the world; there is knit into the fabric of his bones a slowness so complete I marvel that his hands work.

And yet I can't say if he is stupid or not, if those pauses are genuine, if it really takes him that much time to fish up strings of thought, old tires, boots of thought, before he gives his answers. For, you see, his answers often have a wisdom that I don't want to admit has anything in it of the intellectual. Often when Leo speaks, it seems as if a tree spoke, as if rocks gave out weather reports. Or —I don't want to say it—as if a beast had learned conversation. His gestures have the depth of an ox's lowing, and the comfort. In the medieval plays I like to read, I like best the Nativity. Always a point is made by someone you know you can trust about animals, about the animals' warm breath warming the Infant. I will marry Leo because I think he will keep Linda from danger. In its oxordinariness, his breath will keep her safe.

The wisdom of the dumb, of animals, has its terrible lapses. Leo loves guns, for example: he does not believe in gun control, although above his bed there are colored photographs of both dead Kennedys. To hear him try to defend himself on the issue of gun control is at once touching and grotesque, like the Special Olympics, in which victims of cerebral palsy shoot baskets from their wheelchairs. No gun is as deadly as my deadly tongue when I uncover, shattering flesh, the sweet kernel of his stupidity. And yet he says things no one else remembers to say. Often he tells the one part of the truth without which all truth is a lie.

For instance, he was the only one who told me I would have to kill the bats with a shovel and then clear their droppings out of the attic. Cyprian suggested mothballs, as did the County Extension agent, but neither of them told me what would happen after that, that the bats, disoriented, having left the attic, would lie on the ground flapping, poisonous, unable to fly because they must drop from something in order to fly and I had made the environs of their perches uninhabitable. Only Leo knew what would happen, and when he told me I didn't believe him.

When he sold me the mothballs, he told me I would have to go out early the next morning, for the bats would be out on the lawn. Nonsense, I said, if that was true, Cyprian or the County Extension agent would have told me. Do it for my sake, he said. Get up at dawn and see if they're there. If they are, you'll have to hit them with a shovel, and make sure you get them, every one, and crush their skulls because they may be rabid, and you know how your little one likes not to wear her shoes.

Because Leo had been my lover for eighteen months, I did what he said the morning after I scattered the mothballs around the attic. So strong, so piercing was that smell that I believed it would overcome everything. I doubted Leo; I thought I had done enough.

But I did as he asked. I woke at five. The grass was gray green with wetness, the sky, grown waxy with light, took on some color; gold came through, then a throaty, embarrassing red. And in that operatic light, changing like music as I walked, I saw them. Devils. They were blind, they flapped; they had no eyes, they opened their scarlet mouths; they made no noise. Then they hissed; they showed their teeth, the teeth of movie vampires, small and theatrical. I forced myself to count. There were sixteen bats, trying to lift themselves off the ground, trying, failing, bringing their wings together in desperation, raising themselves an inch, two inches, then falling. They moved their heads around, following me as I walked, as if they could see me. I thought of Linda's feet, her round translucent toenails, rose-colored, like shells, the perfect circle of her heels, her soles, tough but no match for all this.

They were all I hoped to keep her from. Terrified, I picked my shovel up and walked toward them. Then I heard a car come up the road. It was Leo. He got out of the car, holding a shovel identical to mine. Silently we walked onto the lawn where the bats lay. We crushed each body with the underside of our shovels and wandered carefully to be sure more had not hidden in the grass.

Leaning on my shovel, I turned to him. "You still want to get married?" I asked him.

"Sure," he said.

I am marrying him partly for silence. God knows there have been silences enough in the houses we have built here on this property, but they have been female silences, dreamy or murderous, or the menacing silence of the one man here. Leo's is the silence of a man who finds the physical world truly absorbing. It is the only male silence that isn't dangerous. Is it unusual, my sense of danger? Surely all women are born knowing the men they love could kill them in a minute, that we are kept alive by kindness, that we are always in peril. This is the source of our desire for obedience, fo the inherited knack, the alert readiness—even in women who rage or live their lives in solitude—for giving in.

It is for shelter that we marry and make love. For years, the first years of Linda's life, I tried to use my body, my own soul, as a shelter against life. And she was life. I closed my heart to her. I would not give her the milk in my breasts. Having given her life, I offered her no other kindness.

There are some neglectful acts for which there can be no forgiveness: the damage is too great. I neglected Linda; I neglected her shamefully, but she is all right. I have read that a mother's rejection can cause autism and schizophrenia, can create a child of violent rages who commits small acts of cruelty, which later, when the child's physical strength is greater, grow into assassinations, anonymous murders, sex crimes of such monstrosity that we forget the details. Now, of course, I think of the mothers of these criminals with understanding. I think of mothers who leave their babies in shopping bags in the post office, like any other parcel wrongly sent. I understand mothers who starve their children, who beat them, who allow them to live in their own filth. It is life they want to starve, to torture, to abandon. Life that was once their life. They speak of the betrayal birth is for a child, but what of the mother who, until then, simply by being herself, with no more patience or intelligence required than the growth of hair demands, effects a perfect nurturance, a home the child will yearn for all its life?

And then the child is born. Desired or not, it is still full of need, and the mother, looking down at the child in her arms, knows she is unnatural as the sweat breaks out on her lip, as, when the child pulls at her breast, she feels that she will die of boredom. I understand mothers who want to take their babies' lives. It is life they must punish, for cheating them, for trapping them in the oldest trick in the world, the female body; for telling them, often children themselves, "You are tied to this life now; your life is over." The miracle is that so few do it. That I did not has nothing to do with me. That Linda is alive is a miracle, but not of instinct. Not of my instinct, in any case. She was kept alive by my mother and her friends, people who had rigorously worked to banish instinct from their lives. They circled her, they warmed her with their breath when I couldn't bear the touch of her skin. They said, as if they knew, "Later you will want her. Later it will be all right."

As if they knew the terrible hunger of love that overcomes me now at the sight of her, even of the top of her head, which I see from the second-story window where I sit, the panes reflecting the blue bowl of apples, reflecting the late summer roses I have picked for the green vase, and touch the glass that lets through the clear image of my little girl.

The day I came home in the taxi with the three dogs, my mother, as she said later, knew something was up. We had never had a dog, and I arrived with three golden retrievers on a complicated leash. I stood in the doorway, ill with misery, and the dogs lay miserably at my feet. My mother, whose instincts are always perfect, said, "Home for the weekend?"

I was so distressed that I sat on the floor. This was not a gesture for a person like my mother to accept without remark.

"You look tired," she said. "Are you sick?"

And, making the most heartless statement of my life, I said to my mother, "I'm pregnant."

"Get up," she said, in her irritated, not her desperate, voice. "And get those goddamn dogs out of the kitchen."

My mother is not a fastidious woman. I've always suspected that at that moment she held the dogs responsible for my pregnancy.

I took the dogs into my almost bare bedroom. My mother followed me.

"How could you be pregnant? Someone like you, for God's sake."

"I just am," I said.

"You can't be," she said. She left the room and closed the door as if she had disposed of the problem.

I lay on my bed and fell asleep. In an hour I was awakened by my mother's knocking at the door.

"I made chili," she said. "What do they eat?" She pointed to the dogs, as if they were members of a sect with strange but rigid dietary laws.

"Dog food," I said, in the listless voice I used for two years after that.

"Well, come and have something to eat first. Then you can get something for them."

I walked to the table, the dogs following me.

"They always follow you like that?" my mother asked.

"They have nowhere else to go," I said.

"That's a very bright answer. Very smart. That's the kind of thing they teach you in college nowadays."

She put a bowl of chili in front of me.

"I'm not hungry," I said.

"Chili is good when you have no appetite. All those spices get the juices going."

I ate for a while to please her. After we had finished our silent meal, she said, "I should never have let you go up there to Columbia. I should have known they'd take advantage of you."

"Nobody took advantage of me, Mother."

"Then how did you get in this condition?" she said through her teeth.

"I got into this condition because I used the wrong kind of birth control."

"Don't talk about that in this house."

I had forgotten: in my mother's canon, practicing birth control was worse than having sex.

"Whose is it?" she asked. "That goddamn professor, right?"

"I'm not sure."

"Don't try and protect him. I know *you*."

"I'm not sure whose it is, Mother. I slept with two people. I'm not sure which one is the father."

"Fine," said my mother. "Very nice. Just beautiful."

That was the last she has ever spoken about the father of my child. There was not a word of forced marriages, not a mention of paternity suits. Which is remarkable, since she is, if nothing else, a woman who believes in convention, whose imagination has been nourished by the reports of blood tests of the stars, huge sums won by victim-women forcing admission through the law.

"We'll have to go away someplace and have it," she said.

This was the beginning of her entirely appropriate use of the first person plural in relation to my pregnancy. Over time, she took on all but the responsibilities it was physically impossible for me to relinquish.

"Should we tell anybody or just go away?" she asked.

It had never occurred to me that the whole thing could be kept a secret. But I hadn't even thought about people's good opinion. Whatever happened, my life was over.

"We have a while to think about it," she said. "I can't think straight when you throw this kind of thing at me. What are you going to do about those dogs?"

"I'll keep them in my room."

"There's not enough room for one dog, no less three," she said, in her angriest tone so far.

"They're used to being crowded. They've spent their whole lives in an apartment."

"The city is no place for dogs that size."

"I'll walk them a lot."

"I can just hear Cyprian," my mother said, looking suddenly worried. "What do you think he'll say about this piece of news?"

"Maybe he doesn't have to know."

We sat at the table, frozen in fear, imagining Cyprian's face, his voice, his terrible accusing eyes. Imagining, worst of all, his disappointment.

"Who do you think he'll blame?" my mother asked. "Not you, of course."

"Why not me?"

"He always blames me. He always has."

"For what?"

"Forget it. For everything. For living. For marrying your father."

"Maybe he won't have to know."

"Maybe it'll be Christmas in July."

I don't know if it was that night that my mother called Clare, but she was there the next morning when I woke up.

"The important thing is to get a good doctor," she said. "Forget about O'Hara."

"He's all right," said my mother.

"He's not all right for this kind of thing," said Clare.

She took out her address book, a beautiful morocco leather, with thin pages gilded on the top and a little ribbon, as in a missal.

"This is the man that did my operation. He does obstetrics too. He's very good."

"I'll bet he costs an arm and a leg. Look at that address," said my mother.

"Don't worry about that part of it," said Clare. "You have enough to worry about."

I knew it was decided: I was going to keep the baby. I believe that was the last clear thought I had for seven months.

I went to Clare's doctor, an elegant, well-dressed, tactful man. He called me Mrs. Taylor and made not a single reference to a husband in the half dozen times I saw him. But in the end he didn't deliver the baby, because in the fifth month of my pregnancy, plans changed, or rather the real plan was formulated, the plan that we are now living out.

No one could see that I was pregnant and it gave us all false hope. All of us who knew, that is—myself, my mother, Elizabeth and Clare. We didn't tell Mary Rose; she was spending a lot of time with Joe Siegel, and we were afraid the news would reflect badly on her and make Joe think he was making a bum connection. We all knew, or thought we knew, the hazards of keeping up a romantic relationship with no consummation in sight. We believed, wrongly, that the balance of their alliance was delicate. And I think that despite our practical steps, we had a magic feeling that if my pregnancy was not visible and we didn't talk about it to outsiders, it might go away.

But in September, my body changed radically. I was no longer someone who could pass for thirteen, or perhaps I was, which was why the visibility of my condition was so shocking. I don't think my mother cared about the neighbors. Having looked down on them, the women in particular, for twenty years, having considered them idle, trivial, and provincial, she didn't value their good opinion. Having parodied their kaffeeklatsches, she couldn't care that she and her daughter now made up the substance of the conversations that went on there. What made us decide to change our plans was that it became clear that our lives had changed. We needed a change of venue.

They decided to call Cyprian. I went into my room so I wouldn't have to hear my mother talking on the telephone. In ten minutes, Elizabeth came in to get me.

"Is it all right?" I asked, wanting a quick bulletin.

"Better than we could have dreamed," she said.

My mother sat triumphantly at the head of the table.

"What did he say?" I asked.

"What a man!" my mother said, coming as near as someone her size and temperament could to a swoon.

"He's amazing," said Clare.

I knew what the three of them were thinking: "We have been right all these years to love him."

"He said," said my mother, with the zest of one who knows she is about to deliver a really good line, "that perhaps all this will spare you greater sin."

The three of them smiled, radiant, girlish, justified in their great love. Perhaps I was simply too depressed to share their joy, but it was not the sentence I had wanted most to hear.

"He said we should go there to have it," said my mother. "And live up there until we figure things out."

"What about your job?" I asked my mother.

"I'll quit. I'll be sixty in November. I can get part of my pension. There'll be no trouble about the Gaspirinis. They've been hinting they want this apartment for their married daughter. I'll get something part time up there after a while. With my experience, I'd be an asset to any insurance company. I know the ropes a lot better than some of those snips right out of secretarial school."

"And I can draw my full pension any time," said Elizabeth. "I've been sixty-five since February. There's no reason for me to stay in New York, the way it is now."

"I can contribute something. And there's the rest of Felicitas' college money," Clare said.

"Cyprian said he and some guys can have a simple house finished in a month or two if we have the cash," my mother said.

"We have the cash," said Clare quickly.

"Okay, then it's all set. Thanks to Cyprian," said my mother.

"Thank God," said Elizabeth.

"He always comes through when you need him," said my mother.

"He's like no one else," said Clare.

No one asked me what I thought, but that was all right, that was the way I wanted it. I was so relieved that Cyprian was not murderously angry that I was ready to go along with anything. I now see that my pregnancy, my illegitimate motherhood, was the only thing that could have kept me near him, near to all of them, in fact. Nothing could, in that way, have served them better. But it was a scandal and a burden and a shock, and I was in great need. They could, in the course of helping me, have insulted me, condemned me, made my misery deeper than it was. But they didn't. They stood by me and defended me. I no longer believe in looking too closely into people's motives. Kindness is a rare thing, and having been saved by it, I no longer choose to mar its luster by too close examination.

In three weeks, everything was done. We got rid of our apartment and with it all the furniture we thought would be too small for our new house. We knew exactly what the house would be like because it would be identical to Muriel's. More important, my mother quit her job at Tom O'Brien's insurance agency, where she had worked for thirty-five years. One day, she came to work and gave two weeks notice. Tom O'Brien, an Irishman who had made a lot of money by having sentimental eyes, was really a dry man with a just and cynical nature. But he lived up to his eyes when my mother told him she was leaving. He wept, then she wept. It was the first emotional display they had shared in thirty-five years of office life. They loved each other with what is probably the most dependable love in the world, the love of people who work well together. A year after my mother left, Tom himself retired. He said he could never replace her; he wrote monthly asking her to come back, making outlandish offers of salary and benefits. Two years after his retirement, he was dead of rectal cancer. My mother blames herself.

We drove up to Orano, as usual, in Clare's car, the four of us and the three dogs, who were wonderfully docile. My mother quickly became devoted to the dogs, as did Clare and Elizabeth. I think the presence of the dogs made us feel more normal, and perhaps we fantasized that everybody thought we were moving to the country for the dogs' sake. My mother realized, as we got on the Bronx Whitestone Bridge, that we couldn't arrive at Father Cyprian's door with three dogs named Ho, Che and Jesus. Their names would have to be changed, she said, and she instantly thought of a solution. We called them, from the moment the car drove over the Westchester border, Joe, Jay and Peaches. They have never noticed the difference.

It was chill and damp and sullen that October and November. The dull, gray cold made everybody's features look pinched and ungenerous; the cold came up through our city shoes, and we huddled in the woolens we thought we could leave packed for another month. I was the only one who could bear the long walks I invented for myself, the only one who could stand the burdocks sticking to my clothes, who could find anything to look at in that brown, stunted landscape. The walks gave me the only pleasure I had that year, the walks and grooming the dogs; after each walk I brushed them and I taught them elaborate tricks. Because of that time, they can fetch and run in circles, they refuse food from my left hand and take it from my right, they bark on command and sing in chorus.

On December 20, Linda was born. I remember nothing about it except some pain and then an anesthetic. I wasn't present at my daughter's birth, and when they showed her to me, I felt too ill and drugged to respond. I had only one thought: she must have a name that would make her as similar as possible to the children she would grow up among. I asked the nurse what name had been given to girl children most often that year. She was remarkably cooperative. There had been, she told me, thirty-four female births so far. Fourteen of the infants were named Linda, followed by six Jennifers, five Deborahs, five Susans, four Kathleens. My mother and the women complained that Linda was not a saint's name, so she was christened Linda Ann. It is, I think, a name that will protect her, like a camouflage suit in an enemy jungle.

In February, Elizabeth moved in with us. She and my mother stayed up late at night, talking, playing cards, my mother interrupting Elizabeth's reading to dissect Muriel's latest atrocity. Elizabeth's pension—ample, thanks to the successes of the New York Board of Education—allowed us new luxuries. A television, for one thing, which my mother loved and Elizabeth suffered for the love of her. My mother sat in front of the television like a new bride, folding laundry, mending. We have what is called an all-electric home. Cyprian had arranged for a tiny washer and dryer to be installed in the kitchen. This pleased my mother as it would have pleased a primitive. She washed every day, diapers of course, but she would sometimes do an extra load of dish towels or rags just for the luxury.

I spent most of my days with Cyprian, making bookshelves for Elizabeth's books, a chest for his vestments. He taught me everything he would have taught a son, and he had lost his old impatience. We were usually silent with each other, and when he gave me directions he spoke to me in a humbled, courtly voice, as if the trick of my maternity had awed him. He spoke to me like a diffident rich man trying for the hand of a beauty. But mostly we did not speak. It was nothing like my childhood, when he would talk to me about the mysteries of the Trinity as he showed me a new load of lumber. He could sense in me after Linda's birth a hard, leaden center, upon which the word of God would not catch fire but freeze, making a steel-cold bridge between us where there was now the equivocal access of partners, of men at work.

When spring came, we planted a garden, worried about floods, helped the neighbors get their cars out of the mud. Clare came up every weekend, bringing the first asparagus and strawberries, bringing Linda Bergdorf Goodman clothes, F.A.O. Schwartz toys. Only when Clare was there did I hold the baby. In her city finery, she seemed less a creature of instinct, less mine.

In July, Mary Rose came with Joe, and for the first time I got the idea that the presence of a baby in the house was a simple pleasure. Joe walked around in his white shoes, a city man unsure about which parts of the landscape ought to be appreciated, praising indiscriminately, extravagantly, the most ordinary growths. Mary Rose clucked at the baby, dressed her for fun, remarked every day that she could see my forehead, and wasn't that the way my nose was shaped at Linda's age? She brought with her the conventional responses, the one gift none of the other godmothers had brought to the christening. And Joe kept pretending that the baby would break if he held her, grew alarmed if she cried or kicked. He made me realize that she was fragile. For the first time, I saw her as weaker than myself. Oh, I had always known she needed care, but her helplessness had seemed to me only a burden. Now, seeing Joe, seeing Mary Rose, I noticed her hands, her feet, her snowy skin, which I had been afraid to touch. All the amazement I should have felt at her birth, I felt when she was moving out of the first, the most passive, stage of her infancy.

Mary Rose. I imagine her waving from the window of the Winnebago she and Joe have bought for their retirement. Mary Rose has gone away, has married. She married a week after she learned that Burt was dead. It isn't possible to be married and to be one of us. What will happen when Leo comes here, comes as my husband? I guess it's different with us; I'm in charge of things now, there is Linda, they can all tell themselves I am not marrying for love.

But Joe Siegel, who waited fifteen years for Mary Rose, who bought her a diamond as big as her knuckle, who cannot bring himself either to call Cyprian "Father" or to address him by his first name—there's no place for him here. So we are not all together. Something has been lost to marriage, to convention, to ordinary human life.

It is a great loss. We are all at our best around Mary Rose, as we are at our worst around Muriel. Is it a loss to Mary Rose? We didn't even call her about Cyprian's heart attack; we didn't think of her until the danger was past.

I am troubled by human change; I find it difficult to comprehend, whether it brings loss or healing. I cannot even recall what happened to me, why my own life changed. Someone came for a visit, said the right thing, brought the right gifts, and somehow I was no longer desperate. I began to laugh at my mother's jokes, to argue with Cyprian over politics, to read books on child development. Suddenly the love that surrounded me took on meaning. I cried at a song on the radio about a young wife who died on Christmas day. I began noticing things in the world that made me laugh, like the breakfast menu at the Orano Diner, which offered THE CYCLOPS SPECIAL: TWO POACHED EGGS ON AN ENGLISH MUFFIN.

Cyprian was with me when I saw that; we were getting coffee while we waited for the lumberyard to fill our order. I pointed to the Cyclops Special. We laughed as we hadn't laughed for years, we got back what we were both afraid we had lost forever: our great pleasure in each other.

"What is our responsibility in charity?" he asked, puttin on his deadpan cleric's face. "Do we inform them of their error or allow them to go on in the darkness of their ignorance?"

"First," I said, "we must determine if their ignorance is invincible. If it is invincible, we have no obligation, in charity, to enlighten them."

"And then there is the hardship to others involved, the temptation to sin. In learning that the Cyclops had only one eye, will they be tempted to serve only one egg for the price of two, thus putting their immortal souls in danger?"

"In charity, I think we are bound to be silent," I said.

"Two coffees, please," he said to the innocent waitress, taken in by his calm smile.

Our laughter met, our words clicked like champagne glasses. After perhaps five years, we were free to love each other again. And we began to talk and to argue as we worked; he began to slip books beside my place at dinner; I clipped articles and slid them into the pocket of his shirt like a magician, pretending to borrow a cigarette. Of course it was different now; I was safe from him. Because I had a child, I was no longer quite a child to him; he had to be more careful of me, fearing the effects of a permanent injury.

What a mystery the heart is. The mind is simple by comparison. How can I describe the process of love that overcame me, the gravitational pull of the baby I hadn't wanted to touch? By her first birthday, she interested me passionately; by the end of the following spring, it was a grief for me to leave her in the afternoon.

I bought mobiles to hang over her crib; I put plastic letters of the alphabet in her playpen. Elizabeth and I sang her *"Il était une bergère,"* and *"Sur le pont d'Avignon,"* so she would have a memory of French.

But then it would come to me that I was burdening her, that the mothers bringing their children up in trailer camps, in the insubstantial houses around the foundry, in the coarse and enterprising new suburbs, were not singing to their children in French. So I would set Linda down in front of the television, watch cartoons with her, memorize the names of the characters. I didn't want her to have any extra problems. She would suffer enough from the odd circumstances of her life. At least she should, I thought, be able to talk to the children she would one day be talking to about dolls with wardrobes of wigs and boots, about mice that fly and boys with horses.

I recovered; I loved my child, my mother, Cyprian, the women who loved me. But my recovery gave them leave to grow old. They saw that they could leave things to me, and they began to do it.

Sometimes I am overcome with a terrible loneliness when I realize how much they want me to take charge. I see all their illnesses before me, their deaths; Cyprian's will be just the first. All the people I love are frailer than I. Except for Linda, they will grow frailer still. There is no person I love for whom I do not have to watch out, who can take physical charge even for a little while. And if the physical charge is mine, the moral charge must be mine also.

But now I will marry. And they will be even freer to grow old.

Little by little, I began to have an ordinary life. The town librarian befriended me. She told me that if I got my B.A. I could replace her when she retired; since 1972, I have worked for her part time.

In September of that year, I entered Hiram Wallace College as an evening student. It was ludicrously different from Columbia, this poor new college that looked like a post office on the moon, that assumed that its students would arrive in cars in the morning and leave in cars at night, docile workers learning under fluorescent lights. There was no history of brash young men walking in perfect boots under extravagant trees. Everyone was there for a reason: they saw degrees as leading to money. Walking through the halls, one could see written in large letters on the green chalk boards words like "Cost Accounting" and "Problems in Dialysis." In the evenings, it was worse: tired office workers and hospital workers who needed college credits for advancement fell asleep in the cafeteria, their heads on their books. And then there were the unattached, the singles, who took painting or psychology to find a mate.

Elizabeth went with me at first; we signed up for a course on the nineteenth-century novel. That first night the professor arrived, as tired-looking as his students. He was a small, slight man of forty-five with the doomed head of a pretender to an Eastern European throne. Everything he did was accompanied by a small sigh. He handed out index cards before he let us know his name, which he never said aloud but wrote morosely on the blackboard.

"You're here for the nineteenth-century novel?" he asked in despair, a weary captain longing for the relief of mutiny.

We nodded; he passed out copies of his mimeographed syllabus and asked us to write our names, addresses and phone numbers, the hours we might be available for conference and whatever courses we had taken in the humanities. This made me nervous. I didn't want to reveal myself as someone who could read Latin and Greek, who had studied Molière in French and medieval history. I didn't want the preferment of this despondent, charmless man who had spent the last twenty years teaching in a third-rate college. But like the others, I wanted a degree so I could get a job. It would be against my interest to conceal my achievements; to make up for them, I decided I would have to be perfectly silent in class. But my fear was unnecessary: the professor gave me no special attention, except to write on each of my A papers, "A solid critical job."

I even made a friend in night school, Bonnie Sickler, a Kentuckian who works in the food stamp office. Her life is based on her husband, a handsome, faithless seller of aluminum siding, for whom she left the South. She is, in fact, responsible, honest, even diligent. She pays her taxes and her electric bills; she is unaware of the considerable male attention she arouses; she is—that test of solid American determination—going to night school. Yet she gives off the air of someone whose behavior can at any moment shade into criminality. She looks like those pictures of kidnappers' accomplices who lull the fears of women victims by pretending to be Avon ladies and giving them sample lipsticks to gain access to the house.

Both of us know, although we never say it, that if we lived in a larger city, if our lives had more prospects, we would not be friends. But as it is, we *are* friends. I admire her primitive female loyalties. Her idea of marriage comes out of a country-and-western song, but I am impressed with anyone who can live a corrupt ideal with diligence and passion.

And we're friends because I am the only woman she thinks her husband is safe with; she believes I am the only woman in the world whom Bobby cannot seduce. I don't know if this inspires her admiration or her contempt, but it puts her mind at rest. And she is devoted to Linda, loves her with the sharp, almost sexual hunger of a childless woman. She would like nothing more than to have a child, but, as she told me two weeks after we met, Bobby had a vasectomy "to punish his first wife." He insists that she tell people she is sterile; he thinks that people will imagine he's impotent if they know he had a vasectomy, and he believes this would be bad for business. Bonnie agrees to this; she says he has his reasons.

I'm grateful for Bonnie's presence in Linda's life. She gives it an edge of danger and illegality, which I do not dare to give it. Early on, Linda knew that she could sneak into Bonnie's room and play with her make-up. Bonnie gives Linda her old high heels to play in; she lets Linda sit in her lap in her parked convertible and pretend to drive; she takes her out to lunch and lets her order whatever she likes and doesn't insist that she finish it; she takes her shopping and lets her pick out her own clothes. If Linda spends the night, Bonnie lets her dress herself no matter how long it takes. Because of Bonnie, I have some hope that Linda will grow up, unlike me, generous-hearted.

Linda is my child; I see her looking with my eyes, the watchful eyes of a child whose family life is peculiar. But it is easier for her than it was for me; she is less frightened. I am more careful than my mother. I would have liked to spare her the fate of the family hope, but how can I, when she collects even the hopes of strangers? The fatherless mystery of her birth makes her for many, it seems, a miracle child. They can attach to her their longings and their faith; she becomes a vessel in which is transformed the thick deposit of their disappointed hopes. It isn't what I wanted for her. Often as a child 'I would, as I was embraced by one or another plangent adult, want to say, "Don't love me so much, don't love me so much." That isn't true; I never wanted to say that. Adoration is addictive. It is also corrupting; there is no way out of it except a radical life.

Bonnie introduced me to Leo, although, of course, I knew him from the hardware store. I had always liked going there, liked the sloping wooden floors, the poor lighting, the metal trays of bolts and screws, the long lengths of green hose, the rubber stoppers, the housewares section, which promised a future of incredible domestic efficiency. It was a place distinctly male in its order; it suggested safety through the right equipment and the use of skills acquired early and kept up with watchful and yet automatic care.

At a party of Bonnie and Bobby's, I was seated across from Leo. We were the only unmarried couple. Bobby was at his worst that night. He's a wonderful host when he isn't thinking about it, but he is one of those large, good-looking men who is spoiled by consciousness. At his business parties, he produces gag favors for his guests, which usually embarrass them, or he makes Bonnie build the party around a theme: Hawaiian night, at which he give out leis and she garnishes everything with pineapple, or Western roundup, at which everyone wears cowboy hats. At the party where I met Leo, Bobby stood beside his chair when everyone was eating his shrimp cocktail and said, "I've got to read you this. It's really something."

A pained and fretful look came over the company, but he didn't notice.

"A smoking saga," he began. "One Kool morning, Virginia Slims, who works for Benson and Hedges, was walking down Chesterfield Lane in Salem County when she met Philip Morris from Marlboro country. He took her to the Parliament Hotel in Newport. He drove her there in his Bel Air. When they got to the hotel, they climbed into the Old Gold bed, and he put his king-size L & M into her flip-top box. Now, in nine months if she doesn't look like a Camel, it will be a Lucky Strike, 'cause he didn't use a filter."

Bobby expected good-old-boy raucous laughter from the men and excited giggles from the women. But there was a dismal silence. They were too sober not to pretend to be above it, these people who went to Disney World on their honeymoons and now dreamed of moving to Atlanta, these women who had only just replaced the plastic anemones on their coffee tables with trailing spider plants. I heard Bonnie laugh, the painful laugh of pure loyalty. I made myself laugh, and so did Leo. The others looked on, and I was conscripted into a defense conspiracy I didn't want any part of. The next week, Leo called me for a date.

I refused and gave no excuse. Three months later, when I was asking his advice about rust-proofing, he asked me to have a cup of coffee. Why did I go with him? Why did I continue to see him? We had no conversation; Leo is one of those men whose only happy days were spent as a boy, alone in the woods with another silent boy, cutting trails and lying still to watch the animals. He is only interested in a relationship that has some hope of repeating that tone. So we went for walks in the woods. I am not a patient person; I sometimes wonder why I continued to spend time with him, so much of it in silence. It must be that, like many plain women, I am overly impressed by beauty. Not that Leo is beautiful as Robert was; he is a tall, thin man of thirty-four with red hair, a red beard and the apologetic eyes of the youngest child of a large, cruel family. But he is the most desirable man in our area, and even I knew it meant something to be chosen by him. I wonder what abuse a woman has to go through at the hands of a man before she gives up the inward flicker of delight, like the click and flame of a cheap cigarette lighter, at being chosen? Where did we learn that definition of honor? As long as it is there, we are never really independent.

And now I will marry him, after two years of walks and movies, after two winters of his plowing our long drive, lending me tools, picking Clare up at the airport, bringing me lengths of hose, extension cords. Now I will be married; I will do this ordinary thing.

I am afraid of marriage, the diminishment, the safety of it. I am afraid it will make me lose my edge, will cover my bones in obscuring flesh, will move me from my desert landscape. Will I be one more woman who lives in the country, is good around the property, occasionally reads books? I've met two of them, mothers of Linda's classmates, but I always felt confident that no one could mistake me for one of them, standing at the door of the school with their good teeth, their long, shining hair, their heavy legs, their jeans embroidered with sunrises or flowers of their own design. I was *singular*. My daughter and I were excluded from the clear categories of law. Now I will be the wife of the man who owns the village hardware store; my child will be his child. Marriage: it is a choice, not an act of nature visited upon me. For a long time, I have taken pride in my life because I thought I had not just a life but a fate, and I was vain about accepting fate in an age when most people didn't even acknowledge it. Am I losing the fine texture of my own life so that my daughter can have a chance at a more ordinary existence? Or am I marrying for my own shelter?

I fear the consequences of exposure, the toughening of my spirit, the silences of my own heart. And I fear in myself a growing cruelty of judgment I hope sex will keep me from. I have never understood random sexual desire. I like having Leo's arms around me; I enjoy being kissed. But the ardor I seem to inspire in him astounds me. I like to think that I am fond of sex. I'm proud of the pleasure I seem able to bring someone I care for. But sex really interests me only when it's over, when Leo is silent again, when I can feel the beating of his tired heart. The excitement, the high dramatic moments, all seem predictable to me. It is the intimacy I like, the feel of Leo's knees on the soles of my feet, as he sets himself between my spread, bent legs. I like the fact that his knees fit into my arches like some cunning middle-European toy.

I find it difficult to justify my reverence for a man of so little mind. Yet I want a life with him. I want to be more human. And I want Linda to have a father.

I suspect that being fatherless leaves a woman with a taste for the fanatical. Having grown unsheltered, having never seen in the familiar flesh the embodiment of the ancient image of authority, a girl can be satisfied only with the heroic, the desperate, the extreme. A fatherless girl thinks all things possible and nothing safe. I don't want that for Linda. I had Cyprian, but he fathered me as if we were both bodiless, for our connection had nothing in it of the flesh. But I will sleep with Leo, Linda will know that. And Leo will know that Linda is an ordinary child, a child of flesh and bone, since he will, in being my husband, become flesh of mine. So far, Linda is very different from me, from what I was as a child. She is not uncertain; she is not frightened. With Leo for a father, the differences between us will grow.

I've watched him seriously explaining to her the way things work, with none of Cyprian's impatience. I've seen Linda riding on his shoulders, looking for squirrels or cardinals. I've seen him at the side of her bed when she had the mumps, having driven into Orano four times to find an ice cream flavor that would tempt her. I saw his pained incomprehension at her pain; his patience as he played Lotto with her by the hour, taking up the slack of my boredom. There is something in all that that will sustain her. I want her to know the silent protection of a good and ordinary man. I missed that; it was a grief and a loss. I want Linda to feel what I felt when I woke up in Cyprian's arms after the accident we had when I was fourteen; I want her to feel safe, because sometimes I can't bear the thought of my frail child loose in a world of danger.

Maybe I'm getting married, like any of the girls in my grammar school, for safety. Maybe by now it is so instinctive in women that we can never marry for another reason. I hadn't thought I would marry. I thought we would go on, the five of us, living on the property, Clare up on the weekends, Mary Rose and Joe visiting occasionally, dinners with Bobby and Bonnie, Leo in the background. "The constant shepherd," Cyprian calls him, looking under the furniture when he isn't there, pretending to see him behind the armchairs, making Linda shriek with laughter as he shakes out his pocket handkerchief, saying, "I know he's here somewhere." I thought we would go on like that, until Cyprian had his heart attack.

Muriel found him, thank God. She has so little left, she would never have forgiven us if one of us had been the first to come to his rescue. She called an ambulance without telling any of us, leaving us to learn of the emergency from the sound of the siren coming up the road. He was taken to St. Joseph's Hospital, where he occasionally filled in for the chaplain.

We sat together that night in the hospital lobby; five women with nowhere to go. Later Leo came, bringing buckets of Kentucky Fried Chicken and small containers of milk.

We had to contemplate the death of the man who had been the center of our lives. For me, it would be the first memorable death. My father died while I was still an infant. The others would be helped by memory. Elizabeth and my mother had the distinction of widowhood, and Elizabeth had been brought the news of a dead child. All of them had been through the death of their mother, these women to whom mothers were of primary importance. They sat and waited, children born in America of women who had risked everything to get here, women who saw their daughters self-supporting and mistrusted it, because their only real respect was for women who ruled large houses. All of them had been together in these mothers' deaths: Clare had even gone to Muriel in her mother's final illness.

For me the experience was more trying, although it's useless to try to gauge another's suffering. They were waiting for a death, but they had the practice of grief and, with one another, the luxury of free expression of it. But I was in charge of things; I had to keep control. And when the nurse came and said that only one person could see Cyprian, it was clear that I should be the one.

I had seen him ill before, but I was afraid to see him under plastic, tubes in his nose and mouth, lying back with the unbearable patience of the seriously ill.

He put his hand out to me and said, "My dear little girl, all this," and then he began sobbing.

I knew the only way to relieve his sorrow was to make him feel part of a conspiracy.

"Cut it out. If they see you, they'll make me leave. You

know how they are in hospitals, always waiting for the thin edge of the wedge."

He pressed my hand. I had always loved the way he did that, as if he were afraid of losing my attention, but at the same time confident of the power of his physical strength.

"What will you do with the property if I die?"

"I know everything about it."

"You know almost as much as I."

"About some things more, and I wasn't born here."

He smiled; he liked my brash confidence about the house and the property. It was a good trick, and we both knew it, his turning a city girl into a husbandman.

"I don't think you're going to die," I said. "I have a feeling."

"You have too many feelings. But then, you're a modern, you believe in them."

"I'm the least emotional of any of you. I just happened to get pregnant out of wedlock."

He looked worried again. "How's the baby?"

"Fine. Furious that they won't let her in the hospital. She keeps telling us there's a rule, children in first grade and over can go to hospitals. She repeats 'and over' with great emphasis: she thinks the official tone gives her case weight."

He tried to laugh. "It hasn't been much of a life for you," he said.

I was insulted. I thought I had made a good life; I was happier than I had ever been; I thought he admired my life. I was silent.

"My life has been a failure," he said. "All the souls I never touched. Now I don't want to; now I want to be left alone."

I was still silent.

"All the hours I gave all the people, all the time, the enormous time, and what do I have to show for it?"

"Property and a cure of souls," I said.

"The best I could hope for in this corrupt world."

"The world has always been corrupt; you romanticize history."

"I see I will have to stay alive to educate you."

"Yes, but remember, I know more Greek than you."

"That's what I'll do if, as this snot-nosed young doctor says, I am to be virtually immobilized. I'll learn Greek."

"I'll teach you."

"And I'll teach you logic."

"I know logic."

"As much as I know Greek."

The nurse came and said I would have to leave. I knew he wasn't dying, and the doctor confirmed it but said he would have to lead a radically circumscribed life.

It was a great relief. I needed his life; I suppose I will always need it, or the idea of it, at the center of my own. I like to think that I am undeceived about him; I am over my childish adoration and my adolescent rage. I know his mind is not first-rate. He had three ideas: the authority of the Church, the corruption induced by Original Sin and the wickedness of large-scale government. All the rest is instinct and effusion. Yet there is no one I revere more. I revere him for his labor, for his passionate, excluding love, for the dignity of his priestly calling he wears with him everywhere: the habit of his grand, impossible life.

But my mind is not safe with him. His mind is taut and quick, but it is not open, it is not trustworthy. How could it be? He was trained by medievalists; he believes in the final word of authority. I want to consider the most difficult questions, but I must be free to make mistakes along the way. That's not possible with Cyprian; he's always ready to jump on the imperfections of my mind, to blame my education, the inevitable corruption of my generation. Like an insecure lover, he is pleased to note my failures.

This is a problem we have as man and woman. The model is always there: Margaret Fuller and Carlyle. "I accept the universe," said Fuller, expressing stupidly a genuine intellectual problem. "By gad, you'd better," said Carlyle, winning himself an audience through his wrong-headed wit. For he was wrong. Fuller was speaking of volition, of the central human struggle to place oneself in relation to the absolute. It is so easy for men with the kind of mind Cyprian has to make a woman look foolish: the sage as fire in whose flame must burn the fat female mind. My mind is better, more complicated, more responsible than his, but he can, in a minute, make it look childish and uninformed. Our minds can meet only in play. I have no one to talk to about the questions that seriously interest me.

And I cannot talk about God. Of all of them, I alone have no spiritual life. It is Cyprian's fault; he trained me too well, trained me against the sentimental, the susceptibility of the heart. So I will not accept the blandishments of the religious life; I will not look to God for comfort, or for succor, or for sweetness. God will have to meet me on the high ground of reason, and there He's a poor contender.

I am interested in the perception of the sacred. So many humans seem to hunger for it: the clear, the encumbered. I too hunger, but my hunger is specific. If I could see the face of God as free from all necessity, the vision as the reward of a grueling search, the soul stripped down, rock hard, then I would look for Him. The pure light that enlightens every man. If He would show Himself so, then I would seek Him. But I will not let Him into my heart. My daughter is there, my mother, Leo, Cyprian, the women whom I love. I will not open my heart to God. If He is the only God I could worship, He will value my chastity. But I will not be violated; I will not submit myself. I will wait. But I will wait for light, not love.

And so we wait to learn what will happen to Cyprian, fearfully, for we guess the outcome. He has been told he can live a long life if he lives a quiet one, but we don't know whether or not he will court death. We are sensible women; we realize we must be silent, even with one another. Muriel goes on in her bitter, passionate watchfulness. Elizabeth goes on, her mournfulness a secret underneath the pleasures of small tasks and large reading. My mother goes on with her mysterious, absorbing plans. Next year, Clare will retire; she has begun the building of her house. Mary Rose, now Joe Siegel's wife, waits in Arizona for news.

And I go on, the daughter of my mother, the mother of

my daughter, caretaker of the property, soon to be a man's wife. My life is isolated, difficult and formal. It is, perhaps, not the life I would have chosen, but it is a serious life. I do less harm than good.

Charlotte

Sometimes I try to figure out if I'm old. I mean, my age is old, sixty-seven is, let's face it, no spring chicken. At sixty-seven my mother was an old woman, but here I sit in an aquamarine pants suit planning to start a business. The girl Felicitas met in night school, Bonnie, a social worker—she got tired of all the cutbacks and the red tape or whatever they call it, and she wants me to help her start up an insurance business. Her husband has the money and she has the contacts and the charm and I'm supplying the know-how. Of course, we'll have to take the exams, which are no picnic, only forty percent pass, but I'm not worried. So I guess I can't be old. No sense making hay till the sun shines is my motto nowadays.

You could look at us all and say, There they are, five old women waiting for an old man to die, living in the country with a young woman and a kid. When you put it that way it sounds pretty goddamn flat. But you can always make your life sound wrong if you try to describe it in a hundred words or less. We're a lot better off than a lot of people. Look at Rosalie, my sister. Look at her kids—one of them's a Jehovah's Witness, the other goes around with a rock group, God knows where, all over the country, all in the back of a truck, Rosalie says, boys and girls, sleeping there, everything. Well, I think Felicitas is a lot better off than that. Sure, she has a kid and isn't married. But she's taking good care of it, and a lot of the girls give up their kids nowadays. Not her. And she's got friends and her disposition's good, and now she's got a man.

And there never was a kid like Linda. She was a beautiful baby. All babies are nice-looking, let's face it, but she was great, really smart, and good-natured, you've never seen anything like it. I must say she's a more cheerful kid than Felicitas was. Just naturally. I mean, Felicitas was good but melancholy. Melancholy baby, I used to call her. But you could never call Linda melancholy. Felicitas does all these enrichment things with her they do nowadays, so she's smart as a whip, like her mother. But she's a lot more sociable than her mother. She takes after me in that. Felicitas is always running all over the place, taking Linda to her friends and bringing them here. Leo's very good at that, sharing the driving, and it'll be easier for Linda, having a father around. I wonder what it means to her not having a father, but there's no sense dwelling on it. Besides, half of her friends have divorced parents, so it's not that weird anymore. Not like it used to be. Sometimes she asks about it. I was all for lying to her, but not Felicitas. She's always told her, "Your father is one of two people, both of whom live very far away." The first time I heard that, I hit the roof. But I came around to her way of thinking. They have discussions about it. And then, of course, she calls Cyprian "Father." God knows what people think. I hope to God Felicitas will let Linda call Leo "Daddy," that she doesn't get one of her goddamn bees in her bonnet. It would just make everything a lot more normal, which we all could use.

Considering what people put up with, we could do a lot worse. There's Tom O'Brien's wife in a nursing home, nothing wrong with her except she broke her hip and she's a little forgetful. Her and all her children. Tom Jr. too good for the insurance business with his M.A. from St. John's, and all the others with their big church weddings, not one of them sees fit to take the mother in. She writes to me and I write back, of course. She says I never change and I write such a cheerful, newsy letter and I'm lucky to be close to my daughter.

As if that explains it.

Elizabeth

I have never been happier in my life. Perhaps I should have been born an old woman; my talents have never been youthful ones. I have been, for as long as I can remember, cowardly, indolent, in love with luxury and fearful of it, disastrous with money, secretive, afraid of strangers. This makes the losses of old age to me sheer gain.

I seem to do less and less. I read no devotional literature, except for Donne, Herbert, Hopkins, and I wonder if it is the poetry or the devotion I am struck by. As the others sat in silence in the hospital corridor while we waited for the news of Cyprian, I could see their lips moving with the words of the Hail Mary. But I was saying Donne's "Hymn to God My God, in My Sickness":

> We think that Paradise and Calvary,
> Christ's cross and Adam's tree, stood in one place;
> Look, Lord, and find both Adams met in me;
> As the first Adam's sweat surrounds my face,
> May the last Adam's blood my soul embrace.
>
> So, in his purple wrapped, receive me, Lord,
> By these his thorns give me his other crown;
> And as to others' souls I preached Thy word,
> Be this my text, my sermon to mine own:
> Therefore that he may raise the Lord throws down.

What I wanted for Cyprian, even more than physical health, was serenity. If he had to die, I wanted death to find him in a state of resolution. I did not want him to die with a bitter heart. I prayed to John Donne, himself a clergyman who preached most perfectly the Word of God and died beloved. I prayed to no canonized saint and, thinking of that, began my prayers with "Dear John Donne, although you are not canonized." Then I thought of "The Canonization," and just as the nurse came in to say that Cyprian was all right, the words in my head were, "For Godsake hold your tongue, and let me love." And all I could think of was how dreadful I would have felt if he had been dying at that minute, if that had been the news the nurse had brought.

But he didn't die, although we live in dread of it. The loss will be terrible, but I know about loss, and I no longer fear it. What I fear is that the center will not hold, that without him we will lose ourselves, that Felicitas and Leo will move off the land, and Clare will decide that life here is too dull for her, and Charlotte will stay with me reluctantly, out of duty, wishing all the time she could be with Felicitas and Linda. This is the proof of my selfish nature: I see the death of a man I have loved for forty years, who has guided my soul, who has kept me from terror and held back despair—I see his death in terms of the breakup of the neighborhood. It is a child's fear, a child's egotism, and as the thought comes to me, I pray the most childish of prayers: Let things stay as they are.

I have never been able, like Charlotte, to bargain with God. She begins each prayer, she says, with "Look, this is the deal." I cannot say to God, "For the first time, I am happy, I deserve some happiness." Because we all of us deserve happiness or none of us does. Happiness has nothing to do with desert, and if I attribute human happiness to the sphere of God's interest, I must place there human unhappiness as well. Still, I make prayers of petition because I believe one good comes of it: the expression of desire. It is important to know what one longs for, and to know it clearly; in the area of desire, one should not err.

My desire now is perhaps the least generous one: to hold on to what I have. It is change I fear, no longer to live days that give me pleasure. Early mass, Cyprian's mass, the most serious of hours. We keep the Latin; perhaps our motives are bad ones, keeping back the new, but how the language sustains us, buoys us up on those thin, milky mornings. *"Domine, non sum dignus,"* and we take the Host in our mouths, always the same number consecrated, one for each of us, unless Leo comes.

Leo. I watch him take communion with the rest of us, a man among women, a just man, a man of kindness. What is the prayer of a man like that? One imagines it made of words of one syllable. But he cannot be a simple man or he would not have chosen Felicitas. I watch him, kneeling, with his hands tucked under his elbows, and I see the sweetness of his face, his long El Greco jaw, and I think, This is why Christ chose young men; He could be safe with them. The beloved disciple, the sad young man with a talent for loyalty, for silence. I am glad Felicitas has chosen to accept Leo. I wish she was kinder to him, but I know she cannot be. She has no patience with the hesitant; she loves what is quick and forthright and thoroughgoing—she would have to, loving Cyprian. She loves the tone of a clear pronouncement more than she loves the truth. So Leo, who ponders all and gives no quick decree, often exasperates her, as I have at times exasperated her since her early childhood.

I love the long breakfasts after mass, the last coffee with Charlotte when the others have left the house. "Sit down," she says each morning "Let's relax awhile; at our age, we've earned it." She makes another pot of coffee, and we sit, watching the sky take on its full measure of color. When Linda was younger, our attention was engaged with her. For both of us, it was a luxury we had been deprived of because we were mothers who worked, and I because my child was weak and I knew he would die young. Now that Linda is in school, our mornings stretch out with what is for me a delicious interminableness, for Charlotte an excess which now begins to cloy. I am more satisfied with our life than Charlotte is; she is more energetic and courageous and so begins to feel bored. She misses the city.

I do not miss the city, although I once thought of my life as inseparable from it. I fled from New York as my husband fled from me; some marriages cannot sustain the falsehood that a real romance demands. Everyone said that I would miss the museums the libraries, the concerts, the theaters and the churches were I could find a French priest or a ruined Slav saying mass. But the truth is, I am simpler than that. Few people see that; thinking I am fearful, they imagine I am protecting some fragile, complicated desire. But what I like are conversations that are shaped by stories. I have always known that I could not be religious if I were not Christian, for Christianity is the only really convivial faith, the only one with stories like the finding of the Child Jesus in the temple, including ordinary fear and that most ordinary blessed emotion: relief. I have never been attracted to the majesty of God, the fire, the illuminated skies, the angels, swift and vengeful, cutting through the elemental earth.

I pray less here, which is odd, since I live in a community ostensibly formed by a common religious life. I remark upon this change, but I do not worry about it. Occasionally I am still capable of that rare, clear flight, when I am covered over with brightness. Still, I feel the shelter of that intimate breath. It is true that I long for it less, but I am sleeping better now. Often I prayed when I awoke in fear, imagining the fire escape thronged with vicious, smiling boys who would kill me for my pocket radio. Perhaps the old become less spiritual. Envisioning an eternity of spirit all too close, they grow hungry for the company they will perhaps find themselves without forever, for the stories they will never hear if they are not told now, for the feel of hard earth on the soles of feet that will rest motionless, for the ordinary human happiness they will give up for an ecstasy which, being incorporeal, is unimaginable.

Even if I grow ill, I will die happy. So much entertains me; so little is difficult. I have never been a realistic woman. Now I am old, I do not need to try to be. I am happy at my lack of influence; my diminishing powers are a cause for rejoicing. Something may happen in a minute to take it all from me, but I have had this: for a few years I have lived the life I wanted.

Muriel

Apart from him, I belong to no one; no one is fond of me, except perhaps the child, and she would forget me in an hour. I must be seen, after he dies, as a burden, an unpaid debt. I prefer to live alone, but I cannot: all my money went into building this house, and who would buy it, one of three, soon to be four, houses in a circle, five hundred yards up an unimproved road?

So I am condemned to stay with them, a prisoner of a bad dream, homeless in my own home, suffered, borne, worse than a poor relation, for I am tied by no blood. There is nothing to bind me to them, only Cyprian, who has decided to die, leaving us to one another. How long is memory a bond? How long, absorbed in one another, will he be real to them? For me, his death will be the end of life. But not for them, they have one another.

Since they have come, I wake in the night in terror, always wanting to run to his house, to check his breathing, to be sure he is not in pain, not in need of something, thinking it a weakness to call out. And each day when I saw him in the morning at the altar, it was a miracle. I offer my mass every day now in thanksgiving that he has been spared. I believe in the Resurrection and the Life; I believe that we will meet in heaven. But what will be the nature of our meetings, absorbed as we will be in the vision of God? Will there be in eternity particular affections, particular regard?

I fear being lost in the vision of God; I fear being one among many. It is, once more, a sin against faith. I disbelieve the happiness of heaven, the unapproachable light where we are to each other indistinct.

My death will be a relief to everybody. There is nothing more lonely than to look among live faces for the face of one who will live after oneself and mourn, the face that, after one's death, will be changed by grief, and to find contempt or an undifferentiated kindness. I wait for a face to meet my face; I wait for the singular gaze, the gaze of permanent choosing, the glance of absolute preferment. This I have always waited for and never found, have hungered for and never tasted. Even now I hope, a woman in a house I cannot sell. I wait here to be looked upon with favor, to be chosen above others, knowing I will die the first beloved of no living soul.

Clare

The view here is unremarkable, except that it is ours, and there is nothing more beautifying than the angle of property. Like most of this part of the country, the land has been badly used: the hills in the background are indistinguishable from the hills in this or almost any other county in this part of the Northeast. Only sometimes, late in the afternoon at the approach of winter, a blue and solid light falls on them, and they maintain for half an hour a clear, isolated, immeasurable beauty. Then I think, "Of course, this is mine, I will stay here." And my heart lifts. This is not just a saying: the heart can lighten. And I wonder, as one does in the midst of love, how my doubts could have arisen, how I could want anything but this.

So I will bring my old age here, the old age of a gentle-woman, savored like the last *marron glacé* in the hands of an émigré. Perhaps, after all, it is not beauty that moves me, but life. I move toward the warmth like any animal. I will leave the streets, the paintings, the dancers, the women playing flutes, the tortured men playing stringed instruments. In the privacy of my perfect living room, I fear a corruption more thorough than any that could touch me up here: the meagerness of my own life there could seep, like a weak acid, through my spirit. I could die an old woman devoted only to the order of her days.

Here I may be bruised and grazed and wounded by the boredom, by the irritation and the crowding of domestic life. I fear the clips and stings of other human lives, lives less careful than my own. I fear the sound of Muriel's voice, the print of her green curtains; I fear Elizabeth's clumsiness and her uncertainties, Felicitas' rudeness and judgments, the ill-timed demands of Linda, the physical weakness of Cyprian, his bad temper. And now Leo's meekness, his dumb comprehending stares. For twenty years I have lived alone. I have come home to the solace of a room I have created for myself, to the incredible luxury of a room of utter silence. This, I fear, I will lose; I fear they will think my house is their house, that they can come in any time, sit anywhere, use anything. I am taking a risk, but in old age, risk may be the only wise investment.

There is no longer really a place for me in the world I have spent my life in. I am as much an anachronism as Elizabeth, only being anachronistic is no grief to her; she has always been uneasy in the world. I am not bitter, like Cyprian, at my fall from power. I am more prudent than he, more moderate; I see the clues to the future, what they say. I am no longer fashionable. There are no more women like me. I am the end of the line, the last of a dying race: the wise virgin, the well-dressed, clever spinster, interested in style but not in sex. And the world of objects, of materials, has changed. I cannot understand women who come into the store wearing blue jeans and five-hundred-dollar boots; I cannot understand their hairstyles, curled like a dog's or a kindergarten child's and their false doll eyes on top of mouths painted to look like criminals'. I do not understand the plastic buckles on their belts, the buttons missing from their coats, their huge eyeglasses. I cannot fathom their purchase of cars no one is surprised will break down in weeks or months, their conception of foods invented for an adolescent's palate. I am baffled by their T-shirts and their fake fur coats My father made a fortune on the understanding of, the reverence for, material and all its formal rules. Now the rules have disappeared.

I will turn my attention to the house I will build, the land I will inhabit. I chose a site with a view in a clump of high pines, farther from the others than they like. I have spoken with Felicitas about the landscape; we have planned a formal garden. At sixty to become a gardener! I admire my future self, stooped, sunburned, wearing a man's hat. I admire the view I have chosen. This is the greatest gift: to choose a life one can admire oneself for living. For most, it is impossible; they are bowed down beneath necessity. But I am free of necessity, I am an old woman with friends and money. I wait for the surprises of my body, its inevitable lapses and decay. But I wait free of terror, even with some interest. I hope to be awake for my own death.

Cyprian

I die failed in my vocation. A priest. Thou art a priest for ever. *The priesthood.* That comes closer to the sense of it, the grand impersonal nature of the calling, objective as reason or order, a noun majestic as those. Not I, but Christ in me. *Ex opere operato,* not the worker but the work. So that the state of the individual soul counts for nothing in the validity of the sacrament. A priest mad or drunk can make the Body and Blood of Christ. In seminary, we were told the story of the priest who went mad and consecrated all the bread in a Chicago bakery. Was it, asked our professor, lawfully consecrated? Each one of us, even the slowest, knew the answer. It was valid; it was the Body and Blood of Christ. His brother priests had to consume it on the spot. "Forty loaves, no fishes," said Father Evangelist. We laughed, imagining the stuffed priests. In those days, priests had both a sense of humor and a deep sense of the spiritual. Now they have nothing, except a sense of themselves, a sense of what will get them on television.

It was grandeur I wanted, that I left my family for. I was a child. I see that now. Perhaps they should have made me wait. A farm boy, ignorant and smelling of cows, with one good pair of shoes for mass. My family lived what I thought then a life that lacked in exaltation. Even then I stank of pride. What I have seen of degradation, of the degradation of the very priests I left my family for, makes me think I should have stayed there on the farm, working with my father, with my brothers, achieving my salvation in the blessed way of the ordinary, the obscure. Perhaps it would have been my glory, and in charity it was my obligation. Two years after I left, the farm failed. My father died a bankrupt, delivering mail. An old man walking along the road with aching muscles. He had been, like all farmers, rheumatic, but there was something to be won from victorious movement over pain when he was working his own land. At the end of his life he overcame the pain that stabbed his bones only to give into strange hands the messages of strangers. This is on my head. If I had been his son, as Christ was the son of the carpenter of Nazareth, I might have saved him, he might have died on his land. I could not give my family half the hidden life that Christ gave to Nazareth. At fifteen, drunk on the vision of Father Adolphus in his gold cape holding the prayer book, pronouncing the ancient words, I prayed that I would be delivered of my nature in the priesthood. I would not be the son of my father, the brother of my brothers, bumbling and heavy and uncouth. I would be part of that glorious company, the line of the apostles. I would not be who I was.

The monstrosity of it! I left my home, my family, for a life of poverty and of necessity. I believed all this for years, I thought I had found God in the company of the priests, my brothers.

Two others arrived in my year, John Naylor, given the name Wilfred, and Frank Bass, given the name Augustine. And I, Philip Leonard, renamed Cyprian. We were a small order; we had no schools or parishes. We had to depend for our vocations on the boys our men met in the course of preaching parish missions or retreats. Many of the priests in the house were foreigners, keeping alive the fledgling American community. I was blessed in knowing those men. They had the spiritual life that is so much more natural to those whose language has been for years sacramentalized by the life of the Church. How much harder it is for an Englishman or an American, whose tongue is the tongue of commerce, the language of the marketplace. Our souls are naturally coarsened. There are no great spiritual writers in English, except Newman. And even in Newman, there is no straightforwardness. I hear a gentleman speaking, a man who worried about table manners and the accents of his friends. Nothing in him of the great, rough force of the Spanish mystics, or the plain, imperative Bernard, or the authoritative Bellarmine, who ordered kings. How fortunate I was in learning from those saintly men, the Spanish Father Antonio, the three Italian men, each one a master craftsman as well as a scholar. And the German priest who could not eat our bread and lost, in one year, fifty pounds.

From them I learned the spirit of silence, which must be the true environment for every priest, whatever his ministry. I had been a farm boy, used to the silence of animals, of open land, of winter mornings where the quiet was pierced only by single rays of silver light. I thought I knew silence on the hills when the hushed sun withdrew and I, a boy out with the animals, stood, my heart in my young mouth, covered in beauty. I had known natural silence, but in the monastery I learned the silence shaped by prayer and punctuated by it, the purposeful silence of men gifted with speech and with affection for their brothers, giving God the gift of all the words they could have said and wasted. The silence that was, in this modern world, a reproach as powerful as the lacerations of the prophets.

Father Celestine, a Frenchman, told me that a priest should have much silence in his life for the sake of his mass. The canon of the mass should emerge from that silence with infinite power and significance. For nine years I studied, learning wisdom from these great old men who had the innocence and the simplicity of children. They were learned, one a great canonist, one a classicist who could not teach me Greek, but they looked on the world with the freshness of the entirely untaught. The charity of God burnt in their hearts; they spent hours hearing the confessions of strangers, for these were not the men who went out to the parishes and built up, as I did, devoted clienteles. These men heard confessions in the monastery church in the middle of Buffalo, the confessions of laborers and drunkards and wives afraid to take the sacrament in their own parishes.

Theirs is the ideal that I have failed, the great ideal whose model is the mass, impersonal, restrained, available, utterly public and yet full of solitude. In the Roman rite there is no room, as there is in the Eastern liturgies, for the gestures that express the personal enthusiasm, the marvel of the celebrant. We understand that we must disappear inside our own office, subsume our personalities in the great honor of our vocations. This I have not done. In this I have failed them, those old, holy men for whom I left my family.

In their great charity, they did not suspect my pride. They referred to it as warmth of heart, my ardor for the souls who came to me. They did not understand that I loved those souls not in God but for themselves, that I wished to talk to them not only for their salvation but for the pleasure of words given and taken, personal gifts. I have not learned the great lesson of these men: the lesson of silence, the lesson of forgetfulness.

For a young priest, many things are easy. Perhaps it is the grace of the sacrament. He walks through the world, the oil of anointment glistening on his temples. He is patient, for the sins of men are new to him. If his advice is ignorant, at least the terrible burden of repetition is not his: he can hide his failures in his loving heart. They are small still, they will not escape and swallow that same heart or eat his entrails with their bitterness. The young priest is a healthy animal; he is blessed with an animal's short memory.

To the eye of the public, which is not the eye of God, I was successful. The lines in front of my confessional were the longest in the church. I slept little; always some soul waited for me. I held back nothing; I involved myself in families, in madness, in the avarice of businessmen, the cunning of politicians. And always I came back to the silence of the monastery, the healing silence, and the great, health-giving liturgy we lived by, the feasts that marked our sleep and waking. The life among the priests, my brothers, gave me back the soul I gave away to other souls. I was perfectly happy. I believed I was doing the work of God.

But I was nothing but a sham. If some of God's work was done, it was through His grace only. I was as full of myself as any of the Irish politicians I accused of graft. The life of the community had become degraded around me, and I was so absorbed in the work I was so full of that I did not see it till it was too late, and I was able to do nothing.

By the time the war came, the old saintly priests had died or gone back to their native monasteries, or to Florida or Utah, where we opened new motherhouses. It is possible to say that the success of our order ruined us. A typically American error. The rejoicing at mere size is a reflex now as automatic for most people as the push buttons they live by. During the war, the fasts were relaxed and we no longer rose at three to sing the matins. The excuse was that we were an active, not a contemplative, order and that we had to keep up our strength for our ministry in the world. Lies, excuses for the weakness of the flesh. There was less sickness in the monastery when we prayed and fasted; afterwards, all you could hear in the choir was the sniffling of the young men, who were always having colds. In their defense, I will say that the war is supposed to have introduced new foreign germs into the country, virulent strains our systems were unused to. A sign of God: we have never, since then, regained our strength, physical, political or moral.

Augustine Bass was made superior in 1946. After that, the monastery could no longer be a place of refreshment for me. There was no more silence, always the sound of activity, of production, the machine that printed mass cards, that washed dishes, that repaired shoes and waxed the floor. And when Augustine turned an old room where vestments were stored into what he called a rec room. All the snot-nosed boys who thought they would be priests played Ping-Pong now and pushed their dimes into the Coke machine Augustine rented from a local gangster.

Then my vocation failed me. The devil pressed me and I could not resist him. The patience I accorded to the most miserable wretches, the pathetic weak souls who came to me in sorrow, I could not accord my brother priests. The monastery soon became a place of torment for me. I raged against them, publicly and privately. Reginald, my confessor, warned me that I was becoming an occasion of sin. Even kneeling before him, in the sacrament of reconciliation, I called up the memory of the great spiritual riches born of silence and discipline, the mysterious consolation springing from adherence to the rule. Even in the confessional, a penitent, I could not bow my head. "They are wrong," I would say, kneeling, my nails pressed into my palms. "They are living the modern error."

"My son," said Reginald, a saint who suffered, I see now, more cruelly than I the gross corruption of the order, "the source of all error is a failure of charity."

Love left my heart, and that is hell, to be unable to feel the heart, to have the heart a stone, an indigestible hardness in the very center of one's being, so that all movements that sustain life grow full of effort and the dreadful torpor of despair sets in. This is the paralysis the damned are cursed with, and in my paralysis, not yet complete, I struck out with the diseased limbs of my clear rage. I grew impatient with the souls who came before me. Where I once took their suffering into myself was now a stone; the cell where sympathy abode was hardened over with disgust; fellowship turned to boredom. Where I had seen them as wounded, I saw them as corrupt; where I had perceived struggle, I saw pride; where I had seen confusion, I saw only the dull stupidity of vice. This is sin, a blinding, a hardening over. And in my blindness, I did not see myself as standing up for the ideal that I had left my parents for.

It is only now that I, an old man making room for death, forgive them. For years, I carried in my heart the treasure of my grievances, cherishing like a connoisseur the details of my great trove. Over and over I rehearsed the insults of the young priests. They replayed themselves fresh and enchanting twenty years after they had been spoken. I retold in my heart the indignities of Augustine Bass; there I lived, in the cell of my own bitterness, mistaking my own selfishness for holy ardor.

It is only now that I am close to death that I acknowledge the great kindness of my faithful friends. For years, I thought of them as second best. They could not speak to me of the spirit of God; they could not counsel me in my growing bitterness. I could not share with them the great transcendent beauty of a life of consecrated men, receiving from one another's hands the Body of Christ. I saw them as simple and myself as complex. I longed for the refreshment of the monastery; I longed for consolation; I yearned for a brother who could rekindle the heart's flame that burned only in anger now, who could restore to me the blessed peace that fed me in the silence of the monastery.

I saw the affection of these good women as a pitiful travesty of the durable, shining friendship I sought from another man. *O my chevalier,* says Hopkins, the priest-poet, seeing Christ the horseman. When Frank Taylor died, I was inconsolable; I saw myself as left with only womanish affection as a solace, a bulwark against the stinking, petrified disorder of the world. And it would not suffice; it could not solace me.

When the women visited me, I imagined it at first as an intrusion. But my heart lifted at the child Felicitas. Here was a love I saw as clear as the love I had for my brother priests. Each summer when she left, I was bereft. Prayer could not touch the sorrow of my heart. I wanted only her presence, the sound of her sharp, truth-telling voice, her clear objective gaze when I taught her something, the quickness of her splendid mind. And her uneasy laughter, which I won by imitating. like a night-club comic, the parishioners, the storekeepers, the workers on the street. Each summer when she left, I felt the agony of simple human loss, and I berated myself, for I did not love her with a priestly love, objective and impersonal, concerned for the salvation of her soul. I loved her as a human child, my child, with the terrible possessiveness of parenthood. In the Church's wisdom, priests are denied such love, for it is the most consuming love, the most impartial. A priest must love neutrally, must love evenly, and I knew that to save Felicitas, I would give up the lives and even the salvations of a thousand of my ordinary flock.

When she grew older, grew rebellious, I knew the bitterest of Jesus' sorrows: the agony within the Agony of Gethsemene, when Judas kissed and the three faithful slept. Then my heart closed utterly. I wanted only to die. The physical constriction of my heart was no surprise to me. That I did not die astonished me; it was another punishment.

All the years alone in Arizona, in Canada, the years of moral isolation among men I could not speak to, who despised me and whom I despised, men coarse-grained as animals, all those years of loneliness were nothing to what I felt when Felicita drew back from me, embraced the world and looked on me with scorn or with the ancient, ignoble fear of a bad child. When the news came of her pregnancy, my heart opened to her and I turned to her. But she turned from me, from all of us, into the hard shell of her misery. The birth of Linda brought me back to life. And for the first time, I had faith, the simple faith in God, His loving providence, I had when I left my family. I knew we would be all right. I knew Felicitas would come back to us and we would prosper.

I have had to learn the discipline of prosperous love, I have had to be struck down by age and sickness to feel the great richness of the ardent, the extraordinary love I live among. I have had to learn ordinary happiness, and from ordinary happiness, the first real peace of my life, my life which I had wanted full of splendor. I wanted to live in unapproachable light, the light of the pure spirit. Now every morning is miraculous to me. I wake and see in the thin, early light the faces of my friends.

But I fear that in loving as I do now I betray the priestly love I vowed to live by. There is no way in which my love can be objective or impersonal. I am doomed like the rest of my kind to the terrible ringed accident of human love. I am pulled down by the irresistible gravity of affection and regard. These are the people I love: I choose to be with them above all others. These are the countenances that lift my heart. Sometimes I fear that a priest should never be light-hearted; if he lives his vows, he should be the receptacle for the anonymous, repetitive sorrow of the poor race of humans for whose sanctification he is consecrate.

I wake sometimes in the middle of a dream about the monastery, expecting almost to hear the music of the hours, and I realize that I am on the site of my parent's house, surrounded by the muffling, consoling flesh of women. And I think, They have won me, they have dragged me down to the middling terrain of their conception of the world, half blood instinct, half the impulse of the womb. And I have wanted to rise up in the cold night and close the door of my house forever, to leave behind the comfort, the safety, and to walk out into the cold, searching a cave where I could live, starving for visions like the desert fathers. One night, I did leave the house and walked for hours, wishing to disencumber myself. But my bones failed me and the lights of an all-night diner were irresistible. I entered the steamy, greasy warmth, felt the meat smell cling to my clothing. I sat down at the counter and picked up a matchbox. On it was printed ACE 24-HOUR CAFE—WHERE NICE PEOPLE MEET. And tears came to my eyes for the hopefulness, the sweetness, the enduring promise of plain human love. And I understood the incarnation for, I believe, the first time: Christ took on flesh for love, because the flesh is lovable.

The waitress looked at me, an old man with a night's growth of gray-green beard. My eyes, I knew, were feverish, the mad eyes she must have got used to on the late-night shift. She said, "How about another cup of coffee, dear?" I smiled and thanked her, as Tobias must have thanked the angel. And I thought of them all, of all the women, the terrible vulnerability of sleeping women, alone in their dark houses.

Now they will not be alone; Felicitas will marry. When she and Leo came to tell me, I said, "I suppose you're old enough to know what you're doing." What could I say? I gave them my blessing.

I believe the marriage is a good thing. Leo is a fine boy, simple but, like Felicitas, clean of heart. Like many simple men, he seems to be nearly mute, but I suppose Felicitas requires kindness after her terrible experience with that man, whoever he is, who fathered Linda. No one could be kinder than Leo; I suppose that is what she needs. I never pretended to be a marriage counselor; I can only speak in the name of the Church, which could have no objection to their union.

Whom would I choose for her to marry? I have such small experience of good marriages; priests are allowed details of marriages only when they are at the point of collapse. I always imagined her married to someone like William Buckley, a man of great wit and great probity, so they could spend their days in delightful argument and work together on the proper causes. No, I never meant for her to marry. When she was a child, I saw her as a solitary woman, too objective to stoop to the sort of things men want from a wife. In part, I have always had a small contempt for the women who submit to the degradation that men seem to require in a mate. The men also I condemn, but their fault appears to me more natural. I could never see Felicitas submitting herself to the foolishness that makes what the world calls an attractive woman, and she is not simple enough to make an ordinary good wife, a vocation I hold in the highest esteem. The virtues that state requires are patience and obedience, the qualities Felicitas has lacked since birth.

But I never imagined her a mother. The shock of seeing her in pregnancy, her small child's body so distended, was as much a visual as a moral shock. She was so clearly still a child and her maternity so reluctant. But I have never seen a mother I approved of more; I have never seen a happier child.

I think that the love of Charlotte and the other women has sustained her. They all think Felicitas' marriage will be a good thing. The child needs a father, they say, almost in unison, the *choragi,* the women of Thebes. The words fly into my flesh like arrows. She has me, I want to say. Do not think I am proud of this impulse; it cannot be anything but a failure in a priest. Of course it will be better for the child to go into the world protected by legitimacy. The law was created to shelter the innocent. There is nothing I can do with my life to make a shelter for a child, two children, for Felicitas will always be my child.

It is when these feelings overcome me that I know I

have failed in my vocation. When I left my home, my parents and my brothers, I gave up the right to ordinary ties, to loyalties that spring from blood or passion. It is when I face up to this failure that I know it is right that I should die before I do more damage, cause more scandal.

The fifth commandment forbids us to take unnecessary risks with our lives, but it does not require us to take extraordinary precautions to prolong them. I have always taken solace from activity. When I despair, I can look with pleasure at my accomplishments on this land. I have rescued it, brought it from a waste ruined by negligence and circumstance to the cultivated, orderly home of people whose lives are innocent. *Laborare est orare:* to labor is to pray. I fail so badly and so often in my prayer life, at least I have had faith that God accepts the offering of my labor. I cannot sit like an invalid, an old man in carpet slippers, sleeping most of the day, cranky and ridiculously argumentative, to prolong a life which is clearly a great failure, whose only sweetness is derived from the affection of women and children who have nowhere else to go.

And yet sometimes I think that sweetness is worth everything. It is true, I am happier than I have ever been. And when I look out the window and see Linda and Felicitas planting carrots, planting potatoes (Linda prefers root vegetables and flowers that are grown from bulbs), I think it is unbearable that one day I will not see their faces. I fear the moment of death when one longs only for a human face, that beat, that second between death and life eternal when there is nothing, and for a moment one is utterly alone before entering the terrible, beautiful room of judgment.

I do not fear judgment; I do not fear purgatory, where I hope to go; I fear the moment of longing for a human face. And yet I long to be free of this body, only an encumbrance now, to enter into the realm of simple light that is the face of God.

But when I think of the faces of those I love, I am tempted to work to prolong my life. I know they are frightened of my dying, for they will feel alone in spirit, unshepherded. For Muriel it will be the worst, her I have most failed, most wounded. I should have warned her that her love was dangerous, born of fear, the damaged and possessive love that turns on itself. And yet, when I was lonely, I fed off her love. I allowed her to come and live here, for I was afraid, in the solitude that did not serve me, of falling into despair. I did not like her company, but I required her presence. For this I may not be forgiven. This is blasphemy, for I have repented, and the love of God forgives even the sins of our cowardice and of the smallness of our hearts, the terrible temptation to self-hate. Only faith can save us from self-hate. In faith I leave it all behind me, in the hands of God, in the hands of a girl.

Perhaps the greatest grief will be not to see the child grown. I have never understood women who grow bored with their childrn; they must have no imagination, no interior life. Every question, every observation I find fascinating; her simple physical presence is enchanting. Only a week ago, I interrupted her playing mass. She had memorized some of the Latin, and she copies my gestures perfectly. For a moment I was shocked, a girl child saying the sacred words of God. She asked if I thought she was doing it well. I said she had learned the Latin perfectly.

"I'd like to be a priest when I grow up," she said.

"You can't," I said, "you're female."

"So what?" she said, in the tone she defies her grandmother but not her mother in.

"Girls can't be priests," I said. "Our Lord said so."

"Where?" she asked.

"In the gospel," I said.

"Where?" she insisted.

I told her He didn't say it in so many words, but He chose no women to be apostles, and priests are successors to the apostles. That means they would have to be like the apostles.

"But the apostles were Jewish, and you're not Jewish," she said.

"What's that got to do with it?" I asked her.

"So, you're not like them, and you're a priest." She glowed with successful argument.

I thought of all the foolish, mediocre men who were

permitted ordination because of the accident of their sex. And I thought of this child, obviously superior to all others of her age in beauty, grace and wisdom. I told her to pray that the Church would change its mind by the time she grew up.

"You pray, too," she said.

I said I would, but it must be a secret between us. And so each morning, at my mass, I pray for the ordination of women.

Love is terrible. To disentangle oneself from the passions, the affections, to love with a burning heart which demands only itself and never asks for gratitude or kindness. In that I have failed. I have hungered for kindness; I have hungered for gratitude.

But the love of God, untouched by accident and preference and failure, this I long for. *Lumen lumens*. The light giving light.

And yet we are incarnate. I look around me at the faces that I love, at the slant, imperfect sun this evening on the mountains, and I pray neither to live nor to die, but to be empty of desire.

Linda

At night I can hear all their voices. I lie in bed and try to hear them clearly, the words and not the rising sounds, the falling sounds. Some are easier, my grandmother and Father Cyprian. Elizabeth's voice is the quietest. When Clare talks, the others are quiet around her. When Muriel talks, they only want her to stop so they can start again. But when my mother talks, they wait a long time to answer. Sometimes she has to make them talk. "What do *you* think? What do *you* think?" I can hear her say.

I can see my mother now through the window. She

goes by me carrying lumber, carrying a shovel, carrying a burlap sack. She walks slowly. Every time she passes me, she waves. Now she is happy; she is singing. At night we sit by the fire. She opens her knees and makes a cave for me to sit in. I press my back against her and her hands cross in front of me. When she sings, I can feel the humming in my spine. It travels up my spine because I am leaning against her and she is singing.

When I sit against my grandmother, I do not feel my bones. She has bouncy flesh, speckled flesh. The tops of her arms are cool. I lay my face against her and I smell her skin. My grandmother is old, but her skin isn't like paper, like Elizabeth's or Muriel's. I do not lay my head against their skin; I do not rest my head against them.

Father Cyprian loves me because I am a child.

Muriel loves me because nobody wants to talk to her.

Mary Rose loves me better than her grandchildren by marriage.

Clare loves me because I am careful.

Elizabeth loves me, but she loves my grandmother the best.

My grandmother loves me and my mother the same amount because we have the same blood.

My mother loves me more than other people's mothers love them because my father is one of two people.

Sometimes I am frightened. I want to say, "Don't love me so much." I'm afraid if I don't love them enough, they will get sick, get weak, they will get older and older. Even my mother, the youngest.

Now my mother will get married. Now people will say about Leo, "This is your father." He will sleep in the bed with my mother. He could make my mother have a child. I would call that child my sister or my brother, but it would have a father. I will always be my mother's. I will never marry. I will always stay with my mother.

I don't tell my friends that I know four Greek words, ten Latin words, the names of angels. Four other girls in my class are named Linda. We all think that's funny, so we are friends. They like me because I run and catch things quickly and because I have three dogs and a red pickup truck my mother drives. They like to sleep over because I'm allowed to have the dogs on my bed and keep the night light on. They never say, "You have no father." I am afraid they will say it. Some of them think Father Cyprian is my father. Then I tell them priests can never marry. When my mother marries Leo, they will think he is my father. They will forget that once I told them, "My father is one of two people."

Father Cyprian is dying; he will go to heaven. I know death. I have seen dead things on the road, dead things the dogs bring home. They do not look like what they are. I am afraid for Father Cyprian. I am afraid of dead animals. I am afraid of the way their flesh falls off their bones, and of their eyes that look at nothing. One day, I will see in heaven all the people that I loved who died. But if they are dead, they will not be themselves. How will I know the dead ones I have loved? How will I recognize them?

Everyone is old here but my mother and me. All the people my mother loves are old but me. Soon they will die. That's why my mother wants to marry Leo. So that all the people that she loves will not be old and dying. She thinks I will go away and so she has to marry Leo. I tell her I will never go away.

My mother is not like anybody. She can do things and she knows things. But sometimes she is afraid. I am afraid, too, but my mother thinks I am never afraid, so I do not tell her. Sometimes at night I dream of cities on fire, of looking for my mother in the city where the dead people are lying with their eyes looking at nothing. I am afraid of the smell of Muriel's breath and the cookies she gives me with coconut. I am afraid of walking down the road and finding that the houses are strange and it isn't our road and I don't know where I am. I am afraid my friends will remember that one day I told them my father was one of two people.

I am not afraid when I am with my mother. One day all of them will die, though. Even my mother will die. I am the youngest. I will be the last to die, which means that I will be the last alive.

Now I see my mother leaning on her shovel; now I see my grandmother. They are laughing and they see me at the window. "Come out," they say, "Come out and talk to us. We're lonely for you. Tell us something."

I run out. I can feel my heart. I am running toward them They are standing under the apple tree. My mother picks me up and holds me in her arms. My grandmother is laughing. My mother lifts me up into the leaves. We are not dying.

About the Author

MARY GORDON'S first novel, *Final Payments*, a best seller in both hardcover and paperback, was nominated for the National Book Critics Circle Award and named one of the outstanding books of 1978 by *The New York Times Book Review*. Her short stories have appeared in *The Virginia Quarterly Review*, *Redbook* and *The Atlantic Monthly*. She lives in upstate New York with her husband, Arthur Cash, the biographer of Laurence Sterne.

The
Best Modern Fiction
from
BALLANTINE